# ALMOST HEAVEN

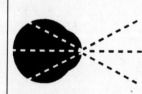

This Large Print Book carries the
Seal of Approval of N.A.V.H.

# ALMOST HEAVEN

## CHRIS FABRY

**THORNDIKE PRESS**

*A part of Gale, Cengage Learning*

GALE
CENGAGE Learning·

Detroit • New York • San Francisco • New Haven, Conn • Waterville, Maine • London

**LIBRARY OF CONGRESS CATALOGING-IN-PUBLICATION DATA**

Fabry, Chris, 1961–
    Almost heaven / by Chris Fabry.
        p. cm. — (Thorndike Press large print Christian fiction)
    ISBN-13: 978-1-4104-3475-3 (hardcover)
    ISBN-10: 1-4104-3475-3 (hardcover)
    1. Large type books. I. Title.
PS3556.A26A78 2011
813'.54—dc22                                    2010050866

Published in 2011 by arrangement with Tyndale House Publishers, Inc.

Printed in Mexico
1 2 3 4 5 6 7 15 14 13 12 11

*To the memory of*
*James William "Billy" Allman*
*and Barbara Kessel.*

*You are both missed.*

In West Virginia, history often repeats itself. Perhaps the fact that our history is so painful explains why it is so poorly understood.

*John Alexander Williams*

Therefore, angels are only servants — spirits sent to care for people who will inherit salvation.

*Hebrews 1:14*

# PROLOGUE

*Dogwood, West Virginia*
*2006*

Becky Putnam stepped onto Billy Allman's front porch, a camera strung over one shoulder and a reporter's notebook in the other hand. She had graduated with a degree in journalism from Marshall University, a minor in English literature, and felt lucky to have a job in her chosen field. But after a few more assignments like this one, she was going to apply at the new Target. She'd heard they were hiring.

A friend of the owner had mentioned something about Billy Allman and his new venture in town. It was a human-interest story, but not one worth telling in detail. She hoped to get a couple of usable snapshots and then head back to work on the obituaries. If there was anything that kept circulation up, it was the obituaries.

A dog growled inside when she knocked,

and she noticed his brown and white coat through the small window by the door. He put his paws up and peered at her, then scratched at the door. She turned and looked at the hillside and the interstate in the distance, car tires whining with the muted wetness of a West Virginia rain. There was nothing like West Virginia rain to bring out the smell of the earth. Of course, she hated the smell of the earth and the West Virginia rain. She wanted to be working in Cincinnati or Lexington. Somewhere that could yield a double homicide or some gang slayings. Instead she was stuck with a promo/puff piece about a guy who had built a radio station in his own house. What could possibly come from this?

The door opened, and there stood Billy Allman. She had expected someone eccentric, maybe with thick glasses and an Albert Einstein look. Wild hair. Or a Stephen Hawking body in a wheelchair. But Billy looked surprisingly normal. He had a crooked grin and hair that barely covered a growing bald spot. He wasn't short or tall, just average with an average build and hairy arms that hung down from a tight T-shirt with sweat stains in the underarms. His jeans had that unwashed look that led her to believe they could stand in the corner by themselves. His skin was washed-out, and she thought of the poem by Edgar Allen Poe that included:

While the angels, all pallid and wan,
Uprising, unveiling, affirm
That the play is the tragedy, "Man,"
And its hero, the Conqueror Worm.

She didn't know why she thought of that, other than the word *pallid,* which was how Billy looked. A tinge of ghost to his complexion. She guessed it was from being inside most of the day.

"You must be Becky," he said. "Come on in. Don't mind him; he'll just lick you to death."

He shook her hand and backed inside, looking about and straightening some newspapers on an old couch. Lined up against the wall was a collection of old radios. She asked about them, and Billy went into a dissertation about the year they were made and how long it took him to restore them. He turned one on and let her hear the sound quality and smiled as he tuned the dial.

More to keep the movement going forward than from a keen interest, she said, "Do you mind if I take your picture in front of them?"

His eyes danced and he held up a finger

11

for her to wait. He disappeared into a cluttered room and returned with what looked like a bookshelf with several tubes and knobs mounted on top. "This is my 1924 Atwater Kent. My pride and joy."

"Great," Becky said.

He knelt in front of the other radios and rested the shelf on one leg as she snapped the photo. Then Billy led her into the control room, and she took a few more with him at the microphone with headphones on.

When she was done, they sat in the living room and she took some notes. He offered her a drink of water, but by the looks of the dishes in his sink, she didn't want to take the chance. The room was stuffy and close, and the odor of sweaty clothes and stale breath and old wood made her eyes water.

"Is there a Mrs. Allman?" she said.

"No, my mother is gone. . . . You mean a wife?" Billy blushed. "No. I've n-never married."

"You must be quite proud of this accomplishment," Becky said, changing the subject. "Not everyone can build their own radio station."

Billy nodded. "This is about the happiest day of my life."

She wondered what was on the opposite end of that spectrum. If this was the high

12

point, what could possibly be the low point?

She asked a few more questions and took one of his business cards with the station's slogan on the front. "Is there anything you'd like to add that I haven't asked?" That was one of those questions they taught you in journalism school.

"You've pretty much covered it, I guess." He walked her out, and as she stood on the porch, he leaned against the door, the dog sitting at his feet dutifully. "I know it's not much. I mean, I know most people probably will pass right over my picture and the news about the station. But I appreciate you taking the time to come all the way out here. I appreciate your interest."

His sincerity almost took her breath away. She smiled and shook his hand again. "It's been a pleasure meeting you, Mr. Allman. I hope you like the story we run."

"I'm sure I will."

■ ■ ■ ■

# PART ONE:
# ALL MY MEMORIES

■ ■ ■ ■

# 1

I suppose you can sum up a man's life with a few words. That's what the newspaper tries to do with an obituary. And it's what that reporter will try to do in her article. "Billy Allman . . . resident of Dogwood . . . lifelong dream to build a radio station . . ." She'll do a fine job, I'm sure. She seemed kindhearted and the type that will get her facts straight, but I know there will be a lot of my life that will fall through the cracks.

I believe every life has hidden songs that hang by twin threads of music and memory. I believe in the songs that have never been played for another soul. I believe they run between the rocks and along the creekbeds of our lives. These are songs that cannot be heard by anything but the soul. They sometimes run dry or spill over the banks until we find ourselves wading through them.

My life has been filled with my share of dirges and plainsongs. I would sing jaunty

17

melodies of cotton candy and ice cream if I could, a top-40 three-minute-and-twenty-second tune, but the songs that have been given to me are played in A minor and are plagued with pauses and riffs that have no clear resolution. I ache for some major chord, a tonal shift that brings musical contentment. I do not know if I will find that.

Throughout my life I have dedicated myself to God. I told him early on that I would go anywhere and do anything he wanted. No holding back. But as time slipped and the conversation has become more one-sided, that plan has appeared haphazard at best. God has seemed massively indifferent to my devotion, if he has even heard my cries.

I suppose I need to put this story down in an ordered fashion to make sense of the silence and to fill in the missing places of my own. Or perhaps I will be able to convince the people who know me as a hermit that there was some reason for the pain. Our lives are judged by a few snapshots taken at vulnerable moments, and I have decided to set my hand to recording the flashes I can recall, the ones revealing my motivations. The look on that reporter's face as I showed her the disparate parts of my life made me want to put this down in my own words. But this is not really for those outside looking in. This is for me.

One of the neighbors described the morning of February 26, 1972, as a cold stillness. I woke up at the first sign of the overcast light. It was my tenth birthday, and as children will do, I did not want sleep to steal any of the good apportioned to me that day. I had invited three boys from my class to the first and last party my parents would ever offer. After that day, Mama never wanted to celebrate a thing, I guess. She had baked a cake the night before and I wanted a piece so bad I could taste it. I can still smell the cherry icing if I close my eyes and think hard enough.

I flipped on the TV to watch the only channel we got in the hollow. Too early for *Johnny Quest* or *Scooby Doo,* my favorites. It was some preacher talking about a prophecy of sudden destruction and how it would come like a thief in the night, like a woman's labor pains. We should be prepared. We should cry out to God now before that destruction came.

At ten, I hadn't committed many mortal sins, so there wasn't much reason for me to think that his message had bearing on my life. But after the fact I wondered if what happened was because I was too prideful or had asked for too many presents. Children will do that — make everything about them, as if some decision they make will change the course of history. If I had prayed right then and there, would things have been different? If I had cried out to God for mercy, would he have changed the course of Buffalo Creek?

I turned off the TV and went to the front window, where the beads of water streaked the awkwardly cut glass and drifted down to the softening wood that tried to hold it all together. In the wintertime the wind whistled through those panes and ice formed on the inside so thick you could scrape your name. Now the water soaked the window through, and streams flowed down the dirt driveway to the road, washing the mud across it. The sight of that misty morning ran cold through me. It was as if the leaves had known better. They had escaped and left the trees looking like sticks on the silent hillside.

Daddy had left the house in the evening to check on the creek because it was up to the top of its banks. He came back to tell us a bunch of people had already gone to the high school because they thought the dam was going to break. The fellow from the coal company had assured everyone up and down the valley that nothing was wrong. We should just stay in our houses. Ride out the rain.

"You think we ought to get over to the school?" Mama had said.

Daddy rubbed his chin. "I think we ought to wait it out and see." Daddy had faith in the company, but not as much as he had in God.

I noticed a muddy spot on the front porch that wasn't there the night before, so I could tell Daddy had been back, but now I figured he was checking the dam one more time. There wasn't much movement on the road, just a few cars spraying water as they passed. And then I saw him, moving faster than usual. My father had a gentleman's gait. He never seemed in a hurry, sort of like my idea of what Jesus must have been like walking along in dusty Israel. He always had time to reach down and give a dog a pat on the head or to pull me close to him with one of those big hands. Like other people who make their homes on the sides of mountains, he took things in stride. He believed that a person in haste usually missed out.

But my daddy walked straight inside the

21

house that morning without taking his boots off. The mud was everywhere, and all I could do was stare at his feet and wonder what had happened because Mama would kill him when she saw it.

"Where's your mother?" he said.

"Still asleep," I said. "What's wrong?"

"Arlene!" he shouted. I heard the bed-springs creak, and he turned back to me before he walked down the hall. "Get dressed quick."

"Is it the dam?" I said.

"Yeah, it's the dam."

I threw on a pair of pants and a shirt over the T-shirt I'd slept in. Though they tried to speak softly, I could hear everything. I heard everything they said about me at the break-fast table each morning and everything they talked about in bed through the thin walls of that tiny house. At least everything I wanted to hear. Sometimes I didn't want to hear a word from them because of the pain it brought about my older brother Harless.

"I don't like the looks of it," he said. "Water is just about to the top. If that thing goes, it's going to wipe this whole valley out. And everybody with it."

Mama pulled on her robe and hurried down the hallway. "Is that what the company's saying?"

Daddy followed her in his muddy boots. Since the company had let us buy the house, he had taken such pride in keeping it clean and neat. He even planted trees and bushes in front.

"I don't trust Dasovich," Daddy said. "He went through again this morning telling us not to worry. That he was going to install another leak pipe. But the top of that dam is like a baby's soft spot. And if I'm right, there's enough water behind number three to stretch from there to the Guyandotte and back again and cover this whole valley."

Mama had the Folgers can out but she wasn't opening it. The cake she'd made sat on a white plate with wax paper over it.

Daddy looked at me. "Get your shoes on."

"Where are we going?" I said.

"Over to the school. Put some clothes in the basket yonder. Just in case. And take it to the car."

"What about the party?" As soon as I said it, I felt bad. The look on his face made me ashamed of being so selfish. But I couldn't help it. And the tears came.

"Your friends will probably be over there," he said. "It'll be one big party. Then when it's safe, we'll come back." He touched my shoulder and nodded toward my room. "Ar-

23

lene, you get dressed and I'll grab a suitcase."

Mama put the cake in a hatbox, and I hurried to get the basket of clothes. I grabbed
my Bible and Dad's mandolin and put them
between the underwear and T-shirts and
jeans, then walked out on the porch and
down the cinder-block steps. Thunder was
under there looking at me. He was our little
beagle who slept outside. Daddy would take
him rabbit hunting and he said he was the
best, but I liked it when he curled up next
to me while I watched TV. Mama would let
me bring him in every so often as long as
he wasn't wet and didn't come begging in
the kitchen. I would scratch his back and
watch his hind legs go to running. We called
him Thunder because of that bellow of a
bark.

I bent down and looked under the porch.
"Come on, boy," I coaxed, but he kind of
whined and his eyes darted left and right,
like there was something beyond me that
spelled trouble.

Daddy came out of the house with the old
suitcase my papaw brought with him when
he stayed with us before he died. My daddy
was born in Omar, and Papaw was from
Austria-Hungary, back before it was just
Austria or Hungary. Papaw always said the

West Virginia hills reminded him of his homeland. He took to mining like a duck to water, though I think he would have lived longer if he'd have just farmed.

Daddy brought out the suitcase in one hand, and in the other was a drawer from the desk with all of our pictures. On top of the drawer was a hatbox holding the cake Mama had made. "Open the door," he said, and when I didn't get to it fast enough, he grumbled and set the suitcase on the car and popped open the door and put everything inside. "Get in. Quick."

Mama came down the steps holding Harless's picture against her chest. She had a look on her face that was pure worry. Mama was an uncommonly beautiful woman of the hills, with long hair that she cared for every evening with a pearl-handled brush her mother had given her. After she brushed it out, she braided it, and I remember it swinging down her back as she made breakfast in the morning. Daddy always said she had the hair of a Tuckahoe Indian maiden, and Mama would smile, but it was true. Her great-grandmother on her daddy's side had been from the tribe during the days when white people were offered money for Tuckahoe scalps.

Just as Mama made it to the car, there

was a sound that echoed through the hills I will never forget. It was like hearing a car crash behind you; you knew exactly what it was, but you didn't want to turn your head and look because you knew there was going to be somebody dead back there. I heard stories later of the people who were higher up the creek and what they saw after the upper dam broke and overwhelmed the other two. Daddy had said the company didn't have engineers building the dam, just a drawing of what it should be, and they turned the guys with bulldozers loose. All the waste from the mines was piled up as high as they could get it, but not packed down like it should be. When all that rain mixed with the water used to clean the coal, it made a lake filled to overflowing — 132 million gallons is what they said later on. That's what was coming toward us, but of course we didn't know that for sure right then.

Thunder barked and ran out from under the house. I jumped out and yelled for him, but Daddy grabbed my arm and slung me back. "Stay in there." He whistled for Thunder, the high-pitched whistle I could never do, and the dog turned and looked at him, then kept running toward the creek like he was after a rabbit.

Daddy hopped in the car and started it up.

"Don't leave him!" I shouted.

"He'll be okay, Billy. Calm down."

We made it to the blacktopped road and headed down the valley, but as soon as we did, Mama looked at Daddy and said, "Other, what about Dreama?"

Daddy gave her a stare that said she was asking too much.

"She brought those kids over last night," Mama said. "The car's right there by the house. She won't know."

Daddy turned our Chevy Impala onto a dirt road that was nothing but mud and slipped and slid up the embankment. Mama asked what he was doing and he wouldn't answer her until he reached the tree line and set the emergency brake. "I'll be right back."

For some reason I still don't understand, he reached back and squeezed my leg. "You be good," he said.

I didn't want him to go. But there was nothing I could do. I just watched him slip and slide down the hill, almost like he was trying to make us laugh, his one hand over his head, his other hand around the cigarette he was trying to keep dry.

"Lord, protect him," my mother said as

27

she watched. She was always praying out loud like that. Just a sentence here or a sentence there that led to a running conversation with the Almighty on everything from baking banana bread to saving somebody's marriage. I imagined my daddy was doing exactly the same thing because he had the same kind of relationship with his Father in heaven.

The rain was still coming, running down the window, so I rolled mine down to get a better look, and that's when I saw Thunder coming up the creek bank barking and sniffing along the edge of the water. I yelled at Dad to get him, but he couldn't hear me. He kept sliding toward the house until he got to the porch. That's when we lost sight of him, but I guessed he was knocking on the door and trying to wake Miss Dreama up.

About that time a car came along honking its horn and that car was just going lickety-split. As the car raced on, I heard something upstream, and through the trees it looked like a semi-trailer was moving fast along the road, except it was an actual house that was coming down the valley like a child will move a toy in the dirt. I stared at it, fix-eyed, my voice caught somewhere inside.

"Oh, Lordy, here it comes!" Mama opened

the door as fast as she could and started hollering at the top of her lungs. "Other! The dam's busted! Get out of there!"

She took a step and fell flat on her behind in the mud and slid. I got out and tried to help her, and when I looked up, Miss Dreama's house was splintering from the wall of water that crashed down. It surged onto the other side of the hill carrying part of the town with it; then it switched back and that black sludge slammed into the side of Miss Dreama's place and lifted it right off its foundation, turning it a little. It was then I could see my father with a little one in each arm, trying to keep his balance. Miss Dreama screamed and Mama screamed and then I couldn't hear a thing. It was like some switch just turned off. I turned away because I couldn't bear to look and caught sight of Thunder just before the black water engulfed him.

My father's face was determined and stoic as he tried to step off the porch while the house moved, but it was swirling fast, like the house in *The Wizard of Oz*. It was all he could do to stay upright. And I thought if he could ride it out, maybe everything would be all right. Maybe if I closed my eyes and prayed, things would be okay and the whole crew of them would step off onto dry ground. But there was nothing dry in that West Virginia valley.

Mama got up and slipped and slid back to the car. When I just stayed there, watching, she picked me up by the arm and almost tossed me into the front seat with her. She started the car and held her foot on the brake as we slid backward toward the raging water, and then I heard my own screams. The car slipped sideways and she turned the wheel sharply so we drifted straight. Miss Dreama's house was moving faster now. I glanced at my mother; she was doing all she could to stop us but we were being drawn like a magnet down. Daddy had been right to put us up near the tree line and if we had stayed there, we would have been okay, but I never blamed her for what she did. She was doing it out of instinct, out of desperate love.

The car slid down and the water met us. I call it water but it wasn't really. It was as thick as gob and just as nasty. A black mix of mud and coal sludge and trees that had been ripped from the bank moving in a torrent that only God himself could've stopped. Once it was loosed from the number three, there was nothing that was going to stop it until it reached the Guyandotte.

The black mess was all over the window

and coming in the backseat. Mama opened her door and tried to grab me, but she fell out and I was pulled back by another wave that swept over the car, caught fully in the weight of the water that treated houses and trailers like my toys. The car door closed and my birthday cake had fallen and mixed with the brackish water. I screamed for my mother, who ran along the bank — though it had been someone's backyard only a few minutes earlier. My breath came in fits, just gasps, and for a moment I thought about the preacher and the sudden destruction he had predicted.

"Help me. Help me. Mama! Help me!" I cried to God and Jesus and my mother and yelled for my daddy, but I couldn't see anymore and the coal sludge was filling up the car behind me.

The back of the car slammed into something that I later learned was a telephone pole that hadn't been swept away yet, and through the windshield I saw another house coming toward me, moving with the water like a boat. Then the car rose up like it wanted to stand on its trunk and I fell into the backseat and saw the open window. I knew right then this was my chance, my only chance to escape what was coming.

From that day to this one, when anyone

asked how I survived, I have told them one story. That it was my birthday. That I didn't want to die. That something rose up inside of me that was equal to or greater than that flood, and that was the human instinct to survive. And not only did I jump out of that car into the swirling water and get to solid ground, but I grabbed my daddy's mandolin on the way out. Most people who heard me play never knew what that instrument went through. It was probably the only mandolin that survived the Buffalo Creek disaster, but I don't know that for a fact.

I was sitting in the mud, too close to the water that looked like cement, when Mama got to me. She hauled me back up the bank to safety and then collapsed in a heap, bawling and rocking back and forth and saying, "I thought I had lost you. I thought I had lost you. And I prayed that the Lord wouldn't take everything."

It wasn't long after I got out of the water that a trailer smashed into our car and took the telephone pole with it and all of it went rolling down the valley like dirt rolls off a car when it's washed. It was just gravity and force and pressure doing what God intended when he made this old world. I was an eyewitness to the whole thing.

■ ■ ■ ■

The water went down in about three hours
or so, and then everybody started looking
for survivors and walking through the
houses that weren't smashed. Mama and I
moved back up to where our house was,
thinking maybe Daddy had gone there and
was waiting. We didn't find him or our
house. It looked like somebody just took a
hand and pushed everything away. There
was nothing left.

The street was mud- and coal-covered,
and people were walking here and there asking if we'd seen this person or that. Some
of the bodies had been found, and men
made stretchers to carry them to the tempo-
rary morgue. People said the National
Guard had been called out but wouldn't arrive until the next day. But everybody
pitched in and did what had to be done.
Hill people are like that. We take care of our
own.

People invited folks into their houses. Just
flung open the doors wide without a care in
the world how they would make it. Some
brought others in for a meal or just to sit
and tell their stories. I don't know that
anything helped more than talking about

what had happened. Where they were when the water hit. How their cousins looked the last time they saw them. And then there were the stories of people going by in houses, standing on roofs, just trying to survive the surge. Those were the hardest for me because I remembered my daddy.

We worked our way to the school, hoping to find him there. We passed what looked like our car raised up on a twenty-foot pile of debris. I could only see the underside of it and the top was smashed in. I couldn't tell if it was ours or not, and anyway it didn't make much sense to guess.

The two of us wandered into the school, and when Mama saw her friends, they just fell into each other's arms and cried. I stood back, watching and wondering what we were going to do. We didn't have a house. Our car was gone. We only had the clothes on our backs and that mandolin.

It was late that afternoon when we finally had something to eat put in front of us, but neither of us was hungry. Every time somebody walked in the front door, Mama would jump. Whoever it was got an earful of questions. She'd say Daddy's name and then repeat it: "Other Alexander Allman." She'd tell them the mine he worked in and that he had a tattoo of an eagle on his right shoulder.

We slept on cots in the gymnasium that night. There was a lot of coffee and talking until late at night, and then the crying started. Mothers crying for their babies. Husbands crying for their wives. Children crying for their parents. Just a whole mass of humanity trying to get through. One man was interviewed by the TV news, and he said he was sorry God had allowed him to live to see what he did.

A lot of people were coming in and out, exhausted from all the searching. I fell asleep and my father came to me in his miner's hat, his face black with coal dust. He had marks on his face and neck where he'd been hit by tree limbs and rocks.

"Where were you, Daddy?" I cried. "What happened?"

Just like that, he was gone and I woke up with the most awful feeling, crying out for him. Mama was there to hush me, saying it was okay. I looked around and others were staring. I just held on to her.

The next day the National Guard came, and they were pulling bodies out of the creek and out from under houses and even out of trees. It seems odd to say that, but the wall of water was that high. It lifted people right up into the trees and left them. There was a church that was moved off its foundation and plopped down a long way from where it used to be, and everybody said wasn't that like God to leave a house of worship alone. But what we didn't know was there was somebody underneath it they found a while later.

I knew my daddy was somewhere in that list of victims, just another body in a stack of people they brought in bags and on stretchers. I didn't want to see him that way. I wanted to keep thinking of him in the good way, him teaching me about the mandolin or holding my hand as we walked to the company store. But the picture that kept coming back was him on Miss Dreama's porch holding those kids and trying to get to safety.

We walked around like zombies all day, and then here came some trucks with clothes and blankets and big boxes filled with cans of Spam and other food and water. I lost all my appetite for Spam about then.

That night there was talk of when the funerals would start. Our pastor came and Mama hugged him and he was in just as bad a shape as we were.

"The Lord has a purpose in this," the pastor said. "For the life of me, I don't know what it is, but I know my Redeemer liveth. And heaven is a more beautiful place because of all these good people who are there."

"Is my daddy there?" I asked.

The man's face was as wrinkled as a paper sack after lunch. "Billy, if your daddy got caught in the flood and died, I know for sure where he is. He's praising Jesus in the presence of God and the angels. You don't have to worry about that."

"Is that what happens when you die?" I said in a shaky voice. I was thinking about the kids in my class who wouldn't be there next week. "You don't go floating off somewhere and stay around in the air; you just go on to heaven?"

"Absent from the body is present with the Lord," he said. I could tell it was something he had memorized because it came out stiff and cold. I knew he couldn't help it. He was suffering right along with us.

When he started talking about Daddy and what a good man he was, that sent Mama into a fit of bawling, and I followed her. He said he was sorry, but Mama said not to be. That we needed to remember. And that there was still a chance, as long as he hadn't been found.

"They found one little baby stuck in a hole up the holler," the pastor said. "It's a plain miracle is what it is. And God ain't done yet, son."

I wished that baby were my father, but I was still glad for the little guy. The pastor asked us if we wanted to come back to the parsonage, that it hadn't been touched by the water, and Mama said it would be better for us to wait at the school, in case any word came.

After the pastor left, she went off in the corner to talk with some women and they'd get to crying and I didn't want to bother her, but I was scared to be alone. All night the trucks and machines rolled in, so we didn't get much sleep, but who can sleep when you have lost everything?

A man in uniform showed up about daybreak and asked in a big voice if there was an Arlene Allman staying there. She hurried to the door and next thing I saw, she was on the floor, on her knees, one hand raised up over her head like I've seen her do in church, just crying and saying, "Jesus, Jesus."

I had been praying to Jesus that Daddy would make it out somehow, but I knew in my heart right then that he was gone. A cold shiver shot down my soul that made me think of what it would be like living without him. I had it planned out that Mama would sleep in her room and I would stay in mine and we'd just go on like other people do when someone is killed in a mine explosion or a cave-in. Then I remembered that our house was gone and so was our car and we were wearing the only clothes we owned.

Mama stayed with the man a few minutes getting information on a sheet of paper, then collected herself and came over and knelt in front of my cot. The dam had burst on her and the tears just flowed and it didn't seem they were ever going to stop. Then I saw something in her face — a spark, I guess. Something that told me to hope.

"Billy, listen to me," she said. "Your daddy's alive. He's not dead; he's alive."

She kind of shook me because I guess my mouth was open and nothing came out. She said something about him being pulled out of the creek and taken to a hospital. Unconscious at first. Then he spoke up and gave them his wife's name and his son's name. She pointed at the paper that listed the name of the hospital. The Guard people were going to try and get us over there, but they were dealing with other injured people and all that came with the cleanup. And there was a lot of that to do.

"He's there waiting for us. They're going to get him all better, so you don't have to worry. Jesus was taking care of him all this time and we didn't even know it."

I managed to say something finally. "What happened?"

"We don't know. But somebody pulled him out of the mud and saved his life. Some good neighbor who was at the right place at the right time."

All I could do was hug her and hang on because even though it was good news, I didn't know whether to believe it or not. Until I could actually hold his big, calloused hand, there was part of me that couldn't believe.

"Your daddy is going to be so proud of you," Mama said.

I picked up the mandolin and held it tight to my chest, rubbing the front of it and hoping it was true and not some cruel joke. That news was like getting Lazarus back from the dead, and to this day I still remember the sight of him, wrapped up in bandages, his arm in a sling, gauze over the eye that got gouged out and scrapes all over his face, lying there in the hospital bed watching *I Love Lucy*, except he wasn't watching; it was the fellow next to him watching. I was still holding the mandolin when I hugged him, and the nurse had to pry me off there because she had to take blood or give him a shot or something.

"Thunder didn't make it, did he, Daddy?" I said.

"I reckon he didn't, Son. But he knew there was something coming, didn't he?"

I nodded.

"He was a faithful dog to the end, but that water was too much for him. But the Lord saw us through it."

"What happened to the people in Miss Dreama's house?" I said.

Mama looked kind of sad at me like I hadn't obeyed her, but I couldn't help it.

Daddy looked down at the covers and sort of smoothed out the sheet a little bit, and a big old tear formed in the one eye that wasn't covered. "It was just awful, Son. I don't expect I'll ever be able to take it all in. It's just tragical."

"Did they make it?" I choked. "Those two little girls?"

He shook his head and looked at Mama. "I don't see how they could have. When we got close to the bank, I jumped down into the sludge and the mess but I couldn't hold on. The current was too strong. I never should have made it out myself, but God

41

must have something more for me to do, I reckon."

Mama's mouth started giving way, her chin puckering. "They found them in the creek, down past the railroad trestle. All of them together except the littlest one. They haven't found her yet."

She put her head down on the bed, and Daddy put his bandaged arm around her and tried to pat her. There with the people on the TV laughing at something Lucy said, my mother and father had their most honest conversation I ever heard.

"I didn't mean for you to get hurt," Mama said. "I just wanted Dreama to know. The last thing in the world I wanted to happen was to see you get hurt."

"Arlene, you listen to me. There wasn't nothing going to stop that water once it made up its mind to come down that valley. You were looking out for your neighbors as you would yourself. I'm just glad you stayed on high ground."

Mama looked up at me, and I knew we were going to keep our secret from him. I knew he was not in a state to hear the truth. So I kept quiet. It was some time before he heard about the car and how I was stuck in there alone. It liked to kill him when he saw how damaged it was, and it wasn't long after that we moved out of the creek.

But all of that time, from my tenth birth-day until the day he died, I never told him what really happened in the car. I told Mama and Daddy what I have written here before, and that is, I just got up enough nerve to jump. But that is not the truth.

My first reaction was not to believe what happened. I was scared that I had made it up. In a little boy's mind it's possible to get the truth mixed up with the make-believe. After I decided I couldn't make up some-thing like that, I was scared that people would think I was uppity. That they would figure I thought I was something special.

But if you want to know the truth about how I got out of that car, I'll tell you.

After Mama slipped out and I was by myself, it was like the world went into slow motion, like one of those old movies of the Kennedy assassination. The black water poured through the back window as a wave came over the car.

I cried out to my mama and to Jesus and my daddy. I had to tell myself to breathe because it was the scariest thing I've ever seen. We hit the telephone pole, and the windshield cleared enough for me to see another house coming toward me. That's when the car rose up and I fell into the backseat.

And this is where my story changes, because I did not see an open window and know this was my chance to escape. I did not pull myself up by any kind of courage or will. There was nothing that rose up in me that was greater than the floodwaters. Like the 125 others who died that day, I would have drowned or been crushed in that backseat if I had been left to my own devices. I did not jump out of that car and I certainly didn't grab my daddy's mandolin.

With the swirling waters around me, thick as a coal milk shake, I was *lifted* out of that car. By some force of nature or the supernatural. Or maybe it was love that lifted me like a helpless little baby out of that window and placed me on the ground where my mama found me. And right beside me was my daddy's mandolin.

Now that may sound far-fetched to you, and if you think I am touched in the head, you can stop all the speculating because I'm as sane as anybody. But I'm telling you, as sure as I sit here and write this, I had no hope of living and I went from the backseat of that car to being on the ground just as fast as you can blink your eyes. I was another dead body in a car about to be smashed. But by some miracle I wound up alive alongside a river of death. Me and an old mandolin. How can you make people understand a thing like that?

# 2

I will not divulge secrets of hidden things. If you are looking for titillating information about how many of us can dance on the head of a pin, you should look elsewhere. I am not here to aid you with insight into heavenly things, but earthly.

I suppose you will want to know my name. I understand that it aids you in your "connection" with the writer and that you must call me something. I have considered using a pseudonym such as "Clarence" because I'm aware of your films that depict bumbling angels. If you must have a name for me, simply call me Malachi, for it means "messenger," and that is what I was created to be.

Just the telling of the story causes me no small amount of consternation, for when I think about what I am missing at other points of the battle, the assignments I might have been given, I can easily become dissatisfied. You must know at the outset that I did not want this assignment. I did not seek it or grasp for it because at heart, I am a warrior, not a scribe. I am a messenger, not an angelic detective. At times, I will admit, it seems that there is such little purpose in my being here, stuck in a back alley of the world watching the life of a man whose existence seems of less-than-grand importance on the human stage. But I know the Creator too well to let myself wander those country roads for long. In the end I simply exult in the truth that I have been given this assignment by the One who knows the end from the beginning, and so I will gladly fulfill my role.

Now, before you begin the logical leap you are probably making, let me say a word or two about the subject of "guardian angels." As I said earlier, I will not divulge the secret things. I will simply say that there are times and seasons when a person may be required to have one or many angels surrounding him or her, just as there are seasons and times for those of us who serve in the Lord's army. We may move from battle to battle, fighting the enemy on various levels, moving back and forth and accepting different assignments, getting a wider scope and variety of the human experiment.

I believed, before this task, that I knew the whole story. I believed I understood the

Creator and His ways. And I have always been able to make some sense of things from the perspective of timelessness. I know that a grain of wheat must fall into the earth and die before it can bring forth fruit.

However, observing this one life, instead of hundreds and thousands, is causing me to reevaluate my concept of The Plan and how each life is used in the grand scheme. And to this I will now turn my full attention.

I promise I will tell you all that I am allowed. The rest is up to you.

Under direct orders from my commander, I left my station and traveled quickly, by cover of night, to the Allman home. How I travel, how long it takes, and other specifics may be of interest, but they are not important here.

It is difficult to explain what happens when one like me reaches a destination given by my Creator. Standing at the battle line, seeing the array of the enemy for the first time, looking into the face of evil itself, provides a sensory experience unparalleled. To know I am exactly where I am to be, fully equipped for the war ahead, provides a feeling of contentment and joy I cannot fully convey.

However, spotting this young boy sleeping and looking into his face, I am ashamed to say that I felt such disappointment. Letdown. I expected to see a cherubic lad, the tousled hair of aristocracy, a diamond in the rough. Instead, I found an unattractive hill child sleeping soundly, his covers askew, an old mandolin on the bed next to his head. I couldn't help but stare at him and wonder. A bulbous nose, his eyes deep-set, and an almost-Neanderthal forehead. For his age, his hands seemed large and his arms and legs gangly. I know the humans grow in fits and spurts throughout their youth, but I couldn't help but wonder, why this child? Why this plain and ordinary dwelling?

The room was Spartan at best, with a few toys and books on an old shelf held up by bricks and two planks of wood. There were worn baseball cards in the corner that looked as if they had been inherited. It struck me then, and still does, that though his appearance was less than pleasant, this was not an ordinary child. There was something in the way things were arranged, a pattern that suggested order. There was also a crystal radio near the shelf that appeared to be something the child had built himself. I later learned that he and his father had put it together. At first, it didn't work. But when his father left the room, Billy corrected the crossed wires. And that was when he was six.

Do not think that we spend our time snooping into your lives. We have better things to do than mull the minutiae of humans. However, I tell you this in advance because the observations Billy has of himself are certainly, at times, askew of the full truth. Not that he is lying; he is simply humble to the point of exhaustion.

I continued invisible to the human eye as the boy awakened and took his mandolin into the kitchen and sat for a time, holding the instrument and going over the strings with his left hand in a silent song. There are times when we are allowed to take other forms for some important task or contact, but I have never had that opportunity, though it has always been my hope to someday experience the feeling.

Sensing a change, I rose above to view the entire scene. Animals walked unhindered and unaware. Having experience in military maneuvers, I have been able to anticipate attacks and assaults by the enemy, and this felt much the same.

I was relieved when the family moved to their automobile, then dismayed when the father ran to warn another family after the explosion. I rose quickly enough to see the onslaught. It reminded me of the ancient flood in Noah's time, when the waters sprang forth and engulfed the entire earth. This dam break was an isolated instance, of course, but the force with which it moved and destroyed was reminiscent of that judgment.

Once the killing force was unleashed, it was my duty to return to my charge. When I am given an assignment, unless specifically stipulated, it is at my discretion how I accomplish that task. In this case, it was clear that the "rules of engagement" were limited to Billy. For reasons I do not understand, I was told to limit my protective efforts.

But with Billy safely in the automobile, I decided to stay with the father, knowing how the child's life would be affected by the loss of his paternal figure. I am not justifying my actions; I am simply explaining the sequence of events.

I stayed with the house as it picked up speed, rumbling along on the surface of the water. The father, a courageous man in the face of the violence around him and the slim odds, held tightly to two young girls and looked for an opportunity to save them. The wall of water that lifted them continued to take the ramshackle and well-built dwellings indiscriminately. But as this home neared a washed-out bridge and debris that had piled high, I sensed something amiss and rose to see the Allmans' automobile being carried along the edge of the stream. You can only imagine the speed with which I made my way there, finding the mother outside of the car, hysterical.

The car tipped up in a sickening display of the water's power and I feared the worst. When I entered it, Billy gasped for air. He was covered with coal sludge and debris and close to death. I debated speaking peace to him but decided that might frighten him. It was time to act. I grasped his arm and the mandolin that had seemed like another appendage to him that morning and pulled them through the open window and onto the ground a safe distance away. His mother found him there and took over, cradling him in her lap and wailing.

When I was sure Billy was all right, I returned to find the home I had been following obliterated near the bridge, mixed now with the debris that piled higher. Scanning the murky stream, even with my abilities to see beyond that which humans can, I could find no living thing and feared Billy's father had perished.

However, after checking once more on Billy and seeing that he and his mother were moving toward safety, I made another trip. The area was devastated. Dwellings and businesses were wiped out as the spillage moved through the area like a deadly snake.

I spotted something moving near the edge

of black water that had pooled. A coal-crusted hand struggled to break through. I could not tell if this was Billy's father because this person was indistinguishable. His clothes had been ripped from his body. Red leaked through a gash on his head near one eye.

Fearing that he would be unable to extricate himself on his own, and being a ministering spirit called to duty with humans, my first reaction was to reach down and pull him up onto a bank. It was such a small thing, really nothing at all, but as I sat near him, watching the water spill from his mouth and his breathing become more and more shallow, I remembered the instructions given and wondered if I had broken some trust between the human and the unseen world. And it was there on that muddy bank that I began to feel in a way I had never felt.

Humans struggle with the underside of the tapestry, unable to see the beauty in their situation, for they cannot know how the trouble of life fits with The Plan. On the other hand, those of us above are able to see a different view and the orchestration with which the world is held together and moved forward. Seemingly unrelated events below the tapestry take on new meaning from our vantage.

But sitting there next to the near-dead body of that man, watching the lives of people destroyed in a few moments of cacophonic peril, brought me close to the human condition. It gave a magnified vision of that which I had only considered from afar. Why would the Creator allow such wanton destruction and loss of life? and to such undeserving people? They had only the most meager of possessions and lives. Their circumstances, when considered, were heartbreaking. Why are these lives taken and those of the wicked and debauched not? I can think of many more deserving canyons on the face of the earth, where water could cascade and not take out one righteous person.

It is written that angels long to look into the things of salvation, and that is true. But sitting beside that man, wondering what future lay ahead for the boy whose only goal that day was a birthday party, I breathed in the utter despair and anguish and senselessness of humanity. It made me glad that I am not a man.

It also brought a sense of fright to me. Perhaps it was there all along, dormant until this moment when the loss of life and deadly waters brought the submerged to the surface.

Doubt.

I have no lack of faith in the Creator's order; I have seen Him work His plan through the ages, through the wars and rumors of wars. I have seen His love poured out on His people to such an extent that I wanted to taste redemption — for I cannot be redeemed. I believed, in spite of what was before me, that the purpose of the cosmos was still in place, that the sovereign hand of God was still moving and able to create beauty from ashes. But though my belief is built upon nothing less than the sacrifice of the One, there was a moment of doubt.

And I feared that would change everything. Like the flood that swept through these people's lives, I feared this might be used against me and, more frighteningly, against Him.

# 3

I have heard that your first childhood memory is telling. Mine is a mixture of scents, sounds, and visuals. Of wood smoke and bluegrass and wrinkled hands on a mandolin.

I can see my daddy's black shoes tapping to the beat. Mama says I would sit on the floor and listen to him and his friends play in the evening. Just sit right there in the middle of the hardwood floor with toes tapping and my hands clapping. We lost the picture in the flood, but there was one of me looking up at them with the biggest grin a kid could ever have, listening to the music. "Sally Goodin' " and "Cripple Creek" and "Old Joe Clark."

That's what is imprinted on my brain: fingers on an old mandolin and people sitting in a circle in hardback chairs tapping on the wood floor and playing music that came from the soul. I believe that's where the music comes from. And it doesn't matter if all those instruments are exactly in tune, but it does help.

You might think that my daddy learned the mandolin from his own daddy or a relative, but it was actually another miner who traded him the instrument for a few of his chickens. From the time I was little, I remember watching his gnarled fingers moving up and down that neck. It was hard for him to get his fingertips in there to play and that's partly the reason why I think he wanted me to learn, so that he could see somebody with smaller fingers do it the way it was meant to be played. He would put his hand on the back of my head or on my shoulder while he was teaching me, and it felt like a warm biscuit back there. My daddy taught me to be a gentle man with such rough hands you could sand plywood with them.

I never really learned to read the notes from the page and transfer that to the instrument. But I did learn the sequence of chords and what strings and frets went with those chord progressions. To me, music is a mathematical equation or a signal flow from the transmitter to the antenna. Daddy taught me to be in the music, to be present with the chord structure and the notes being played by others. In those early days when his friends would come over and he would hand the mandolin to me, it was almost like a bluegrass blues session as his friends presented the musical playground for me and I simply danced and frolicked from note to note. I can still remember the looks on the faces of those miners when I played "Tennessee Waltz" and "Foggy Mountain Breakdown." There are some songs that are just part of you, and I suppose "Amazing Grace" is the other one that not a soul on earth can teach you. You just have to feel it.

Daddy taught me all he could in the years after the flood, but he and I both knew there was only so much he could give to me and that it was something I needed to fly with, like a little bird who is pushed from the nest.

We stayed in Lorado a little while, moving into one of the trailers the government provided. Other people sued the company but not my daddy. They gave him something like $4,000 for everything, and that was all she wrote. He said we were fortunate to get out of there with our lives. The damage had been done to him, though. He already had the black lung, and after the flood it crippled him so that he couldn't walk well. Just kind of hobbled around wherever it was he was going by using a cane.

He finally took the money they gave and left Logan County for good. We moved to a town called Dogwood because some of my mama's kin were there at the time.

We found a place to rent for a good price and moved what little stuff we had inside. Others in the community heard about our plight and gave us some clothes and furniture. Nothing in the house matched, but Mama treated it like a castle, moving an old couch around the living room like it mattered. I can still remember the day we went to Heck's and bought a television. That was a big day.

My daddy would sit out on the porch in a lawn chair somebody gave to us and smoke his Pall Malls and watch cars go by on the interstate, tucked in between the hills like we were. One thing the flood did for us was cause us to take a lot of pictures. I still have photos of my father laughing, though trying not to show his bad teeth. Kind of a half laugh that people of the mountain give you because they are more ashamed of what's behind their lips than they are happy about laughing. There's one of him in that old lawn chair, which would have fallen through with anybody else because all of the slats were rotten, but by then he didn't weigh

59

more than a bird, his body wracked with coughing. He was just a shell of the man I knew when I was little, but he was a survivor.

Dogwood didn't have any coal mines and he didn't have the strength to do much but cough up the black stuff inside his lungs. The only thing he could do with the little breath he had in him was auctioneering. There was an old boy at the feed store who heard he had kind of a talent for it, and he hired him to sell some farm equipment for a family that was going through a hard time. The only problem was my daddy couldn't talk as loud as he needed to, and he worried that he would try too hard and start coughing and that would be the end of his auctioneering.

That year I turned twelve and the more I thought about it, the more I set on a plan to help. One of my cousins was named Elvis and their family didn't have a whole lot more than we did, but he did have this old electric guitar that he'd bring outside and try to play of a night. It was just about the most terrible sound you have ever heard because he didn't know how to tune the thing. I would go over and tune it for him and show him a few chords.

There was also an ancient recorder with a

microphone at our schoolhouse, and I knew it wasn't right when I did it, but one Friday I took the microphone and wound the cord around it and stuffed it inside my pocket and took it home. The only problem was, the plug on the end of it was the wrong kind, so I had to strip it off and do the same with Elvis's guitar cord. I got it ready late the night before the auction and took it to my daddy.

I turned the amp on and the speaker hummed and rattled a little until the tubes warmed up. When I plugged in the microphone and held it close to his lips while he talked, his eyes lit up like a Christmas tree. The next day at the feed store, I borrowed a long, black extension cord and plugged it in. That little amp worked like a charm and Daddy did cough a few times, but he got through it all right.

The people whose stuff he auctioned off got a fair price for their equipment, and I guess one of them heard what I had done because after he paid my daddy, the man took me inside and bought me a Zagnut bar and a bottle of grape Nehi. I'll tell you, I was getting to like Dogwood a lot after that. I fixed the microphone cable back up and returned it every weekend after Daddy used it.

Daddy's health didn't improve and pretty soon he was in bed. By then, Mama was working at the beauty shop part-time, and he sat there by himself all day. I felt sorry for him. He wanted to get up out of that bed and throw a ball with me or just go for a walk, but he didn't have the strength.

I remember one Sunday morning before the end, I found him in the kitchen getting his jacket on. It was October and the leaves had started to turn and the ground smelled like an earth pie you could eat.

"Where do you think you're going?" I said.

"Out for a walk; you want to come?"

"Mama's going to kill you."

He smiled. "Can't kill what you can't catch."

He handed me his walking stick, the one he had carved all kinds of things in, even part of a Scripture verse that says, "Come unto me, all ye that labour and are heavy laden, and I will give you rest." Except some of the words you couldn't read because the letters got knocked off. He grabbed a smaller stick and shook his head. "No, you take that one."

"I got one; you go ahead and take it."

He wouldn't hear anything of the sort, so we walked outside on the road and then up into the woods with the trees sporting the most beautiful colored leaves you have ever seen. It was like an explosion had happened at a Glidden factory and all of that paint fell on the trees. It was such a good feeling to have my daddy walking with me, even if he did have to go slow. I thought he was getting better and that this was the first of many walks we'd take.

"One of these days I'm going to buy this hill," Daddy said. "Such a pretty piece of land."

"What would you do with it if you had the money?" I said.

He laughed. "Now you're talking like your mama. I'd clear off a spot over there on the side of the hill and build us a nice house. Then I'd clear off the stumps and brush on top and have us a garden that would feed the whole town for three winters in a row. Maybe even raise some cattle and pigs and chickens."

"I don't like chickens."

"And why is that?"

"They wake me up. When we lived back on the creek, they'd get me up every day."

Something happened when I mentioned our old place and I wished I hadn't. Just saying things that spark a memory will do that. He sat down on an old stump and leaned on his stick. I offered him mine, but he waved me off.

"There's something I need to tell you. Something I haven't told anybody. Not even your mama."

I knelt in the wet leaves. Looking back on it, I think he was inviting me in, knowing that time was short.

"What is it?"

He took out a cigarette and put it between his lips, leaving it unlit. "Those two little girls at the house, the ones I carried — they died because of me."

"That's not true."

"Yes, it is, because I let go. They were just as scared as pups and they were screaming to go back with their mama."

"But everybody in that house died, Daddy. Except for you. Leaving them with their mama wouldn't have helped. You were their best chance."

"I was a poor excuse for a chance to those girls. Every night when I go to sleep, I can hear them screaming. And then the sound of their voices in the sludge." He looked away and shook his head. "There are some things a man can't ever leave behind, Billy. I hope to God you'll never have anything like that happen to you."

I stared at his shoes. There was a leaf stuck to the underside of one of them. His shoes were like new, only a few sizes bigger than mine. I would wear those shoes on my first day at a real job.

"There comes a time in a man's life when he knows he's been beat. When he knows the world just came up and smacked him across the face. And you can either get up and go on or just lay there and watch everything roll right on by. I think I've come to that point."

"Daddy, you don't have to worry. Mama's got a job, and pretty soon I'll be old enough to maybe work at the feed store. I'll bet I can make enough money to buy this hillside and a few more."

He patted me on the head like I was a dog on a chain that wants to run. "I hope you do that, Son. With the talent you have with that mandolin and the way you can rig electronics, I wouldn't doubt that you'll make it big someday."

"I'm going to be on the Grand Ole Opry," I said.

"I don't doubt that'll happen. Probably up there playing with Bill Monroe."

"I want to play gospel music. Songs that will lead people to Jesus."

He nodded. "That's what I was hoping you'd say. You can get fame and fortune and then you have your reward. But leading

65

people to Jesus is what will bring you the most satisfaction. You remember that."

He pulled out his lighter and opened the top with a *kerthunk.* Then he lit the cigarette and pulled in a few drags of the killing smoke. "You know what I think we ought to do?"

"What's that?"

"We ought to get up one day when your mother has to work a full day and have the neighbors call you in sick to school. Then you and I can go hunting. Get us a rabbit or a squirrel and surprise her by having it cooking when she gets home. Wouldn't that be something?"

"You mean it?" I said. That sounded about the most wonderful thing I could think of, particularly because it meant my daddy was feeling stronger. To think of him going hunting with me was almost too good of an answer to prayer.

"Tell you what. You go over to Elvis's house and see if you can borrow his .410 and some shells."

"Now?"

"No, after we're finished with the walk. But don't tell your mother. She'd have my hide if she knew I was going to keep you home from school."

We made it all the way to the top of the

ridge, where you could look out and see the town and the hills in the distance. It was like having your own private box on God's handiwork.

He put his hand on my neck and held it there. "You see all the beauty out there?" When I nodded, he said, "That's nothing compared to the beauty of a heart that wants to know God and follow him. And you have that kind of heart, Billy. I know you do. So don't you let anything or anyone take that from you. You understand?"

I nodded, but I didn't understand. If I had, I would never have gotten the gun and hid it under my bed that night. I got him alone later at the house and told him Elvis only had five shells, and he said, "That's plenty."

"For squirrel hunting?" I said.

He laughed. "Five shells, five squirrels. You just wait."

The next day Daddy made a special effort to get up before I went to school. He kissed me on the head and his eyes got all watery. When I left, he had his arm around Mama, hugging her close as he watched me walk to the bus.

Mama went into the shop in the afternoon, so she wasn't there when I reached home. I ran all the way from the bus and threw my books down before the screen door slammed. Some of our best times together came right after the bus let me off and I'd sit there and talk with him or I'd turn on the radio in his room and play the mandolin to those songs. This time, I knew something was wrong. There was a stillness to it I can't explain. Like somebody had broken in and stolen something, though at the time I didn't know what.

I walked into his room and thought he was fooling with me. He had pillows up over his head and his arms were down by his side. I noticed Elvis's gun lying on his chest.

"You can't hide from me," I said, bumping into the bed. "Let's go out and get a few squirrels."

He didn't move, so I pulled the pillows away. He had three towels from the bathroom wrapped around his head. I took hold of his arm and he was cold. Then I noticed the red on the towels and the stains on the wall. The towels had flowers all over them, and my heart started pounding when I pulled them away from his face. I can't describe what that looked like, but I can still see it.

I turned away and noticed two envelopes at the foot of his bed. One had *Billy* written on it and the other one said, *Mama.* That's what he called her when he was tender toward her. I opened the one to me.

Dear Billy,

I'm sorry. You have to believe me when I say that. I don't ask you to understand what I've done, but I hope one day you will find it in your heart to forgive me.

I know this is a lot to take in, but I need your help. Go get Ruthie Bowles and tell her to come quick before Mama comes home. She'll know what to do. I don't want your mama to see me like this. I hate it that you will, but I have come to the end of what I can take.

I love you with all my heart, and you and your mama have been the only reasons for me to stay awhile. I just want to go to Jesus now. I'm hoping to see Harless when I get there and those little girls from Buffalo Creek and tell them how sorry I am. I never should have made it, and they should have.

It makes me sick of heart not to be able to see you grow up and make something of yourself. I know you're going to do that. I'll be watching every step of the way and cheering you on.

I know I don't have to ask you to take

care of your mother. She's going to need you now more than ever. You will both bounce back from this. I just ask you to forgive me because I can't take it any-more.

Love,<br>Daddy

I sat on the bed reading his words over and over. It was the only letter he ever wrote me other than a birthday card he would just sign. And then I looked at the gun. No wonder he had told me not to tell Mama. He used me. I found out later that Mama had taken away all the sharp knives and locked up the medicine, but I guess a man who is determined can find a way to do what he wants.

I cried as I ran to Mrs. Bowles's house. Like some of our neighbors, we didn't have a phone, and there was nobody I would have called faster than her. She was known in the community as someone you could turn to if you were in trouble. I'd been there a few times with my parents, so I knew where she lived, but I didn't know her well. When Mama and Daddy got into some disagreement and couldn't work it out, Mrs. Bowles was the one they went to. She'd had her own trouble, I guess, and when people go through hard times, it helps them know how to help others. I remember her sitting and listening, just crying with them about the house and Harless and all our changes.

Mrs. Bowles opened the door and right away took me by the shoulders, looking me in the eyes and asking what was wrong. I couldn't stop sobbing, and when I told her, she hugged me and held on like a grandmother. She called the police, and then we both hopped in her car and drove back to the house.

She told me to stay in the front room while she went back to the bedroom. The police came and I let them in. Then an ambulance came and some men carried my daddy out. He still had his black shoes on, and they stuck out from underneath the sheet. Ruthie called Mama, and by the time she got home, Mrs. Bowles had the room cleaned with the bed made; she'd wrapped up all the bloody pillows and sheets and put them in the back of her car, and she'd found a little vase full of fake daisies and put them on Mama's dresser with the envelope Daddy left propped up in front of it.

Mama started to bawling as soon as she came in the door and just fell into my arms. Mrs. Bowles patted her shoulder and wrung her hands.

"How did he get the gun, Ruthie? I did everything I could. I knew he was depressed and I hated leaving him, but I had to go to work."

Mrs. Bowles held on until she quieted down and then took her into the bedroom, where she talked in a low voice and then Mama would scream and cry. That was the worst day of my life, and I thought it couldn't get any worse than that.

Something happens when your daddy dies and you feel like it's your fault. A piece of you goes missing. From that day on, I felt there was a hole in my own heart that wasn't ever going to be filled.

I stood in the front room looking outside through the screen on the door. There were all kinds of people looking at the ambulance and the police. Asking questions. Wondering what happened. A rumor went around that my daddy had shot someone, and a kid told me later they thought I was dead. There were kids on bikes and men in their coveralls with their arms folded, shaking their heads and looking off. They finally left, but from then on, it felt like our house was marked.

# 4

I went back to school the next week, and I swear walking down the aisle of that bus was harder than the funeral. Kids staring at me and then whispering to each other. My teacher had put a little bag of candy in my desk with a note that said, "With Sympathy." Inside she wrote that she was sorry for the "trial" I was going through and that she was available if I needed to talk. And she'd write real encouraging notes on all my tests and papers and sometimes didn't count my answers wrong even though I'd gotten them wrong, which I thought wasn't fair to the other kids but was also nice of her.

Kids pretty much stayed away from me, as if suicide was something you could catch. I wondered how many moms had told their kids to leave me alone, that there was something wrong with me. I was already a lonely kid without many friends, but that sealed the deal. At lunch you would have thought that I had the plague because nobody would sit nearby, so I took my lunch outside even if it was raining or snowing.

There was only one other student who gave me the time of day. Heather Blanch sat toward the front of the bus and smelled like flowers in the spring. Every morning I just moved past her because she lived in a big brick house and always had nice clothes and looked like she didn't belong in West Virginia. She looked destined for big things, a blue-ribbon pick of the litter compared to me.

"Sit down," she said one morning as I paused, looking for a seat. When I just stared at her, she blew a bubble and patted the seat with a thin hand. "Sit."

I sat about as far away from her as I could get because it scared me sitting next to someone so pretty and smart. She brushed her hair every day and it looked like silk, just as shiny and soft. And she was always carrying these thick books to read. I could tell by the way the bookmark moved every day that she could read fast.

"You want some gum?" she said, handing me her pack of Fruit Stripe.

"No thanks."

"You're Billy, right?"

I nodded.

"My cousin lives near you. Says she hears you playing the mandolin. You're pretty good."

I shrugged. "I try."

Kids talked around us as I sat there, trying to think of something else to say. "I'm in Mrs. Faulkner's class," I said, my voice cracking. "In the new building." They had constructed an exterior building next to the school that had been built in the 1930s.

She shook her head. "I wish I'd have gotten moved out there. I'm stuck inside with the Barn Owl."

Her teacher was twice the age of mine, and she was right, the lady did look like an owl. She wore thick glasses, and the way her hair framed her face made you think she would eat mice at night.

"So you can," she said.

"Can what?"

"Smile. I've always wondered if there was one in there. Now I can tell everybody the truth."

I stared out the window on the other side, my heart feeling something akin to a mixture of indigestion and a sudden, life-threatening illness. When the bus got to the school, I was the first on my feet.

"You're welcome," she said behind me.

I tried to stay as unseen as possible

75

through the day, and I made it to the bus first and sat way in the back. The next day I caught her eye as I passed the seat. I paused and she looked out the window.

"If you're not going to talk to me, you're not going to sit," she said. "I don't appreciate the silent treatment."

I backed up. "I'm not trying to give you the silent treatment. I just don't do well around . . ."

"Around what?"

"Sit down!" the bus driver yelled. He was a wiry, thin man named Scarberry. Didn't weigh much, but his voice was like God's.

I arranged my books and tried to get comfortable, but I was sweating in the chill of the morning.

"You don't do well around what?" she said, her face twisted.

"People like you."

She was clearly agitated, and at the next stop I shifted to get up and move back. She grabbed my jacket in her fist and I was surprised at her strength. "Stay." She said it like she was ordering a dog not to go for a tree, and a boy in front of us turned around and laughed, showing teeth that looked like he'd been eating black licorice.

"What kind of people don't you do well around?" she said, staring at me with eyes the color of the ocean, though I had never seen it.

"You know. Nice people with new clothes and big houses."

She scrunched her face up. "You're prejudiced."

"Excuse me?"

"Do you think people with dark skin are dumber than you?"

"No."

"Are they any less human beings?"

"No, they're the same as you and me."

"Then why would you judge me just because I have new clothes and live in a brick house? Besides, this is not new. I got it last year."

"I'm not judging you; I just don't know how to talk to somebody like you."

"Well then we might have just had a breakthrough in education. You're talking, aren't you?"

I nodded. "But it's not real easy."

"First time with anything is hard. Tell you what, I'll hold this seat open for you every day and we'll practice."

The thought of sitting next to her each day was both exhilarating and sickening. She would be able to spot all the flaws in my wardrobe, which amounted to about three outfits. My shoes were already falling apart.

"Why are you doing this?" I said.

"See, a good question opens the conversation up to new information. You're catching on." She put a finger to her lips. "Why am I doing this? Maybe it's because I feel sorry for you. Maybe it's because I'm madly in love with you. Maybe it's that I don't want any of those kids who get on after you do to sit here." She turned to me. "What do you think?"

"Maybe it's all the above?" I said.

She howled. "*And* a sense of humor. I like it." She held out her hand. "Shake on it. We'll sit together as long as we're still riding the same bus."

I took her hand, a soft, warm thing, and was again surprised at the strength she showed in the handshake. A warmth spread through me, and from that day on, I never looked at a yellow school bus the same.

It was three years later that Mama and I talked about the day Daddy died. She was listening to a Christian radio station that we could barely pull in, the signal crackling and dropping in and out. I had put up an antenna and hooked it to the gutter on the house.

The preacher talked about Lazarus coming out of the grave and how his friends had to take the grave clothes from him and used that to explain how people can help others get through hard times. After the man gave his address and the program was over, Mama turned off the radio.

"Do you ever think about that day?" she said.

"I don't spend one day *not* thinking about it."

"And what is it you think?"

"That if I hadn't done what he told me, he'd still be alive."

"Oh, Billy," she said, and she got that hangdog look. "Your daddy was a good man but he did a selfish thing. I can understand it because he was in a lot of pain, but you can't ever blame yourself. He's the one who chose."

"But I gave him the gun."

"If he couldn't have convinced you to bring it to him, he would have figured out some other way. What did he tell you?"

I told her we were going hunting, and she nearly broke in two. She put her head on my shoulder and the tears flowed. I just sat there, shaking on the inside, feeling like a wet leaf on the ground.

Finally she got her breath. "There were

things he could never bring himself to tell people. Things he saw. You knew he was in Holden 22, didn't you?"

I shook my head.

"He worked the Holden 22 mine before we moved to Lorado. He was supposed to be on the crew that went into the mine that day, but he'd gotten hurt and the doctor said he should take the day off. He would have been in there with the rest of them that morning."

"What happened?" I said.

"A fire. They hauled eighteen men out of there and they looked like they'd just gone to sleep. Two of them crawled out this narrow passage to see if they could get help and they survived it by the grace of God, but all those others died. It liked to break Other's heart.

"Then, a few weeks before your daddy died, he got word that one of those men who crawled out of there had died over in Boone County. He'd become the foreman on the tipple and fell in a coal crusher. I think that's part of what pushed Other over the edge. All the pain he felt inside, and feeling like he should have died several places, and what happened with Harless, it all just did him in."

"What about Harless?"

She let go of me and sat up straight. It was like the windup of a major league pitcher. She was trying to get the momentum to let the words go from another deep hurt.

"When Harless turned eighteen, there was a good chance he would get drafted. More than good. His first thought was to run. And then he thought he'd be a conscientious objector."

"What's that?"

"It just means you don't want to go kill people. Some people have religious objections to it. Harless didn't, but he also didn't want to go to Vietnam. But your daddy said to Harless that it was his duty to serve his country. When your country calls, you go. He always believed that.

"He and Harless fought about it a long time. And after he graduated high school, Harless took off for Myrtle Beach and stayed with some friends down there thinking about it. You probably don't remember any of this."

"I remember how good it felt when Harless would pick me up and take me on his shoulders to the football games."

"He loved you like ice cream and sheet cake," she said, a twinkle of memory in her eyes. "He just marveled at how smart you were, learning to read before you ever set foot in school."

"I wish we still had his picture," I said.

She nodded. "I still have him here." She put her hand over her heart.

"What happened to him after that?"

"He came back from the beach all tanned and ready to enlist. Said he wasn't going to wait for them to come and get him; he was going to go on his own terms. And it made your daddy proud.

"Harless did well in basic training and they said he might be officer material. They sent him over there to Viet Rock, as he called it, and he would send us pictures of himself holding a machine gun and smiling with a cigarette hanging out of his mouth. Your daddy would smile when I'd read him one of those letters where Harless would make sport of the things he was doing. He would never admit how hard it was; he just attacked it like your daddy did the mines."

We sat there awhile. It was good to hear my mother's voice talk about the past. I don't know how she got the strength to do it, and that strength wasn't there much after that.

"I remember the day the man came to our door and you cried," I said.

She closed her eyes and I could tell that

memory hurt the worst. "He was coming home in another week. He'd almost made it through his first tour when a sniper fired from the trees. Hit him in the head. They tried to get him to the hospital, but the man said he was killed instantly. Just there one minute and gone the next."

"And Daddy felt like it was his fault?"

"He bawled like a baby at the funeral and just couldn't shake the fact that he'd been the one to push him. He was like a zombie for weeks."

"What brought him out of it?"

She looked at me and smiled. "You did."

"Me? How?"

"The mandolin. He came in one day from work, all covered up with the coal dust, and took a shower. And he was headed to bed without eating a bite when he heard you playing the mandolin in your room. Just picking out some song they had played in their group. He hadn't been with his friends since Harless died, even though I told him he should invite them over. He stood there listening, and then his shoulders shook and I thought he was having a nervous break-down.

" 'I'm sorry; I'm sorry,' he kept saying. I told him it was all right, that everything was going to be okay. And the next week he had his friends back over and there was music in the house. You were sitting right there in the middle of them. That's what pulled him out of it. You and the music."

Mama put her arm around me and snuggled close. "Your daddy always said that God had given you a great gift. He said he could hear the Lord pass just listening to the sounds that instrument could make."

"Is that what you think?" I said.

"More than ever," she said. "The Lord has given you something special, Billy. But it's not really your talent."

"What do you mean?"

"The people you read about in the Bible who are the special people aren't really all that special. They're just sinful people like you and me. What makes them special is the Lord himself. He delights in using the weak things and the despised things and things the world doesn't have much time to notice."

"Like coal miners and their families."

She hugged me tighter. "Especially coal miners and their families. I think God has something special in mind for you. I don't know what it is. I don't know where he's going to lead you, but I know God is going to work in you and through you."

I wanted to tell her about the day of the

84

flood and how I hadn't jumped, but I just said, "What makes you so sure?"

"Because I don't think God trusts just anybody with so much heartache. The world has not yet seen what God can do with a man who gives both halves of a broken heart to him. And I don't doubt that a man like that can change the world . . . or at least a little part of it."

Mama and I never talked much about Harless and Daddy after that, except in her final days that were even more of a heartache. But after that day, I was determined to be the man she was talking about. I wanted to be the one with the broken heart God would use. I didn't have any idea how he would do that, of course. It took me a long time to realize what was right in front of me.

# 5

Time hinders the human condition, but it does not touch me. With our Creator, one day is like a thousand years and a thousand years a day. We feel the onslaught of time only as it is experienced by those in our charge. To us it is only a discipline. Time holds no sway, has no bearing on our resolve to achieve our assigned duties.

However, I will admit that at the beginning of my sojourn with Billy Allman, I began to count the days and spend the hours of his slumber in contemplation of his life's unfolding events. There was something about him that caused me to ponder time in a new way.

Time hinders the humans because their lives are lived on two slopes. Their early lives consist of the upward climb to what they are trying to attain. They press on through education and strive to reach a point where they feel satisfied, where they have "enough," always just beyond their grasp. They neglect what they say is important and strive for sand that so easily slips through their fingers.

The crest of the hill is always unseen. And as the descent begins — indeed, even at the end of days when the eyes give way and the hearing diminishes — humans continue to grasp for what they cannot have. *"If You were a just God, You would give me what I ask."* In that cry, they show that it is not the glory of God they desire, but the want and need in their own heart.

In the mind of the enemy, if they can push a human away from Truth, whatever the means, then they succeed in the continued separation of the created from the Creator. If that human is a follower of the Way, if he possesses a real faith that casts his entire being on the goodness and mercy of God, the evil one will make every attempt to thwart that life and bring it to naught. To discourage and keep that person disconnected from Life. Get him to settle for much less than what the Creator desires for each of His children.

It was along this striving, undulating path that Billy's father was brought, both by physical and emotional turmoil, to the end. I heard his hacking cough during the day, when I would occasionally observe him sitting alone in the front room, the gas heater turned on high in hope of getting warmth to the bone.

Nothing warmed him. He brooded over the past and choices made, speaking to no one.

I did not notice the enemy's approach at first, for I was focused on Billy. Call it complacency if you must.

The enemy congregated around Billy's father, egged him on, whispered to him about his lack of value, his lack of faith, and how everything would be much better if he were not in the picture. They accused him about his older son. The man began to believe he was worthless.

Nothing could have been further from the truth, of course. That boy needed him. Though he felt like half a man, he was everything to the boy, and I wondered if events that would proceed later in Billy's life would prove that postulate true.

When I think of the differences between the way their Father in heaven works with them and the way the evil one tries to use them for his own selfish ends, it astounds me that more humans cannot see the ruse. At every turn, the Creator has endeavored to lead and guide His creation into Truth and Knowledge, but in the corner of those turns has been the enemy seeking to detour humans and cloud their thinking, twisting the good things the King has offered into diabolical traps. The evil one is crafty, and he is every bit the lion seeking to devour.

I dispatched a message to my superior and gave a full report of the enemy's activity. He sent a return message that I was to be on guard but I was not to intervene in any extraordinary way. I was instructed not to risk myself in combat against these forces and to focus on my charge.

Of course, this caused me to think about my actions long ago at the flood. If I had not acted, Billy would have been spared the trauma of seeing his father on the day the demons won. But he would have also missed the time they had together after the flood.

The room took on a palpable darkness, even to Billy, for I saw him several times as he approached and then turned away, as if he could perceive something amiss. Each time I found the enemy at the father's bedside or next to the rickety chair by the gas heater, I would disperse them. But like flies, they multiplied in the return and the onslaught continued. I never once feared their retaliation, for these were merely harassers of the soul. They feared me and where I might send them. But the taste and smell of death in that room lured them time and again, and when they saw they were winning the battle over the man's emotions and will, it only incited them, like fresh blood in a pool of sharks.

I tell you this to prepare you for what I saw at the funeral. Billy handled the day as well as could be expected. There was an initial shock that came over him and seeped into the countryside. Not many came to the service for his father. A few made the long trek from Buffalo Creek and tsk-tsked about his untimely demise. Billy's mother, of course, was in no shape to comfort her only living son, but she did the best she could. And the pastor of their local church did a much-less-than-adequate job of giving hope from the Scriptures.

The final straw was the imp I found sitting on the pile of dirt above the freshly dug hole.

"Have you no decency?" I said, teeth clenched.

He dodged my lunge and skittered away to a nearby tombstone, where he sat enjoying the anger he had caused. "Actually, I think not. Decency was the last thing handed out, and my plate was already full of greed and avarice."

There was something familiar about his voice and demeanor, but I couldn't place him. That he was alone surprised me because the death of humans is something the enemy delights in. They love to see the crying and grief-stricken families. But it is also normal to see many like me at such occasions because the death of one who is loved by the King does not bring sadness, but joy. The enemy sees this as the end, but in truth it is only the beginning, the opening of a new door into a new existence that will last for all eternity.

"You should not be angry with me," the demon said, simpering on the tombstone. "You should be angry with yourself for not preventing such a tragedy. Or if you really want to channel your anger at the one who deserves it, you would be upset with your own Leader, the One who sent you here. Didn't He forbid you to intervene?"

I suddenly recognized the imp. He had been there, aiding and abetting the father of lies when the sickness had been brought on the righteous man Job. When he had broken the pots in order to scratch at the boils on his ravaged skin, this one had been there, mocking the host of heaven as we looked on, silent, unable to act because of the decree.

I flew to the demon, sword unsheathed, and held the tip of the blade to his neck.

Eyes wide, he gulped and stammered, "Now who has the lack of decency? It's a funeral, after all."

"Leave this place now, demon, and do not return."

I let him get up from his awkward position,

but then he turned to me. "This is not the end of trouble for your charge. We know the reason you were chosen." He tilted his head sickeningly, too far, almost turning it all the way around. "Your Leader has left you vulnerable, just like the boy. He was abandoned by *his* father. And so have you been abandoned in this wasteland."

I drew closer. "There is no abandonment with the Most High. There is not a word on your tongue that He does not hear." The demon shrank back as I spoke the words from David, of old:

" 'Whither shall I go from thy spirit? or whither shall I flee from thy presence? If I ascend up into heaven, thou art there: if I make my bed in hell, behold, thou art there. If I take the wings of the morning, and dwell in the uttermost parts of the sea; Even there shall thy hand lead me, and thy right hand shall hold me.' "

The demon turned his head as if trying to block the words. When I was finished, he turned back and pointed to the grave.

I glanced at Billy, whose eyes were filled, brimming and running freely. His mother sat, stunned and unmoving, by his side. It was a picture of abject grief, the kind that sinks to the bone and takes hold of a life and alters it forever.

The demon's voice changed to whispered tones, and his confidence chilled me. "We know the thoughts of your Most High God for your charge and you. They are thoughts of evil to bring destruction upon you. And though you may call upon Him, He will not hearken unto you. The boy will seek His will but not find it, though he searches with all his heart. His is a future without hope."

I turned and gasped to see a thousand demons congregated in that valley of death, with more behind the edge of the trees, all of them grinning as if the victory was won. Having a warrior spirit, I knew I could fight and defeat the assembled foe if called upon, but I also knew it was imperative to inform my superiors, to say nothing of my concern for the boy and his mother.

I sprang from my position and the demons followed. I was not running from the fight but taking it to a different plane. But as I ascended and signaled my comrades, I couldn't block the demon's voice. Did he really know the plan? In the case of Job, that was true. Satan had conferred with the Most High, and it led to devastation. Though in the end, Job was not killed and his life proved a testament of the faithfulness and sovereignty of the One, I wondered about Billy's life. The seed of doubt that had begun to grow had sprouted. The demon had used my own lack of knowledge and trust against me.

The war that day was fierce and I was joined by many of the host to battle these unholy ones. We fought them all the way to the pit, where they scattered and abandoned the struggle, shrieking and screaming. And when I returned to the home of my charge, his mother sat in front of the television, entranced. Billy sat in his room with the mandolin, playing a sad and mournful tune.

# 6

My sophomore year in high school was my first year at Dogwood High. Back then freshmen still went to junior high on the hill overlooking the high school.

One afternoon in the spring I was sitting in the little control room in Mr. Gibson's class that we used to record ourselves for the local radio station. Every week they let us have a ten-minute show that would air on Saturday afternoons. We recorded it on a reel-to-reel Wollensak that clunked when you hit Record. I was always the engineer and editor for the program and never got to talk much.

We called Mr. Gibson "Buzz" because he wore his hair closely cropped at a time when everyone else wore it long. And he was painfully short, which must have been hard for him because most of the guys who walked in towered over him. He had hands that looked like they belonged to a beauty queen, and for a West Virginia born and bred man, he had an eye for fashion. He wore shiny cowboy boots and pastel-colored suits with floral-print shirts that stood out in pictures. He had a way of walking with a purpose the rest of the teachers and administrators didn't have.

"I didn't know you played," he said, stepping into the room as I shut off the recorder. I had hoped to get away with playing the mandolin without discovery.

"I'll erase it."

"No, play it for me."

"I'm not any good; I just fool around."

He looked at the small mixer we had that was hooked up to an eight-track player as well as a turntable. "What were you playing?"

"Just playing along with a record I bought."

He leaned over the turntable and his Brut aftershave swept through the room. "Bill Monroe," he said, his head moving as he read the name on the record. "Can you keep up with him?"

"You know bluegrass?"

"I'm a closet fan. There's a fellow at my church who plays in a group. Can you keep up with Bill Monroe?"

"I can stay with the tempo okay."

"Let me hear it."

"It's not any good."

"You said that already."

The kids on the bus made fun of me for bringing my mandolin. They called me "Flatt and Scruggs" and it killed me because I hated the attention. I didn't have a case for it; I just kept it strung over my shoulder and hidden under my coat. When I sat down next to Heather the next morning, she spotted it. There was not another kid on the bus I would have handed it to, but when she held out those slim, milky-white hands, I unstrapped it and gave it up. She plucked and strummed and smiled. Something happened to my heart.

One of the kids behind her grabbed it and held it over his head, hooting with glee. It was Earl Caldwell, a hulk of a boy with a penchant for crude remarks to young ladies and violence toward any male smaller than him. He would draw his middle finger behind his thumb as he walked down a classroom aisle or on the bus and flick his knuckle at the skulls of unsuspecting victims. The echoes of bone on bone still haunt me.

"Looks like old Scruggs here won't be making any music," he howled.

The bus driver glanced in the mirror and then looked back at the road. Mr. Scarberry was not a disciplinarian to those who were taller than he was, and he was of the same stature as Mr. Gibson. I looked back and saw the equivalent of a vital body part being tossed about by a gorilla. One kid suggested that Earl toss the instrument out the window, and for a minute I thought he was going to.

"Hey!" someone shouted. "Give it back. Now!"

It was Heather. She stood, the curlers still in her hair. She was David against the Philistine, the little engine against the big mountain.

She held out her smooth hand, her jaw set, just real determination. "I said give it back."

Earl pursed his lips as he handed the instrument to her. "Ought to be ashamed, having a girl pick your fights, Allman."

"Shut up, Earl," Heather said.

She took the mandolin and handed it back to me, then as calmly as ever began unrolling the rest of her curlers. I could feel Earl's breath. Smell it too. But I didn't turn around.

"I have to stay after school today for practice," she whispered. "My mom can give you a ride if you want."

"Cheerleading?"

"Season's over," she said. "The school play. I got a little part. You shouldn't carry that on here again with these cretins."

I rode home with them that afternoon. Her mother didn't recognize me at first, but when Heather said, "Billy needs a ride," a wave of pity came over her and then she smiled.

"You two have a good day?" Mrs. Blanch said.

Heather shrugged and cracked her gum.

"Yes, ma'am," I said.

"You should take a cue from Billy and have more manners," Mrs. Blanch said.

"Billy's going to be a star," Heather said. "Mr. Gibson said he's bringing in some bluegrass guy to hear him tomorrow."

"Is that so?" her mother said. "Well, I'll look forward to hearing you on the Grand Ole Opry."

Heather turned and winked at me, sticking out her tongue and laughing.

"Billy, how's your mother doing?" Mrs. Blanch said.

"Better than expected, ma'am. Thanks for asking."

"I saw her at the beauty shop last week. She's doing a good job over there."

She made small talk until Heather flipped on the radio. I apologized for them having to get their car muddy pulling into our driveway and got out as fast as I could so they wouldn't see the laundry hanging inside our front porch. I thanked them for the ride and Mrs. Blanch said, "It's no problem at all, Billy."

Then I watched them drive away. Mrs. Blanch seemed to be lecturing her daughter about something she couldn't talk about when I was in the car. I watched them until they topped the hill and their taillights went out of sight.

At the start of sixth period the next day, Mr. Gibson turned up the volume of the recording I had made and played it through the classroom speakers. He rewound it twice to play specific riffs I'd done on a chorus. Stuff I'd made up that wasn't what Bill Monroe had done. Kids made their way back from lunch and cupped their hands over the window to see who was inside, which always drove Buzz crazy because they left greasy handprints.

The man he'd told me about was with him. Vernon Turley was an associate pastor from a big church in Barboursville. He was chubby with a kind face and a no-nonsense attitude. I knew his last name from his family's group, creatively titled The Turleys. He had branched off and formed his own group that toured area churches. I was in the presence of someone in the music ministry.

"How'd you learn to play like that?" Pastor Turley said after the song ended.

"My dad taught me," I said. "I pick up stuff here and there."

"Can you read music?"

I shook my head. "Can't make heads or tails of the notes, but I can look at guitar chords and fit them to the mandolin."

Buzz chimed in. "Why hasn't Mrs. Heck snagged you?"

"There's not much call for a mandolin in the marching band, I don't think."

"He's probably right," Pastor Turley said, scratching his face. It was smooth, and it looked like he was the type of person who had trouble growing any kind of a beard. "I'd like to hear you play."

Buzz pointed to the mandolin. "Take that on out to the front."

"I gotta get to gym class," I said.

Buzz waved me off. "I'll send a note to Coach Hall. It's time to see how you do on-stage."

It wasn't my class out there. It was one

filled with kids older than me. Juniors and seniors. Heather was the only one the same age as me, and she was in the front row, acting like she fit in with everybody, which she did.

Buzz was well-known for not sticking with the lesson plan. He took roll quickly, and then, sweeping his hand out like a ringmaster at the big top, he said, "Ladies and gentlemen! How many of you knew that Dogwood High has a musical genius in its midst? That's right, a gen-u-wine hillbilly prodigy walks these halls every day in work boots and denim."

Everybody looked at me. I hated gym, but I wanted more than anything to be out of that room. Of course, there was no use fighting it once Buzz got his act going.

"Now I have been in and around show business all my life, and I have seen them come and seen them go. But I have never seen fingers as fast on a mandolin as I saw in the control room back there yesterday. I've invited a real musician to judge his talent, and then he's going to speak to you about performing and stage presence. But first, a musical interlude. What do you say?"

The class hooted and cheered. " 'Free Bird'!" somebody shouted.

"It's not going to be that gospel bluegrass

crud, is it?" Paul Davidson said. He was the center on the basketball team and could say things to teachers nobody could get away with. If Paul said it, the teachers couldn't wait to get to the break room to talk about it.

"In fact, our guest today does play that gospel bluegrass crud, but it is only the finest gospel bluegrass crud," Buzz said, making some of the kids laugh.

Buzz had me stand at the podium, and I stared at the floor, looking like a kid who had worn the same shirt and pants to school every day since August, which was not true because I had two identical shirts and pants I switched out. Heather clapped politely and so did a few others, but it was clear this was going to be a tough sell. Pastor Turley stepped out of the control room and folded his arms.

Buzz briskly walked to the control room and started the record, but one of the channels was muted and he couldn't get the song on the speakers. After a couple of minutes I put the mandolin down and went in and showed him. When I passed the front row coming back, Paul stuck out his leg and tripped me. I fell flat on my face with my hands outstretched and the whole room busted loose. Heather glared at Paul and actually helped me up.

"You ready, Billy?" Buzz said into the talk-back.

Paul just grinned, his dimples showing.

I nodded and Buzz started the record. He turned the music up loud enough for everybody to hear, but low enough so it wouldn't drown out the mandolin, which can be a problem. It's not the loudest instrument, but I think it's the most beautiful way to interpret a song.

Daddy said the best thing a musician could do was give people a pure experience. Help them feel the music and become part of it. And that's what I did as soon as the needle hit that record. I closed my eyes, and even though I could hear some giggles and mocking from the back of the room, I just shut that out and strummed along with Bill Monroe.

There are a lot of players who talk about being "in the moment" when they perform. When you're fully running inside a song, when it's part of you and you're part of it, you can take chances, try things, and I guess that's the best way to describe what happened. I let my fingers work out what was in my soul. Somebody else who was there might have a different opinion, but for me it was pure joy. I let go of the nerves, I let go of who was watching, I let go of what Buzz and Pastor Turley might think, and I just became a mandolin evangelist. I showed them all why I love that instrument and what I could do with it.

When I was done, the kids in the room responded. A lot of them clapped, and when I opened my eyes, Heather was smiling bigger than I'd ever seen her. She looked genuinely happy. I'm not saying everybody was converted. Certainly Paul didn't throw away his Styx records. But there was a certain respect he gave me later as he walked down the hall and nodded. He'd never so much as made the distinction between me and a bug on the sidewalk.

The truth was, I could play even better. I wasn't holding back, but you can only do so much with one song to show your musical skills.

Buzz talked with Pastor Turley in the control room, and then he wrote me a note and told me to come back after the last period. I told him I had to catch the bus, but he said it was important. I flew down the hall to gym class, and Coach Hall was fit to be tied that anybody would be late, but the note calmed him.

When the bell rang after seventh period, I went back to Buzz's room. The kids from

105

the play were milling around and Heather was talking and laughing with some friends. Something inside me hurt when I saw that. The people talked about their lines or the upcoming game or a dance or a party at somebody else's house. You don't know how lonely you are until you hear people with normal lives talk about theirs. Maybe that's why I've kept away from crowds.

I stayed as long as I could, but I knew the bus wouldn't wait, so I headed for the hall. I met Buzz as I turned the corner, and he handed me a record and said I could keep it. I thanked him and kept moving.

"Wait; don't go," he said.

"The bus is leaving."

"I want you to stay while we practice. I have something for you to do."

"I need to get home."

"You have a job?"

"No, it's just that Mama expects me to be home when she gets there."

He put a hand on my shoulder. "This is important, Billy. I want you to listen to this record in the control room. Play along with the songs and record it. I'll get you a ride home. Does anybody in the play live near you?"

I mentioned Heather, but as soon as I did, I remembered her mother talking with her as they drove away.

"Good, I'll ask her," Buzz said, glancing at the clock. "Now get in the control room. You'll have at least an hour, hour and a half tops, to record."

"All of it?" I said.

He rubbed his chin. "Just start the record and hit the recorder and see what happens."

I studied the picture on the album. There were five men in striped suits standing next to a hay wagon. The title of the record was *I Saw the Light,* and the men were holding their instruments and smiling really big. I never figured out why they were out in the barnyard for the picture, but looking later at all the other album covers, it was clear they had exhausted their range of locations.

The man in the middle of the cover was the only one who wasn't holding an instrument. He was large, and the stripes made him look like the statue outside of a Big Boy restaurant.

"That's Pastor Turley, isn't it?"

"Billy, most every weekend he and his group are out on the road playing and singing."

"What's that got to do with me?"

"They lost their mandolin player a few months ago. He's interested in you but wants to see how you react to their music.

Do you think you can give it a shot?"

I looked at the list of songs. It was a pretty standard set. I knew all of them but one and figured that was an original.

"I can try," I said.

He closed the door and I got out the mandolin and began. The truth was, if I could have chosen anything in the world to do after school, that's what I would have done. When I got home each day, I would usually find something to eat and get out the two Realistic recorders I had repaired. Recording on the Wollensak sounded a lot better.

The record he gave me wasn't well produced. They'd found some cut-rate studio where the first good take got slapped on the record. But truth be told, the musicians weren't that bad. "I Saw the Light" was the first song, and it was mainly a banjo tune. I found the runs right away and figured out what they were doing with the chorus and turnaround. It wasn't rocket science.

I got lost in those songs and was on the last one, "Mother Left Me Her Bible," when everybody returned from the auditorium. Buzz took Heather aside, and she glanced at the control room and shook her head like she was really sorry about something.

He came in as the reel flapped. He had

his jacket and briefcase in hand. "You ready to head out?"

I put the reel in a box and handed it to him. "All done. There's some good tunes on here."

He slipped it in the briefcase, and we walked to the teachers' parking lot, which looked out on the river and the old covered bridge. He drove a little VW bug that chugged to life like a lawn mower engine.

"I appreciate you doing what you're doing," I said.

"How did you feel about your performance?" he said. "You looked pretty comfortable up there."

I shrugged. "I guess it was all right. I was nervous at first, but then when the music took over, I was okay. I could have been better with a little more practice."

Buzz smiled. "Do you think you could do that in front of a bigger crowd? say, a few hundred people?"

"If I can do it in front of people who hate the music I'm playing, I guess I could do it for just about anybody."

He flicked on the radio and tuned it to the local country-and-western station, WDGW. There was a Don Williams song on and Buzz said he liked the man's music.

"There's something so smooth and clean

about his recordings," I said. "The voice lays into his songs just right."

The signal got stronger and he pointed out the antenna. "I know the manager of that station. He actually hired another one of our students to work there."

It was a white metal building that looked like it could have been a sausage factory or a warehouse. I'd been past there a hundred times and never really noticed the antenna. He flipped to another station and we listened to Kenny Rogers's scratchy voice. I gave Buzz directions, and as we passed neighbors' houses, I got that bad feeling when you know somebody from the outside is going to look in at your life.

Buzz parked next to the road because our driveway was a mud hole. Mom's car was in the grass by the back door. I took him around back because of all the laundry still hanging up on the front porch.

"Where have you been, Billy?" Mama said. "I was worried sick."

"Mama, this is Bu— uh, Mr. Gibson. He's one of my teachers."

Mama wiped her hands on her apron and shook his hand. "Nice to meet you, Mr. Gibson. Is there something wrong?"

"Not at all," Buzz said. "I kept your son after school working on a project. Do you mind if I come in and talk about it?"

"Not at all," Mama said, backing up the cinder blocks. "Can I get you something to drink? All we have is Diet Shasta."

"Love it," Buzz said.

Mama got him a glass bottle and he sat at the kitchen table. I'd never noticed how many cracks in the walls there were, how the linoleum was turned up in the corners, and how the wood was rotted around the doorjamb until somebody new sat in the house.

"Can you stay for supper?" Mama said, cracking open the bottle.

"I would love to, Mrs. Allman, but I have a dinner date with my wife tonight. I can only stay a few minutes. I want to talk to you about your son."

Her face fell and she sat down on the one chair with the rooster painted on it. "He's done something wrong?"

"Your son isn't in any trouble," Buzz said, reaching a hand out and patting my mother's. "He brought his mandolin to school today and played for the class. He's very good. Exceptional talent. I invited a friend of mine to listen to him who has a gospel group. The Gospel Bluegrass Boys."

Mama's eyes lit up. "Is that so?"

"They've been around a few years," Buzz

said. "They travel all throughout West Virginia, Ohio, Kentucky, and a little into Tennessee."

"I've heard about their records," Mama said, masking a smile. "But I never thought a teacher in Dogwood was part of them."

"No, you don't understand. I'm not part of the group. But Vernon is — he's in our church — and when I heard Billy, I invited him to hear your son."

"I see," she said. But I could tell she didn't. Her mind wasn't all there at times. Part of that was all she'd been through and part of it wasn't.

"They play mainly in local churches and revivals. But they have done shows as far away as Cincinnati and they've opened for some name bands. It's not just a hobby; it's serious, but the music is a ministry. It touches lives and encourages people."

"I'll just bet it does."

"Teaching is a love of mine. Helping kids learn and grow is a passion. And when I see somebody with Billy's talent, I try to help them channel that in some positive direction."

"Well, I appreciate all you're doing."

"I tell you, Mrs. Allman, your son has something special. A gift. And since all good gifts come from the Father of lights, I don't think we should hide it under a bushel basket."

Mama sat back, relaxed, like someone had given her a full-body massage. "Well, what do you think about that! I knew from the moment he was born, he was special. It's just good to hear somebody else come around."

"You have reason to be proud," Buzz said. "You've done a fine job raising a son who's respectful and attentive."

"His daddy taught him the mandolin," Mama said. "And he's good at electronics, too."

"I know you've been through a difficult time in the past few years. And I want to make you a proposal." He smiled and sat back. "Not that kind of proposal."

Mama chuckled and covered her mouth with a hand. Being a woman of the hills, her teeth were not in the best shape.

"Billy made a tape of himself playing along with the band's songs. I want to take that to my friend. They lost their mandolin picker a few months ago and haven't re-placed him."

"And if they like me?" I said.

"If they approve — and I don't have any reason to believe they won't — I think they'll ask you to join them. Come to practices. And eventually go on the road with them. Vernon has to be at the church on most Sundays, so usually it's Friday and Saturday nights that they're gone."

My mouth dropped open. Mama turned to me with a smile that didn't fit the situation. "Well, that would pretty much take him away every weekend."

"Eventually. But he would be able to choose when he wanted to go and when you'd want him to stay. Now, their ministry is not-for-profit, so they don't actually pay their players, but they use the money from record sales and their honorarium to buy clothes and instruments and sound equipment. They'd probably get Billy some new clothes and maybe even help out here at the house with repairs you might need."

"That's real kind of you to think of Billy, Mr. Gibson. Why don't you let us talk it over?"

"I think that's a fine idea," Buzz said. He took a final swig of his soda, screwed on the cap, and tossed the bottle in the trash. "This would be a great opportunity for your son, ma'am. He'll gain confidence, get some great experience, and help out the group. And there's no rush. Just let me know what you think."

I stood on the front porch and watched

Buzz drive away. Mama was still sitting at the table running her hand over a crack in the plastic tablecloth. I leaned up against the wall and didn't say a word. Sometimes it was better to wait her out.

"Your daddy would be proud of you," she said. "He always thought you had a natural talent."

"But?"

She sighed. "People are out for themselves, Billy. What's in it for this Gibson fellow?"

I stared at her. "There's nothing in it for him. He just gives a hoot."

She shook her head. "It doesn't work that way. People are always in it for something. You don't know people like I do."

I looked out the window at the hill behind the house. A red squirrel flitted from one tree branch to another.

"I don't know that it's time. You have a lot of growing to do before you get into this kind of thing."

"Mama, I may only get a chance like this once."

"I doubt that. Maybe it's just me not able to let go. I just don't have a good feeling."

"Good feeling? Well, if you don't have it, I do. And Daddy would let me go."

"Now that's not fair, dragging your father into this."

"You brought him up yourself. You said he would be proud of me."

"You ought to be a lawyer, that's what you ought to be." She smiled. "What would this do to your studies?"

"I'd make sure I had all my homework done before we went on the road."

"Where do they practice? We don't even know that."

"Probably at the church in Barboursville."

"And how would you get down there? I can't drive you every week."

"I can get a ride from Mr. Gibson after school. And then Mr. Turley could drive up the interstate and drop me off at the bridge. We'd work it out. No big deal."

"You've figured it all out, haven't you? You're already counting on it." Just as I was sitting down at the table, Mama got up. "I've got to make supper."

I took hold of her arm and held on. She finally sat down.

"Mama, something happened to me today. I got up in front of people and played. Kids my own age. They don't even like the music and they enjoyed it. They noticed me."

"Getting people to notice you is not a good reason to join a group. Pride goeth before the fall."

"It's not pride. It's finding myself. I feel

116

like I looked out a window I didn't even know was in the building. And outside was a world I could fit into."

"A world of fame and fortune?"

"This is not about becoming famous. It's about doing what God made me to do. When I got up there with the mandolin, I thought, this is the thing that makes me feel alive."

"What about electronics and building things?"

"They go hand in hand," I said. "Don't you see? I could probably help the group with their sound system. I could wrap cables and repair instruments if they need it. Please, Mama. I want to do this."

She looked out the back door and a mist came over her eyes. "Maybe it *is* the right thing to do, to let you fly and try out your wings."

"I think the Lord has ordered all this. What are the chances that Mr. Gibson would teach at Dogwood High and he'd overhear me playing in the back room? and then talk to Mr. Turley?"

"Now there's where you need a little bit of faith," she said. "The Lord doesn't need Gibson or Turley to help him find you. He can do that by himself."

"I'm just saying it feels like something

God designed. He can use people like me if we'll yield to his will."

Mama stared hard at me. "That sounds like something an old man would say. Do you trust this Turley fellow? That Gibson seemed kind of squirrelly. Nice, don't get me wrong, but squirrelly."

"He's one of the best teachers at the school and well-liked. I always learn a lot from him." That wasn't totally true, but I said it anyway.

"Let me pray on it," she said. "You go cut us some firewood."

As I went through the screen door, she yelled, "And take a jacket; it's cold out."

I kept going in my shirtsleeves, unhindered by the chill in the air, almost floating, imagining what traveling with the group would be like. We'd probably eat at restaurants. Practices would be a lot of fun. And I wondered about the clothes. Would I be able to wear them to school?

I broke a sweat swinging the ax and chopped enough wood for the two of us. It was the time of year when you could sense the turning of the earth from casket to incubator. The trees were bare, but I knew the buds would soon be breaking out and the green would replace the gray and brown.

I brought an armload of firewood to the

back of the house. Mama was standing in the kitchen with her hand against a hip, stirring a pot of macaroni on the stove, looking out the window. Tears streaked her face.

"What's wrong now?" I said.

She shook her head. "Just another spell, I guess. All these thoughts swirling around in my head."

Ever since Daddy had taken his life, Mama had been going downhill. It was as if her mind was so full of things that they overflowed at times and bubbled up like macaroni that's been turned too high on the stove. He had left her a miner's pension and a little from Social Security and me. That put everything on her, and the weight of it made her a different person at times. I'd catch her talking to herself in her bedroom, brushing out her hair until there were clumps of it in the brush. I just chalked it up to all the shock she'd been through.

"You'll probably be bringing young ladies around now, won't you?" she said.

"Excuse me?"

"That pretty thing you sit by on the bus. What's her name?"

"How do you know who I sit beside?"

She rolled her eyes. "Doesn't take Dick Tracy to know you're growing up, Son. And I work at a beauty salon. What's her name?"

I told her. "But she's not my girlfriend or anything. She's in another league."

"Don't sell yourself short, Billy Allman. You belong in any league you choose, you hear?"

"Then can I be in the league with the Gospel Bluegrass Boys?"

She started to cry. Finally she said, "Letting go is always hard. I thought it was hard with your daddy and with Harless, but it's even harder with you."

"Does that mean I can be part of the group?"

"It means you can think about it. I'm not giving my blessing yet, but you can think about it."

I hugged her so tight she came up off the floor and dripped hot water on my shirt. "Don't worry; maybe the guys won't like me," I said.

"There's not a chance of that," she said. "Get washed up for supper."

We ate together and watched TV all evening. I was only half-there because I wondered what the group thought of me. I rehearsed what I was going to say to Pastor Turley if he called. That night I dreamed I was onstage at the Grand Ole Opry and Ernest Tubb introduced our group, only it wasn't the Gospel Bluegrass Boys taking the stage; it was Billy's Gospel Bluegrass Band. The crowd went wild as we stepped up to the microphones, and by the time I was finished, smoke was coming off my fingers and the crowd loved every song. It was a nice dream.

Of course, it didn't work out that way. Life generally doesn't. I wish it would have, but I guess God had a different plan. What he was thinking and doing about that time of my life, I don't know. I don't think I'll ever know. And part of me doesn't even want to know.

# 7

I observed many subtle personality shifts in Billy during high school. His interaction with peers was not affected as much as their interaction with him. They presented a limited acceptance that surprised me. Among these was his interaction with "the girl." And he developed a deepening disdain for bullies who tread upon lower life forms.

All of this fascinated me because I knew the truth. There was something different about him, something the Almighty would use, but his classmates could not get past their makeup and fleeting athletic prowess. Their crowns and achievements were meager, but they clung to trophies and memories as if they were truly an eternal weight of glory. This is the malady of the humans, that they can hold on to that which is fleeting and of little consequence and call it everlasting. They focus on awards, achievements, and what can be done in their own strength while the Almighty desires to work through their weakness. Very few humans, from what I have observed, ever realize how weak they really are, let alone surrender their limited abilities to the power of the One who can transform that weakness into spiritual strength that can alter the world. Billy was such a man, though from an earthly perspective, he did not have much to show for his submission.

I also observed Billy's growing fascination with music and performance. The pastor who befriended him allowed Billy to practice, travel, and play with their group, but there was something about him that troubled me. In the small settings of mold-ridden sanctuaries, Billy used his gift to praise the One who had given it. His shell began to break a little more each time he stepped to the microphone. Still, I wondered if this was the best use of his talent.

About this time I was called away to another assignment. A battle that had continued for many seasons had intensified. I was summoned, given orders, and dismissed. But my questions surprised my commander.

"I thought you would be glad to be released from your charge, if only for a season," he said. "You have grown fond of this young man?"

"I have grown to understand him and his

motivations. And I have become fascinated with all aspects of the human experience."

"You want to see how the story progresses."

"I want to protect him. I'm not in this simply for discovery."

"Of course not, but part of your fascination has to do with the way each life moves forward and interconnects with others. Observing how his friendships change in high school. His romantic relationships when he is young become much more complicated. The relationship with his mother. The political and social upheavals pressing in. The speed with which all of this happens, without those on the human plane being aware, is astounding, I would think."

"You speak as if you have been given a like assignment," I said.

He smiled. "When I was given a charge during the events surrounding the glorious life and work of our Creator, I was even more convinced than you that a mistake had been made. I was built for battle. I was created for warfare, not protection. I did not want to become a human babysitter. Particularly in a place like Tarsus."

"Paul," I said.

"Yes! Saul of Tarsus, who later became Paul. Being sent to him meant that I missed much of the earthly life and ministry of our

Lord. I longed to observe the life of Christ, but there I was, watching this young Jewish boy at his lessons day after day, protecting him from an errant horse-drawn cart while the whole world was turned upside down. I could see no rhyme or reason in the assignment.

"And then, after the Death and Resurrection — I only heard of these things; I didn't see them firsthand as you probably did — my charge became vehement in his opposition to those who followed the Way. I had been protecting someone who was actually *against* the very One I had sworn myself to serve. It made less than no sense, but I was stuck."

He turned and stared into space. I could sense emotion welling up.

"You questioned your assignment?"

"I did, and in doing so, I doubted more than my assignment. I doubted the One who had given it to me. But I faithfully protected him, though at the time there was little opposition. This man was doing the bidding of the evil one without the encouragement of demonic forces. But as soon as he met Jesus on that road, all the forces of hell were unleashed. I had my hands full from then on. He endured imprisonment and false accusation and ship-wreck — what a storm that was — and discouragement and strife among his brethren, arguments and false teaching. I was equally as dismayed when he was in chains, thinking that I had failed somehow. I did not see that a greater good was coming from this isolation. Now, I understand."

He paused, sensing some concern of mine. When he asked about this, I replied, "If I were beating back the forces of the enemy each day as you did, I would be less concerned. However, he hasn't needed my protection and watchcare either from physical or demonic forces."

"You are restless, then."

"I am eager to fulfill my role."

"So was I with Paul. I saw no rhyme or reason for my presence in his life before his conversion, and then afterward, the years of imprisonment . . . it made little sense to me."

"And you stayed with him to the end?"

He nodded. "His last moments were . . . memorable. And though there was great pain, in the midst of that was a hint of a smile at his final breath."

"Is it difficult to watch the demise of a charge? For you, was it something you had to turn away from?"

He tilted his head. "You are becoming attached to this charge, are you not?"

"Billy is compelling. There is no arrogance or pride in him, I don't think. Even animals sense his gentle spirit and are attracted to him. Perhaps one who has seen such difficulty and loss is better suited to humility. But I've often wondered about his future. If there were some way to encourage him about what will be. How he will be used. I feel like there is something ahead for him."

"And if you leave him now, the plans for your charge will be thwarted?"

"I know that is fallacious thinking. The Most High is sovereign over the affairs of all mankind. And I know that though my time away from him may bring trouble, nothing is outside the realm or influence of the One who loved him enough to die for him."

"Precisely. He knows the beginning from the end, every hair of every head, every sparrow that falls. You and I know this intuitively since we have chosen to follow. Humans learn this experientially, which is what your charge will now need to learn more fully."

"So he is going to go through more difficulty?"

"I have yet to see a charge who finds smooth sailing through life. In fact, the ones He seems to use and love most must go through deep valleys. The Sovereign loves them infinitely but allows them to pass through trouble. This keeps them from complacency."

"How long must I be away?" I said.

"That, too, is not known. Any more than I

could tell you how long you would be with your charge to begin. But let me give you ample warning." My superior stared at me with what seemed pity and a bit of emotion I could not understand. "When you return to him, things may be . . . different. Do not blame yourself. These events to come must occur, though we do not know what they are or how they will affect your charge. Do you understand?"

"No. How can you tell me of future things when you say you can't even tell me how long I am to be away?"

"Because I have been instructed by One who holds the future in His nail-scarred hands."

His words troubled me, but I left and traveled to my post, carrying out my duties as a warrior in the army of the Lord. I had no trouble transitioning to the battle and leading our forces against the enemy. But in certain moments I could not help thinking of Billy.

I had no idea a life could change so quickly.

■ ■ ■ ■

# PART TWO:
# PAINTED ON THE
# SKY

■ ■ ■ ■

# 8

The orders came for me to return to Billy when the battle concluded. A long assignment had led to another that spread to wider regions. The more I was given to do, the more evil was unleashed, the more content and focused I became. It may seem strange that I would use warfare as my praise to the Almighty, but that is my specialty and I work tirelessly.

Still, though I was glad to return to those hills, part of me felt estranged. I felt I had missed great chunks of Billy's life, though in his time and space it was only a few years. When I finally settled into my routine of observance, I discovered Billy was in his own battle.

Early on in Billy's life he was forced to become a man, a provider, and he rose to those responsibilities. But he always retained a childlike quality. Not all humans have the ability to live in such a way. There was something about Billy's imagination, the way he stopped and noticed small things, the extent to which he would go to help a friend or a stranger, the simple way he would return a shopping cart to the front of the grocery.

There was a wonder to his life, and I could not tell if this childlike quality was a product of Billy's upbringing, if it was endemic to his personality, if something spiritual led him on this path to a more simple way, or if there was some point in Billy's life where he had become "stuck." This quality could be deemed a two-edged sword because it made him a wonderful human being, but it also left him quite vulnerable. My experience has been that innocence does not fare well when pitted against evil.

Not long after high school, the girl from the bus came back into his life. I assume humans considered her beautiful based on the way they deferred to her and doted, from teachers and administrators to members of the community. This beautiful one returned to that small community about the time Billy was studying at a nearby technical school. It was much less expensive than college and more practical. The truth was, Billy knew more than most teachers at the school, but he dutifully attended classes.

The girl was enrolled in a beauty school (which seemed entirely appropriate to me), and since she had no automobile, Billy offered her a ride. Upon a cursory investigation of her home situation, I learned that her family was punishing her for some unseen infraction. She had studied at a prestigious university in the east and squandered her opportunity or money (or both) and was now paying the consequences. She was learning a trade, hairdressing, and worked odd jobs in the evening. Billy never learned how "odd" these jobs were.

Every month or two, Billy would go to her home for a haircut. The first few were ghastly, but he always acted pleased. He would put on his baseball cap and then tip her more money than he would have paid in a salon.

There were days when Billy did not have classes, but he would drive her anyway and wait at the nearby library until she was finished. Other times he would work overnight at the radio station where he was newly employed and make it back to her home just in time to pick her up, drive her all the way back to the school, and then drive to his own home for sleep, setting his alarm to pick her up again.

On more than one occasion, the girl would come from the building laughing and joking with new friends, telling Billy that she wouldn't be needing a ride that day. She was headed to a movie or dinner or a bar. Billy was always gracious.

I had heard from others of my kind about this type of relationship. In the lull of battle they would regale us with stories of strong Christians who were enticed and drawn away by the love of a beautiful woman or, more often, the strength and danger of a handsome, rugged man. Foolishly, they believed they could reform this person and somehow cause them to believe. Sometimes, in a few isolated instances, that occurred. But more often, the enemy uses this passion and desire for the forbidden to draw the Christian from the deep water of faith into the shallow end of the pool.

I feared for Billy because it was clear the girl had no inclination toward the spiritual. I thought of ways I could thwart him in his pursuit of her, believing that since I was sent to protect, this would be approved. A flat tire here, an injured dog there, a stranger broken down on the side of the road — all of these things would have diverted him, but only temporarily. I did not come in contact with the enemy in relation to the girl. She was already being pulled away by her own passions — I assume that is why the enemy left her alone. When an auto is in neutral and rolling down a hill, one does not need to shift into gear and push the accelerator.

But Billy did not see. His heart was romantically intertwined. He had never so much as held her hand, other than to help her up when she was in a drunken stupor. His lips had never touched hers. She had shown him no encouragement, which is commendable, I suppose, though she did rely on him for encouragement in her dark times. He even loaned her money, if you can fathom that. Billy, without so much as a dime to his family name, loaned her the money to continue schooling. He was, in my estimation, the only person on the horizon of her life that she could truly count on for stability. The phone would ring early in the morning and Billy would rouse from his slumber and retrieve her from whatever party she had attended the night before. More than once he was summoned to the county jail.

Call it what you wish, infatuation or wishful thinking, but the unrequited love of a beautiful woman is exhausting.

Finally Billy somehow dug inside and had the nerve to tell her how he felt. The revelation was met with a cool response. I looked over his shoulder and read the letter she sent.

I sensed that you felt more for me than I did for you. I love you as a friend, Billy. A very good friend who would go out of his way to help. And I want you to know how much I appreciate everything you've done. But I just don't feel the same way, and for that I am sorry.

Billy wept as he read. But he still drove her to the school until her training was complete. As a graduation present, he bought her, with his own savings, a used car to drive to work. He even paid for her first six months of insurance, which she couldn't afford. I suppose it saved him having to drive her, but I did not see the reason he would spend so much money without hope of a return on his investment. Perhaps he believed he could still win her heart. This is the way of humans, to hope in something out of reach. That hope was dashed the day his mother sat him down and told him the news that the girl was getting married.

The most heartbreaking scene I can relate came in a park, on a summer Saturday. Billy parked far from the venue, near the tennis courts on the other side of the hill. He walked the long way around and finally stopped at a spot overlooking the garden, which was almost in full bloom. The afternoon sun warmed the ground, the scent of roses filled the air, and Billy sat in an area scattered with pine needles and tall grass. Here he was unseen.

Everyone was dressed nicely, and folding chairs had been arrayed. A flower girl spread rose petals on the walkway between rows as a string quartet played the familiar strains of Beethoven and Pachelbel.

The music lifted above the valley floor, but when it reached him, I was sure it sounded more like a dirge. The groom and best man appeared in their finery. From the back came the bride with a brilliant white dress, which I was sure she did not deserve. She took her place beside the groom and they both said their vows, which they had written themselves, amplified by the small, tinny sound system.

"I promise to cherish and care for you as long as we both shall love."

Billy shook his head. He stayed on the hill, engulfed by the green trees, leaves, and pines, even after the service ended. A dog came near, sniffing at him, off the leash and wandering. Billy called the dog over with a wave, and the dog let him scratch its ear. The couple who owned it called, and the dog seemed reluctant to leave but obeyed after licking Billy's hand.

After most left for the reception, the bride and groom remained for pictures. They stood in an arch surrounded by roses, a bridesmaid and the best man with them. Smiling, always smiling for the camera, and then hurrying back to a waiting limousine.

After they were gone, Billy made his way down the hill through the thick birches and scattered maples. He crossed the asphalt road and walked through the rose garden, where three men wearing ties folded chairs. It was the bride's father and her brothers. Billy started at the back and began folding until the older man stopped and recognized him.

"Didn't see you at the ceremony, Billy," he called. "What did you think?"

Billy kept his head down while folding. "It was real nice, Mr. Blanch. Perfect day for a wedding."

"It was hotter than blazes," a brother said.

"Yeah, you're lucky you didn't have to get dressed up in this monkey suit," the other said.

The father came back to Billy. "You don't have to do this, son. We've got it."

"If it's all right with you, I'd like to help. I'd feel like I was doing something for her."

The man smiled. "All right. We appreciate it." He went back to folding the next row, making small talk. He suggested Billy would one day conduct weddings, as "religious" as he was.

"I don't think I'm cut out to be a pastor," Billy said.

"Why not? You seem to know the Word just as well or better than most reverends."

Billy smiled. "Now how would you know that?"

"My sister-in-law has kids who attend your Sunday school class. They say you could teach a mule the Romans Road."

"Teaching kids and teaching adults are two different things."

"I expect they are, but they both spring from the same well."

Billy nodded. "I expect so."

The father stopped his work and looked at Billy. "I'm real sorry about this. I know you did the best you could for her. And if I had any say in it, I would have told her to give you a chance. But you know daughters don't listen to their fathers in matters of the heart."

"I appreciate that, Mr. Blanch. The truth is, I was just a friend — and not a very good one."

The man shook his head. "I don't think so. You were the best friend she ever had."

Billy pulled something from his back pocket and handed it to him. "I'd be obliged if you'd give this to the bride and groom for me."

"Why don't you come to the reception? I know she'd be happy to see you."

Billy went on folding the chairs. "I don't think that's a good idea. But you fellows go on. I'll finish up here."

"We couldn't let you do that."

"No, I insist."

The man sighed. "Well, all the chairs go in that hauler over there. You can just lock it up and leave it. We'll come back later and take them to the church."

"Thanks, Billy," one of the brothers said, grabbing his jacket from the back of a chair.

Mr. Blanch shook Billy's hand. "I'll make sure she gets your card. You're a good man, Billy."

Billy nodded and returned to the chairs as the three drove away.

I had not thought it important to look at what Billy was writing when he filled out the card in the parking lot of a Walmart. He had spent an eternity looking through them, choosing just the right one, and then made some mistake in what he had written and returned to buy an identical one. I knew I should have paid closer attention when tears flowed as he licked the envelope closed.

On the outside he wrote, "To the Bride and Groom."

As Billy drove home afterward, I moved to the reception and found the mound of gifts and cards. Mr. Blanch placed Billy's on the stack and it remained there. I returned to Billy and found him alone in his living room listening to one of his favorite albums and eating a fish dinner he had ordered from Long John

140

Silver's. If he only knew what that food did to his arteries.

Two months later, Billy got a small white envelope in the mail. He seemed to recognize the handwriting that did not include a name, just the return address from North Carolina. He walked slowly back to the house and dropped the ads and bills on the kitchen table, then made his way to his shop. Billy worked on electronics and woodworking there, things he used his hands to craft. He did not enjoy fishing as much as his friends at the local diner, but when they showed him the artificial lures that drove the bass crazy, Billy took the broken lure he was given and brought them an even better one the next morning. The men around the table, friends from his church, marveled at his ability and asked for more.

In the midst of the dust, wood chips, and solder, Billy sat in his squeaky chair, surrounded by old equipment, half-started projects, schematics, and letters from the FCC, and stared at the small card before him as if it were some talisman that could bring back the past.

His mother knocked on the door lightly, in her right mind on this day. "Is everything all right?"

"I'm fine, Mama."

"All right, now don't work in here all night. I'll have supper ready directly."

"I'll be there."

When she closed the door, he carefully tore open the envelope, holding it close enough to sniff at the lingering scent. He pulled out the small note. Her familiar handwriting was there, only a few sentences with flowery script that filled up the space easily.

Billy,

Thank you for your note. Your friendship means a lot. Thanks for being there through some hard days. We're going to go out to dinner and use your gift!

Sincerely,
Heather

Billy held the card close to his chest and looked out the small window at the front of the house. " 'Fare thee well, my own true love,' " he sang. " 'And farewell for a while.' "

He picked up the mandolin and strummed a few chords and sang along, picking out the bluegrass melody he had apportioned to it. At the end, with tears falling, he smiled and put the instrument away. He placed the note in the envelope and opened the top drawer of the old military desk he had bought at auction. The drawer was cluttered with all kinds of gadgets and used electronics, switches and diodes and circuit boards, as well as paper clips, rubber bands, loose change, and grease pencils. He stashed the note deep underneath the junk and pushed the drawer closed.

When he stood, it was like a weight had fallen from his back. And this ended another sad chapter of the life of Billy Allman. But the sadness would not end, of course. Neither would the longing or the searching and striving.

# 9

Floods leave gaps in the wake, fissures and clefts of memory that songs cannot reach. And so it is with my life. There are things I cannot revisit. I find it easier to edit these scenes and shove them away and pray they will not haunt me. Sometimes you have to just shovel away the locusts that have eaten your life and move on the best you can.

My diabetes diagnosis is one of these. I choose not to remember the darkness of those days, my inability to deal with the reality of the disease, and the many consequences of my decisions. But there are other events that have no diagnosis, no name to hang on them in my limited lexicon. Forgive me for jumping over these. It is not because I am trying to be dishonest.

I feel like just about everything I touch in life goes bad. If there is a syndrome for people who pick up bruised fruit, I have it. That may sound like a pity party, but I don't mean it to be. It's just the truth. And there are worse things that can happen in life than to watch your mother die, but not many. To see the one who gave you life, who suckled you at her breast, wither away both in mind and body is terrible. But it is even more terrible to think of her in some other place than the home she kept for thirty years.

Mama's health had been declining for years. She had to quit work at the beauty shop because most days they had her coming in, she couldn't make it, and when she did, she chased business away because of her attitude. I don't know if the death of my father triggered it or if it was going to happen all along, but somewhere in the long trail of her DNA, something came loose like laundry from the clothesline. And once a sheet gets caught by the wind, there is no telling where you will find it.

I woke up one winter day and found her outside in the snow in her slippers. Her feet were red from the cold and she was walking along the edge of the hill I'd finally made a down payment on, moving from one tree to another calling for a childhood dog. I hollered but she said not to come closer, that no dogcatcher would take her beloved Sugar away. By then I knew better than to try and convince her that I wasn't the dogcatcher.

She was crying when I caught up. "I can't find him anywhere. And he gets so cold. I'm afraid I'm going to lose him. I'm afraid he's not going to make it."

She scratched the living daylights out of me when I picked her up and carried her back to the house. Her nightgown was wet — and not just from the snow. It is one thing to drive your mother to the doctor. It is quite another to clean the mess when her bowels let loose.

In the steady decline that seemed to accelerate after that, I knew some hard decisions had to be made. I asked Macel Preston to come by one day the next November. She was the wife of the local sheriff, and my mother and I had known her from church for years. She spoke to my mother kindly and sat in the rocking chair, listening to her carry both sides of the nonsensical conversation.

"You remember back before we moved to the creek, how hard it was to get persimmons off those trees over at the Fizers'," my mother said.

"No, Arlene, I don't remember," Macel said. "Why don't you tell me?"

And she would. She'd just take off on a thought and turn a corner and pretty soon she was on politics or something she'd seen in the newspaper or something about spaying and neutering Bob Barker's cats. Macel listened until Callie Reynolds drove up.

Callie worked at the post office and delivered our mail. Every now and then she'd bring us dinner. We went to the same church, but since Mama had gotten so bad, it was hard for me to do anything but get to work and back every day. I usually spent Saturdays and Sundays at home.

Callie lived in a trailer on the other side of the Dogwood County line. Because of that we had gone to different schools, but I'd gotten to know her a little. We were about the same age, and she had taken an interest in Mama and helping out. She was a tall woman with a wide nose and teeth that had a mind of their own. One eye wasn't set right and she had a way of looking at you but not looking at you at the same time. It was a bit unnerving to have a face-to-face conversation because when she stared right at you, it was as if she was looking at something behind you and you always wondered what was so interesting back there. She wasn't heavy, but she walked without a lot of grace, as if her arms were tree limbs. She was just a common, good woman.

I tried to pay her for her time with Mama,

but every time I'd shove a twenty-dollar bill in her hand, she would get offended and say she wasn't doing it for money. People from the hills are like that. I think it springs from a heart that believes a good turn deserves another. If you have felt that kind of love from God in your life, you want to pass the grace along.

She came in and put a casserole dish in the oven and fussed over Mama. I told her I was going to walk Macel to her car and run an errand or two, and Callie said that was fine; she'd take care of things.

Macel stood in silence by her car and just stared at the hillside. It reminded me of all those years ago when my daddy died and how people just seemed to stand and stare off.

"Billy, you're going to have to do something hard one of these days," she said.

"She's not going to leave that house," I said.

"She can't stay here by herself. It's not safe. She's going to hurt herself by trying to make a fire on that stove, or she'll go out and climb that tree on the hill thinking she's making a deposit at the First National Bank."

"Callie is helping me out as much as she can, and I stay with her full-time on the weekend."

"Callie told me you tried to pay her and that she wished you'd stop doing that."

"She's been a big help."

"Unless they're paying you more than I think down at the radio station, you don't have that kind of money. You're still working for the local station, aren't you?"

"I work part-time at WDGW, but my full-time work is down in Huntington."

"From what I've heard of the owner here, he's more tight-fisted than a monkey with a banana in a jar. I hope they pay you well at the other one. You chief engineer now?"

"Makes it sound like I'm a train conductor, doesn't it?"

She chuckled. "You always had a knack with electronics. I used to love hearing you play that mandolin, too. Do you ever pick it up anymore?"

"Sometimes when it's bad with Mama. It's just about the only thing that will soothe her. It's like David playing for King Saul, only King Saul didn't wear a nightgown from Walmart."

She opened her car door and threw her purse in. "Billy, sometimes love looks a lot different than we think it should."

"Ma'am?"

"You have the idea that to love your

mother well, you have to do everything for her like she did for you when you were a baby, and if you don't, you're a failure as a son. And I'm here to release you from that prison you're building."

"Bible says if you don't take care of your family —"

"You're worse than an infidel; that's true. We're to take care of those who took care of us. But there is not a person on the face of this planet who has cared more for their family than you, Billy. I don't know who has been accusing you, probably some voices you ought to shut out. You do not have to listen to them. You have been a model son. You have taken care of your mama and added to her years. You've sacrificed your own happiness."

"I didn't sacrifice anything. It was my pleasure, my duty to take care of her. I'm all she has left."

Macel looked at me. "What happened, Billy? Why haven't you gotten married? Isn't there anyone you're sweet on?"

I looked at the mailbox, then at the ditch. "Women aren't knocking down the door to get to my place, if that's what you mean."

"But there was someone, am I right?"

I nodded. "Long time ago."

"And what happened?"

"Some things don't work out like you plan. Like you want them to."

"You care to elaborate?"

"I wasn't exactly her type, Mrs. Preston. I think it's kind of hard to find my type."

She jingled the keys and got ready to go. "I don't know what God did with the mold after he made you, but I'd like to find it again."

I smiled. "You've been a good friend to us. You and your husband both."

She put a hand on my arm. "When it comes time, you call me. I'll be here. And don't ever think that you're a bad son just because there's this hard thing you have to do. Your daddy would be proud of you."

"Thank you, ma'am," I said.

I went to the store to pick up a few things but wandered around looking at the shelves and thinking. It's funny how aimless a person can feel at times, even when they know God is in control.

When I finally pulled into the driveway of the house, it was dark and Callie's car was gone. Not unusual, but I thought she would have stayed. The sun reached the edge of the hills earlier and earlier in those November days.

I couldn't get out of the car. The past can come up over me like that flood, surprising me with the power and force of time and experience. Images floated by, people and things and situations that were pulled by memory's current. Not a day went by that I didn't think of my daddy, those people back on the creek, that girl who sat by me on the bus, the smell of her hair, the chances squandered. I suppose we are all a collection of such surges and hopes and dreams. There are probably some people who don't have any of that stuff haunting them, but I halfway think that those people are heavily medicated.

There was no movement in the house, so I got up the nerve to go inside. I flicked on the light when I came in the back door, and bugs scurried across the kitchen countertop. There was a pile of dishes in the sink and the casserole dish that Callie had brought was in the middle of the table, half-eaten and left like the Rapture had come.

I called out for Mama and listened. No response.

"Mama, I'm home. You doing all right?"

She wasn't in the bathroom or the bedroom to the left. But I noticed the gun cabinet was open and my .22 was missing. I breathed a little prayer and kept going. The living room was pitch-black, and as I reached for the light, a voice startled me.

"Stay right where you are, you ugly thing." She didn't say *thing;* she used a much uglier word.

I flicked on the light and saw my mother, naked, huddled in the corner and holding the rifle on me. It would have been a shock to anyone else, but to me it was as normal as coming home to see your mother eating oatmeal and watching *Wheel of Fortune.*

"Mama, put the gun down."

She cursed at me with words so foul I could only close my eyes and take a deep breath.

"I know what you're up to," she said. "I called the bank about my savings account. You took everything, didn't you!"

I sighed. "We've been over this. I took all of your accounts and moved them into one."

"You have no right to do that."

"Yes, I do. You gave me the power to take care of you. I'm trying to do what's best. What happened to Callie? You didn't run her off, did you?"

"I don't know what you're talking about," Mama spat. "But I know this: if you don't get out of here, I'm going to blow you to kingdom come."

The phone rang and when I moved to it, she raised the gun. I ignored her and went for the black phone that had hung on the

153

kitchen wall for years. It was caked with dust and grease and felt like an old friend when I picked it up. They don't make phones like that anymore.

"Billy?" Callie said when I answered. Her voice was strained, like she was trying to hold something in a gunnysack that wanted out. "You need to get out of there."

"What's wrong, Callie?"

"It's your mama! Is she still in the house?"

"Yeah, I hope so. She doesn't have a stitch of clothes on." I heard movement behind me but didn't turn around.

"Billy, she found the box of shells. I don't know how she did it, but she found them and loaded that .22 and took a few shots at me before I got out of there."

I noticed a couple of holes in the plaster by the phone.

"She's not well. You have to do something. But first, get out of there."

"I'll take care of it."

"I love her like she was my own mother, but I think she's going to hurt somebody."

"Thank you, Callie."

Callie said something else but I only heard her voice breaking into a cry as I reached to hang up the phone.

"I'm going to blow your head off, you lying cheat."

"That might be the best thing you could do for me, Mama."

"You're selling my antiques, aren't you?" she seethed. "I can't find any of my cutlery. And the car's gone. You sold it right out from under me."

I was still speaking to the holes in the wall, trying to keep my voice calm. "Mama, I sold your car because you can't drive safely anymore. You took out every mailbox from here to Benedict Road. I'm using the money to take care of you and pay for the medication you flush down the toilet."

"You're trying to drug me. That Callie is in on it with you!"

"Callie just cares. And the cutlery's stored away so you don't hurt yourself. We've been over this."

"Stay right where you are!" she yelled.

I sat down at the kitchen table and stared at the casserole.

"You never did love me," she said. "I saw the papers you had drawn up! I saw them in your shop! And don't try to tell me you didn't. I read the whole thing."

"I showed you the papers myself. You signed them of your own free will back when you were in your right mind."

"Oh yeah? Well, I have something to say to you, Mr. High-and-Mighty. I'm taking back that power of attorney, and you'll be out on the street! How do you like them apples? All of a sudden the shoe's on the other foot and it don't feel so good, does it?"

"Mama, calm down and get your robe on."

She moved closer and poked the gun in my face. "You don't boss me around anymore. You're not the man of this house. You *killed* the man of this house."

Her venom finally struck and I looked up, wounded.

"That's right," she said. "I figured it out. You knew your daddy was having troubles. You knew how fragile his mind was. So you sneaked and got that .410 and some shells and put it where he could reach it when he got low. And when he was in the ground, you never cried like somebody who loved their daddy. You just went on as if it never happened. Just picked up the next day and kept moving. I should have seen it at the time, but I didn't."

"Mama, you don't know what you're saying."

"If you had loved your daddy, you would have helped him. You would have become a better man!"

She was shouting now and it was all I could do to resist grabbing the barrel of the gun and ripping it from her hands. She looked like she didn't have the strength to pull the trigger, but the holes in the wall betrayed that thought.

"Mama, you're not thinking straight. Now get your robe on and let's talk about this."

"Talk, talk, talk," she snapped. "That time is over. You've been talking with those nursing home people. You've been talking with the county. Don't think I can't hear you on the phone."

I had tried to keep my conversations with the authorities as discreet as possible. It had been a long series of delayed decisions and questions about the cost and the logistics of such a move. I hadn't made the final decision because the house was my mother's castle. She lived for that house, as old and broken-down as it was.

"We've been talking about what's best for you."

"What's *best* for me? You can't even run your own life, let alone mine. You go running after a split-tail bed thrasher and then boohoo about it, moping around here like some wounded dog. Just get up and get out. And don't come back."

Blue and white lights flashed over the hill, and I put my face in my hands. "Mama, get dressed; the police are coming."

"You called the police?" she shouted.

"No, I think Callie probably did after you used her for target practice. Now unless you want the sheriff or one of his deputies seeing you in your birthday suit, you'd better give me the gun and get your robe on."

She turned and looked out the window, and if the scene hadn't been so serious, I would have laughed at the sight of her jiggly, saggy bottom. She glanced back at me with an icy stare. "I can't believe you called the cops on me. That just proves what kind of low-life scum you've turned out to be. Billy, you are the worst son a mother could ever have. I hope you know that."

"Yeah, I know it, Mama. You tell me that every day." I stood and walked out the door without looking back.

The squad car pulled into the driveway and sank. I leaned against my truck and watched Sheriff Hadley Preston put on his hat and step out.

"How goes the battle, Billy?" Sheriff Preston said.

"You chose the right words, Sheriff. I'm all right. Yourself?"

"I'd be a lot better if I was back in the kitchen eating trout. My wife knows what

to do with a rainbow and some red potatoes."

"Sorry to set your weekend off to a bad
start," I said. "You can go back home. I
think the worst is over."

"From what Callie Reynolds told the
dispatcher, she's lucky to be alive."

I nodded toward the back window of the
house. "And there she stands, Grandma
Rambo."

Sheriff Preston stared at the window and
made a face. "Nice outfit. I thought you
kept the guns locked up."

"And the bullets, too. Somehow she got
into both. That won't happen again."

"Billy, you know how much Macel and I
love your mother. We'd crawl all over this
hill to help her in any way we could."

"And you have, Sheriff. She can't tell you
herself, but I know she'd be grateful for all
you've done."

"Well, she ought to be grateful to you.
You've been the best son anybody could
hope to have. But you know somebody's
going to get hurt if you don't do something."

"She found out I was having her committed. That's what triggered this."

"Is that so." He took in a breath and just
stood there. "When?"

"I'll do it Monday. I can take the day off work and get the county people to come in the morning."

"Custer's last stand," the sheriff said.

"Can't say I blame her. I don't think she really understands what's going on. She went off her medication. Knows something is about to change. She's just scared."

Sheriff Preston nodded. "I think we all have an internal detector of sorts that helps us know when things are about to change. Good or bad, it's there. Wish I'd have listened to mine a time or two."

"This is the hardest thing I've ever had to do."

"I expect it is."

"But I did it to the letter with the lawyer. Crossed every t and dotted every i."

"Have you actually talked with her about it?"

"I've tried to. She signed the power of attorney a year ago when she seemed in a better place. But every time I try to bring up her moving to the home, it's like talking to a stone that wants to argue about the weather. Nothing that comes back makes any sense."

"Poor thing." He said it with a bit of compassion that choked me up.

"Yeah," I said, looking at her. Mama had

pulled a couple of the chairs from the dinner table against the back door and then sat down next to the stove and stared out the window. She was in such a mind that she didn't realize the door opened out and the chairs would be of no use.

"Maybe they can give her some help in there. Get her on something that will help right the ship."

"I'm afraid the ship has turned over on its side, Sheriff. I should have done this a long time ago, but I just couldn't. She gave her whole life for me. Least I could do was hang in there with her to the end. But I guess that won't happen."

"You'll still visit her. She'll come around."

"Yeah, but it won't be the same. She won't be here. This house was everything to her. After you lose everything, any little thing means a lot. This was all she had after Buffalo Creek. It wasn't much, but it was hers, even with all the bad memories of my daddy."

He shifted and the leather on his holster creaked. "Hard times notwithstanding, she shot at Callie."

"You know Callie won't press charges."

Sheriff Preston pushed back his hat and scratched his head. "You're right. That woman would slog through hell and back for your mother. And I think she'd do it because of you."

"What do you mean?"

"She's sweet on you, Billy. You can't see that?"

I waved him off. "She's just a good friend."

He rolled his eyes and sighed. "Well, Callie wanted to make sure you and the neighbors were safe from Annie Oakley over there. All you'd need is for her to take potshots at the neighbor kids like she was shooting ducks at the carnival. We need to get that gun away from her."

"I can get it."

"Why haven't you?"

"I didn't want to scare her. Plus, maybe I thought I'd get lucky and she'd actually hit me."

"Sometimes I feel the same way. Just put me out of my misery."

"Yeah, but then you got that trout waiting back home."

"You got a point there. The love and cooking of a good woman will keep you going." He gave me a long look like he wanted to ask me something else, but he held his tongue. "Well, to be honest with you, Billy, your mother doesn't seem scared to me. Looks like she's ready for a fight."

"Give me a few minutes. If it works, you come in and get the gun. If it doesn't, bring a gurney and wheel me out."

"I'll be there," the sheriff said.

Using the truck to shield me, I walked unseen to the porch and entered the front door. The floorboards creaked, but I picked my steps to make as little noise as possible. The front room was an office of sorts, with scattered parts of old radios and things I'd worked on over the past few months. My original Atwater Kent I restored when I was thirteen. A couple of CB base stations and my ham radio and straight key, building plans for a radio station I had salvaged, and what would pass as junk to most people but felt like treasure to me. A pastiche of a solitary life of broken dreams and shattered hopes all strewn about on a workbench.

In the corner, behind a stack of records I hadn't even looked at in years, was my old friend. I pulled it out and went into the living room and sat in Daddy's favorite chair. The strings were rusty, but it didn't take long to get them going. I played her favorite, "In the Garden." Daddy used to play it for her and she would curl up beside him on the couch and sing along.

The kitchen light was still on and I could see her reflection in one of the windows. As soon as I started picking out the tune, she sat up and her head cocked like an old dog that smells a coon or a rabbit but doesn't have the energy to follow the scent. She made it to a standing position by holding the gun out in front of her and came walking, stiff-legged, back through the darkened hallway. I saw the silhouette of an old woman holding a gun across her chest, a geriatric soldier pushing up one more hill. It is one of the endearing images I still have.

When she got past the bathroom, she stopped and put the gun on the floor. As soon as I heard her voice, I found the spot where she was singing and played along.

When she got to the third verse, she reached the couch and stretched out.

"I'd stay in the garden with Him
Tho' the night around me be falling,
But He bids me go;
thro' the voice of woe
His voice to me is calling."

By the time she sang the last words, her voice quavered. The back door opened and the sheriff entered.

"Play it again, Other," she said. "You play it so pretty."

I started over again, and in the little light

there was, I pointed to the ground where Sheriff Preston walked. He saw me and picked up the gun.

Mama sang the words softly again. " 'I come to the garden alone, while the dew is still on the roses.' " I could tell there was something going on with the sheriff. He just stood there looking at the two of us in the darkness, as if this surreal image would be stuck in his mind.

He moved back to the hallway and mouthed, "I'll put the gun in your truck."

I nodded and kept playing.

And He walks with me,
And He talks with me,
And He tells me I am His own,
And the joy we share
as we tarry there,
None other has ever known.

She went to sleep on the couch and I brought her covers and put them over her. I slept in the chair beside her in case she woke up and tried to leave.

# 10

On Sunday afternoon I told her we were
going for a drive. I dressed her in her best
outfit, the same one she had worn to Daddy's funeral. She had lost so much weight
that it just hung on her like a jacket on a
scarecrow. I brushed Mama's hair and tried
to tie it in a bun like she always did, but it
just came out looking all whopperjawed and
I let it hang down her back.

She didn't protest or turn mean, and she
even took her pills, which was a blessing. I
wanted this to be a good day. I helped her
out to the car and buckled her in, talking to
her and reassuring her that she'd like the
surprise.

We drove to Huntington through the
streets that had scared her to navigate when
Daddy was having tests and doctors' appointments nearly every week. To her this
was a big city with mysterious, tall build-
ings. But I had gone to technical school here

and had been working in town for years.

We drove to Sixteenth Street and turned right on Fifth Avenue and worked our way into an industrial area. The smell of chemicals hung heavy. Mama had her window cracked and she sniffed at the air. "Mmm. Smell those hot dogs."

Stewarts is one of the landmarks of my childhood, and one of the hot spots in Huntington since 1932. The tiny building that the original owners built in the middle of the Depression still stands. And the secret sauce Grandma Gertrude developed is still hand-cooked.

Mama once said that the hot dogs were so good here because they rolled each one of them up in a napkin. That kept the bun soft and the sauce warm. I'm not sure whether it was the sauce, the onions, the type of bun or hot dog, or if the whole thing was simply the power of memory over the taste buds, but every bite seemed to bring back something good. There are times when I will pull into this little orange shack and sip from a frosty mug and the tears will roll because of what comes back to me. I think that has less to do with the cuisine than it does the past, but the two seem to be inseparable in my mind.

We pulled into the Stewarts parking lot,

and a young girl came to put a ticket number on our windshield. She looked into the car and smiled. "Welcome to Stewarts. What can I get for you?"

I ordered five hot dogs for the two of us and a gallon of root beer to go. The girl wrote the order on a green pad and walked off to stick it on the metal wheel inside.

"Stewarts always made the best hot dogs," Mama said.

"Do you remember coming here with Daddy after his doctors' appointments?"

She smiled. "He just loved these hot dogs, didn't he? And you did too. The four of us could go through a dozen of them easy because Harless always had such an appetite."

Harless had died long before we ever pulled into the Stewarts parking lot, but I let that go. The girl brought us the jug and a bag of hot dogs.

"You give that pretty little thing a good tip, Son," Mama said. "He's single, you know."

The girl bent down and smiled at her. "You have the prettiest hair, ma'am. Just as pretty as a picture."

I handed her back some of the ones from my change and she thanked me. We turned around and went back up Third Avenue, the smell of the hot dogs making my mouth water. Marshall University was to our left, and Mama marveled at the stadium and the campus. I turned left on Hal Greer Boulevard and headed back the way we had come, but before we got to the interstate, I turned right and wound through the small, two-lane road that ran to Ritter Park. I found a good place to park near a picnic area and helped Mama out of the car.

There was a slight breeze, but the sun was out and warmed us. We sat at the table and I poured her some root beer. She took a sip and closed her eyes like she had tasted a fine, aged wine.

"That's what I remember," she said. "Now give me one of those dogs."

She unwrapped a hot dog from the napkin and the look on her face when she took her first bite was priceless. A little smile showed at the corners of her mouth, along with a healthy bit of chili sauce.

Sitting there with her, it felt like some of the hard times just melted away, like butter in her cast-iron skillet. She was back with me. Sitting there with the sunshine on our faces, the sound of children on the playground as our sound track, I wondered if I was doing the right thing sending her away. Perhaps we could make this work.

"You know what this makes me think of?" she said. "The time we went down to Lexington for our anniversary. Do you remember that?"

"I can't say I do, Mama."

"You took me to that big hotel, the one with the suites, and there were two big rooms and two big beds." She threw back her head and laughed. "Oh, we had a time. At least you did."

I unwrapped a third hot dog while she told me more about that weekend. Though I tried to silence her, she gave intimate details I didn't want to hear. I sat there, blushing and ashamed for her, but also knowing there was nothing she could do to control these detours of the mind.

She finished her story and the hot dog at the same time and mashed the napkin into a ball.

"Do you want another one?" I said. "We still have one left."

She shook her head vigorously and looked away, her muscles tensing. A tear escaped one eye and traveled a long, wrinkled path down her cheek.

"What are you thinking, Mama?"

She shook her head some more like she was trying to get something unstuck from the drain of memory. Suddenly she got up and walked toward the trash can to throw away the postage stamp–size napkin and then moved toward three children who had a box and a sign: *Puppies for sale.*

"Want to buy a puppy?" a girl said to her. She couldn't have been more than ten. She wore a torn, ratty jacket and shoes that should have been tossed long ago. "They've all had their shots."

My mother looked inside the box and oohed and aahed at the mangiest-looking dogs I had ever seen. To say they were mutts would have been too kind to them and their mother. They were scrawny and wormy-looking things that could hardly stand on their own.

"They're only fifty dollars each," a boy said. He was a little younger than his sister and appeared as mangy as the pups. "We have to get rid of them today or they're going to the pound."

"That's a real shame, but I don't think we're in the market for any puppies," I said kindly but firmly. "Come on, Mama."

Mama was transfixed. She kept looking down and bending a little further, reaching out a hand to one brown and white pup whose fur seemed to curl at the end. The runt of the litter and surely the first to expire when he hit the doors of the pound.

"Can I hold him?" she said to the boy.

More quickly than a bass will strike a june bug, that boy had the dog out of the box and in my mother's arms. I whispered a prayer under my breath because the child surely did not know what he had done.

The dog licked my mother's fingers, probably driven wild by the hot dog sauce. She giggled and held him to her chest. "Such a nice puppy. Looks just like Thunder, doesn't he?"

He didn't look a thing like Thunder, but I wasn't about to say that. "Let's put him back now, Mama."

She turned away and carried the pup toward the picnic table.

"You gonna buy it?" the third child said. It was hard to tell whether it was a boy or a girl, but the voice gave him away. His nose ran like a flooded river.

"No, I'm not going to buy it, son," I said.

"Eeewww," the girl said, and she pointed and the three of them laughed. "She's going pee!"

I turned to see my mother with her legs apart. I ran to her and tried to get the puppy away.

"Mama, we can't take that dog home."

Like a child who has just found a toy she will not part with, she clutched the thing tightly. The dog's eyes bulged.

"Mama, let go. You're going to hurt him."

The three children gathered around us, getting upset. "Give him back if you're not going to buy him."

Mama stared daggers at me and spoke through clenched teeth. "I'm not letting go."

A few parents at the playground looked on as we moved like a flock of geese across the manicured lawn. My mother's socks were drenched with urine and the smell was overpowering.

"Just let him down to run," I said. "Let's see how fast he can run."

The pup yelped in pain as her grip grew tighter.

"She's going to kill it!" the girl shouted. "She's crushing him!"

I took out my wallet. I only had two twenties left from our trip to Stewarts. I handed them over.

"You're ten short," she said.

"I owe you," I said.

Mama walked toward the car across the wide-open field, the dog yipping and yelping.

I hurried to the picnic area and grabbed the last hot dog and handed the nearly full gallon jug of root beer to the kids. "Take this home with you. And come back next weekend. I'll bring the rest of your money."

The kids ran back to their laundry basket, and I caught up with my mother. She had calmed a little and the frightened pup could breathe again. Inside, I buckled her, but she wouldn't let go of the dog. I unwrapped the last hot dog and tore off a bit and fed it to him. The pup ate it ravenously. Mama took the hot dog and started feeding the mongrel herself, tearing off just enough so the hungry thing wouldn't choke to death. She was getting chili all over her dress, but she smiled and cooed and it seemed to pacify her.

As we neared the house, the dog got sick and all of that hot dog came back up again all over Mama's dress. The perfect end to the perfect day.

That night I tucked Mama into bed and sat down next to her. She'd kept the dog with her the whole evening. I managed to get it away long enough to let it do its business outside, but Mama followed me to the back steps and watched. I didn't want it sleeping in bed with her, but the little thing seemed to calm her.

"We have a big day tomorrow, Mama," I said, brushing her hair.

She smiled and patted the pup's head.

"Every day is a big day, Other."

"Did you like the hot dogs?"

"I love Stewarts," she said. "Will you play for me again?"

I brought the mandolin to her room and played her favorite in the darkness. After she fell asleep, I tried to get the pup, but it was fast asleep, content and snuggled warm against her bony body. I stood and listened to them sleep, dreading the morning.

I awakened to a knock at the front door. I can always tell when new company comes. They go to the front door when everyone knows we don't use it. A car was parked in the driveway and a white van sat next to the road with the name of the nursing home on the side. Two men in white jumpsuits were behind the woman at the door.

I took a deep breath and invited them in. The county worker had paperwork to sign. It was all businesslike and matter-of-fact, like buying a used car. Sign here and here, initial there, and you were on your way.

"I need to get her ready," I said. "We had a rough day yesterday."

"We'll wait," the woman said. As I stood, she stopped me. "You need to know you're doing the right thing. This is what a loving son would do." She said it by rote, like a flight attendant will tell you how to buckle your seat belt and look for the exits around you. I've never been on a plane but I've seen that stuff in movies. I nodded and left the room, thinking it was not the right thing to do.

Mama was at the window holding the pup. It had peed on her nightgown.

"Mama?" I said softly.

"They've come for me, haven't they?" There was something dead in her voice. Resignation.

"We just need to get you to a place where we can take care of you. Everything's going to be okay. Let me help you get dressed."

She turned and looked at me. "If you've decided to take every bit of dignity from me and put me away, the least you can do is let me get dressed by myself." She said it with all the clarity of a Supreme Court justice. It was as if, for that brief moment, she had stepped back into herself and was fully there.

"The last thing I want to do is take your dignity," I said. "I just want to take care of you and I can't do that anymore. I'm sorry. This is the only thing I can think to do."

Something like love shone in her eyes. And hurt. She searched for more words but they wouldn't come.

"All right," I said, putting a hand on her feeble arm. "Let me take the pup while you get your things on."

"No, let him stay. He'll be fine."

I left the door ajar and went back to the front room. Sheriff Preston had arrived and was talking with the men in the driveway. I told the county health worker that Mama would be ready in a minute, and she looked at her watch. "All right. But we need to move this along. It's not good for her to prolong the process."

"I understand," I said.

I joined Sheriff Preston outside. Callie Reynolds brought corn bread and chili. People in West Virginia who care usually show it with food. She said she was going to leave it on the kitchen table and asked if she could help.

"Mama's insisted on getting dressed by herself," I said. "Maybe if you were there when she came out, it would help. A familiar face."

Wiping away tears, Callie nodded. "I'll be there. I'm so sorry you have to go through this, Billy."

Callie went in the back door. Instead of shaking my hand, Sheriff Preston put an arm around me and led me to the street. "It doesn't get much tougher than this, Billy. I

177

don't know if that brings any comfort."

I told him about the trip to the park and the pup we brought home. He listened and smiled when I said she wouldn't let go of it.

"Animals have a way of getting to your heart when nothing else can," he said. "I'm not surprised she latched on to something like that."

"I think she knows, Sheriff. I think she knows it's time and this is the right thing to do. But that doesn't make it any easier."

He crossed his arms in front of him. "Knowing and doing are two different things." He said it like he was talking about himself. "Sometimes, when you know the right thing to do, you simply have to do it, even though it breaks your heart."

The wind picked up and a semi passed on the interstate behind us.

"The older we get, the more like children we become," he said. "Maybe you can keep that dog and take it to her at the home to brighten her day. I'll bet she'll look forward to it. Little dog like that can give so much more than it ever receives."

We stood there not talking until the county health lady came to the door and looked out. Callie pushed past her holding the puppy we had yet to name.

"Is this your dog?" she said.

"Mama and I got it yesterday. It's a long story. She wouldn't take no for an answer. Did she give him to you?"

"No, I found him in the bathroom."

"Mr. Allman, I think we ought to move ahead," the county health worker said.

It was like those last few moments before they close the casket on the dearest person in your life. You just want one last goodbye, one last vision of how the person used to be. Something to hold on to for the lonely years ahead. I could hear in my head the ugly words she was about to say to the men as they helped her to the van.

"Yes, ma'am," I said, taking the pup from Callie. He trembled in my hands.

"You need to sign these final release forms," the health lady said. "I'll make sure she's ready."

I cradled the dog in one arm and signed the blurry pages. I never knew a signature could be so hard.

The sheriff put his hand on the page to steady it. "I know it's hard to believe right now, but this is for the best. You know that in your heart. It's just going to take some time for the truth to sink in. Believe me. It will."

I nodded quickly and handed the paperwork to the older man in white. He smelled

179

like Pall Malls.

"We'll take good care of her," he said with an emphysemic cough.

"I know you will."

We must have looked like quite a conglomeration of humanity right about then. All these disparate people, mostly strangers, shoulder to shoulder to help bear out an old woman who couldn't take care of herself. You could hear the floor creak with every footstep and the second hand on the old clock Mama had bought when we first moved. The sun had faded the face of it to a burnt orange.

The health worker came out of the bedroom with an awkward gait, like she didn't know whether to come outside the room or stay in. She came to me, and things seemed to move in slow motion.

"Mr. Allman . . . how long has your mother been dead?"

"Dead?" I rushed to the room and Callie followed. "She's not dead. She's just getting ready."

I pushed through the bedroom door and saw my mother on the hard floor with an arm cradled under her. There was no blood; she hadn't fallen and hit her head. She hadn't squirreled pills away or found shells to another gun. It was as if she had just decided that nobody was going to take her and given up the ghost right then and there. I handed the pup to Callie and felt my mother's neck and arm for a pulse. Nothing.

"She just spoke to me," I said, choking back the tears. "She wanted to get dressed herself. And yesterday we went out together . . ."

"I've seen this before," the health worker said. "Probably happened when she heard us in the front room. When the truth finally hits, they just know it's time. There are statistics . . ."

The woman continued but I couldn't hear. I felt a hand on my shoulder.

"I'm so sorry, Billy," Callie whispered through her tears.

I picked up my mother's limp body and placed her on the bed, her head perfectly positioned on the white pillow. Air escaped her lungs in a final breath and I stared. There was nothing else to do. No place to go. The world felt empty and sullen. A planet that had stopped spinning. How do you live in an empty hole in space? Where do you go from nothing? What do you do when the floorboards of life open up and swallow you?

Sheriff Preston came in. "I'm sorry for

your loss. Would you like me to call the funeral home, Billy?"

I nodded. "I guess that's what we ought to do now, isn't it?"

"I'll get them on the phone."

The county health people left and were replaced by funeral home people. More things to sign. More questions to answer. More strangers taking care of the mother I didn't have anymore.

I asked the man from the funeral home if he had ever seen this type of thing before. "I've seen just about everything. You couldn't surprise me anymore. But your mother went real peaceful. I can tell that looking at her face. I think she felt loved in the end."

I covered my face with my hands and lost it. Right there in front of the couch, I knelt and out came a flood of emotion that burst and filled that house. The outburst scared and shocked me, not only the intensity, but the duration.

You come into this world naked and you go out of it the same way. But in all of that time, from my birth to that day of watching my mother voluntarily give up the right to take a breath, I had never felt alone. I had always felt that God was walking with the two of us, helping us claw our way back

182

onto dry ground. I could have had a million friends and they could all have been around me with their hands on my shoulder, and it wouldn't have amounted to a hill of beans. I was alone in the world and I knew it.

They carried my mother out of the home she loved in a body bag on top of a rolling gurney that left little marks in the dust on the wood floor. I was prepared to watch them take her away, but not like that.

When everyone was gone and I had told Callie for the last time that I didn't need any company, I went back to my mother's room. Her underclothes had been tossed on the floor. I picked them up and put them in the closet and closed the door. It felt like a final slap, a reckless and insulting end to the day. "That's life," she would have said.

I spent the rest of the day trying to figure out what to do. I found a pad of paper where she had made a to-do list. It must have been years in the making. I remembered to call my boss and told him what had happened. He offered to give me a few days off, but I said it would be better if I worked until the funeral on Thursday.

The pup with no name kept me company. I didn't have the wherewithal to write *dog food* on the list, so I gave him some chili with corn bread crumbled into it, and he gobbled it down and licked the plastic cereal bowl. It was a choice I would come to regret in the middle of the night, but after all I had been through over the weekend, it seemed like a small price to pay for a little companionship.

I shut the dog up in the laundry room with a bowl of water and some dry food I borrowed from a neighbor while I went to work. He was whining before I ever got the door shut.

At work, people were kind and there was a card signed by everybody in the office that said *Sympathy* on the front of it. One woman from the newsroom who I knew was a believer wrote, "I'm praying for you, Billy. May God sustain you through this trial. Psalm 23."

In the days to come, I got a few cards telling me what my mother meant to the people in the community. I was surprised at how many people were at the funeral. My boss from work. Beulah, who ran the beauty shop. Sheriff Preston and his wife. My pastor from the Bible church welcomed everyone, and we sang about coming to the garden alone. Mama would have liked that. The pastor spoke about the blessed hope we have in Jesus. Then he asked me to come and say a few words. I would not have done it for any other human being on the planet, not in a million years. But she would have loved seeing me up there.

"I want to thank you all for coming. Mama would have liked it that she brought you all together.

"My mother did not have an easy life. It felt like she moved from one storm to another. Some of you know we lived along Buffalo Creek down in Logan County when that dam broke. She lived through that. She helped Daddy through his illness. She saw a son die in Vietnam. She lost her parents early on.

"And she always told me, when her mind was right, that the struggle of our lives was not a sign that we were failing or losing. The struggle was a sign that there was still life. If you stopped struggling, that's when you needed to be worried. The fight meant God was helping you keep going one more day even if you didn't think you could make it.

"I believe that, even when I don't."

Macel Preston wiped away a few tears and I felt my chin quiver. But I held it together long enough to finish.

"The other thing she would have wanted you to know is that no matter how hard things get, God is there. I can see glimpses of that even in her worst days. I can see the ways that Jesus was working all of this out, even though it's hard to make sense of it.

"Mama loved me to the end in the only ways she knew how. Even through the sickness of her mind, she was caring for me. On the day before she died, we passed some kids who were selling mangy puppies. She picked one of them up and wouldn't let go. I had to buy it so the kids wouldn't call the police on us."

Everybody laughed.

"I think Mama knew I would need something in the house after she was gone. She was providing for me even in the darkest hours."

I paused and gathered the pieces of paper I had torn from my mother's to-do pad. With tears in my eyes I said, "I loved my mama. And she loved me. I don't think a son could ask for more than that."

I started to leave the lectern and then stopped. People wiped at their eyes and stared straight ahead. I put my hand on the casket and looked at them. "Someone came up to me last night and said they were sorry that I had lost my mother. And I appreciate that. But I want to set the record straight. I haven't lost her. I know exactly where she is. One day I'll see her again."

Macel came to me after the graveside service and clutched my hand in hers. "Your mother would have been so proud of all you said. It was just beautiful, Billy. I'm so sorry for the pain you've been through."

"We went through some deep waters together. I'm glad she's at peace. And I'm glad I know where she is."

She nodded. "The Lord has something good in store for you. I can just feel it."

"Feels like I'm turning a page, Mrs. Preston. I don't know what's on the other side, and I know it's going to be hard, but I think I'm ready."

"I'm going to send Hadley over with a casserole or two in the coming days."

"I look forward to it, ma'am. I appreciate your husband more than I can say. Compared to some lawmen I've been acquainted with, he seems to have a real heart."

"He does. He's a good man, Billy. Pray for him. He needs to know the Lord."

I nodded. "What's holding him back?"

"The past. The future. He's a wandering soul with a lot on his mind. I've had the church praying for him for years, but there doesn't seem to be much going on. I have enough faith to trust the Lord is going to do something there, too."

"If there's one thing I've learned, it's that God has a way of working on his own timetable. And it usually is a lot different from ours."

"That's the truth, Billy. It surely is."

"I'll be praying for your husband," I said.

"I appreciate that. And I'll be praying that God is close to you in this time."

I went back to my car after everybody left, but I just sat there and watched the workers lower the casket down and then cover the hole with dirt. After they finished and made their way from the cemetery, I got out and took my mandolin over to her grave and played one last time. Music had been such a part of our lives and I knew she would have liked it.

I believe that absent from the body is present with the Lord. The pastor back on the creek had said that after the flood, and his words rang true to me all those years later. If you are "in Christ," the moment you take your last breath is the moment you are in the very presence of God. So I really wasn't playing for her. I was playing for the memory of her. The memories of all the years and the hard times and the choices I'd made and the way we both had to deal with them. Wave after wave of memories swept over me and carried me to unexpected places along the creek bank of my life. A restaurant where my mother let me order food we couldn't afford, my first day of school in Dogwood when she trailed me to the classroom — as unable to let go of me as I was of her — sitting together near the empty grave at my father's funeral, and the day she gave me the news of Heather's wedding.

Before the sickness took over her mind and body, I had seen her at the point of despair only a handful of times. She was always such a woman of faith, someone who believed that God was who he said he was and would do what he said he would do. But that day I remember her face fell and there seemed like something had bittered up her soul.

I had just come home from an overnight shift at the radio station. It was only part-time, but I was happy to be doing something I really enjoyed. I sat in one of the kitchen chairs and she sat next to me and folded her hands across the table as if in prayer.

"Billy, Heather's mother called me today."

"Really? What for?"

"She wanted to let us know some news."

I nodded. My mother had a flair for the dramatic, and this pregnant pause was one of her devices to drag me into a story. "News?" I finally said.

She rubbed her hands, pursed her lips, and finally let it escape. "Heather is getting married this weekend. Down at the rose garden in Ritter Park. Her mother wanted you to know. I'm so sorry, Billy."

I swallowed hard and scratched at something on my neck. "Married, huh? Who to?"

"She didn't say. It came up all of a sudden, I guess. I don't think they knew she was even serious about anybody. I don't think it was anybody from around here."

I tried to laugh. "Well, I don't know why you'd think I would be upset. We were friends, but it was never anything more than that."

She kept looking into my eyes. "Is that the truth?"

I got up and went to the sink and ran the water. I washed my hands for no particular reason other than to put my back to my mother so I wouldn't have to endure her eyes.

"Actually, I'm real happy for her, Mama."

"Say what?" she said.

I dried my hands on a paper towel and turned. "I'm glad she found somebody. It was always my hope that she'd be happy. My biggest prayer was that she would know

Jesus. But I also prayed that she'd find somebody who would be good to her. Maybe that's who she's found."

"Well, nobody knows much about him. I think it was somebody she met on a trip. I doubt it will last."

"I hope you're wrong. What God joins together should stay together." I tossed the paper towel into a Foodland bag on the floor. "I can't say I'm all that surprised. She was always unpredictable." I put a hand on Mama's shoulder. "Thanks for telling me. I'm going to get some sleep."

"Billy?" she said when I hit the hallway. "If you need to talk, I'm here."

"Thanks, Mama."

I smiled at her and walked back to my room and shut the door. I took off my shoes and jacket and collapsed into bed. A swarm of memories collected around me like bees to a hive. Memories that I wanted to both forget and cherish. I knew from the day I sat down beside her on that bus that I had no chance of winning her heart. And something was tearing at the soul of that girl. That she would run into the arms of someone who could give her some comfort from life's disappointments was expected after all she'd been through.

I lay there on the pillow, the sun coming

up over the hills and bringing warmth and light. My body was exhausted, and there was a deep ache that only comes when hope and love meet a brick wall.

"Lord, you know why Heather is running," I prayed. "And you know the heart of this man she's going to marry. I release her to you and ask you to draw her to yourself. Bring her into a relationship with you, and do the same for her husband. Show them there's no better place to live than in your will. I don't know how you're going to do it, Lord, but I pray you would."

I guess some people wondered over the years if I even had those kinds of feelings because of the type of person I am. Solitary. Working alone most of the time. That's why I'm writing it down. Those feelings have been there and come up now and then at unexpected times. I guess that's part of the struggle. Part of living in a world filled with hurts and disappointments.

I patted the loose dirt on the grave and picked up a flower arrangement that had fallen. Then I said good-bye to my mother for the last time and headed home.

# 11

The Sunday after Mama's funeral, I took the pup to Ritter Park. I had an ample supply of Stewarts hot dogs as I looked for the kids. When I couldn't find them, my heart grew heavy. I opened a can of tennis balls and the pup chased one around for a while, bumping it with his nose and rolling over it with his paws.

I picked him up and headed for the rose garden. This time of year its beauty was masked, but the meticulous gardening still stirred me. I could see the expanse of the park from here, the fields and playgrounds and trees that seemed as old as time itself. I spotted three kids with a box at the end of the park and hurried to reach them.

I was out of breath but managed to get their attention before they crossed Thirteenth Avenue. Their eyes lit up and they came running, the dogs thumping against the sides of the box.

"We didn't think you'd come back," the girl said.

"Yeah," the younger boy said. "Our mom said you ditched us."

"Well, tell your mother that Billy Allman always keeps his word to a friend." I pulled out the ten-dollar bill I had in my shirt pocket. "Looks like you still have all of your pups. Didn't have to take them to the pound?"

The girl looked up sheepishly. "Mama told us to forget the pound and just chuck them in the river, but I couldn't do it."

"Well, I'm with you," I said. "They just need a good home."

"Your pup looks like he's doing okay," the girl said.

"He eats like a king," I said.

"What happened to that old lady who was with you?" the younger one said. "I thought she was going to kill that dog."

"She was sick, actually. I didn't know how sick. She crossed over the river this past week, so she's in a better place."

"She went to Proctorville?" the boy said.

Any other time I would have laughed out loud. Instead, I smiled, the hurt still there. "No, she passed away." When the three of them shot me bewildered looks, I explained that she had died and that her funeral had been Thursday.

"I ain't never knowed anybody who died the same week they bought a puppy," the girl said.

I gave them the box of hot dogs and the gallon jug of root beer, and the girl said they would have them for dinner. "Mama will freak out. We don't have much food in the house."

"You tell her a satisfied customer came back to pay his debt."

"You wanna come eat with us?" the younger boy said.

The girl shot him a mean look like he had just uttered a blasphemy.

"I don't think I could stay to eat, but I'll give you a ride home. How far away is your house?"

The girl pointed. "About a mile or so over thataway. But Mama wouldn't like us getting a ride from a stranger. Did you hear about that little girl who got kidnapped?"

I'd been listening to the news stories. A young girl had been abducted from Dogwood over the summer, according to her mother. I had volunteered on a search crew a few months back, scouring the countryside, but there had been no sign of the child.

"Tell you what, you put your puppies in the back, then, and I'll follow you home so

195

you don't have to carry them."

The girl thought a minute. "I don't think she'd mind you giving us a ride."

They all scrunched into the truck and we drove past the brick homes of Huntington's upper crust and into an area of houses with rotting roofs and overgrown yards. The kids gave conflicting directions, and we wound up at some apartments that looked like they were too run-down even for college students.

The kids hopped out, carrying the dogs and the food and drink, a lightness to their step. "Mama, it's him! He came back and paid us!"

I stayed at the truck and waited for the mother to invite me in or call the police. Through an open window next door, I heard bluegrass music. I recognized the group and wondered if it was the radio or a CD. There weren't many stations in this area that played that type of music.

The mother came to the door barefoot, wearing faded jeans with holes in the knees, the sign of the bottle in her eyes. They were hollow and empty, like the life had been sucked out of them.

"What are you doing around my kids?"

The younger boy pulled on her hand and

told her not to yell, but she pushed him away.

"I didn't mean to upset you, ma'am. I just wanted to pay my debt and do something nice for your children. I didn't have the money last week when I saw them —"

"You one of them perverts who steals kids?"

"No, ma'am, I —"

"Stop calling me ma'am. I'm not some old lady."

"I know that, ma'— I mean, I'm sorry. I didn't mean to upset you. That's just how I talk to people."

Her hands were on her hips and her posture said she was ready for a fight. A curtain pulled back in another apartment. We had an audience. The kids were at the screen door. I didn't want an argument with her or anybody else.

I explained what had happened. How I didn't want to buy a puppy but my mother insisted. And how guilty I felt for cheating her children of those ten dollars. "My mother passed this week, and I think it was God's way of letting me have a little companionship. I remembered this morning that I owed them, so I thought the least I could do was give a little food and something to drink for their gift to me."

"We don't need your charity," the woman spat.

"Mama, he's nice," the girl said through the screen.

She yelled something so mean to her that it cut me to the heart. The lady told her to close the door and then turned on me. "Get out of here and don't come back. Next time I see you around my kids, I'm calling the cops."

I backed away to my truck. I wanted to explain more or at least say I didn't mean any harm. I had the good sense to know this wasn't really about me, but I still felt the shame of being there with people looking.

When I drove away, the kids were at the front window eating those hot dogs. I never drove by Stewarts again without thinking of them and their mother so scarred and scared that she couldn't see something good when it stared her in the face.

I go back to that event and what happened with the children as what started my dream. Hearing that music coming from the apartment and knowing how people identified with it, how much it could seep into a soul or break a stony heart, gave me an idea. I'd seen it happen before, the message of the music cutting through, even though the people who played it weren't perfect. I'd seen music change people, the words and the melodies working their way like a vine into the spirit, winding around their lives until they had to respond.

The next week, when my manager called me into his office, it was like a streak of lightning across the sky of my life. I didn't see it that way then, but it struck me later that God was moving the course of my life.

"How are you doing, Billy?" he said, speaking slowly as if he were reading a script. His name was Karl Stillwater, and I have never been able to get over the irony of that last name.

"I'm all right, considering. Thanks for asking."

Karl was not a big man, either in stature, resolve, or heart. The cowboy boots made him a little taller, but they also seemed like props. He lived on a farm outside of town that had no animals in the barn or crops in the field. It was just country veneer. All look and no corn.

There had been several painful conversations when I first began working overnights for him. He said I'd never make it — even in the hills — as an announcer. He just wanted me to play the music along with the voice-overs of the image IDs and stingers that played in between songs, which was a little like taking a girl to a movie and sitting in the row behind her.

So I threw myself into the technical and watched others with better voices and less to say shuffle through the control room. It has always seemed to me that what you say is more important than having a good voice. You can have all the panache in the world and a smooth sound and professionalism, but if there's no heart, people can tell. But that is not the way the world works, I guess.

"Were you finally able to buy that piece of land down in Dogwood?"

"I'm paying on it every month."

"Did your mama leave you anything to help out with that?" he said, folding his hands like a preacher about to deliver a sermon on hell.

"Mama didn't have much of anything. She left a few trinkets but no money. But she loved me with everything she had. I think that's better than a big inheritance."

"No property or . . . ?" he said with a grimace, like what he was about to say would have been easier for him if she had a big life insurance policy.

I shook my head.

"Well, Billy, we've kind of come to a

crossroads here. And I hate to do this at such a time, but I think we need to go another direction with the station."

"Another direction? Format change?"

"No, we need to hire a different chief engineer. With the economy what it is and our ad revenue down, we've had to make some hard decisions. Like I said, I hate to do this to you at such a hard time. I know you'll understand."

"I can take a pay cut," I said.

He winced. "It's not just the pay issue. It's the whole package. You understand."

"No, I don't understand. I haven't been late to work; I haven't shirked my duties. Can you tell me the last time the station was off the air because of equipment problems? The only downtime we've had is the lightning strike at —"

He put up a hand. "I'm not saying you've been negligent. This is a financial decision pure and simple."

"Karl, you have to have an engineer. You said you were going to hire another one. There's nobody on the planet who's going to work for less than I do."

"We're looking at somebody who could come in part-time, maybe. Might not pay benefits. The benefits are killing us."

"Then let me do that," I said. "I'll cut

back to three days. Even two, if you want."

He shook his head. "I don't think so. Now, I'd be glad to give you a recommendation, a reference as you job hunt. You might make money fixing TVs and such. You can fix just about anything. But I think we need to move in another direction. I'm sure you understand."

"Stop saying I'll understand."

"I'm sorry, Billy."

"Don't do this."

"I truly am."

He stood up and reached a hand toward me.

"Is this about your brother? Is Jimmy the one you're going to hire?"

He looked down at his desk and took back his hand. "I'm sorry."

I took my jacket and stood. When I turned to leave, something struck me. With my hand on the doorknob, I looked back at him. "The old Gates board in the production room. It's been unhooked for a couple of years. Would you consider selling that to me?"

He made a face and laughed. "That thing has been around here longer than I have. What do you want with it?"

"Would you sell it?"

He rubbed his chin. "Well, we have to give

you two weeks' severance, but if you want it, I think we can work something out. Clear out your desk and I'll have Kathy put it down in writing. Don't want you suing us or anything."

I didn't smile.

"Oh, go on and take it with you today if you'd like."

I nodded. "I do thank you for giving me a chance, Karl. You didn't have to but you did."

"It's been a pleasure having you with us, Billy. I wish you well. Let me know what works out for you."

I closed the door and collected my things. It didn't take long. I had one of the announcers help me carry the heavy mixing board to my truck and load it in the back. I gave the key to the building back to Kathy, who had tears in her eyes.

"I'm so sorry about all this, Billy. I don't know what's going on around here these days."

"I'll be okay. I thank you for your kindness."

It felt like I was losing part of my life and that the long march on my personal Bataan was continuing. Looking back, I was just starting on a new adventure that I couldn't see. Jesus said in the Bible that unless a kernel of wheat falls to the ground and dies, it stays a single seed. But if it dies, it can produce a bunch of seeds. That means a lot more wheat can only come from a dead kernel. I think that's what happened.

# 12

A man with a singular vision is difficult to find. One who seeks with a whole heart to give his whole self to God, no matter the cost, no matter the pain, is a human anomaly. I've heard of such people, and those men and women have changed the world, not because of their great strength and abilities, but because of the relinquishing of their own desires.

If there is a wholly unreserved man on earth, I have not seen him. But I have come very close in Billy Allman. For when the dream of his life and the love of a woman and all that he had planned failed, as simple and unsatisfying as that would have seemed to someone who believed happiness was contingent on finding "the good life," Billy was set free. He was released to run in the playground of God's will. Of course he did not immediately do this. He squandered much time and zeal by the swing sets before he could even begin to understand the scope of his opportunities.

Humanity is not easy for a being like me to understand. In our battles, there is no acquiescence to defeat. But on that time-bound planet, the goal for the human believer is not found in every victorious triumph, but in the elusive relationship with the Father that then leads to ultimate victory.

It is becoming much clearer that there is a veil of understanding on both sides of the eternal chasm. They do not understand how things in the heavenlies are ordered because they have no ability to *see* into our world. And there is an equally opaque veil for those of us who look on from this side of heaven's wonders. We cannot understand the ways of the heart. We cannot fully experience the strength of a loving Father carrying one through desperate times. For the human followers, it is in losing that they finally discover. It is in failing that they see. It is in the abandonment of the trail they believed would lead them to lasting joy that they set out on a new path. It is much narrower and overgrown, but in the journey through this wilderness of the soul, they discover more about themselves and Him than if every prayer of their wayward hearts had been answered in the affirmative.

I say that Billy was released by this event, the losing of what he deemed his true love, and by other events that were soon to come.

But release is always a process with humans. Though he began to run and plan and dream in the space given him, though his spirit became more free in the years that followed, it seemed he was hobbled, saddled with something from the past that I had not observed. This came in flashes, outbursts of anger, destructive behavior. Billy did not eat well. He was not a drunkard, but what he chose to consume daily made me think he was punishing himself. Anything from the past could be blamed — his father, his mother's death, the loss of his "love," or something else entirely, but I could never discover in any of his correspondence or discussions with his few friends the specific reason.

There was a period of time when I had been called away, the time at the latter end of his high school years that prevented me from being in his presence, but I had been through the general ebb and flow of his life. As Billy began his second "career," as he would call it, I set myself on a path of discovery to find that piece of the puzzle. If I had failed in some way to protect him, I wanted to know. And though I feared the discovery, I feared even more the source where that information would come.

# 13

There was a man of God I listened to every day on the radio, and after I lost my job, I got to hear him twice each day. His voice was like a bullhorn to my soul because even when he just read the Bible, it felt like my heart stirred. And when he told stories and sprinkled in his understanding and wisdom, it was like he had a pipeline right into heaven. I named my dog Rogers because of him.

In my early years in Dogwood, I had not traveled farther than the state line, with the exception of a few trips across the Ohio River to visit my mother's relatives, and once to Kentucky. With all the pomp and promises of the Gospel Bluegrass Boys, we wound up visiting two other states, but just making short jaunts, so I did not consider myself a world traveler. It's not that I didn't want to go places. If I could have driven to Memphis and visited that pastor's church, I would have done it in a minute, but traveling very far from home caused problems.

A year or two after my mama died, I heard this pastor was speaking at a church in Charleston on a Saturday night, and I drove up there to hear him and talk with him. I put on my best clothes, which wasn't saying much, and walked into that big auditorium with all those seats and people wearing ties and suit coats. I felt pretty small. The service was thrilling, but something happened afterward and I got turned around in the lobby trying to find this pastor. He left out a side door and I followed but got into some hallway with a lot of plants and got confused. A man spoke harshly to me and said I couldn't be back there, and I went the other way and wound up in a sea of people.

One usher found me wandering near the sanctuary and must have thought I was out of my gourd. When he found out I had the sugar diabetes, he took me back through those doors and sat me in an office. There was this little refrigerator under a desk and he got me a sandwich and a little box of juice. He said he could tell from my eyes that something was wrong. I checked my levels and they were dangerously low, so I had a couple more of those juice boxes.

"You feeling better?" the man asked.

I said yes and thanked him, my head clearing, and told him the real reason I had come.

The man winced. "That may be a little tough. He's gone."

"Already?"

"He and his wife went directly from here to a hotel. They fly out early in the morning from Yeager. Is there something I can help you with?"

"No, I appreciate it. I feel like the Lord wants me to talk with him."

The man nodded. "I understand."

"Can you tell me which hotel he's in?"

"I don't think I should. I want to help. But the staff would probably be upset I even told you —"

"It's all right," I interrupted. "I don't want you to do something you don't feel is right. He deserves his privacy."

"Believe me, I would if I could. And I'd be glad to help you myself."

I got up and the room spun, so I sat down again and caught my breath. Then a thought occurred to me. "You don't suppose you could answer me a different question, could you?"

"What's that?"

"Well, if I was from out of town, which I am, and if I wanted to get to the airport early in the morning, do you have a recommendation for a hotel in the area?"

He smiled at me like I was a dog that had just fetched the morning paper without getting any slobber on it. He opened a desk drawer and got out a pad of paper and wrote something on it. "Turn right out of the parking lot and at the first light turn left. It's down on your right. The address is right here."

I thanked him and my eyes stung. "I could have just asked God to direct me, I guess, but who knows where I would have ended up. Probably in the Kanawha River."

"We wouldn't want that," the man said. "Tell me your name."

I told him.

He handed me a card with his name on it. It read, *Charles Broughton.* He was some kind of salesman and it was real professional-looking. "If you ever need anything else, Billy, I want you to call me."

I felt a bit of hope as I drove to the hotel. It was a fancy place with lots of leather furniture in the lobby. I felt just as out of place there as I had at the church, but after a few minutes I used a phone to dial the operator and asked for his room. The fellow hesitated, then said he would put me through.

A woman answered and I asked to talk to her husband. She was real nice and asked me to hold on. My hands started sweating and I had to wipe them off on my shirt.

"This is Adrian," he said. That voice. Unmistakable. Just like I had heard on the radio. Piercing and clear. "Hello? Is there anybody there?"

I finally got up the gumption to speak. "Hello, sir, uh . . . I was wondering . . . I was at your meeting tonight and . . . I don't want to bother you . . ."

"Who is this?"

"My name is Billy Allman, sir. You don't know me."

"Well, Billy Allman, go ahead and ask whatever you want; you're not bothering me."

I took a breath. "Well, is there a way you would sit and talk with me for a few minutes about something?"

"About what? the weather? theology?"

"I'm born again, Dr. Rogers. Washed in the blood. But I have a big decision to make. And I feel like the Lord wants me to get your opinion. I'm not a pastor or a teacher or anything. It's just that he's put something on my heart and I can't seem to get shed of it."

It sounded like he put his hand over the

phone and said something to his wife. When he came back on, he said, "Where are you?"

"In the lobby of your hotel."

He chuckled. "Well, you made it easy on me, didn't you. I'll be down in ten minutes. Find us someplace quiet where people won't disturb us."

"I'll do that. And thank you, sir. Thank you."

The hotel had a breakfast area that went all the way around the corner and I set up shop there. I was like a kid waiting for Christmas. Of course, I had just seen him at the service, and I'd seen his picture a few times before that, but I swear I would've known him just by the way he walked. It was like he had authority that other people didn't. He scanned the lobby and moved toward me when I waved. He stuck out his hand and shook firmly.

"Billy, it's nice to meet you. Where should we sit?"

I showed him around the corner to the table. I couldn't do much but stare. "I can't believe I'm actually talking with you. I've listened a long time."

"I appreciate that. Let's get to it then."

I had made notes on a couple of three-by-five cards that covered the front and back. When I looked at them, he motioned for me to put them down. "Just share from your heart, Billy."

I looked him full in the face. "Pastor, I feel like God has given me an idea to help people in my Jerusalem. It's nothing earth-shattering, but it is kind of risky and I don't know whether to go through with it."

"What's the idea?"

"A radio station. I've gone through the application process with the FCC, and I have a bead on the rest of the equipment, but there are fees to pay and an antenna and tower to buy, and all of that is pretty expensive."

"What do you want to do with the station?"

"Run some programs like yours, but mostly play bluegrass music that speaks to people around here. Gospel-oriented music that gets them thinking about things above."

He nodded. "Do you have experience in radio?"

"I've been doing it all my life. I'm more into the technical side than the microphone side, but I can do both."

"Well, I certainly think that's a worthy dream. One question I always ask is, are other people doing the same thing you plan on doing?"

I shook my head. "No, sir. There's a

bluegrass station in Huntington and one in Charleston, but the signal is spotty in our hollow down in Dogwood. Plus, I want to do some things they don't do."

There was a napkin on the table and he moved it around and stared at me. "What do the people who know you best think about this idea? Are you involved in a church?"

"I am now. For a long time I didn't go because of my mother and her sickness before she passed. There was a falling-out of sorts, too. Your program fed me through that time."

"Well, you need to have people around you praying for this radio station. And you'll probably need some people who will support you. How much do you need to get this off the ground?"

I told him.

"Do you have any debt?"

"Just my house and the land behind it, but I've been paying on that a few years."

The man closed his eyes and brought a verse from memory. He always quoted in King James. " 'A man's heart deviseth his way: but the Lord directeth his steps.' "

"Proverbs 16:9," I said.

His eyes opened wide. "Billy, I meet a lot of people with a lot of dreams. And most of them are just things they want. They want a bigger house or a better wife or a wider ministry, tada, tada, tada. But I can tell you love the Lord with all your heart."

Tears came to my eyes. "I do."

"And you want to please him with your whole heart."

"Yes, sir."

"Do you have a wife?"

"No, sir."

"Any family?"

"My mother was the last in her family and my daddy died years ago."

"Well, let me ask you this and I want you to answer honestly. Billy, do you believe God loves you? that he wants the very best for your life?"

"Yes, sir, I do."

"And do you believe this idea you've had for some time has been given by him and he's put you in a place to see it come true, with his help?"

I nodded. "I don't know how I'm going to raise the money or get the rest of the equipment, but yes, this is all about him."

"All right. Then if he has truly planted this vision in your heart and has given you the inclination and the ability to run it, and if he provides the resources to accomplish it, I don't see why you shouldn't put your whole heart into it."

I put my head down on the table and he put his hand on my shoulder. It took me a minute to look back up at him.

He locked eyes with me and raised a finger. "This is what I'll say to you. Go back to your church and the pastor and the leaders there. Humble yourself before that fellowship. Clear up anything that's between you, okay? Now, if they're not holding God's Word as a standard, you go someplace else."

"That's not the case. They preach the Word."

"All right, then the problem was probably some personality difference or communication?"

"They invited some people to sing there that I didn't think was a good idea."

"Well, you go clear that up and don't go at this alone. You need people to stand with you. You need people to pray. There might be people there who would become partners in the work."

"I never thought of it that way, but you're right. I'm almost cheating them out of the blessing."

"Exactly. Plan it well, pray it through, follow the Lord's leading, and in time, he will direct your path and set you on a firm foundation."

I couldn't help the joy that flooded my soul. It felt like fresh rain on a dry and thirsty land. "This is what I needed."

"Now don't go on my word and recommendation. You have to have the faith it takes to believe what God has called you to do. That's not going to come from something an old preacher like me can say."

"I know that now. Even if you had said it was the dumbest idea you'd ever heard, if God gave it to me, that's going to be enough."

"That's it. Now if you start hearing voices telling you things, that's a different story." He laughed and his face scrunched up and there was a light there. "Can I pray with you?"

"I'd like that a lot," I said.

And then he prayed a prayer that made me ashamed because it felt like I was intruding on a holy conversation he was having with almighty God. Part of me felt I shouldn't even have been there. But I was, and by God's grace he was too.

Before he left, he asked me to write my address on the napkin. "I'd better get back before my wife wonders if she's missed the Rapture." Then he laughed and took off across the lobby.

"Dr. Rogers?" He stopped and turned back to me. "Thank you for what you mean to us."

"Thank the Lord, Billy. And thank you for your devotion to the King."

Two weeks later I got a white envelope in the mail with a return address from Tennessee. It was a card signed by Dr. Rogers with Proverbs 16:9 written in his own hand. *God bless you, Billy. So glad we got to meet. This is a little something to help you dig the first shovelful of dirt for the antenna.* It was a check for $1,000.

It was the only check I would receive. I did go to the pastor of our church and some of the leaders and we talked through some things. I told them my dream and that Dr. Rogers had met and prayed with me. The pastor was not as hard on me as the others — he was actually supportive to a point — but the reaction from the others was clear. There was no way they were ever going to get on board the leaky ark I was about to build.

The pastor said he would pray for me and do anything he could to help. They put me on the prayer list. But to be honest, I knew I had to go at this more like the Lone Ranger. That did not deter me. I deposited the check from Dr. Rogers in the bank under the name Billy Allman Enterprises. A local lawyer and CPA who was in my graduating class helped me incorporate the business with the state and I was rolling. Any check I got from my work on TVs and radios I would apportion to the mortgage and paying the utilities. Whatever was left over at the end of the month went into the radio station fund.

It was a long, uphill climb with as many setbacks as I'd ever had with anything I'd tried in my life. They say that anything that's good is going to be hard, and if you measure success by the amount of work it took, that station was a success long before I went on the air.

I began construction of the control room first since I already had some equipment. I took the door from Mama's room off the hinges and cut a rectangular hole in it that the old Gates board with rotary pots fit perfectly into. I put up foam from an old mattress top on the walls to deaden the sound so my voice didn't bounce around too much. As long as Rogers didn't bark at the squirrels in the trees and nobody flushed the toilet on the other side of the wall, it was pretty quiet. Nobody did that, of course, because there was nobody there but me.

Now when the trains would go through in the morning and the evening, that was a different story. You could hear that leak through the window, but I like that sound a lot and I figured I'd use it.

I kept looking online and in the trades for a deal on a transmitter. You'd be surprised what you can find on the Internet. I found one I thought I could afford, but it would have eaten up all of my savings, so I decided to build it myself.

For the antenna tower, I only had enough money for the top section. I decided to run the line back on the hill so the signal would be stronger, but I couldn't afford to install a tower. Finally, an old boy who lived in the hollow, Earl Cummins, heard about what I was trying to do and said he had a telephone pole that they'd disconnected just sitting in a field. He said he'd pull it down and I could use it. We worked one Saturday getting it back on the hill. I fixed the top section to it and we set to digging. With a chain, a couple ropes, and a pulley, we managed to get it about halfway up before the pole swung down and nearly killed Earl. He managed to escape getting squished.

We cut the pole in two to make it more manageable and that meant I didn't need such a tall ladder to work on it. It was something to see that antenna on the hill. Most people never noticed it, but I would drive up to the next exit on the interstate and slow down when I passed and just look up and shake my head. My dream was coming true.

People in town would ask what I was doing and I'd tell them as much as they could handle. It's hard letting other people in on your dream when most of them think you're crazy. There were times when I thought I was in way over my head. At one low point, I had run out of money and all I had to eat was one box of macaroni and cheese. I didn't even have the milk, so I just used water. I told Rogers I was going to have to start eating from his dish and he wagged his tail. It's a wonderful thing to have a companion like that who just wants to sit by you while you work.

One night I was working late with my soldering iron in what had become master control. I had gotten all the XLR cables done and was down under the table wiring up the console to the reel-to-reel tape players that would have been obsolete at any other station. I was working as hard as I could, but I was tired and hungry and about ready to give up. I started thinking about Heather and wondering what had happened with her. I hadn't heard anything after the wedding. And down there in the dust and dirt I thought about how much my life felt like it was purposeless and how I was useless to God or anybody else, and I'll be honest with you, I about lost it. The tears just rolled and I knew I was feeling something real, though part of me wondered if I was getting low with my blood sugar. Rogers scratched at my side and whimpered, and I sat up.

Maybe it was the blood rushing to my head or just the way my body was reacting to all the stress and grief, but right then I smelled the sweetest odor I have ever smelled. I never burned candles or had perfume about the place. Mama had a couple of bottles stored away in the closet, I suppose, but it couldn't have been that. The windows were closed and I didn't have a fan or the heater on. It smelled like a mixture of wild lilacs and honeysuckle from heaven.

I went from crying and feeling such despair to actually smiling and laughing. That sweet smell was like God saying to me, "It's all right. I'm here with you." It smelled just like the house would have smelled when Mary took the perfume, which was called pure nard — and I do not have any idea what *nard* is — and then poured it on the feet of Jesus and wiped his feet with her hair. The Scriptures say the whole house was filled with the aroma. I could imagine the angels asking why anyone would waste perfume on the likes of me, and that was part of why I was laughing and crying at the same time.

I've never told anybody about that because I didn't want to puff myself up or make people think I'm something I'm not. At that moment I just realized it wasn't really about me anymore; it was about God's love and his call.

# 14

The next day Callie Reynolds came by the house with a couple of paper bags full of food. Part of a ham, fresh Mexican corn bread muffins she had baked that morning, a huge Tupperware container of chili, and even a little chocolate cake she said was low-carb and made with artificial sweetener.

"I know you can't have a lot of desserts, but I also know how much you like it," she said.

I told her it wasn't so much the sugar; it was the carbs in the cake that got me. "If I dose right, I'm fine."

All the stuff on the table made it feel like Thanksgiving, and the aroma was almost as good as what I'd experienced the night before.

"Why'd you bring me all this?" I said. I could tell the question hurt her somehow, so I clarified. "I mean, why did you bring it today?"

Her demeanor changed. I think she thought I was upset with her. I didn't feel that way at all. In fact, I was just starving.

"I had half a day off today from work and I asked the Lord what I could do that would make a difference in somebody's life, and you popped into my mind. I knew with all the work you're doing over here, you probably don't have a lot of time to work on supper."

I took one of the muffins and it was still warm. The thing just kind of melted in my mouth like West Virginia manna. "Well, I'm sure glad you have such a tight relationship with the Almighty. This will keep me for a week."

I gave her a tour of the house and realized halfway through that I hadn't bathed for a while. She didn't let on, but I had another thing to put on my to-do list. I was wearing the same clothes I'd had on for the last week, but when you live alone, there's not much reason to change. When I got focused on a project, I would go a couple of days lasered in on whatever it was. It was the same when I was a kid, whether it was working on a jigsaw puzzle, an Erector set, or a Heathkit radio.

She made a big deal about everything I showed her, but it looked like rubble. She pointed above the door of Mama's room and asked what the hole was for, and I told her I was wiring the on-air light. "Any time the microphone goes on, that will light up."

"This is going to be real professional," she said.

"You have to have an on-air light if you're going to run a radio station."

"Where did you get it?"

"I've been doing some work for WDGW in town, and the manager offered to pay me in used equipment and a microphone and cable. He said I could have the light outside the production room that didn't work anymore."

"Can you get it to work again?"

I smiled. "Oh yeah. I can get just about anything to work again. The line from the transmitter up to the tower is coming from them too. They had almost exactly what I needed."

"This is exciting, Billy. It's like the Lord is making all this happen."

"I've been working hard, but I can tell you he's the one providing. He even provided the food."

She laughed at that. The tour didn't take that long, and we walked outside to her car. There was a chill in the air, and she crossed her arms and stood by her car door. I thanked her again for her kindness and bringing the food.

"You're more than welcome, Billy." She put a hand to her head like she was nervous about something. "I was wondering . . . as involved as you're getting with the station and getting it up and running, I was trying to think of some way I could help out. You know, support you. I don't have money to buy equipment, and I don't know much about radio stations, but I do know how to cook."

"Well, I agree with that."

"How about if I cooked for you? Just packaged things up for your meals through the week. I'd freeze it and you could store it and then follow the directions? 'Put such and such in the oven at 350 for an hour' — that kind of thing. If you can wire up a whole radio station, you should be able to do that."

My heart jumped as soon as she said it, but then I started thinking about the old camel's nose under the tent. If I let her do all this, what else would she want? And how much would I owe her? There was no part of me that was romantically interested, but I'll admit my stomach was having second thoughts.

"I think it's a great idea, but I wouldn't

want you to do all that for no pay. It wouldn't be right."

She crooked her head back one way and then the other. "No way. You hush your mouth. I wouldn't take one red cent for helping you."

"Then I can't accept. It wouldn't be right for me to just take from you."

She leaned back against her car and I could tell she was hurt. "You took the gift from Dr. Rogers, didn't you? What was different about that and what I'm offering?"

"How'd you hear about that?"

"The pastor told me."

I thought about it a minute. "Well, I guess there's not much of a difference in practice, but you'd be coming here every week and giving me stuff instead of a one-time check. It doesn't seem right."

"So it's a matter of your pride. You don't want a woman coming around doing things for you."

"No, it's not that. I just don't want to take advantage of you."

She looked away and then put her hands on her hips. "Billy. I'm investing in the work you're doing just like Dr. Rogers did. I want to be part of the blessing this is going to be. I've told you, I can't write a big check. But the Lord impressed on me that my gift is making food. It's something I can do."

"And where are you going to get the money for all that food?"

"I plant a garden every year. You know my daddy has cattle on his farm. I get a portion of beef from him that just sits in that big old freezer of theirs. Now for you to refuse this gift is downright cruel."

I was beginning to see her point and I felt bad that I had offended her. The longer I waited to speak, the more uncomfortable the silence became.

"I won't force my food on you anymore. I just think it's a shame you won't take something the Lord is offering you." She opened her car door, then looked back. "Is it that you think you'll have to start liking me? I've resigned myself to the fact that you don't care in that way."

I put up a hand but she wasn't finished.

"I don't serve my food with strings attached. It's a gift from the Lord. I swear, Billy, you act like you're all alone in this, and you're not. There's people out here who just care, and I don't see why you won't let them show it."

"Can I talk now?" I said.

She crossed her arms again. "Go ahead."

"I know you're telling me the truth. About the strings. And I don't want you to feel like I don't appreciate what you've done. The truth is, I've been so focused on my work that I haven't had much time to eat, let alone get to the store."

"That's why it makes sense to let me help."

"Can I finish?"

She rolled her eyes and flicked her hand, which made me chuckle because that's what my mother would do when we got into some argument.

"I accept your offer. And I'm grateful to God that you thought of me. I can't do this alone. But that's all I've known for a long time and it's comfortable for me. Me and that dog."

She softened a little and nodded. "I can understand that."

We stood there in the chill and she glanced at the back of the house. "There's enough in there to last you about five or six days. I'll be back with more on the weekend. Do you have another freezer?"

"No, Mama always talked about getting one but I never did."

She bit her upper lip. "My mama bought one of those little ones at Sam's Club. I don't know why because it doesn't hold much. But it would be perfect for you. Only problem is it stopped working. They put it down in the basement and just stored it."

"What was wrong with it?"

She told me.

"Maybe a condenser. I could take a look at it for them."

"No, you'd be doing them a favor if you would just take it. The dump won't take it without charging because it's got that freezer juice in it."

"Freezer juice," I said, shaking my head and laughing.

"Freon or whatever goes through the coils. I don't know what you call it."

She laughed at herself then and I knew we were going to be okay.

"See you on the weekend, then," I said, reaching out a hand.

She shook it like a deacon at the start of an all-church supper. "I'll ask my daddy to bring that over to you. He'll be tickled pink to get rid of it."

Two days later I was working on the transmitter when Mr. Reynolds pulled up in his old Ford truck that rattled and choked. He was a chunky man and I could see where his daughter got her nose. He'd been to church off and on in the past few years but not regularly. His wife and daughter were always there, though, as if joined at the hip in praying for him.

"Callie says you're building yourself a radio station," he said as I helped him pull down the freezer. It was a lot bigger than what she had let on but light.

I told him what I had planned.

"Well, I don't go in much for religion, but that music is part of me. I expect I'll listen and give it a try once you get on the air."

"I'd be pleased to dedicate a song to you."

"You know, my son-in-law is a whiz at those computers. Callie's sister's husband. I don't understand it myself, but he says there's people who do radio stations right on the Internet. Be a lot cheaper. You ever thought of that?"

I held the kitchen door open with my foot until we got the freezer past it. "I've seen that myself, and it's probably good for some. But most of the folks up and down the hollow here can't afford a computer or the monthly charge for the ISP. If all you have to do is turn on the radio and listen, that's a lot easier than going through that Internet rigmarole."

"You got a point, Billy. Can't take the computer in the truck with me."

I took the back off the freezer while he was standing there and got my voltage meter from the workbench and started testing.

"Callie also tells me she's going to be cooking for you. Is that right?"

I nodded. "Made me an offer I couldn't refuse. She's a real good cook."

"Takes after her mama."

"It's a bad power supply," I said. "These things can get a surge and burn out fast. I can fix it for you for next to nothing."

"No, there's no fixing to it; it's yours."

"Well, I'll get good use out of it. Thank you for going to the trouble to bring it over."

I showed him what I was doing with the house and the spooled-up antenna wire. "You should have no problem hearing us on the farm."

He lingered down at the shop, looking out the window at the road. "Just one thing, Billy."

"Sir?"

"Don't hurt that girl. That's all I ask. She's as sweet as summer squash. Somebody beat her with an ugly stick, but if there's one thing I've learned, it's that beauty is not just on the outside. People have it inside, too. I think that's probably in the Bible somewhere, isn't it?"

"Sure is — 1 Samuel. Story of the prophet sorting through Jesse's sons to find the next king. Before the prophet went, God reminded him not to be swayed by how they looked — told him that man looks at the outward appearance but the Lord looks at the heart. That's the same thing you were saying."

"I wish people would do that with Callie. Look at her heart instead of her face."

I didn't say anything, just kind of stared at the floor, noticing a pill bug crawling along.

"She'd kill me if she knew I was talking with you, but I thought I'd mention it. She cares an awful lot for you, Billy."

"And I wouldn't do a thing in the world to hurt her feelings, sir."

"I know you wouldn't. You're a good man. Get that freezer fixed and use it."

"I'll do it," I said.

Sometimes I wonder if God looks down on us from some parapet in heaven, all us little beings doing everything we can to control our bit of the world. There are times when it feels like all the working and striving is only for us and not for him. All of the wishing and hoping and planning that gets washed away with a big rain or a gust of wind is just for our own comfort or feeling of accomplishment. But then I come back to the fact that he has placed us on earth for a purpose, and that is to fulfill whatever mission he has. And I remember that he walked among us, God in flesh and bone, working and sweating and eating and drinking and laughing. When I got down, I'd think of that and go back to building a radio station in my house.

I didn't have any idea what would happen. It was just like the fellow in that movie about building a baseball diamond in his cornfield. Or like Noah building his ark. Most people looked at it as some kooky guy with a pipe dream. I'm sure some of them thought I was a conspiracy nut who wanted attention.

It wasn't anything like that. It was a slow, methodical process to praise the God who loved me. I wanted to tell other people about that love. When I'd get finished with one project, one room, I'd get another part-time job and make enough money for the next phase. I was as happy as a coon in a cornfield putting it all together because I could see it in my head.

But it didn't become real to me until the day the license showed up. I just stood at the mailbox and stared at the envelope, half-afraid to open it. I was approved for a commercial FM license at 96.3 MHz with full power at 6,000 watts. Rogers and I ate like kings that night in celebration. I left the food Callie had brought in the freezer and drove through the nearest Hardee's for burgers. I was dangerously low on money and most of my freelance had dried up.

The next day I called that Charles Broughton fellow at the church in Charleston, thinking about his nice business card, and I asked if there was someplace that could do the same thing for me. He asked why I wanted them and I told him my dream. Then he asked more questions and we must have talked a half hour. I told him I needed cards so I could sell time to prospective advertisers.

He told me to hang on and not go to the local quick-print place until he had a chance to work on it. I knew I could just print it off myself, but there was so much other stuff to be done and I didn't want it to look cheap.

Two days later a car pulled up in front of the house real slow and a man got out with a paper bag under his arm. He walked up to the front door and knocked.

"Are you ready?" he said, his smile about as wide as the Cheshire cat.

"Ready for what?"

"Your business cards and stationery."

He pulled a little box out of the bag and inside were five hundred white business cards with my name, address, and phone number. Over top of my name it had the call letters of the station and an antenna with a beacon in the shape of a cross. Underneath it said, *Good News Bluegrass: Music for the soul, a message for the heart.*

I about jumped out of my skin. Then he pulled out the stationery that had the address and the same thing written at the top and bottom. Plus, he had printed up a rate card for spot announcements with the cost left blank so I could just write it in.

"How did you do this?" I said, my mouth still hanging open.

"I have a friend in radio sales. He gave it to me and I copied it. My wife and I worked on the logo, and the printer turned it around in a day. I think they did a pretty good job."

"*Pretty good* doesn't even come close," I said. "How much do I owe you?"

"Just put me down as the charter member of your fan club, Billy. My only regret is that I won't be able to hear you unless I'm passing through."

I didn't have the words to thank him, but I did invite him to stay for supper. He wouldn't hear of it and said he was going to take me to the diner and I could order the biggest steak on the menu, which I did. Rogers wasn't too happy with me leaving, but I wasn't about to pass up a good meal.

We talked about my business plan, which I didn't have. He gave me tips from his own business and how I needed to approach the owners of places around town with the chance to get in on the ground floor.

"You'll be reaching people in this hollow that these businesses can't. Let's say you sell a spot for ten dollars to the local grocery. For a hundred dollars they can run ten spots each day. And you can tell them, if they get on board now, before you go on the air, you'll double their spot load for signing up early. For every spot they ran, you'd throw one in free. If they buy a week's worth, you'll throw in another week. If they advertise for a month, you'll throw in the second month. Six months' investment now could buy them a whole year."

"I'd thought about running a special to begin."

"Are you able to produce the commercials yourself?"

I nodded. "I can just use the audition channel of the board and I'm good."

"So you can tell them the production won't cost them a penny because you'll be doing all of that free. Unless they already have something to play, and most of these places won't."

I chewed on my rib eye and wiped my mouth. "I've been working on the music end of things off and on, but I hadn't really thought that far ahead about the commercials."

"Well, you need to, Billy. I know you're not in it for the money, but you're also going to have extra bills. And there's the mortgage to think of. How much money do you have in the bank right now?"

I told him and he winced.

"All right. What do you need to make each month to keep yourself afloat?"

"I don't have any idea."

He got out a piece of paper and wrote down the approximate amount of bills I had each month. Some of them were a month or two behind.

"Who are you going to hire to help you run the station and sell the time?"

"I'm going to do it myself. I can't afford to hire anybody. If things take off, maybe I can."

He looked around the restaurant. Things had thinned out a bit. "Do you know the owner of this place?"

I nodded. "Of course. There's not many people in town I don't know."

"Why don't you ask him to come over?"

I got the server's attention and asked her

to tell Albert I needed to see him. They called him Fat Albert after the cartoon character, but he wasn't really that over-weight; he was just short and stocky.

He smiled and shook my hand as he sat down and I introduced my friend from Charleston. "Everything all right with your food?"

"Our compliments to the cook," I said.

Charlie took over. "Albert, it looks like you have a fine place here, but you could use an uptick in business, especially at din-ner."

"It gets slow about this time on weeknights but picks up on the weekend. Breakfast is our big draw."

"Well, Billy here wants to offer you a chance to increase your business and vis-ibility."

"This have anything to do with that sta-tion you're building?" Albert said to me.

"I'm set to start in less than two weeks."

"In order to make this thing take off, we need local sponsors who will advertise," Charlie said. "You could track the response by having some kind of special you only talk about on the radio. See if it increases traffic. And since you're the first business Billy's approached, if you'll agree to sign up for a month of advertising, he'll match every spot you buy for another month. Plus, the production work is free. You don't pay anything extra for that."

Albert listened intently and asked a couple of questions before he said, "Mr. Broughton, if I had an unlimited supply of money, I would advertise on the local country station and have a billboard by the interstate. The truth is, I'm struggling just to pay my servers."

"And Billy can help you with that. A bump in business on the weeknights will more than compensate for anything you spend."

"How much are they each?"

I handed him the sheet of paper where I had written in the amount. He looked at it and frowned. "I couldn't afford half of this, even if I wanted to."

"The trick with radio is saturation," I said. "People respond to stuff they hear over and over. It takes a few times hearing it for them to decide to come here. So you have to load up on the morning and afternoon drive and then sprinkle the spots in throughout the rest of the day to get the best effect."

He shook his head. "I don't know. I'll have to think about it."

"Absolutely," Charlie said. "But remember, Billy's giving you first chance at this, and as the schedule fills up, the price will also go up. Don't wait too long."

We drove back to my house with Charlie telling me this was my big start. He was impressed with the way I had taken over and said if I could pitch like that to other businesses, I could have the first year of funds in the bank.

"Don't be discouraged when they say no. They'll probably say that more often than yes. But one in ten will say yes, so keep knocking on doors."

"What kinds of businesses would be best?"

"Any business that depends on people knowing about them. And that's every business."

"Would a realty company be a good sale?"

"You bet. You want listeners to bond with that business. So you might have them come to the studio and record their own spots."

"What about your realty business?"

"Me?"

"Yeah, there's probably people here who have no idea how much help you could be to them."

He smiled. "You're going to be a natural at this, Billy."

He wrote a check for two weeks of spots. I had him write down a little bit of what he wanted said. When he left, I had more of a feeling of what I had gotten into. My original vision was just to play music and tell people the good news. I could focus on the technical side of things like I always had and pass for an announcer, but the sales area had scared me. Now I had a vision for this side of the business and what I needed to do before I pulled the switch.

A week before I was scheduled to go on the air, I dressed in my Sunday best and hit the road. I had called ahead to set up appointments at Foodland, the drugstore, the print shop, and the mini golf. Other places I just stopped.

The owner of the gas station laughed at me. "Billy, people aren't going to come to my gas station because they hear you talk about me on the radio. They're going to come by here because they need gas."

I got that reaction a lot and by the end of the day I was exhausted, discouraged, and getting pretty low. I stopped at the diner and ordered a glass of orange juice to bring my sugar level back up. I paid the server and was about to walk out when Albert sat on a stool at the counter.

"Do you really think you can increase my business in the evenings, Billy?"

"I don't know for sure about anything but

death, taxes, and the grace of God. But if you'll try it out for a month, I promise I'll give it my best shot. And if in the middle of that time, you don't see results, you can cancel and I'll give the rest of your money back."

"All right. I'll take a week's worth. Ten spots a day. You throw in the second week and we'll go from there."

I shook his hand and went home with my second account. I recorded the spots the next day and had them in the cart machines and ready to go.

It was hard to sleep on those nights before the station started. Slowly the rest of my freelance work had dropped off until the new station became my only source of income. It was like God was weaning me from the teat of what I had always known. A paycheck. Benefits. He was taking me into uncharted waters and I was buoyed along by my vision and his grace.

I've heard it said that the best place to be is in the will of God. Every night as I tossed and turned, with Rogers lying at the foot of the bed, I prayed that's where I was. I wanted this to be something that could only be explained by God's intervention. Those days I walked by faith and not by sight. It was the most exciting time of my life.

# 15

On the day Billy began his second radio career, he was forty-four years old. He could hardly sleep the night before, preparing the music reels that would loop and play continuously when there was no thirty-minute program. He had set the looping up so that if all of the reels were full, he could leave the station for four hours. Four hours of sleep at a time was all he would have for years, which wreaked havoc on his health.

In those early days, he ran on adrenaline, instant coffee, and Callie's food. It was clear to me how she felt, and clear to everyone in their church, but for some reason Billy remained uninterested. Perhaps there was only one love of his life. Perhaps he believed God had called him to singleness.

My theory was not any of the above. I believed Billy was somehow "stuck" in his mind-set, settled into a way of thinking and a way of life that was not wholly chosen by him, but determined by past events. I am not discounting the fact that he was a committed follower of the Way. There is no question that his motivation for the things he did with his life was to bring others into the truth about God. But in the lives of many humans, there is an event that brings them to a point of irreconcilable difference with themselves, and the enemy uses this to mire them in despondency and despair. This clouds their vision of the future and what might be with things that are not. The evil one loves to distort what *is* by looking through the prism of the past. It could have been the flood that did this to Billy or possibly the rejection he'd experienced from Heather, but I had an inkling it was something else.

I sent word to my superior and asked for any explanation or lead. I explained my theory and posited that someone may have witnessed a crucial event during those years when I had been absent, but the response was less than satisfactory. There was no record of past events given.

For the moment, I had little choice but to abandon this line of questioning and merely observe Billy as he settled into his new role with the station. There seemed to be no enemy activity around him during this time. This concerned me, for there should have been at least some opposition to Billy's radio venture. It appeared the forces of evil did not regard his efforts as worthy of an attack.

In an intuitive move, I visited Callie and there discovered a shockingly different story. Sometimes the evil one casts a frontal assault, but at many others he uses unconventional means. He stages a peripheral attack.

Callie lived alone just across the county line in a double-wide trailer. She spent her days at a job she did not enjoy with people who vexed her. These she faithfully prayed for and treated with as much kindness as she could muster. She had a vision of the future that was not commensurate with reality. (I know this from several diary entries, not from reading her mind.) She believed Billy was the one for her and that he would eventually discover the truth that they were meant for each other. She had helped with his mother out of an equal amount of kindness and longing. After he began his radio station, she would listen each day, setting her clock radio to hear his first words.

I discovered an imp bent on Callie's destruction at her home. Simpering and twisted, he was frightened at the first sight of my light.

"What do you want with me, servant of the Most High?" the evil one seethed.

"Why do you torment this woman?"

He cocked his head. "Why do you protect worthless human debris? Why do you spend your days tethered to a man whose life is of no consequence?"

"Every life has consequence. Every beating heart. Every tortured soul. They are worth something because the King places His worth on them."

"Save your tripe," he spat. "Even you don't truly believe *every* life has value. Not even your Leader believes that, for He has destined some to us. He chose some to believe and let others fall."

"He is not willing that *any* should perish," I said, tight-lipped. "He proved His love by the sacrifice of His own Son."

The imp backed away, but there was a sneer in his voice when he said, "You exult in His sovereignty, but all I see is chaos. The One who orders the universe is incompetent. Look at the calamity and the bloodshed and the tears." He was emboldened by his own words and moved closer. "And with all of the battles to be fought, with all of the skirmishes between yours and mine, you continue to follow an inconsequential, dithering, inept human. Has your Sovereign forgotten your power and skill?"

"I do not answer to you."

"Agreed. But wouldn't your experience and

expertise be better suited for battle? If you would come to our side, you could serve a being with such great power. He is responsive to those who call to him, not negligent and uncaring."

"Your *leader*," I said with contempt, "has only the power given him by the One on the throne. The King does not love the darkness, does not skulk in the shadows and tear down. He dwells in the light and has at His heart the best interests of His creation."

"The light, the light," the imp said dismissively. "You should see what men do in the darkness. That makes a much better story."

"Tell me why you were assigned to this woman," I said, disregarding his repulsive tongue movements.

"I don't have to tell you anything," he seethed, then softened. "But I will. Yes, I will because my superior said you would approach one day and that when you do, I am to tell you what will happen."

"You have no knowledge of the future."

"And yet you are interested."

When I did not respond, he continued.

"The end of this woman is fast approaching. And her demise will be even worse than that of your charge's father." He inched closer, his eyes wide. "Your charge seems to have a black cloud following him. Those he touches wither."

The imp moved up to the room where the woman now sat in a worn recliner, a cover over her to break the chill, a tissue to her nose. "Look at her. He has already caused her depressed state and will contribute to her end."

"This woman will not fall to your devices and plans. The King loves her too much."

"Ah, so *you* know the future! Or were you given special revelation? Wouldn't you have said the same about his parents?"

"I know this: whatever befalls her is not outside the loving watchcare of the One who called her according to His purposes."

"The old crutch comes out." He laughed. "Every time there are problems or something you hadn't anticipated, you pour these into the melting pot of the Almighty's purposes and stir and simmer them. While teeth gnash and children die and spinsters shrivel into shells, you call on God's goodness. How convenient. Why do you let your Ruler off so easily?"

"Be careful, evil one. I will chase you to the pit where you will spend your eternal destiny."

"My, you have the script memorized. God's little angel on a string, dancing to and fro in order to please the One who pushes and pulls. How sad not to have the freedom to live for yourself. For something much bigger."

The longer he spoke, the more I realized this demon believed there was a crack in my armor. If he could get me to turn from serving the King, if he could not just sway me in my desire to follow but also get me to turn and fall away from Truth, he would have done something he had never been able to accomplish in the realm of battle. Defection from the ranks of the elect.

"Your Leader does not really care about you, your charge, or this poor woman," the imp continued. "It is all about *His* glory, *His* name. *His* eternal purposes. That seems rather self-possessed, wouldn't you agree? I would much rather follow a leader who can give you a measure of power to exercise on your own, at your discretion, than blindly follow One who only has His own interests at heart."

I knew this to be false on the face of it. The imp had no discretion whatsoever. He was chained eternally by the knowledge of eventual defeat. But he was also chained by his superiors. If there was anyone who had freedom, it was me. The ability to act justly and with honor is freedom, a truth that would be lost on this one.

He turned to the woman, who had pulled her knees to her chest, her body wracking with sobs. "It is only a matter of time," he continued. "Your charge puts her through such torment. Even more than I can inflict."

"Go to your superior," I said. "Tell him I demand a meeting."

"So you can get me to leave my charge?" He chuckled. "I may look inept, but I'm certainly not going to —"

I grabbed him — actually touched the foul-smelling beast — and held him close. He turned his head from the light and shielded his eyes.

"I said you will go now and tell your superior, the evil one I spoke with at the cemetery after the father's funeral. I need information."

He struggled to get free. "What information? He will ask me. He will send me back. It will only take longer if you don't tell me."

"The past," I said. "My charge's past while I was away. What happened?"

"And you think he would know?"

"He will know."

I threw him and the imp skulked into the night. I stayed there with the woman, watching her weep, sensing the anguish in her soul. She kept a hand on her forehead, massaging her temples and going through a box of tissues.

Legally, meaning according to my rules of engagement, I could do nothing to aid her. But just the departure of evil seemed to soothe her. Or perhaps it was my presence that brought peace. I like to think that is the case with humans, that when those who are charged with their protection or ministering to them from beyond the veil appear, they respond physically to our presence. But I know that even those who call themselves followers of the Way sometimes do not put much stock in our reality. There is too much of the here and now to begin thinking of what might be going on in our dimension. If they only knew. If they only believed the love of the Almighty for them, in the midst of the suffering and depression.

Weary and cold, the woman staggered to her bedroom, the cover still draped about her. She paused at the nightstand and turned the radio volume low, as if reaching out to a friend to keep her company through the long night.

Callie fell into bed and drew herself into a ball and wept again. She shook and trembled. With the music playing softly, she finally gave up the struggle and sleep overtook her. A peaceful rest.

I stayed with her there until her eyes closed and her breathing evened. Watching. Waiting. Wondering if things I knew and believed about their world and mine would survive what I would discover in the days ahead.

# 16

The station got some local press at the start. The small article written by Becky Putnam listed the frequency, my name, and a little bit about my vision. "Allman says he wants to reach the people of Dogwood and beyond with music of the hills that will touch their hearts and give them a longing for something more." I thought that was pretty good. With what little information she had and the time it took to snap a few shots, I was pleased with the outcome.

I didn't have the money to start a Web site, but I did give out an e-mail address where people could reach me. I had only one phone line, but I was given a used Telos interface from a fellow in Huntington who heard of the station. There is a brotherhood of sorts among radio people, especially those on the engineering side, and we all hate to throw out things that are broken when they might find a home and be useful someplace else.

I didn't have much time for fixing things, however. Running a station twenty-four hours a day usually takes multiple people. I had a grand plan to do local news every hour throughout the day by recording it, but I abandoned that pretty fast. The lineup consisted of music, running the big reels I had recorded, but sprinkled through the late morning and afternoon were half-hour programs. I was able to get local businesses to sponsor some. Others I just played because I thought they fit and I got something out of the messages.

My big production was the morning show that lasted about three hours, depending on my mood. I picked out a mixture of CDs and records I thought would speak to people. I used my own devotional thoughts and read the "Our Daily Bread" from RBC Ministries each morning. I had this idea that what people wanted from their radio was not a deep-voiced announcer or a slapstick show with jokes, but just a person to sit beside them with a cup of coffee and talk about life. Real life. The stuff people in the hills go through with kids who get in trouble and friends who get hooked on the bottle or some illegal substance.

Most people in Dogwood get up, do

whatever chores they're supposed to, go to work, come home, have supper and a couple of beers, maybe do something with their kids, and go to bed and get up and do it all over again. Just an endless cycle. On Sundays, if they darken the door of a church, it's out of obligation. To many, God is not someone you know but something you try to get off your back.

My hope was that I could show listeners what it meant to allow God entry into life's every nook and cranny. My postulate was the old concept of input and output I had figured out as a kid. If you have clean wires going in and out of the transmitter, you have a power source to work from that can keep you going. God cares about every aspect of our lives and I wanted to show them that.

When I met with the Realtor from Charleston, Charles Broughton, one question he asked was "What is success going to be with this station?" At first, I thought that success would mean being able to stay on the air, pay the bills, and have a little money left over at the end of the month to buy another piece of equipment or upgrade the transmitter. Then, as I got to thinking about it, I realized success can't be measured in those terms, especially when you're working on something that has a goal of reaching people's hearts. Success has to be measured one person at a time, and since I have no way of knowing what's going on in hearts, I have to leave that up to somebody who does. So every time I got an e-mail or a phone call that said a certain song came at just the right time or that something I said in the morning made a difference, I'd toss a quarter into an empty five-gallon water jug in the corner of the room. I called it my "Success Can." Some days when I got several responses, I'd just toss a dollar in.

Whenever I got tired or discouraged because somebody dropped their sponsorship or I felt like there was just nobody listening (and there were a lot of those times), I took a look at the can in the corner. I probably had no more than five dollars in there at any one time because I used the money for food and such. But the sight of it kept me going.

When businesses would ask what kind of listenership we had, I'd always tell them how loyal the people were to advertisers and how many showed up at the diner for the pork barbecue special the week before, but it got increasingly hard to sell time. I dropped my prices, but even that didn't help. I just kept getting up each morning. I think that's all any of us can do.

■ ■ ■ ■

It was about this time, when everything felt like it was being held together with duct tape and paper clips, that Callie came by. I was sitting at the console when she pulled in, and the way she sat in her car let me know something was up.

I met her at the back door. She tried but the smile came hard. She kind of looked at me and then over to the freezer really fast. I asked her what was wrong and she shook her head and put away the food she'd brought.

"I baked you a chicken for tonight and put some biscuits in. Low fat. Just keep it in the refrigerator until you're ready and you can heat it up in the microwave."

She finished storing everything and closed the refrigerator door. Then she stood there in the kitchen and I could see the little girl in her. What she must have looked like at Christmastime waiting to open a present she knew she wouldn't like. She just kept looking at her hands or the floor, I couldn't tell which.

"I can't do it anymore, Billy," she finally said. Her voice was almost a whisper. "It's just too hard."

"The meals? I can cook for myself now that the station is up and running."

"No, it's not really the meals and the cooking. You know I like to do that for you. It's just . . ." She ran a hand up and down one arm like she'd lost all feeling in it. "I hope you'll understand."

That sentence triggered something and set me off inside. I wasn't about to just let it go. "No, I don't understand. What's going on, Callie?"

She didn't answer. I heard the program wrapping up and I needed to manually start the next one — on Saturday mornings I ran some children's programs, dramas that I thought the kids would like. That's about the only time the phone would ring, when I'd do a contest and the same kid would call four times in a row to be the fourth caller. "Can you wait until I get through this break?"

She nodded and went into the living room. When I had the next half-hour program started, I found her looking at the pictures on the mantel. She held up a shot of me and my brother. We had lost all our pictures, but a friend had sent it to us from back in Buffalo Creek.

"Do you remember him?" she said. "Harless, wasn't it?"

"Harless Winslow Allman."

"What was he like?"

"I can only remember flashes, like picture postcards in the brain. His strength. He played football and he'd come home with bruises and hurt ankles and the next day he'd be running for the bus. Tough as nails. And girls seemed to like him. He used to bring girls to the house and sit and watch TV, and he'd get so mad that I wouldn't go to bed.

"One night, just before he left for Vietnam, I had a couple of boys over to sleep out in a tent in the backyard. Now this is more than a flash for me. This is in living color. We were talking about the future and what was going to happen. And I said one day we would get to the point where you could walk around and carry a phone with you wherever you went. They asked how that would work, and I told them I didn't know, but a radio works and there's no wires coming to your house for that.

"The others said I was a blockhead and just laughed, and that's when Harless jumped out and scared us half to death and we rolled around in our sleeping bags laughing and accusing each other of peeing ourselves.

"Harless sat there and looked at us, like

261

he wished he could be our age again. Maybe part of him wanted to go off to exotic places, but I think he just wanted to stay in the hills. I guess he had heard us talking because he put his arm around me and pointed a finger at the other two.

" 'This is a brilliant kid. You're going to be shining his shoes someday. He's going to cure cancer or the black lung or come up with an invention that's going to revolution-ize the world. So stop making fun of him, you hear?'

"Those boys got real quiet after that. And when he left for Vietnam, it was like a part of me left with him."

"Did he write?"

"He sent letters. I wrote him something just about every day early on. Then, as time wore on, I kind of let it slide, thinking I could just talk to him when he got back."

A few moments passed and she put the picture back on the shelf. "I've never heard you talk that much about anything personal, Billy. Other than when you're on the radio."

"Radio will do that. It kind of scares me a little, wondering what to say every morning. Wondering if anybody's listening. If I'm making a dent in anything."

"You're doing a good job. People really appreciate the things you say."

"You want to sit down?"

She moved to the couch, and I took Mama's chair and turned it a little from the TV. It had been a while since I talked with anybody at the house. We sat there and listened to the program playing in the next room. Rogers came in and hopped up beside Callie, and she stroked his head. Finally I couldn't take it anymore.

"So what did you mean? What's too hard?"

She looked out the front window and there was mist in her eyes. "I wish I could explain it, Billy. It's about you and me and the whole world."

"No wonder you can't explain it."

She gave a bittersweet smile. "I guess I lied. To you and myself at the same time."

"About what?"

"The strings. I told you there were none attached when I started bringing you food. I truly didn't think there were. I thought this was something the Lord had given me to do and I was just going to do it for him." Her chin puckered and she pushed a fist to it and kept going, her voice cracking a little. "But every week for the last two years I've come over here hoping things might change. I listen to you on the radio every day and I feel close to you. I want to help. But it's just a one-sided conversation."

263

I rubbed my hands together and listened. When Job's friends came over, it says they sat with him seven days and didn't say a thing. Then, when they opened their mouths, they showed they weren't the best friends. So I just listened.

"I said the Lord was offering you a gift, and I did it because I care about you. But I don't think I can care anymore. Not that I won't pray for you and think about you and listen to you. I don't think I could stop doing that. But I don't think I can keep up with the cooking because of the feelings I have inside."

She finally looked up at me and there was more than just longing for a friend there. The look scared me, shook me to the core. Rogers even stared at me, like he sensed something.

"Callie, I don't do very well with this kind of thing."

"What are you afraid of, Billy?"

"Afraid of? I don't know that I'm afraid of anything. Maybe making the payments on the house each month and the land."

"No, I mean inside. You talk a lot on the radio. About the Bible. You tell funny stories you've heard. You want people to have a relationship with God, but something's holding you back from connecting with people. You know, in the real world. What are you afraid of?"

"I don't know," I said.

The program kept going in the other room and I wished it would stop so I could go back there.

"Is it that you're scared of being rejected?"

I didn't know whether Callie knew about Heather or not, but I figured that's what she meant. "That could be part of it, I guess. I'm just not ready."

"Billy, we're both in our forties. If you're not ready now, when will you be?"

"It's complicated. It's not like I can just turn a switch. This kind of thing is harder for some people than others."

She leaned forward with her elbows on her knees. "Is there any part of you that wants to take a chance? to have something more?"

"Sure. But I like what I do, Callie. It's what the Lord called me to. And I know it's not much, but I get to speak to people that —"

"I'm not saying that what you do is not important. I agree that the Lord has given you this. You have a gift. What I'm asking is if you're going to settle for this the rest of your life. You sit here all alone each day and tell people what a wonderful friend they have in Jesus, you go to church and sit in the back, you eat alone with your dog, you go to bed alone at night, and you wake up alone. Do you want something more?"

I sat there like a stump. She could not have known what feelings she had stirred. She could not have known how much I hated having feelings stirred. "I don't know."

"You know what I think?" she said, and there was an edge to her voice. A bit of righteous anger. "I think you're afraid of having somebody really know you. I think you're a little boy who's afraid. Just a boy stuck in a man's body. You're scared."

I laughed but it felt like nerves. "How can somebody who's on the radio be afraid of having people know him? Tell me that."

She shook her head. "That's just veneer and you know it. Polish on the shoe leather. And that doesn't mean what you do is not important. It is. But there's something deeper, Billy. You don't have to go through all of this alone. And maybe I'm not the one for you. But it breaks my heart to . . ."

Her voice cracked again and she put a hand to her mouth. Rogers sat up and looked at me, then put his head in her lap.

"I've heard you during the day when you'll play the wrong programs. I know it's your sugar levels. I worry about you not

266

waking up someday. And what's being done to your body since you don't take care of yourself."

"Oh, you don't have to worry about me," I said, and as soon as I did, she shut down. "I think I've done pretty well taking care of myself."

We just sat there, Mama's clock ticking.

"I do understand what you're saying about having a deeper relationship," I said. "It's the same way with God. You can just go to church on Sunday and sing the songs, or you can take it seriously and really walk with him. That's what I try to do every day."

"Don't patronize me."

"How am I patronizing you? I don't even know how to patronize."

"I'm not sure if that's the word. Don't turn this into something spiritual and feel like you can get off the hook."

"I don't want to get off the hook, Callie. I like you. I truly do. And I appreciate everything you've done. But my life is set now. I like speaking into people's lives and making them a little hungrier for God."

Callie sighed. "Have you ever considered that you might be able to know God better with somebody else by your side? somebody who could encourage you and show you real love? who could challenge you and knock off the rough edges?"

"I have considered that."

"That probably sounds judgmental and selfish. I don't mean it to be. It's not that I know what's best. I'm in the same boat. I've held out for so long, scared you'll think I'm too ugly and not want anything more to do with me."

"You're not ugly, Callie," I said.

She closed her eyes. "I've said enough. Probably too much."

The theme music was playing and I told her to wait. I got into the next program, but when I came back out, Rogers was looking out the back door, his tail wagging. Callie was in her car pulling out of the driveway.

# 17

I thought a lot about what Callie said over the next few weeks. Of course, my diet changed without her cooking, and that probably affected my mood. I ate a lot of macaroni and cheese and Stouffer's frozen dinners. But I knew the itch on my soul was more than just getting my belly filled. There was something to what she was saying, but I pushed it down. I told myself I had been alone for this long and there was no way I could change. And God could use a cracked pot like me, something weak. I sure count myself like that.

The diner had stopped advertising because their business had all but dried up. I wound up trading out some spots for a meal or two here and there. When my truck broke down and I couldn't fix it, I made a deal with the auto shop to pay half in cash and half in spots. The electric, gas, and water companies were less favorable to such an arrangement. I managed to pay them and still stay up on the mortgage, but it was tight.

I could set my watch to Callie coming around each day. Her old Subaru would rumble up the road, going from mailbox to mailbox like a honeybee to flowers. She'd needed muffler work done for quite a while. Since she had talked with me and stopped bringing food, I hadn't had any kind of word from her except the times when I owed money on some piece of mail. Most of the time she'd pay it and I would put an envelope with some change in the box. I'd write a note on a scrap paper saying, "I hope you're doing well" or something like that, but I hadn't heard anything.

One afternoon she drove up and I got this feeling that I needed to go out there and talk. She saw me as I came off the front porch and slowed down right at the driveway. Her car was plastered with mud from the recent rains. She sat in the passenger seat and straddled the console in order to deliver the mail, using her left foot to hang on to the brake or move ahead. Both flashers going. The radio was up pretty loud, playing my station, and it made me feel good to hear it.

She turned the sound down with fingers that stuck through leather gloves she had cut. She had on an old Cincinnati Reds ball cap with her hair tied through the hole in the back. She kept her hair up with rubber bands — the same ones she used for all the big stacks of mail she banded together.

"Howdy, stranger," I said.

She grabbed a plastic box from behind her and dragged it up front. Without looking at me and without emotion, she said, "Hey, Billy. You got another package today."

"Those publishing people send me books, asking me to have their guests on, but I don't do stuff like that."

"You ought to just write and tell them to stop. What kind do they send?"

I ripped open the bubble-wrapped package and pulled out a brightly colored book.

She opened her eyes wide. "I've heard about that one."

"Here, take it. It's yours."

"No, I couldn't accept that."

"I just cart them over to the church library every few weeks," I said. "It would save me a trip. You go on and take it. I'll have done something for you for a change."

She thought a minute, then took it and put it by her foot. Her eyes were kind of bloodshot and I mentioned it.

"It's that time of year. Allergies. Not much I can do about it but take a bunch of pills

271

and feel my head swell up like a balloon."

She sat there for a moment, and I couldn't think of anything else to say and I guess she couldn't either. A car pulled in behind her and she looked in the mirror. "I'll be seeing you, Billy."

She pulled forward and took the outgoing mail as the other car pulled into the driveway. Then she turned around and headed back down the muddy road.

I could see my reflection in the tinted window of the shiny car and wondered who in the world could be inside. I stood and waited until the window rolled down.

A man took off his sunglasses and stared at me. "Billy Allman, is that you?"

I stepped toward the car because I didn't recognize him at first. But when I heard his voice, I knew it was Vernon Turley. His hair was longer and gray and it looked like he'd had some work done. His face looked tight. From newspaper reports, he had become a much bigger deal than when I was traveling with the group. And he wasn't a pastor anymore. I knew that much from his Web site.

I was so shocked at seeing him in my driveway, I couldn't speak. But I guess he didn't need me saying anything because he just lit into the conversation.

"I heard about your station. Been listening to it on my drive over. Doesn't have much reach, but the mix you have is real nice, Billy. I like the one instrumental to the two vocals. That Andy Falco is something else, isn't he?"

"Yes, sir, he is."

"Congratulations. Your own radio station. That's a big accomplishment. I always knew you would do something with your life."

I stared at him, tongue-tied. It felt strange to hear his voice since I had been hearing it in my head for so long.

"I always wondered how you were doing after you left the band. How's your mother?"

"She passed."

"I'm sorry to hear that. I remember your daddy passed when you were young. I know that was a tough time for you." He held out a CD in shrink-wrap that was too loose. "This is our new album. Has some of the old standards and a couple of originals. This is really getting some good airplay around the tristate."

I stared at the picture on the front. They were definitely using a better photographer than when I was with them. Back then we had the Dobro player's sister who lived in Red Jacket, and we drove half the day just to get to her place; then when we got there, she couldn't get her flash to work, so we wound up outside next to a chicken coop. That didn't make a whole lot of sense to me, but I wasn't about to say anything.

"The ministry is really exploding with the Internet," he continued. "We're getting requests from all over the country. No way we could get to all of those places. It's a lot different than when you were with us."

I stared at the CD and let the memories wash over me. Riding in his fifteen-passenger van with the little trailer hitched to the back of it. Stopping at Wendy's for a burger and a Frosty. Then we'd play in some little church way out in the sticks and finish tearing down around ten and then head to the next little church or for home. It was not a glamorous life, but we made some good music.

"So do you think you could work us into your rotation?" he said.

I scratched my head and handed the CD back to him. "I'm sorry, Mr. Turley. I don't think so."

He took off the sunglasses and put them over his visor, then stepped out. "Why not? This is the music the people around here resonate with. It's right in your target."

"I understand that. But I already have my

playlist. I spin songs onto reels the old-fashioned way."

"Then when you make a new reel, you could use some of these." He held the CD back to me and I reluctantly took it.

"I don't think so."

He held up a hand. "Okay, I don't know much about running a radio station. But in the mornings you play music from CDs, right? during Rise 'n' Shine?"

He had been listening, which was flattering on one hand and a problem on the other. "That's right. I just don't think it will work, Mr. Turley. Sorry."

"Why don't you just take a listen? Maybe you'll change your mind."

I stared at the CD. "I can't promise you."

He put one foot on the higher part of the lawn and his loafer sank into the mud a bit. "I don't understand, Billy. Is there something wrong between us? I tried to give you a chance you never would have had. People said I shouldn't, that you were too young, not stable. And some in the group were against it, but I spoke up for you. I thought you appreciated what I tried to do. I thought we were friends."

"I'm not saying I don't appreciate what the group did for me. It gave me a chance to play some good music. Be a part of something bigger."

"Everybody was sad when you left. We had people come out at concerts after that and ask about you. I think they wanted to see you more than they did us." He sighed. "Do you still play the mandolin?"

"Every now and again. But not in front of anybody."

He shook his head. "I don't get it, Billy. Talent like you had going to waste. The Lord holds us accountable."

"Mm-hmm."

"And then to think you won't play any of the best music around. It just doesn't make sense. It's like a restaurant that won't buy the best bread in town for their sandwiches."

"Well, I understand it doesn't make a lick of sense to you. That's just a decision I've made." I turned to go back in the house.

"All right. Let me ask you this before you go."

"I need to get back in and check things."

"This kind of venture doesn't happen on its own. You have to have funds to run a radio station. Pay your bills. I imagine the electric bill alone is off the charts."

"Doesn't cost that much more."

"The transmitter has to pull a lot of electricity. Where'd you get it?"

"Built it myself. Used a filing cabinet and

took the drawers out and cut a hole for the door. You can find the tubes pretty easy because people throw a lot of that stuff out. But the transformer is the hardest part."

"You have enough money coming in each month?"

"I have sponsors."

"Not what I heard. People around town say most of them have dropped off."

"Every business goes through ups and downs."

"True. But when times get tight, it's good to have advertisers who are there to take you through, wouldn't you say?"

"What are you getting at?"

"Well, if you won't work us into your rotation or play us in the morning, maybe we can work out some kind of sponsorship. I'll sponsor a section of music during a daypart and you can just drop in a song or two. You could say the following set of music is sponsored by the Gospel Bluegrass Boys. And then backsell it and maybe mention where people can buy the latest album."

I shook my head. "I don't think so."

He stepped closer. "Billy, I'm offering you hard cash. I'll pay you $1,000 for an hour-long special that uses our music. You can choose whatever songs you want. Now surely you could use $1,000 to pay some bills."

I shook my head. "I don't care how much you fill the blank with, it's not worth it. I have to keep my integrity."

"Your integrity? What's that got to do with anything?"

"I don't want your help."

He crossed his arms. "I don't understand."

I turned my back to him and walked toward the porch. "Yes, you do."

"Listen, just think about it. Okay? I'm willing to pay top dollar for spots or however you think you could work in the songs. I'll even spring for a new computer that will let you go digital. You come up with the cost of it and I'll help you. How would you like that?"

I opened the screen door and turned back. "I like my station the way it is. And the people who listen don't care if a song is on the computer or a CD or on a tape machine. They just want to hear songs they love."

I let the door bang behind me. He called after me again but I didn't turn. He was one of those people who could always get what he wanted, no matter what. If a church didn't give enough in the love offering, he'd have the pastor go back out and make one more appeal. Guilt was like a lead guitar in his band.

His door slammed good and tight, like you would expect out of an expensive car. The mud spun under his tires as he backed out and drove away. I watched out the shop window, and as I passed the trash can, I tossed in the CD.

I thought my days had been dark with my mother and father, and they were. But these days were lonely and soul crushing. The financial stress of having to make it on my own was overwhelming, and the loss of Callie's cooking and friendship made me feel like a hollow log, but I held on to the verse in Psalm 46 that says, "Be still, and know that I am God." One of the preachers I played said that literally meant that we needed to take our hands off the situation and relax.

So every day when Callie would bring me a new bill from whoever or a second or third notice from a dental bill for an abscess I had to have fixed (I didn't have the money for insurance, of course), I would open it up and use a thumbtack to put it on the wall. I called it my Wailing Wall because every time I passed it, I would let out a moan for all that I owed. That's where the verse came in handy. There was no part of that station that I owned because it was all God's. I'd dedicated it to him and given it over to him and told him that anything he wanted to do with it was okay with me.

That's why it was hard to understand what happened next.

I had to do routine maintenance with the equipment to keep things running well. I cleaned the heads of the tape players twice a week, but keeping the transmitter going was another thing. Even though I was the only one in the house, I kept a padlock on the file cabinet door because of the high voltage in there. I didn't want anybody who visited to reach in there and get shocked.

I had noticed some irregularities in the signal strength and saw one tube was giving way. It took me a few days to locate one. It wasn't much, but I didn't have the money for it and the jar in the corner was empty. I looked around for anything of value and finally decided to sell the old mandolin. I figured it was not a bad trade — a handful of musical memories for a tube that would keep us on the air. It felt like I was selling a friend when I handed it to the man at the pawnshop, but I walked out of there with enough for the tube and some groceries.

Before I went to bed one night, I played the legal ID alone with my announcement, saying that the station would be off the air momentarily because of routine maintenance. I opened the transmitter door and took out the tube, then retrieved the box in the living room. I was gone only a few seconds but that was enough. I heard a yelp, and the lights went out, plunging me into total darkness. My stomach dropped because I knew what had happened. I kicked myself for leaving the door open. I took out my Maglite from my pocket and switched it on. Rogers was still twitching and his fur was burned. He must have sniffed at the transformer and the current killed him instantly.

To those who don't understand it, it is hard to describe what a dog can mean to somebody who does not have much in the way of human companionship. A dog can be the comfort God uses to tell us that things are going to be all right. Rogers was there waiting for me at home anytime I left. He was there at the foot of my bed when I got up in the morning. Sometimes when I fell asleep at the console, he would lick my hand at just the right time to wake me up. And to think at the beginning I didn't even want him.

Of course, Rogers reminded me of my mother. He reminded me that though I felt alone at times, I really wasn't. He never asked for one thing except for food and water. And that my carelessness led to his death was almost too much to bear.

I finally got the power back on and the transmitter fixed. On the morning show I told folks about Rogers and I suppose I got a little emotional, especially the part about taking him out back on the hill by the tower and digging his grave and putting him there with his favorite blanket (which happened to be my favorite blanket). But I got through it and played an instrumental version of "Amazing Grace" that I thought was appropriate.

Just so you know how the Lord works in mysterious ways, the next few days I got the most e-mail and calls ever about anything. People wanted to tell me about their animals and how much they were like family to them. With all the misery in the world, it was clear to me how pure and good the love of an animal is. It was recounted to me over and over.

One lady wrote and asked my advice about what to do with her cat. I thought it was humorous that someone who didn't own a cat and really didn't like them would be asked to help an older woman get the courage to put it out of its misery, but I wrote her back and tried. I told her not to go alone to the veterinarian and that her cat would understand, in the end, that she was just trying to love her.

Her last e-mail was the most heartbreaking thing. She said her cat was gone and that I had given her the strength to let her go. After I read it, I turned on the tape machine and went into the kitchen for another cup of coffee. I saw Rogers's empty food and water dish and I was done for just about the whole day. I know some people will not understand this, but I don't apologize for loving that old dog. And after he was gone, I felt such an empty place in my soul that I'm ashamed to admit it, but there it is.

# 18

My curiosity piqued, the way ahead of me paved with good intentions, as well as the justification of believing that the fight would be better fought if I had full understanding of Billy's past, I took leave of my station and traveled across enemy lines for the meeting I had requested. I was reluctant to leave Billy so distraught about an animal that meant so much to him. I wondered if events such as these were "ordered" or were simply allowed to take place. The dog's death had caused great consternation in Billy, but I felt the meeting in the nether regions would finally give answers.

There is no place on earth or in the heavenlies that the Almighty, the Creator of the universe, is not. But there are areas where His presence seems to have less effect — where pervasive evil appears to hold sway, and it was to one of these places that I traveled.

The risk of humans speaking about the evil one is that they will get him and his power out of perspective. Let me say this to clear up any misconception. Satan is limited. He is not ever-present or all-knowing. But, of course, he is a force to be reckoned with, and his legions of followers are not the stumbling, bumbling oafs that many depict. They are a malevolent army trained in terrorism of the soul.

I knew going in that I was dealing with an enemy that would seek to confuse and lie. He and his minions would do anything to deter me from protecting my charge. And I truly believed that was what I was doing in attempting to learn more about the past. I sought answers to why he would choose to live alone and isolated, why he had given up the musical gift.

The demons seemed busy about their tasks and mostly ambivalent to my presence. Perhaps they expected me. Perhaps they had been told to ignore me. But I believe they were acting as they always do, for this is the effect of evil — a retreat into a world of one's own, thinking of nothing but self-preservation. As I looked on, I saw how trapped these creatures were, and something inside wanted to sing, wanted to exult in the goodness of the Holy One, who allows His creation to live and move and have its being in unfettered allegiance to an unending Kingdom.

From the darkness came a voice calling my name. I recognized it and stood my ground, knowing it would be a mistake to go farther.

The demon's face twisted in the light, as if in pain, and he shielded his eyes. "Can't you do something to tone down?"

"It is my nature. How can I do otherwise? I do not apologize for it nor will I change it."

"Ah, the superior attitude. Don't you find it annoying? Darkness has its positives. Especially when discussing the human heart."

"It is written that men loved darkness rather than light. Your leader loves darkness because all who do evil hate the light and refuse to go near it for fear their evil deeds will be exposed."

"Spare me the biblical exposition. If I wanted preaching, I would listen to that simpering charge's radio station." He studied his fingernails and said in a monotone, "What is it you want to know?"

"I was called away from my charge at a vulnerable time in his life. When he was beginning his tenure with the musical group. Did you or any of your kind witness what happened?"

"Why don't you ask your superiors? Why come running to the enemy?"

"I've been unsuccessful in discovering what happened."

He raised his eyebrows. "I thought *all-knowing* meant *all-knowing.* Hmm. A little problem with that attribute. And this has meaning to you for what purpose?"

"It is information that I believe will help me in my tasks."

He twisted his head in that impish way that always repulses me, but I tried not to show it. "Why would I want to cooperate in any way?"

"I do not appeal to your goodwill, for I know you have none."

"Flattery will get you nowhere." He licked his lips grotesquely and moved away from the cavern behind him. "You know, if the few people who actually listen to this radio station knew the depths to which he had fallen in his younger days, I doubt one of them would even come near the signal. They wouldn't waste their time listening to his babbling. It is because of this that we have decided to allow his flailings and machinations with this venture. With what little harm it can do to us, we should be able to use it in the future for much greater harm against him and, ultimately, the One he purports to serve."

The imp edged closer and lowered his voice. "You see, your charge makes a big deal about how much freedom he has in Christ, how much victory and power he has in following your Leader. But he is enslaved. We have him trapped between the past and the present, all those memories, all those evil deeds that run like the infernal tapes, round and round and round. There is no end."

While the demon spoke, I reminded myself that he was a liar and his father had invented the activity and raised it to an art form. Still, like any communiqué from the enemy, there were shreds of truth. I struggled to separate fact from fiction.

"How could you know any of this if you weren't following my charge?"

"This information does not come from me, but from a colleague familiar with that history. He gave a full report of the activity surrounding his own charge who, at the time, had interaction with yours."

"Explain."

"As a youngster your charge was included in a musical endeavor with several others, and it was one of them who, shall we say, led him astray."

"How so?" I said.

The imp chuckled. "You really do want the juicy tidbits, don't you?"

"I want to know the story. What happened?"

"I would have to read you reams of files. It would certainly cause you to distrust not only your charge and his motivations but also the very One who called you to protect him. Tell me this: why would the Almighty be so interested in one who had fallen so far? one who had so degraded himself as to become involved in a bevy of immoral behavior?"

"Perhaps my charge repented. This is something the Almighty delights in doing — forgiving those who have trespassed against Him."

The imp rolled his eyes and his tongue as he said, "Forgiveness. The great mantra of the whole race. They want to forgive everyone. They want to absolve the murderer and the child rapist and the jaywalker and put them all on even footing. And if someone does evil to them, they tie themselves in knots because they cannot truly let go of the anger and resentment. It is such an insidious spectacle. Lucky for you and me that we don't have to entertain any of those thoughts, eh?"

As the demon spoke, I had a fleeting thought. While all of this was happening to Billy — if it did really happen — I was engaged in battle. Our side had again been victorious. But at what cost to Billy? And who had ordered me to this post, knowing the danger Billy would be in? knowing there was someone in the group who would lead him astray?

God Himself.

I focused my thoughts. "We are different

from the humans; this is true. But the Almighty says He uses the weak things of this world to praise Him."

"If I hear that one more time, my insides will explode. It is one thing for the humans whose eyes are clouded by their limited vision to believe that twaddle about the low being high and the high being low, but for you — an intelligent being who can *see* — for you to believe it and defend it stretches the bounds of credulity."

I didn't answer, for my insides roiled with answers that sprang from the ages. I could have spent the next hour recounting the stories of humans who had fit into the holy rubric he demeaned. But this information also brought the questions focused on one life instead of the great circumference of humanity. I was learning about Billy and how his life intersected with the purposes of his Creator. I pondered all of this but kept silent, and he read my silence as a victory.

"He is ours," the demon said. "Totally and irrevocably. Your charge pretends to serve his heavenly Father, but he is really serving himself. He is trying to expunge all of the things in his past for which he feels remorse. He is making up for everything evil he's ever done or thought about doing every day he gets up and strives and does his service to the King. He is not praising God with his being; he is selfishly assuaging his guilt through his own power and confession." The demon laughed derisively.

"Perhaps the most important thing is not what he has done but what was done to him."

"Victim status, then. 'Woe is me; I've been violated by evil people. I had no control. I had no say in the matter.' If I were to read to you the transcript, I'm sure you would never look at your charge the same way again."

The demon retrieved the report, or what he purported to be the report, and it was then I realized the truth. The demon had agreed to this meeting, had engaged with me, to keep me from the task I had been given. He was plying me with information to ensnare, not for an attack on me, but on Billy.

I hastened my return to the hills with the demon's voice echoing its accusations. It does not take long for an attack to become effective. What I found there showed what a tragic mistake I had made in listening to the evil one.

# 19

When a new mailman showed up driving the route one Monday, I didn't think much about it. He came late in the day, but few people are as fast as Callie in their sorting and delivery. She took time off every now and then and was off every other Saturday. But when he came earlier the next day, I went out and asked what was going on. He was a young fellow from Barboursville who had started part-time and was now full-time in Dogwood. He said Callie hadn't been to work since Saturday and they hadn't been able to get ahold of her.

I called her house but there was no answer, so I called her parents and her mother answered.

"Billy, we've been so worried. Her car's gone and the door is locked tight and there's no movement in there at all. She's never done anything like this before, not letting us know where she is or if she's okay.

I've called the hospitals . . ." Her voice broke. "We just can't find her. I swear I don't know what to do. Have you heard anything from her?"

"No, ma'am." I told her about the last time I had seen her at the mailbox.

"We're real worried. I think something's happened. We called the sheriff, but he said they have to wait a certain amount of time and that she'll probably show up."

I took a deep breath and looked at the programs ready to go on the machines. "Tell you what. Let me go over to her place and see if I can find out anything."

"Thank you, Billy."

I started the next preaching program and set up my reels of music. The way I'd set it up, if there was more than twenty seconds of dead air, the first music reel or whatever was on machine number one would automatically start. To play music in the afternoon liked to kill me because I knew I'd get phone calls from people telling me they missed the second part of some message, but I saw this as an emergency and knew the people would understand if they knew the situation.

Sometimes I'd get a call from Callie on her cell phone when I played the wrong program. Half the time I was just mixed up, but many times it was because of the fatigue or my blood sugars that were out of whack. She was an angel on my shoulder trying to keep me on track.

Callie's trailer was supposed to look white and blue, but mostly it was a rusty red. One of the metal panels had come loose from the roof and turned up like a cowlick on a country boy. I checked her mailbox and there was a pile of stuff. I knocked, but there was no answer and the metal door didn't have a window. I pulled a loose cinder block over to the trailer and stood on it to see into the kitchen. The sink was full and on the table was the book I had given her. But there was no sign of Callie.

I cupped my hand over the window and looked closer. By the sink was an open prescription bottle. My heart skipped a beat. I carried the cinder block to the living room window. The drapes were open there, but she wasn't on the couch. Then I moved to the back bedroom and looked in the window, but the blinds were closed. The window was the kind you crank open and there was a little crack there. I pulled it open a couple of inches.

"Callie? You in there?"

A familiar sound came from the room —

my radio station playing through the tinny clock radio. The preaching had stopped and the music was going.

I had to pull at the blinds through the ripped screen and broke a couple of the slats. I let my eyes adjust and saw her unmade bed. There was a long lump on it that I thought was her at first, but I realized that was one of those body pillows under the covers.

"What do you think you're doing?"

I grabbed my chest and took a breath. I hadn't noticed the woman standing at the end of the next trailer. "Just trying to find Callie."

"She ain't here," she said. Her voice was like gravel and her stare could have stopped a freight train. She had one hand in her apron pocket and the other flicking a cigarette.

"Are you sure?"

"Haven't seen her for a few days. Who are you?" It was more of an accusation than a question.

"A friend of hers. I talked with her mother and she told me she was missing."

"A friend don't go breaking in to a house."

I finally noticed there was something making her apron stick out. Something hard. And it was pointed right at me.

"What's your name?" she said.

"Billy Allman."

She squinted. "You the fellow on the radio?"

I nodded.

"Say something else."

"It's fifty-three degrees in Dogwood, relative humidity is 73 percent, and we should get a shower a bit later in the day."

She took her hand out of her apron. "You *are* him." She laughed and a cough accompanied it. "You sure don't look like I thought you would."

What do you say to the expectations of casual listeners?

She wore a tight-fitting smock and shuffled through the crabgrass in faded pink house shoes. She held out nicotine-stained fingers and shook my hand. "Opal Walker," she said. "I've known Callie since she moved in."

I recognized the last name. Her son, Graham Walker, had gotten in trouble with the law and was doing time at Pruntytown. Anybody who knew about her pretty much stayed clear of her. That Callie would befriend her was not a surprise. She was always the one to believe the best about people and see them as needing the Lord. To be honest, Opal was right in my target audience, though she didn't know it.

"You listen to my station?" I said.

"Anytime I was over at Callie's, she had it on. She talked about you something fierce. Just a walking billboard. Like you hung the moon over the mountain."

"When was the last time you saw her?"

She thought a minute. "Saturday. She came home from work and then went out in the evening."

"I don't want to alarm you, but I saw an open bottle of pills by the sink, so I'm trying to get inside and make sure she's not lying in there."

Her jaw fell. "Well, I got a key." Opal turned and hobbled back toward her trailer. "She gave it to me just in case."

She returned with a key ring that had a frog on the end of it. Callie always liked frogs for some reason.

Opal followed me to the front door and I had to work on it to get it open. When I did, an odor hit me and I turned. "That doesn't smell too good."

Opal cursed and grunted as she pulled herself up into the house. I picked up the medicine bottle and didn't recognize the type of pills they were. Opal, however, sounded like she should have been a pharmacist. She knew they were for depression and surmised that Callie hadn't told anyone about it.

I studied the bottle. There were still pills inside. "If she'd wanted to OD, she would have taken all of them, wouldn't she?" I said.

Opal grunted.

I moved past a sink piled with dishes. The drain was stopped up and the water standing there could have explained the smell. At least that's what I hoped. I went through the living room and could tell Opal followed by the creak of the floorboards. I prayed the cinder blocks would hold.

The bathroom door was closed tight, but all the other doors were open. I saw into the tiny laundry room, a pile of clothes sitting there in front of the stacked washer and dryer.

I put my hand on the bathroom knob and stopped. There was something in that trailer other than the smell. Something dark. I don't much go in for the warfare stuff and praying the devil away, but it was almost like you could cut it with a knife. I breathed a prayer and asked God to keep my mind clear.

"Callie?" I said.

Hearing my own voice just about made me jump and I could tell Opal was skittered by it. She was breathing hard behind me, a mixture of asthmatic breaths and phlegm.

"Go on and open it," she wheezed.

I turned the knob and pushed.

A small tub with the shower curtain drawn. All Callie's hair stuff by the sink in a basket. So much hair stuff.

I moved across the linoleum, praying, *Please, God, don't let her be in here.*

I took the shower curtain in my hand and like that scene in *Psycho* where Janet Leigh finally dies and grabs it with one hand, I pulled it back.

Empty.

I let out a sigh and Opal did the same. "I thought for sure she was going to be looking up at us from that tub."

I left the bathroom — Opal had to back out for me to get past her — and checked the bedroom and the rest of the house again just to make sure. Callie wasn't there. I turned off the clock radio and went back to the living room.

"It's a peculiar thing," she said. "I knew she was in a bad way, but I never thought she would up and leave."

"What do you mean, a bad way?"

"She always took such good care of herself. But of late she just let her hair go and she'd wear the same outfit days in a row. Wasn't like her."

"What do you think happened?"

She shook her head. "Your guess is as good as anybody's. My big concern is . . ."

"Is what?"

"That she took that Subaru off the side of some back road somewhere and nobody's going to find her until hunting season."

"Callie wouldn't do that."

"She would if she was desperate or depressed, and it looks to me like she was. I don't know what was going on. Maybe she was having trouble with her bills or there was some man."

"Was there a man?"

"None that she talked about other than you. And if she didn't hurt herself, what do you think happened?"

"I don't know." I looked around for any clues, like some bumbling detective, but I had no idea what to look for.

"Well, if you figure it out, you let me know," Opal said. "I better get back. *Wheel of Fortune* is coming on."

"I'm going to do these dishes. I'll bring the key back to you when I'm done."

I left the front door open and cranked the kitchen window so I'd get some cross-ventilation. She didn't have a disposal and there were a bunch of vegetables caught in the drain, which had made the smell. I got the dishes washed and put in the rack beside the sink. I hoped Callie would be able to see what I'd done for her, just so she could see that somebody cared.

I went through the mail and most of it was junk. Stuff from a credit card company and ads for the grocery store. A water bill. Electric bill. A catalog filled with quilting stuff. A Christian book catalog with apocalyptic fiction. Something from a doctor's office. I opened it and saw he was a psychologist. It said the bill was overdue and asked for payment immediately.

I put all the mail in a neat stack on the table and fidgeted, looking out at the driveway and praying she would just drive up and the biggest problem we'd have was me explaining why I was sitting in her kitchen.

Before I left, I decided to check the refrigerator. There was a little bit of milk in an outdated carton, something on a plate covered with tinfoil, and three Coors Light cans that looked as out of place there as a pitchfork in a preschool. I could tell the three had been six, due to the plastic connector. My mind raced. Callie had never been one to drink. She had seen the ravages of alcoholism in her own family. Why would she have the beer in her fridge?

I looked under cushions and in the pages

of the Bible she had on her coffee table. Then I got an idea and went back to her bedroom. There was another Bible in there by her nightstand and under it was a spiral notebook. Something inside told me I should stop, that a woman's private thoughts should stay private, but I told myself there might be something that would help me.

The notebook was half-filled. On each page there was a date and a listing of a passage read and her reaction. Some kind of application she wanted to make. Then a prayer. In fact, the prayers went on and on throughout the notebook. Maybe it was pride, maybe it was just a man's curiosity, but I started looking for my own name. It showed up on the third page.

Lord, I feel such despair. It feels like everything is pushing in on me and I can't see what you're doing. I don't see any hope with Billy, but I give him to you and thank you for him. You know the longing in my heart. You know how long I've prayed. I think it must be time to just let go and let you have him. Use him in people's lives and keep him safe. Help him take care of himself.

I looked at the date on the entry and saw it was right around the time we had talked in my living room. The next few pages were filled with much the same, mentioning me here and there, people at the church she was praying for, her job, different people on her route she was lifting up. I felt almost ashamed reading it. I always knew she was a deep well, but I had no idea how deep until I was wading through her thoughts.

Toward the middle of the journal, the dates got more sparse. She'd miss a day or two, and then a week would go by. She'd apologize to the Lord for not being in the Word. Her handwriting changed. Early on it was flowing and flowery but toward the end of her entries it became more angular, like chicken scratch. Even that was a far sight better than my handwriting, but it kind of scared me.

Dr. J thinks I ought to make more friends and go to the singles group at a bigger church. It's hard to even think of anybody but Billy, but maybe he's right. The world is a big place and there has to be somebody out there who would want a woman like me. I know I'm not much to look at, but I would try hard to make somebody happy.

Sometimes you see things that put everything in perspective real fast. War will do that. A trip to the emergency room. Something said in a church service when you ask God to speak to you and he does. Reading her heart was like falling down at some altar. I took a deep breath and turned the page.

Toward the end, which had stopped nearly two weeks earlier, she began talking about another fellow. Some of the words were just printed now.

Lord, I pray you would get hold of L's heart and give him a vision of what you can do with him. He could be so much more if he'd give his life to you. Draw him to yourself, and if it be your will, give him a love for me. I keep thinking about what you could do with the both of us together, but I know it's wrong for me to fall for him and be unequally yoked. Still, you know how he tugs at my heartstrings.

The final entry seemed more pleading than worshipful, more desperate. She talked about being tired of being lonely and how convinced she was that if she could just spend more time with L, he would understand the message and want to respond.

Lord, I feel like this is my last chance.
When I'm around him, something inside
comes alive. And since you came to give
life, I can't help but think he's a gift
from you.

I closed the journal and put it back under
the Bible. I just sat there a couple minutes
thinking and wondering.

I locked the front door, my mind searching for answers. Opal came to her door
when I knocked, but it took her a while. I
handed the frog back to her and she put it
in an empty ashtray. I gave her my number
and asked her to call me if she saw Callie or
had any news.

When I got back home, the light was flash-
ing on my answering machine. I changed
the music reels and made an announcement
that I would play the preaching programs
beginning at 7:00 and I apologized for the
inconvenience.

I called Sheriff Preston's house and talked
with Macel. She was alarmed about Callie
and I asked her to have her husband call
me.

I cooked up a macaroni and cheese tray in
the microwave and listened to the messages

while I ate my supper. The first two were asking about the preaching programs. The last one made me sit up.

"Billy, this is Vernon Turley. I've been thinking more about your situation there and I want to offer you another chance. . . ."

I hit the Delete button and the machine beeped at me. I had to keep my hand to the task. Before I went to bed, I got in the car and drove over to Callie's again, listening to the station on the way, some of the songs speaking right to me as if God himself was trying to send me a message. I pulled in and let the headlights illumine the driveway. I could tell by the tracks in the mud that no one had been there since I had left.

Back at home, another message had come in; this one was Sheriff Preston. He said to call him no matter what time it was and I took him at his word. I explained what I had found out at Callie's place, and he said he would start investigating in earnest. He asked if I knew the license plate number on her Subaru and I told him I didn't, but I could find it.

"I'll drive over to her parents' house in the morning," he said. "Hopefully she'll turn up before then and everybody can just relax."

"I don't think that's going to happen,

Sheriff. This is not like her. Something is wrong."

"All right, Billy. We'll get the ball rolling. I appreciate you calling and your concern."

Sleep did not come easily. Usually when 11 p.m. came and I began the overnight music — a soft and soothing blend of instrumentals and vocals that didn't have the fast pace of some bluegrass tunes — I could barely make it back to bed before I was asleep. This time, however, I lay there piecing together what I knew, thinking about the last time I saw Callie, her cutoff leather gloves, her hair pulled back. About where she might be and what had happened. I'll admit it's easy for me to think the worst because when my mind runs, it runs to the low places, where the water goes first. What kind of flood had Callie gotten herself into? Or had it overwhelmed her all on its own, without her help?

I drifted off but never fully slept and then sat bolt upright at 3 a.m. A better man would have made coffee and just stayed up praying for her. I started my morning show each day at 5:30, so I could only get about two hours of rest, but I changed the reels and then fell back into bed and dozed.

I awoke sweating, my body shaking, and I

knew I was low. It's a feeling I can't describe. A craving deep down in the soul for something to bring me to normal, as if anything could. I always thought it was interesting that the Lord would give me the sugar diabetes with the way my life worked out. An inner realization that I didn't have everything I needed, and there was no way in the world to get it by myself.

That's what I talked about that morning on the radio as I opened the microphone. I usually gave some devotional thought from Oswald Chambers or some other preacher. Just a few words to stir up the soul for hardworking people who had to pry their eyes open at that hour of the day. But that morning I played an instrumental tune underneath and read from my journal, with some new thoughts mixed in.

"I have known a hunger in my heart during the early morning hours that can't be helped with a drink of juice or a carbed-up bar of some kind. When I wake up shaking and wondering how I'm going to make it to the kitchen without passing out, and with my feet and legs tingling like a thousand pins are sticking me, I think this is the kind of hunger we all have. Most of us try to fill ourselves with something. Stuff or food or drink or pills or sex or whatever feels good at the moment.

"Some of you may be shaking this morning, not from lack of sugar, but from a lack of knowing God loves you and has some kind of plan in the middle of what you call a life. It can get cloudy and misty at times, so thick that you aren't able to see much of the field he has planted you in. And if that's where you are, I'm here to tell you that you're in a good place. It probably doesn't feel that way, and you may be about to turn off the radio right now because you think I'm a nut. But God has you right where you need to be. Because it's not where you're strong that he will use you; it's where you're weak.

"I have lived long enough and have seen enough pain and problems to take me on a journey I would not have picked. And you may be right there with me. You didn't choose what's happening. And you know deep down that there's no relief from it. You may have forgotten that childlike feeling of hope you once had, that things could work out okay, could work out different. But that hope is there and available, even if you can't feel it. Sometimes you have to hold on to the hope that God has for you instead of the hope you can dredge up yourself.

"We read in God's Word, in the book of

Romans, that we have been justified, or made right with God, through faith in Jesus Christ. And because of that, we have peace with God and can rejoice in the hope of the glory of God. Now get that straight — we don't have joy because we have hope; we rejoice *in* the hope God gives, and the object of that hope is his glory. Everything points back to that, the glory of God, and if we don't realize that, then we're going to be shaking and passing out all of our lives from the hunger. God alone is the one who deserves the praise and the glory because this is all his deal anyway. And it says in that passage in Romans, chapter 5, that if we put our hope in God and we focus on his glory, that kind of hope will not disappoint.

"I've known a lot of disappointment. I've known a lot of disappointed people. Things didn't turn out the way they thought they would. God didn't heal their child or keep their baby from going to jail. God didn't bring a husband. And when he did, he didn't bring a very good one. Or some woman has been praying every day for her husband to come to Jesus and it hasn't happened.

"The truth is this: you don't need your circumstances to change in order to give praise to God. In fact, the best place to live the Christian life and participate with God in the plan he has for you is right where you are. So whatever task he has for you to do, whatever job you have, or if you're just out looking for a job, I don't care what it is, God wants to work through you today, right where you are."

I pictured in my mind's eye what it was like to be waking up to my voice. Women in curlers and men sitting on the side of the bed trying to shove to an upright position. Or husbands and wives with coffee at the table and the morning paper. I thought of Callie, too, and wondered if there was any way she could hear my voice. All of these images coalesced and gave me the urge to conclude.

"There's one more thing I want to say and then we'll get to the music, which is why most of you turned on the radio today. But if you're one of those who says, 'God can't love me after what I've done,' I want you to hear me loud and clear. I don't care what you've done. I don't care where you are. I don't care what mistakes you have made or what laws you've broken or what sins you've committed.

"No matter what you've done or what consequences you face for your actions, there is great hope in God. So don't ever say you're too bad for him to love you. That's like saying the ocean isn't big enough to fit a rowboat. His love and his mercy and grace are so much bigger than anything you could ever even imagine doing wrong. Come to him and ask him to forgive you and he will. You can bank on it."

I took a deep breath. "Now I told you that was all I was going to say, but there's one more thing that's weighing heavy on my heart this morning. Some of you know Callie Reynolds. She delivers mail here in Dogwood. Her family and friends are real worried because we can't locate her. If anybody has seen her or knows where she is, please let us know. She drives a green Subaru with a muffler problem."

I told people if they had any information to please call me at the station. I gave the number and waited. I had installed a little light on the phone that lit up red instead of ringing when I was on the air, and I stared at it as I talked, willing it to light up. But it didn't.

I prayed a short prayer for the people who were listening, that God would give them peace in the midst of whatever storm they were going through. And that someone would come to know God personally that day. I prayed that Callie would be okay and that we'd be able to find her. Then I started playing music and just sat there and watched the phone.

I mentioned Callie again during the next break and gave all the information about her that I could and asked people to be on the lookout for her Subaru. I started the next set of songs and the light flashed. It was a little girl, and I thought at first she was pranking me, like some of the kids did around town. But I could tell by her voice that there was something different.

"I heard you mention the mail lady and I had to call," she said.

"Do you know Callie?"

"I talk with her on Saturdays or when I get sick and stay home from school. I like to stand down by the mailbox and wait for her. She's really nice."

"Well, I agree with you. I think she's a special lady."

"My grandmother says you're probably sweet on her or something to make a big fuss like this about a missing person."

"Your grandmother sounds like a smart lady. I would listen to her if I were you."

"Are you going to marry her?"

I laughed. "I have a hard time understanding women. My first priority is to find her.

We'll have to see where we go from there. But you're wrong about the missing person. I've talked about another one before — that little girl who went missing a few years ago. One of the first things I did when I started this station is share prayer needs, and she was at the top of the list, even though she'd been gone for some time."

The girl got quiet.

"Did I say something wrong?" I said.

"No. It's just that I'm that little girl. My name's Natalie Edwards."

"Is that right."

"In the flesh," she said.

"Well, I'm sure glad to talk to you. There were lots of people praying for you during those years."

"Thank you. I live with my grandparents now. They take care of me. I don't talk about it much because it upsets my grandmother."

"You mean when you talk about being gone, it upsets her?"

"Yeah, the past is a hard thing. I guess because my mama took off before I came back and she never returned. I think I kind of remind Mamaw of all the time she spent praying and hoping I'd be okay."

"I expect that was a difficult few years."

"It was. But I was okay."

I heard the bus pass the house and said something about her needing to get ready for school.

"No, not today," she said. "My grandmother is taking me to the dentist or whatever you call that fellow who gives you braces. The kind that go on your teeth to make them straight?" She ended some of her sentences with a question, making the words go up. "They say I need something called an expander."

"I always thought the prettiest girls in school were the ones with braces," I said.

She giggled. "You're just saying that. I don't think I have to get them yet, but it's probably not far away. I don't want them because they cost a lot of money and I don't see the point in it, but Mamaw said it was worth it to see my smile straight and that I'd appreciate it once I get to high school. I suppose she's right."

We talked a little more, or I should say she talked a lot more, and then I asked her why she had called, if she had information about Callie, and she said she did.

"Actually I wanted two things. One was to tell you what the mail lady said to me last Saturday when she went past here and the other was to ask if you'd play me a song."

"What song?"

" 'I'll Fly Away.' That's my favorite. I don't care who you get to sing it; I've never heard it sung in a bad way."

"I'll sure do it. Just let me find it and I'll get it on as you and your grandmother drive to the doctor's appointment."

"That would be great. We'll be leaving in about twenty minutes."

"What did Callie say to you?"

"She called me 'sugar babe.' She always does that when she drives up and I'm standing there. And she said she bet I had boyfriends all over."

That sounded like Callie, taking notice of a little girl on her route.

"And I asked her about her boyfriend, and she laughed and said the old one didn't pan out but there might be a new one. She said she had to get home and get ready for her date, and I asked if it was somebody from her church because she was all the time talking about her church, but she laughed like it was the funniest thing she had ever heard, and then she said no, he wasn't the churchgoing type."

"Did she say anything more? like where they were going or where he lived?"

"She didn't, though she did say that she would fill me in on everything the next time she saw me. And I haven't seen her since.

What do you think happened?"

"Well, I don't rightly know, but I sure want to find out. Do you remember anything else?"

"Not that I can think of right now. If I do, I'll call you back."

"You do that. This has been really helpful, Natalie. I thank you for calling. Will you call me back someday?"

"I sure will," she said.

A half hour later I played Alison Krauss's version of "I'll Fly Away" from *O Brother, Where Art Thou?* As I thought about Natalie riding along with her grandmother, I couldn't get her words out of my head. I also wondered if somehow I had been part of the problem or if I was to blame for anything bad that happened.

# 20

It is a popular misconception that angels can read the minds of humans and see everything at every moment. It is true that we have a more advantageous perspective from which to view events, but we are not like the Creator. We cannot know all. I know I have made that point several times, but I cannot say it enough.

So it was with urgency that I returned to Billy and felt that my absence had in some way produced or at least permitted an unfolding tragedy.

Though it would seem to the casual observer that Callie's actions were an uncharacteristic departure from her character and nature, it was obvious to me how her life's progression had led her to this point and to desperate measures.

Some also think demons can read minds and in turn anticipate events. Do not misunderstand me; they are intelligent beings who can learn things and wreak havoc. They cause great confusion and pain, even in the lives of believers, but they are limited in power. They cannot tell the future or invade the minds of humans without the human's approval. They must in some way be invited or allowed access by thoughts and actions. And in like manner, the peace of God can either be welcomed or shunned. Angelic help can come, but it must be requested. One must ask.

For Callie, the invitation of the evil one came through an innocent friendship with an acquaintance. Reading between the lines of the diary, which Billy did not read thoroughly, and having seen her despondency in my earlier visit, aided me in discerning what had happened. However, the location of this "friend" was not as easily discovered, and while Billy went about his tasks throughout that day, keeping a close eye on the telephone and praying constantly, I left him — a calculated risk I was willing to take — and scoured the countryside for Callie's automobile. Some would believe I stumbled upon it, but in the economy of the Almighty, there is no stumbling. No, I was led to the country road in a neighboring state, discovering her automobile parked and abandoned near a dirt and gravel driveway of a shack that could have been used as an outpost for hunters. Near the cabin was a huge truck, parked haphazardly, as if it had barely made it.

Inside the cabin I found them, and by this I mean the evil ones who had congregated there. I might have been able to prevent this had I continued at my post. I could have thwarted their evil intent, perhaps, but this is another aspect of humanity I have learned. They spend much time second-guessing and wondering *what if.* The angelic host does not deal in the supposed, but in truth. We are much more cognizant of what *is* rather than what *might have been.* And so I assessed the situation and determined that the prayers for Callie were well-founded, for she was in grave danger, both from the evil ones and her human companion. Intertwined like grappling vines, she and this man lay together far removed from reality.

The imps laughed and hurled insults at her, but I sent them on their way and stayed until Callie stirred. She stared at her naked body as if it were new to her, then quickly covered herself and slipped into the bathroom. There she wept. She pressed at her temples, as if the memories would not subside. What memories those were, I could not tell, but with the anguish came another round of assaults by the evil ones. They shouted and taunted and slung all kinds of murderous thoughts her way, encouraging her to end her life. At this, my anger boiled and I hastily dispatched those enemies of God, but not so soon that Callie wasn't affected.

She gathered herself and stumbled to the room. The man awakened and she ran for the door, but he was on her suddenly and dragged her to the bed.

Laughing and hissing came from the rafters of the home as the demons watched. Wherever there is evil in the world, there is glee in the minds of the fallen.

Callie struggled at first and then, like an animal in a trap, gave in to the pain and degradation. I wanted to speak to Callie, to attend to her when the man rose and retrieved a syringe and sent her into a stupor. When her body stilled, he dressed and went to his truck, leaving her without clothes or belongings.

I rose above, wondering if there might be a house nearby, but in all directions there was wilderness. She was trapped, at the mercy of the man who had used her. Lifeless, without a phone, no way to contact the outside world, curled on the bed, she was alone.

It is in such situations that I long to be able to appear to someone like Callie, but I had not been given that directive, nor did I have it at my discretion. I could not scribble directions on Billy's wall, either, for that did not lie in my purview. So I watched, not wanting to leave her for fear the onslaught of the evil ones would continue. As helpless as she, I stayed there with her, whispering comfort and encouragement, protecting, and wondering what I could do to intervene.

# 21

That afternoon I spoke with Sheriff Preston about Natalie's call. He said a coworker at the post office mentioned a new friend of Callie's. "They didn't know much about him and I only got a first name."

"What is it?"

"Larry."

"That narrows it down," I said. "Must be a million Larrys around here. Have you talked with anyone at the church?"

"I spoke with the pastor and her parents and the folks in her small group and nobody has a clue. If she brought him up, they can't remember."

After I hung up, I got an idea and drove over to Callie's trailer and knocked on Opal's front door. She opened it, snuffed out a cigarette, and put on her glasses.

She finally recognized me and said, "You heard anything from her?"

I shook my head. "Everybody's looking,

though. I did get a name. Do you remember her mentioning anybody named Larry?"

She squinted and rubbed at the white whiskers that grew from her chin. "Seems to me she did. Yeah, it was the night she came over for a cup of sugar and sat through the rest of *Desperate Housewives.* We talked about my son and got to talking about forgiveness and if a person can change. And she said she had a friend named Larry who had a past of sorts. That's what she said."

"Did she say where she'd met him? a last name?"

"I don't remember any last name. But I thought . . ." She opened the door wide and I noticed a cat curled up on the kitchen table next to some dishes still out from breakfast. "I think she said something about him being on her mail route. No, wait, that's not right. She met him when he pulled her out of a ditch. That's what it was. He's a truck driver for some outfit around here. Said he was real nice. And half-joking, I said since things weren't working out between you two, why didn't she give this Larry a chance."

"What did she say to that?"

"It was just a passing thing. Poor girl, she was just all torn up about her life and not being able to find love."

"Did she say who he drove for?"

She thought a minute. "I don't think she did, but I assumed it was the wholesale place up on Virginia Avenue."

I nodded. "If you remember anything else, would you call me?"

She picked up another pack of cigarettes. "Sure thing. You be careful now, Billy. It can be a mean world out there."

My heart pounded as I drove up the winding, two-lane road to Callahan Wholesale, a distributor of food to restaurants and supermarkets through the region. It was hard enough to call on businesses to advertise, but to go looking for some guy about a suspicious disappearance made me more than nervous.

Most cars were gone from the parking lot, but there was an older man hovering over the engine of a Ford F-150, his hands greasy and a baseball hat pushed back on his head. He saw me as I drove up and turned to me as he wiped his hands on a handkerchief he had stuffed in his back pocket.

"Can I help you?"

"What's wrong with your truck?" I said.

"Seems to be electrical. I'm hoping it's the battery and not the alternator, but the signs are a-pointing that way."

I offered to go back and get a tool from my house to help him check the voltage on the battery.

"That would probably be a help. But I don't want to put you out. What can I do for you?"

"You work here?"

"Going on twenty years. But they're not hiring. They laid off a bunch of people about a month ago. The economy, you know."

"I'm not looking for work; I'm trying to find a guy who works here named Larry."

"Got four or five Larrys. What's he do?"

"He's a driver, I think."

"That whittles it down. I know two Larrys who are drivers. I don't pretend to know everybody, you know. What's he look like?"

"I'm not sure. He pulled a friend of mine out of a ditch some time ago."

"Why are you looking for him?"

"I think he might be able to help me find that friend."

He scratched at his bald spot, the baseball hat flopping like some pelt hung up to dry on the side of a barn. "Well, there's Larry McCoy. He's about my age. Lives down Route 34 near Lincoln County. He has a haul each day."

"What about the other one?"

"That would be Larry Childers. He was one they laid off. I don't know exactly where he lives, but most days after work you could find him over at the Dew Drop Inn."

"What's he look like?"

The man smiled and coughed, showing some crooked teeth. "Not much. Kind of dark hair and a belly. He probably still has the company hat."

"I'll head over there and then bring back the voltmeter."

"No, don't bother. If you could just give me a jump, I'll get it home and worry with it there."

We hooked it up and the truck fired to life, which made me think it was probably the battery.

"One more question," I said over the roar of the rusted-out muffler. "What's he drive?"

He told me and I headed back the way I came. The Dew Drop wasn't that far as the crow flies, but you had to go the roundabout way to get to it. It made me wonder if this really was the fellow I was looking for. Why in the world would Callie go for a guy who sounded so far from the type of person she was?

The Dew Drop Inn had taken several manifestations in the many years it had been open in Dogwood. At one point, revival had broken out in some of the surrounding churches and there were picket signs every day talking about "Demon Rum" and "Beware the Asp's Bite," and that discouraged some of the regulars. A year into that, the owners gave up and sold the dilapidated building to a group of people in the community who tore down the sign, painted the building white, and turned the bar into an altar. There were stories about that church that said they were known to bring snakes into a service, but I never investigated.

But you can't keep water from seeking its own level, and the Dew Drop opened under new management in a less-populated but still-accessible area near the newly installed power lines where nobody wanted to live. I pulled into the gravel parking lot and counted eight vehicles, one of them matching the description I'd been given. There wasn't one part of me that wanted to go inside, but I kept telling myself I was doing this for Callie.

The bar was dimly lit and it took me a few seconds to adjust. I thought of the verse that says men loved darkness instead of light. A jukebox in the corner played something by Hank Williams Jr. There was a musty smell, and smoke hung heavy. In some places you have the aroma of cooking meat to squelch the stale beer, but nobody came to the Dew Drop to eat. The closest thing to a square meal you could get was the crunching peanut shells under my feet.

There were a few people scattered at some tables and three men at the bar who turned and looked at me, then went back to their business. The bartender was a scrawny man who looked like he had experience with the product he sold. His voice was high-pitched and gravelly.

"What can I get for you?" he said.

I waved at him and nodded. "I'm good for now. Just looking for somebody."

A guy at the bar turned and said, "Who you looking for?"

"Larry Childers," I said, but evidently Bocephus's voice on "A Country Boy Can Survive" drowned me out.

"Who?" the man yelled.

I said the name again and a guy a few tables away stood. He had a pretty big belly and his arms hung in front of him like a gorilla's. The Callahan Wholesale hat was pulled low on his forehead and hair snaked out behind him in a tightly tied ponytail. His face was framed by reddish-brown stubble. His chest hair stuck out over the shirt collar and gave him the appearance of a man-bear.

"What do you want?"

The music seemed to get louder and I motioned for the door. "You mind stepping outside?"

He shook his head. "Whatever you need to say you can say in here."

"Got that right," one of his friends at the table said.

I held up my hands defensively. "I'm not here for trouble. I'm just looking for a friend of mine. Heard you might know her."

"Her?" one of the guys said. Then he laughed and so did the other two.

Larry shoved his chair back and moved toward me. His fists looked like sledgehammers and his legs were like tree trunks, stiff and resolute. From the way he held himself, I had no doubt he knew how to use those sledgehammers.

"What's this about?" he said.

I leaned forward and said, "It's about Callie Reynolds. Do you know her?"

The muscles on one side of his face tensed. He glanced at the door and I read that as an invitation. He said something to the men at the table and then followed me outside.

"You her brother or something?" he said, following me to my truck.

330

I leaned against it and crossed my arms. "No. I just know her. I care about her."

He scratched at his chin and dipped his head with each sentence, like a duck walking toward water. "Okay, then listen up. I don't know anything. I helped her on the road once when her car slid into a ditch. That's it."

"You never went on a date with her?"

"I'm married."

"A friend of hers said she mentioned you. That something was going on. Not that I'm accusing you. I don't care about that."

"Get out of here and don't come back." He pointed at my chest with a fat finger and turned to leave.

I grabbed at the back of his flannel shirt. "Wait. I need your help."

He stopped and turned, leveling his eyes. "What you need to do is leave. You understand? Don't bother me again. I don't know anything about where she is or what happened."

I returned his stare. "How do you know she's missing?"

He glanced away and cursed under his breath. I stood there, my legs and arms trembling, and at first I thought it was my nerves or fear of getting hit, but as he walked back into the Dew Drop, I realized I hadn't had anything to eat since breakfast and my levels were low. I kept a plastic bag with a couple of energy bars in the truck, but when I checked it, I remembered I ate those the last time I felt the trembles.

I stumbled into the bar, hunting for carbohydrates, my breath short. I could feel the blood draining from my face, like the last trickle of water in a dried-up reservoir.

"There he is again," somebody said on my right.

I ignored them. "I need a Coca-Cola," I said to the bartender.

He looked at the men coming toward me. "You need to turn around and go right back out that door."

"I'm a diabetic," I said. "I have to raise my sugar levels or I'm going to —"

"You're out of here," one of Larry's friends said. He grabbed me and threw me toward the door. I hit it face forward, but he opened it and pushed me the rest of the way out until I stumbled in the gravel. I threw out my hands to catch myself and cut them.

He yelled something at me, but I was going in and out. It's hard to explain to somebody who's never been through it. Think about the time in your life when you were the hungriest. When you felt like you could grab a banana and eat it peel and all. That's what it's like when you go low, and there's nothing you can do but try to satisfy the craving.

There were two others behind the man. They stood at the door with their hands on their hips. I tried to get up but my head spun and I had to stay down. I prayed and asked God to help, and then I remembered the cake frosting in my glove compartment. I crawled my way to the passenger door and fumbled around inside, knocking out the tire pressure gauge and the title and insurance papers and some tissues. The music from the bar subsided and I noticed the men had gone back inside. I grabbed the white tube and unscrewed it. Just some of this on my gums could work its way into my bloodstream enough to keep me coherent. But when I got the top off, my heart sank because the end had to be cut off. I chewed on it, but it was too thick. As I reached for my pocketknife, I felt myself falling, my body needing a jump start just like the Ford earlier. My eyes blurring, air coming in short gasps, I lay back on the gravel and called out to God for help. *Send me an angel, Lord. Send me somebody.*

I heard the "disappearing dreams of yesterday" line from "Sunday Morning

Coming Down" and then saw a couple of cowboy boots coming toward the truck.

Whoever it was bent down to me and lifted my head. It was a gray-haired man with an open can of Pepsi. He held it to my lips and I took a long drink and felt the sugar and carbs hit my bloodstream. I drank the whole thing in two gulps and sat up and belched, then said, "Excuse me." I was still trembling, but that would give me the jolt I needed and send me up.

The man smiled at my burp. "I had a son with the sugar diabetes, and I know what it can do to you. You got type 1 or type 2?"

He had breath that would have knocked down a steamroller, but if this was the angel God could use, I was okay with it. I held up one finger.

He nodded. "You feeling better now?"

"Can I get another one?" I said, some of the feeling coming back to my body. "Or maybe orange juice? You think they would have that in there?"

He smiled. "Just stay right here."

I pulled myself up to the seat and tossed the cake frosting back in the glove compartment. I made a mental note to get another tube that was easier to open. My body felt tingly and hollow, almost like I wasn't really living in it anymore, just renting. It had been a while since I'd gone that low.

The man came back with a can of cold orange juice and I sipped at it, wondering how low my levels had gone. I needed something solid. I needed to get back to the station and put on some new tapes. But I needed to find Callie more.

The man leaned forward against the truck in the twilight. "You have many spells like this?"

"Not in a while. I'll go low when I'm home sometimes, but I'm always close to something that'll bring me back. Just kind of got caught out here." I stuck out my hand. "Billy Allman."

He shook with me, and by the shape of his hands I guessed he was a tradesman. Maybe drywall or concrete. "Pleased to meet you, Billy." He thought a minute. "You're not the guy with the radio station, are you?"

"One and the same."

He chuckled. "Gotta tell my wife I met you. She listens to that all the time."

"Just don't tell her where we were."

He looked toward the door. "What was that all about? I don't think I've ever seen Larry so upset, unless he's losing at poker."

"Do you know him?"

"I drink in the same bar with him every

afternoon. If you can know a person that way, then I do."

"A friend of mine is missing. To be honest, I don't know if he knows anything or not, but I'm just trying to follow the trail and it's getting cold."

"A woman?"

I nodded.

He scowled. "Larry's married. Maybe that's why he wouldn't talk to you. Probably thought you were spying on him for his wife."

"I'm not here to get anybody in trouble. I got a friend who hasn't been to work in a few days who hasn't missed a day in years. Her family is worried sick. I'm just looking for clues."

The man nodded. "Stay here. Let me talk with him."

"I appreciate it," I said. "If you don't mind, I'm going to the gas station down the road and get a PowerBar."

"See you in a few."

He patted the front of the truck like you would the head of a dog you wanted to catch a rabbit. When he disappeared inside, I drove to the gas station. I needed to get a read on my levels so I could dose, but at least I wouldn't be going low soon. When I got back to the Dew Drop, the gray-haired man was sitting on the step outside. He came to my open window and ran his tongue around his bottom teeth.

"I might have something for you. It wasn't easy, but I got Larry to tell me he saw your friend last Saturday. Said they got a bite to eat and talked. It was all innocent."

"Uh-huh. And did Callie know he was married?"

"We didn't get into that. But he did say toward the end of the talk, after they'd had a little to drink, they met up with another friend of his, and when Larry took off, those two were still together."

I grabbed a yellow pad of paper I keep on the dashboard. That Callie would be drinking at all alarmed me, but I wasn't in judgment-passing mode. I wanted information.

"His name is Clay Gilmore." He gave me the man's number. "Larry wants you to make sure you don't mention him when you talk with him. He doesn't want any of this coming back on him."

I put the pad back on the seat and turned to him. "Scripture says the deeds done in darkness will one day come into the light."

"Does it now? You sound like my wife."

"I don't mean to. I appreciate what you did. I don't know what I'd have done if you hadn't helped."

"You'd have made it, Billy."

I started the truck and it fired up like an old friend. "My guess is your wife at home is praying for you."

"I expect you're right about that."

"Tell her I said hello. And tell her I'll be praying for you too."

I put the truck in reverse, and he turned and stepped toward me. "One more thing I didn't mention. Larry said this Clay fellow ain't right in the head. And he carries a gun. You be careful, Billy."

# 22

I went home and switched the reels, then checked my levels, which were above 400 — not good. I gave myself a correction shot, wondering if what people said about the pump being so much easier was true. I barely had enough money for insulin and I reused my needles.

I got on the computer and did a reverse lookup on the phone number the man had given. MapQuest showed me the way, and it looked like Clay lived in a remote area of Dogwood County. I called the number but there was no answer.

It was dark when my headlights hit Clay's muddy driveway, and I drove all the way up to the Massey Ferguson tractor that had been parked there for a while. Weeds grew all around it. The house was dark and there was no outside light, so I kept my truck running and the lights trained on the front yard. Calling it a yard was being kind.

I made it as far as the tractor before an old hound came running out from under the wooden stairs, barking and growling. The hair on the back of his neck stood straight, and he sniffed at me like he was sizing up a T-bone steak. I held out a hand and knelt down. He darted away. Pretty soon he came around, sniffing at me and finally licking at the back of my hand. When I stood up, he growled again, and it was a good five minutes before I could get him to trust me enough to let me get to the front door.

I knocked hard but nobody answered. That sent the dog to barking again. I went around the back and found some farm equipment the hard way. I cupped my hand against the window. There was a little night-light on near an old telephone and papers on a desk, but no one moved inside.

I tried the door but it was locked. Same for the front door.

"Callie? Are you in there? It's Billy."

Nothing but crickets and a panting dog behind me.

I thought about kicking the door in, but then I had another idea. I backed up and drove down to the road and went around the bend, then turned my lights off and parked where I could see the house. If there was anybody in there, a light would come on soon. I turned on the radio low, but I couldn't get my station out here.

Sitting there in the dark at the side of the road, I let my mind wander. I kept my eye on the house, waiting for any light to come on, surfing through the dwindling channels on the FM side and listening to the raised ionosphere do its number on the AM band, pulling in stations from Chicago and all over. But what was going through my head was that this whole endeavor had been a failure. I don't mind telling you that I believed the station would be a lot bigger deal than it has become. The fact is, it speaks to me every day. There is something in the music or the teaching that reaches down somewhere and makes my soul sit up and beg for more. But I guess not everybody is the same as me. Sure, I've had some people say that the radio station was important and helped them, but most people had only heard of it or maybe tried it once, and outside of the hollow, like here, you can't even hear it.

Sometimes God has his hand on people in spite of their trials. He walks with them through the fire and they know they are on the right path. At other times, God gives people over to their own desires, and the problems and difficulties they find are of their own accord.

But then there are people like me, who think they are doing exactly what God wants them to do, and they plow through everything that is thrown at them and in the end they're nowhere closer to God than when they started.

That's what I was thinking right then, and I guess the other thing, if I was to be honest about it, was that the love of a good woman had been wasted in the process. I had just spent the past few years digging a lonely hole, and there was nothing at the end of it but four sides of dirt and a long way to climb.

You get to thinking that way and there's not a person in the world who can pull you back. You have to come to your senses yourself through the power of God. His ways are not our ways. The way he guides is not the way we would do it. Look at Job and the senseless things that happened to him. In the end, Job found out that God was the one in control, even though he'd allowed Satan to buffet his servant. And every time I think about Paul chained to a Roman soldier or two, I keep thinking he must have felt like everything he was doing was just spinning his wheels in the sand.

Once I got on that path, things made more sense. I wasn't doing something for nothing, even though at times it felt like it. In the middle of all life had thrown at me, God seemed to be doing something good with my heart. Why was I out here in the middle of nowhere looking for somebody who was just a friend? Was God trying to tell me that Callie meant a lot more to me than I was willing to let on?

I was about to get out of the truck and walk around the perimeter of the house again when two headlights shone behind me, coming around the bend. The car slowed when it got to me. I rolled down the window and could see by his dashboard light that it was an older man, unshaven, a bulge in his jaw.

"Can I help you?" he said with a West Virginia drawl that would have curled a northerner's hair.

"Just looking for Clay Gilmore. He lives here, right?"

The man spat moon-glistened brown juice onto the road. "Been right up there since the day he was born. Crazy Clay."

"Why do you call him that?" I said.

"Not just me; everybody does. You know him?"

"Not really."

"Figures. If you knew him, you wouldn't be sitting down here next to his driveway. Boy ain't right in the head, if you know what I mean. Comes and goes at all hours. We usually just stay out of his way when we see him coming."

"He have family around here?"

He spat again. "Not a one. His mama and daddy died in that house and he buried them in the backyard the next day. Nobody found out about it for a few months when we didn't see them sitting in their lawn chairs."

I opened my door and stood in the road. "I'm looking for a friend of mine. A woman friend. You haven't seen Clay with a lady, have you?"

He laughed and it rattled around in his throat. "Last time I saw a woman go near Clay's house was when a female police officer came out here to investigate some missing person report. One of his dogs pert nigh took one of her legs off."

Something inside didn't feel right and I got the worst feeling about Callie. "I don't see his truck up there. You have any idea if he's here?"

"If his truck ain't there, he's not there."

"Know where he could be?"

The man shook his head. "Your guess is

as good as mine. I hear he spends a lot of time down at the Dew Drop. If it was in the fall, I'd say he was at the hunting cabin he has in Kentucky."

"He has a hunting cabin?"

"Yeah, as if he needed it. We got enough deer and squirrels around here to keep the freezer stocked. That's if you're a good-enough shot. I hear the cabin isn't much, but it's remote."

"You ever been there?"

He blew air through his lips. "Right. He'd never let anybody get near that place, I don't think. Maybe some of the fellows he goes hunting with."

"Like who?"

He spat again and rubbed his chin with a hand. "There's an old boy up the hollow who may have been there. Oakley Chambers. He went to school with Clay. Until eighth grade, when he dropped out. He might know something if anybody does."

He gave me the backwoods directions, including a tree I would notice and the driveway that had a gate at the end of it. I thanked the man and he drove away. Before I left, I thought about getting into Clay's house and making sure Callie wasn't there, but from what I could see, nothing had stirred inside since I'd been sitting there.

■ ■ ■ ■

The glow of a television lit the inside of
Oakley Chambers's house. He was watching something on ESPN and carried a
Coors Light can with him when he came to
the door. I mentioned the fellow's name
who gave me his address and that I was trying to locate Clay Gilmore.

He tossed the can past me into the yard.
"What for? You trying to dig yourself an
early grave?"

"Not at all. I'm trying to find a friend of
mine. Somebody said Clay might know
where she is."

"She?" he said.

"Yeah, our mail lady, Callie Reynolds. She
lives over in Dogwood."

He pursed his lips. "Can't help you."

"Please," I said, putting my hand on the
door as he reached to close it. "Callie means
a lot to me. The old guy said Clay has a
cabin in Kentucky. Can you tell me where
it is? give me a phone number?"

"That place doesn't even have electricity.
No phone. And even if you could find it,
your friend's not going to be there."

"How do you know that?"

He rolled his eyes. "Because Clay don't

take chances like that."

"What do you mean?"

"Just what I said." He leveled his gaze at me. "You got a death wish?"

"No, I'm just desperate. Can you tell me how to get there?"

He shook his head and I reached in my back pocket. The man ducked behind the door and I put up my hand to show him I didn't mean any harm.

"I don't have a whole lot of cash, but I could write you a check. I'm willing to pay for directions."

"Right. And they find your body and trace you back to me."

"Please," I said. "I have a bad feeling about this, and any help you could give would be appreciated."

He went back inside and the kitchen light came on. Someone said something to him as he rummaged through a drawer. "Some crazy guy wanting to know how to get to Clay's cabin."

Finally he came back with a yellow legal pad and turned on the porch light. He stood in his bare feet and drew a line representing I-64. He gave a primer on how many miles it was across the state line, which exit it was, and then which road to take. "It's been a while since I've been back there. I doubt you're going to find it, even with this."

I thanked him and stuffed the page in my pocket.

"Don't say I didn't warn you," he said. "If you don't take something to defend yourself with, you're a fool."

"All right," I said.

I went back to the house and changed the reels so I'd have at least four hours before the station went off the air. My body was feeling the effects of going low and I was exhausted, but I felt adrenaline kick in. I contemplated calling Sheriff Preston, but in the end I figured it best to keep pushing. Plus, he probably would tell me to just leave it to him and I wasn't about to do that. I made sure I had enough food to get me up if I went low, and I took off.

A light rain had begun as I started out. Following the directions carefully, I exited I-64 and twisted and turned until I came to a dirt road, then what looked like a logging road or something gas drillers had constructed to get in and out of the Kentucky hollow. Several times I came to an impasse, or it looked like the road had ended, and it made me think I was on a wild goose chase and I would get stuck. Believe me, there wasn't a tow truck on the face of the planet that could find me back in those woods. But there was something urging me onward that to this day I can't explain. It was all so fragile now that I think about it. I could have just stopped because I was tired or because it wasn't worth the effort, since I didn't know what was at the end of that path. But that unseen force kept me going, along with the fact that the two tire tracks I was following led farther back into the woods and seemed fresh. I used them to stay out of the muddy places.

After I went by a tree that looked like a backward L, like Oakley had said I would find, I hit my watch light and saw I'd been gone more than two hours. I had promised myself that I would turn around as soon as I hit that mark because the station would go off the air if I didn't. But I went a little farther, knowing from that tree I was on the right path. Then the road forked and I had no idea where to go. Oakley hadn't told me about this.

Just as I was looking for a place to turn around, my windshield wipers on intermittent, my headlights shone on something green and metallic. I shouldn't have even seen it — it was just a reflection of the lights, but I pointed the truck a little to the right and there it was, the top of an old

Subaru. My heart about jumped out of my body.

Quickly I switched off my lights, rolled down my window, and turned off the truck. The sounds of the night and the whip-poor-wills and crickets and frogs should have made me feel at home, but there was something wrong here. Maybe it was the intense darkness along the road, but it felt like God had turned off the lights to this place and gone away a long time ago.

I tried to open my door quietly, but it creaked and moaned like an old ghost. I turned off the dome light inside and just left the rusted door partly open as I stepped onto some wet leaves and the soggy grass. My feet sank into the mud and I had to step away from the road to get firmer footing.

I pulled out my Maglite, which any engineer worth his salt carries, and climbed over the piled mud near Callie's car. I knew it was hers. The mud splatters on the quarter panels. Balding tires. A crack in the windshield that ran from the passenger side all the way past the driver's. I shone the light in the back and didn't see anybody. What I did see were several empty mail containers and her cutoff gloves on the passenger seat.

I shone the light around and came back onto the road. That's when I spotted the cabin down the hill. There was no light coming from it. I listened for any dog that might come out, but I figured if it didn't hear the truck when I pulled up or the rusted door, the dog was either nonexistent or stone-deaf.

As it turned out, the cabin sat in a clearing across from a marshy area with cattails and tall grass. A crow cawed in a treetop, and that gave me a bad feeling. A black bird is just as bad as a black cat if you're superstitious, which I am not, but you can't help thinking of those types of things. I looked around for Clay's truck but didn't see it. Either he had it hidden well or he wasn't there.

There comes a point in every man's life when he has to fish or cut bait. I'm not a fisherman. To me, it's more whether you're going to plug in the power cord or just sit there and go over your solder points. There have been plenty of times through the years when I wished I had checked my wiring again, but that's another story. I had to either go in whole hog or just stand on the mushy ground and wait.

I stepped up on the rickety wooden porch that felt like it would give way. I clicked on the light for a second to see the doorknob, then grabbed it and turned, but it didn't

351

budge. I moved to a little window at the right — there weren't many on the cabin — and flashed the light once. It was a kitchen area, and I could see an empty pizza box, plus beer cans and some dirty paper plates overflowing a trash can.

I couldn't see anything else, so I moved to the back and found a bathroom window. It was halfway open and I forced it up all the way. If I had to, I could crawl through, but I wanted to make sure I wasn't climbing into trouble. An overpowering smell hit me, and that's when I stumbled onto the bathtub in the backyard. It was just sitting out of place in the woods and was full of water and something that smelled like lye soap. It looked like there was animal hair on the edges, and my hope was that Clay was getting rid of some doe he had shot by mistake, leaving it there to decompose.

Around the other side of the cabin, my heart pounding, legs tingling, I found the biggest window that looked in on the living area. I peeked my head over the sill. If Clay was in there awake, he had seen me because it was lighter outside than in. When I didn't see any movement, I turned the light on and let the beam pierce the room.

Right next to the window was a bed, and on top of the covers was the nude body of a woman. Her skin was pale and lifeless. On a round table next to the bed were a couple of syringes. I swept the light around the room but didn't see anyone else. I found a piece of wood and put it down to stand on and that raised me up far enough to see the woman's face.

"Callie?" I whispered, even though I knew she couldn't hear me. I pecked on the window and kept the light trained on her face. She didn't move.

Some other man would have put a boot right through the front door and knocked it off its hinges. I thought about it, but I decided to go through the bathroom window — which made me think of the Beatles song, of course. I knocked down some stuff from the windowsill over the tub, but at that point I wasn't concerned about noise.

I went straight for the bed and put a hand against her face. It was chilly in there and so was her cheek; I took off my shirt and put it on her.

I smacked her a couple of times like you see in the movies, trying to get her going, but no response. I felt her wrist for a pulse but couldn't find one. Then I tried her neck and there it was, faint like a little bird's. A shallow pulse is much better than none at all. I noticed her necklace, the cross her

Sunday school class had given her years ago that she always wore. I was praying now, asking God to keep her alive, to help me get her out of there, to help me know what to do.

I stood up and looked for a phone and then remembered what I'd been told. I had always shunned cell phones, saying they were just another sapling on the slippery slope to convenience and I would never own one. Of course, that far from civilization, it probably wouldn't have connected anyway, but something inside me said I should get one.

I looked for a light switch but gave up. Because of the night chill, I grabbed the sheet on the bed and the spread that had fallen to the floor and wrapped her as best I could, tilting her body one way and sealing her up like a mummy. Something fell out as I was doing that and hit the floor. I felt around for it, then shone my light down. It was a frog key chain. I slipped it in my back pocket.

There was no mistake — Callie was not going to win the thinnest-mail-carrier-in-the-world competition, but I was surprised at how easily her deadweight fit in my arms. I have never been a strong man, though I can lift my end of the casket if needed.

While the other kids were playing ball and lifting weights or whatever they did to get pumped up, I was in my room restoring the Atwater Kent radio I found at the junkyard. But holding Callie this way and struggling to the front door, I felt a little of what a firefighter must feel when he carries a child out of a burning building. I was so happy to have found her but also concerned about getting help.

I struggled with the doorknob and finally got it open. When I stepped onto the porch, one of the slats gave way and cracked like a man's rib in a prizefight. It was then that I saw light swaying through the trees and heard a diesel engine of some monstrous truck in the distance.

"We gotta get out of here, Callie," I whispered.

I took off to my right and went around the back of the house, momentum carrying me. I stumbled over some old tires and nearly fell, but I kept my balance, passing the stench of the bathtub and on to the edge of the cabin. Whoever was coming was trying to get around my truck. The headlights were pointed up and shone through the tops of the trees.

I knew this was my chance, so I held her tightly and headed through the underbrush to the tree line. One foot in front of the other, just leaning forward and moving until we came to a little ditch where I could rest. Behind us came a scraping sound. I looked back to see my truck whopperjawed in the road and a huge truck coming over the hill and sliding through the muddy marsh. The headlights shone on the cabin's open door. I stayed down as the truck stopped and a wiry man jumped out and ran inside.

I had to make a decision right then and there whether I was going to chance getting to my truck or just head through the under-brush. If it had been me alone, I probably would have gone through the woods, but I had no idea how bad Callie was or if she would survive whatever drug she'd been given. As the man disappeared through that door, I headed to my truck. The extra weight made me sink in the mud and I slipped and slid up the hill. Just when I thought I was going to make it, my feet flew and we went down in the muck and mire, and the jolt brought a groan from Callie.

"It's all right. We're going to get you some help."

I glanced back and saw the guy running like a madman, shouting, "I'm going to get you!"

It was all I could do to stand on my own

two feet, but picking up Callie was next to impossible, and I knew I had only seconds. I grabbed her arms and dragged her through the mud toward the truck. It was smacked up pretty good in the back and the bumper hung loose.

I got Callie to my door and opened it wide, the hinges creaking. I couldn't get to the passenger side because of the way the truck sat on the hill. Her hair and the bedspread were caked with mud. I managed to pull her up to the seat, then turned her around and the cover fell off. I let the cover and sheet fall and pushed her across the seat; I needed to get her out of there any way I could, and being delicate and modest was not important.

As soon as I shoved the key into the ignition, my windshield shattered in front of me. It looked like a hailstorm. I figured Clay had used a shotgun from below and the pellets glanced up. The glass didn't break — but I couldn't see.

I glanced out the window and saw the guy reloading as he walked toward us. I turned the key and the engine turned, but I forgot to pump the gas pedal a couple of times, so I did that and then ducked as he shot again, hitting the headlights and knocking out both.

He was at the marsh now and coming up beside us and I knew I had one chance.

I hit the key and she roared — a great sound to my beating heart. I threw the truck into reverse and spun the wheels, and mud flew in through the open window. The back end fishtailed and slammed against a tree.

Clay cursed at me as he moved through the marsh and ended with "Get out of the truck!"

It felt like the moment when the water and sludge reached its zenith back at Buffalo Creek. But there was no miracle now. Just me and this fellow and Callie's lifeless body.

He advanced up the hill, his shotgun pointed at me. I shifted into drive and gunned the engine, flying past him down the hill as he jumped back. A shot rang out behind me and the back window shattered. This time glass rained. All over Callie's body and onto the truck's dashboard. It took me a second to discover whether I'd been hit or not as I fishtailed next to the cabin and slid around with my front pointed toward the hill.

I stuck my head out the window and saw him running toward me; then he slowed as I gunned the engine, heading straight for him. That caught him somewhat off guard and he retreated. My tires spun but I picked up speed and then ducked as I got near him. A shot rang out and then another. He'd shot my tires out, and when I looked through the back window, the diesel was pulling out. He caught up with us quickly but I kept going, using the momentum to propel us down the hill. There was no way he could pass us on such a narrow path, so I tried to keep the truck on track, though with no headlights and unable to see through the windshield, it wasn't easy. Steam poured over the hood and that sweet smell of antifreeze leaked through the window. We were in a heap of trouble and I had my doubts as to whether the truck would even keep going, let alone take us home.

It was the slowest chase scene because we bounced along at a maximum of 30 mph, and I had to put a hand on Callie's legs to keep her from falling onto the floorboard. She was cold to the touch, and with the wind whipping through the window, I flipped on the heater. I prayed the bumpy ride and the chill didn't make her worse.

Clay shot at me once from behind, but it was a wild shot that didn't hit anything but the trees overhead. Then he slammed into us and my head shot back, but I stayed in the path. The blown-out tires seemed to give more traction than I would've had otherwise. Either that or there was something else going on to keep the truck going the straight and narrow.

We came to the fork in the road and then the L tree, and the road widened. Clay streaked forward like I was sitting still. He had his passenger window down, and when he came next to me, he raised the shotgun with his right arm and leveled it at my face.

It's funny what you think of in the moment of your death. Seeing those two gun barrels — and I swear this is true, though it may be unbelievable — for some reason I just thought about the frailty of the mandolin and how such a small instrument can make or break the sound of music. Just the pluck of those little strings can add something to the mix that can't be calculated. I don't care how much you add or subtract to the music of your life, if you don't have the mandolin playing somewhere in there, the music is just not the same. When Jesus said he came to give life abundantly, I almost translate that as him saying, "I came to provide the mandolin in the sound track of your life. And to give you a really good part." That may seem sacrilegious to some people, but it speaks in the language I understand.

I must have hit the brake at just the right moment or maybe he was a bad shot because the gun fired and the pellets whizzed past me and blew out the window on the other side of the truck. This boy was playing for keeps, that was for sure.

I slid to a stop and watched him skid sideways on the hillside. Since I could see better in reverse, I backed up to the L tree as fast as I could and swung around in the mud and headed back down the road toward the cabin. He must have gotten stuck because his lights didn't follow.

Callie stirred and tried to push herself up. When she couldn't, she put her legs down and looked over at me, as if I were something from a bad dream.

"Don't worry. I'm here. It's all right, Callie. Go back to sleep."

She curled up in the corner running her hands all over to try and get warm. She swallowed hard and rasped, "Close the window, Billy."

"I wish I could, darlin'," I said.

"Thank you, Billy. Close the window." Then she was gone again, her head jiggling against the door.

The fact that Clay wasn't following us both excited and troubled me. I slowed and stopped, listening to the radiator hiss. Surely the antifreeze was running out. If this road was a dead end, Clay would have caught up to us by now. Unless he had gotten stuck or gone over the hill somewhere. Unless this road was just a loop connected to the other one and he was coming to meet us that way or was waiting.

I kept going until I settled close to Callie's Subaru, then turned off the truck and heard the diesel chugging. Unsure how far away it was, I ran to the Subaru and pulled her keys from my back pocket. There wasn't much gas left, but it fired to life. I threw it into four-wheel drive and backed it out quickly, grabbing Callie and sliding her into the passenger seat.

"It's so cold," she said. Her eyes were rolling back.

When we hit the fork in the road, I knew this decision might be one I'd regret the rest of my life. Or it could be the one that would release us.

I'm not the kind of person who says the Lord talks to him. I don't believe you can hear an audible voice that tells you to do things or not do things because I just don't think he works that way. But I do get impressions about things and the impression I got right then was the single word *wait*.

362

So I sat and waited and prayed like there was no tomorrow, which was entirely possible for the both of us. "Please, God. You know this fellow is going to kill us if he gets the chance. He's half killed Callie the way it is. You know he does not want the truth to come out about what he's done. Deliver us, Lord. Help me find a way out of this hellhole."

I always close my eyes when I pray, but that time I made an exception. I kept them open and watching for the truck. I had my window down to hear and it was good to be able to see again, even with the crack in Callie's windshield.

Then, like the sun coming up on Easter morning, I saw the flash of headlights on the trees to our right, coming back toward me on the fork I had taken. I started the car and slammed it into drive and took off on the other fork, knowing Clay couldn't have seen me with the lights off.

"Yes! Yes!" I said. "Thank you, Lord. Thank you for your deliverance and your mercy." I was all but whooping and hollering. You cannot know relief until you are in a place where your life is literally hanging in the balance and you finally have a glimmer of hope that everything is going to be okay. Relief is a flood I don't mind going through.

I only stopped once, at an all-night truck stop to get enough gas to make it to Huntington. The car was on fumes when I coasted in, and I swore if I saw that truck pull in or pass us, I was going to call the police. But I never saw it and we went on our way to the emergency room. I suppose Clay gave up or he put another plan in place, but I imagined with as serious as he was about getting rid of Callie and me, he wasn't too happy with us.

My station had been off the air for a while, but I wasn't worried about anything but Callie. When you're in that kind of situation, the stuff that's important bubbles to the surface and your priorities change. That a few hill people couldn't wake up to gospel bluegrass and Scripture reading took a backseat to getting help for someone I cared about.

Callie was still slumped in the seat, and I

prayed God would help me get her to a hospital fast. I was just praying up a storm and the tears were falling, partly because we'd gotten away and partly because I knew she had more hurt inside her than any tests would ever reveal.

I drove up to Cabell Huntington's emergency room entrance and told the orderly inside I had a friend in the car who didn't have clothes. They brought out a wheelchair and a blanket and loaded her in. In the dull light of the early morning she looked pale, and her face was drawn from hunger and whatever drug she'd been given. She was beginning to come around, and all I could do was watch them wheel her back to a curtained-off place and then go give what little information I knew to the lady who needed it. I told her Callie was a government employee, so she had to have insurance, but I didn't know much more than that. And I promised I would pay for anything she couldn't cover. It was a promise I intended to keep, though I had no idea how I would do it.

As far as I'm concerned, nurses could run the world a lot better than doctors, lawyers, or politicians. Put them in charge of just about anything and it seems to get done. And fast. The nurse helping Callie went to work hooking her up and checking this and that, and then the doctor came swaggering in, looking at papers. I told him the short version of the story, and he nodded like he'd heard it before, but I don't have any idea how you could have heard that kind of thing. Somebody must've phoned the police because they came a little later and asked questions and it seemed they didn't believe me at first. That's when I called Sheriff Preston and he got there lickety-split. Because he vouched for me, the local police backed off.

"Why didn't you call me, Billy?" Sheriff Preston said. "I would have helped you."

"I know, Sheriff. I wish I had. But when you're in the middle of it, you don't think straight."

"You could have both been killed out there."

I nodded. "That's a fact. We probably should have been."

He said he'd call Callie's parents, and I asked if I could do it. I dialed them from a pay phone in the hallway and Mrs. Reynolds picked up. It wouldn't have surprised me a bit if she'd been up all night praying.

"Billy, what's wrong? Did you know your station is off the air?"

"I know, ma'am. I've got some good news.

I found her."

"You did?" She said it in a gasp, and then she started crying and whimpering. "Where? What happened?"

"I'm down here at the hospital with her."

"Hospital? Is she okay?"

"I think she's going to be, but she's been through a lot, Mrs. Reynolds. Some of it I don't even know. I knew you and your husband would want to come down and be with her."

"As soon as I can throw some clothes on, we'll be there. What happened, Billy?"

"I don't know for sure, but I think somebody was holding her against her will. It's a long story, but if you come down, I think it would be good. Sheriff Preston is here."

"Sheriff Preston," she said, like she was in a daze. "All right. You know that your station is off the air, don't you?"

"Yes, ma'am. I'll fix that as soon as I get home."

The locals said they would need to get in touch with the Kentucky State Police to investigate further. Sheriff Preston worked it out with them to do the tests they needed done on Callie and he would take me back to Kentucky to show them the cabin. I said I needed to get back home and put my station on the air. They kind of looked at me weird, but Sheriff Preston explained.

"I'll run him back up to Dogwood and then we'll meet the state police," Sheriff Preston said.

"That fellow's gonna be gone before you get back," one of the locals said.

"We both know he's probably cut loose already," the sheriff said. "I'll coordinate it."

I stared out the window at the mist rising from the morning dew on the mountain as the sheriff drove me home. He waited in the living room while I changed the tapes and did a station break. I threw on the headphones and thanked people for tuning in, and I asked them to pray for me and my friend Callie Reynolds, who was in the hospital. I don't know if anybody heard me, but I threw it out there hoping someone would. Then I started another four hours of music and kicked myself for not getting some kid from the neighborhood to come in and help me out. Surely I could have found somebody like that, but I was so intent on doing stuff myself that I guess I let pride get in my way.

I tested my sugar levels and I was pretty much in range, give or take. There wasn't much to eat in the house, so Sheriff Preston drove by McDonald's and got me a couple of sausage biscuits, and that perked up my system. He even let me listen to the station as long as we could. I didn't know it, but I fell asleep as we drove back toward Kentucky. The sheriff woke me as we met up with some officers from there. They followed as I showed the way to Clay's cabin.

The road looked different in the morning light. My truck was still there where I had left it, and I pointed out the shot-up windshield. I waited in the cruiser a tense few minutes while Sheriff Preston and the others surrounded the cabin. Over near the marsh there were tire tracks dug deep into the mud and I shook my head when I thought of how close Callie and I came to dying here. Sheriff Preston and the others said the cabin was empty. I showed them where I'd found Callie, the syringes, where the shots were fired, and the bathtub in the backyard. In the light of day it became clear that the horror in the tub wasn't a deer. A couple of the Kentucky police fellows strung the whole area with yellow tape and another fellow put the syringes in a plastic bag.

When I'd told them all I could, Sheriff Preston took me back to the hospital and we found Callie's room. Her parents were outside the door and Mrs. Reynolds hugged me.

"How is she?" I said.

Mrs. Reynolds's face was a mix of sadness and hope, which is the way things ought to be in a weary world. "She's awake. The doctor's in there. She asked about you. I don't think she remembers much of what happened last night."

"She slept through most of it," I said. "Doesn't surprise me. Can I see her?"

The doctor came out and talked with her parents, so I walked in. Callie was sitting up in bed. The nurse was doing something, but when she saw me, she pulled the curtain and left us alone. I sat down next to Callie and she reached for my hand.

"I guess we had an interesting night," she said.

"An interesting few days," I said.

"How did you find me?"

I smiled. "I'm a bloodhound at heart, darlin'. Get my nose to the trail and it's hard to kick me off."

"Or the woman who lost the coin."

I squeezed her hand. "Just like that. She didn't know what she had until she lost it."

She turned her head a little. "How are you, Billy? I've been worried about you."

I shook my head. "Here you are in the hospital hooked up to tubes and you're worried about me. If that don't beat all, I don't know what does."

"He could have killed us both. The police said we were lucky to be alive."

"Luck didn't have a thing to do with it, Callie. It was like I was being drawn to that cabin. I can't explain it. All along the way the Lord ordered my steps and I don't have any doubt he guided me." I leaned closer. "There's something I've never told anybody. Back in Buffalo Creek when I was little, the flood . . ."

She leaned closer when I couldn't talk. "What is it, Billy?"

"I've just felt like the Lord has had his hand on me to do something, and maybe this was it. Maybe this is why he kept me alive all this time. To get you out of that place."

A tear leaked out of her eye and ran down her face. I reached over with a finger and wiped it away, and she held my hand there.

"I think there's more for you to do than this, Billy Allman. And I think you've been doing it all your life."

I shook my head. "This is not about me."

"It's true. You've been a good friend. The very best. And I've put too many expectations on you. I'm going to start cooking for you again as soon as I can get out of here."

"I think there are going to be a lot of changes for us," I said. "But you take your time. We all need you back on the route. I keep getting mail from across town."

She laughed and it was like the sound of the doves flying in the morning light. Just soft and warm and good. I asked what the doctor had said about her condition, and that led her down a path I could tell she didn't want to go.

"Stuff happened out there, Billy. Some really bad stuff."

"I know."

"No, you don't."

"I mean, I could tell it was bad from what I saw."

"You don't know how bad." She put a hand to her head and squeezed her temples. "I don't remember much, but what keeps coming back makes me cold inside. It was awful. Evil."

Her eyes filled with tears. I hate it when a woman cries. I really do. I remember it happening with my mother and how I needed to just go away when she would have a crying jag. But something told me to stay with Callie and not turn. And what sprang to my mind came out in fits and spurts, but it came out just the same.

"Callie, God didn't turn his back on you the past few days. I hope you don't think he abandoned you."

"It didn't feel like he was there," she said.

"He was. Right through the worst of it."

"Then why didn't he stop it? He could have."

"True. And in the end, he did."

"But it's too late. I can't change what happened to me. That man took something from me and I'll never get it back."

I took her hands in both of mine. "Darlin', what happened in those woods does not define the rest of your life. People might look at you and say, 'There's that woman that was taken to the cabin in Kentucky.' But God doesn't look at you that way. He says, 'There's my daughter. There's my spotless bride that my Son died for.' What happened out there does not have to follow you. You don't have to live in its shadow."

She nodded like she understood, but I don't think it sank into her soul. I wanted to find out more about her condition and how long she'd be in the hospital, but the doctor and her parents came in and I had to leave.

Sheriff Preston took me home. He said we were both lucky to be alive and I told him the same thing I'd told Callie. He smiled as if he knew I was going to say something like that.

Of course the station had gone off the air

again, but it didn't bother me. It was time for the preaching programs and I put one on and took a shower. I figured I would let people know more about Callie the next morning. As soon as my head hit the pillow for my nap, I was out and I didn't wake up until the whistling of the off-the-air alert.

I slept through most of the evening, waking up every four hours or so to keep the music going. Mr. Reynolds called and asked if I wanted him to bring me something to eat. "The missus is staying with Callie, but I can drop you by something if you want."

I thanked him and said I was okay. Then he told me what the doctors said. I could tell he was holding some stuff back because it was feminine and private, but reading between the lines, I knew that though she'd been through a lot, she was going to be okay. At least physically.

As I was drifting off to sleep in the wee hours of the next morning, I couldn't help but replay some of the things I'd said to Callie. The stuff about not having the past follow you. Not being defined by the things that happen to you. I realized those words were for her, but I didn't know then that they were every bit as much for me.

Dating is not something I had ever done

seriously. I have been in the company of women before, but to be honest, the pretty ones made me more nervous than anything, and it was just easier to go about my business and not deal with the heartache and letdown. When I think about all the money I've saved over the years on flowers and dinners and haircuts, it's a fair amount. Of course, I spent a lot on Heather and maybe that jaded me about romantic pursuits.

Callie and I sat together in church on Sundays, and some of the older ladies began to whisper. We decided not to let that deter us, but it was a powerful detriment to my worship, especially when Callie sat close and my neck turned red.

I'm not much one to go to the movies because I can't see spending so much money on something you could watch on video for a couple of dollars. If Callie had wanted to, I suppose I would have taken her, but I figured she'd agree with me. For our first "official" date, I took her to the most familiar eatery in Huntington — Stewarts. We ordered two mugs of root beer and six hot dogs and sat in the parking lot and ate off the tray they put in the window. We talked awhile about the radio station and her work and people at church. I felt like I could talk with her about anything, which is a good way to begin a relationship. Not that I had ever had one, but I'm just assuming that's true. If you can talk with somebody about anything, it means you'll probably do all right down the road.

There was a lull in the conversation and my thoughts turned toward more serious matters. Without much warning I just kind of blurted it out.

"I don't know what you're looking for in a man as far as financial stability." I unwrapped one of the napkins from around a hot dog.

She licked some chili sauce off her finger. "What do you think I'm looking for?"

"I suppose you deserve somebody who will put food on the table and pay the mortgage."

"That'd be a start," she said. "But that's not all I'm looking for."

"I can't buy you fancy clothes and a new car every other year."

She turned and looked in the back of the truck. "I didn't know there was anybody around here asking for that." Then she got quiet. "You think that's what I'm looking for?"

I shrugged and took another bite. I swear there is nothing as good as that sauce with the onions and the steamed bun.

Some sauce dribbled down on her blouse and she tried to wipe it off. It was a stain that would last, but she didn't seem to mind.

"Why don't we talk about you?" she said. "You're acting like I'm this hard-to-please woman. I'm not."

"I can tell by the company you keep."

She looked hurt.

"I meant me. I just think you deserve more, that's all. More than I can give."

"Why do you sell yourself so short, Billy? You've got a lot more to give than most men combined."

"You think so?"

"First off, you're handsome as the devil."

I took a pen from my shirt pocket and put a napkin on my knee. "Let me write this down. Sounds like it's gonna be good."

"You only have a few fears, going out in public being one. You love the Lord. You have integrity. You pay your bills on time, as far as I can tell. You loved your mother. And you know how to treat a girl. How did you know I liked these hot dogs so much?"

"I didn't; I just hoped you did."

"Now, you don't take such good care of yourself as far as the diabetes goes, and that could prove costly down the road. That would be the only thing I'd change right off."

"Now you're sounding like my mother." I took a swig of diet root beer and it stung my throat. My blood sugar was rising from the carbs in the bun, but I didn't care. "Would you like spending more time with me?"

"What does that mean?" Callie said.

"You know, going out and doing things together from time to time."

"Oh. I thought you meant something else. Sure. We should spend time getting to know each other better, but the jury is in as far as I'm concerned."

"About what?"

"About you."

"And what's the verdict?"

She just stared at me and smiled, and I focused on her left eye. There was something there that warmed me deep down, and I knew things were going to move fast from there.

I drove us through downtown and along the riverfront. We stopped at a Dairy Queen and sat on a bench and ate a banana split together.

"Aren't you going to dose for that?" she said.

I smiled at her and pulled out a needle. "You're not going to get squeamish on me, are you?"

She rolled her eyes. "I grew up on a farm, Billy. You can't do one thing that would surprise me."

I gave myself the shot through my pant leg and then ate half the banana split. She held her own with that plastic spoon and I halfway wished we'd have gotten two of them. I could count on one hand the number of times I had been to the riverfront like this. And I'd never been there to just sit and talk with somebody. I got a chill all over that could have been mistaken for the ice cream, but I knew it wasn't.

"Callie, I've always been able to look at some piece of equipment and figure out how it works. How to follow the signal path. If I can see a thing, I can build it or install it. A vision. But then I look at you and me and I don't have any idea how two people who are older would ever make it."

"You think you're too set in your ways?"

"I think I'm a weird buzzard, yeah. I work at my own house every day. Only time I go out is to take a walk or go to the store."

"You think I don't know that?"

"I think you don't know what you're getting into."

"Both of us are weird buzzards, Billy. You don't live alone this long and not get into some comfortable ruts. But that doesn't mean it can't work. Just means you can't see it."

That made a lot of sense. But what didn't was the rejection I was about to get.

# 24

I will not bore you with the details of what I did at the cabin and in the surrounding countryside the night of Callie's rescue. It is best left to your imagination. Suffice it to say that the forces of hell itself were arrayed against Billy and Callie, and it was invigorating to finally *do* something that aided them. That is the nature of evil — to inflict suffering on the innocent, to imprison and destroy. But the good news is that they don't have half the power they believe they possess. Greater is the One we serve, praise His name forever, than the enemy who seeks to kill and steal and destroy.

If Billy could have seen what he was up against in that lonely valley of despair, if the heavens could have scrolled back and his eyes been opened to the angelic realm, he would not have been able to achieve the task. In fact, at every step he was mocked and scorned by those lined against him, but he continued, step after agonizing step, as he climbed into that hellish cavern.

I've often wondered why the Almighty set things up this way, the humans unable to witness what we can clearly see. Perhaps this is why it is written that His ways are not their ways. He gives truth and at the same time protects and shields them from what they clearly cannot process. That is the wisdom of God, to allow them enough information to act but not enough to deter them out of abject fear. The human experiment is a process of one step that leads to other steps. You cannot rush them into the future or pull them from the past too quickly.

I do not pretend to understand the ways of the Maker or what He is attempting to achieve with the continual wooing and drawing. But the small advances of the Kingdom, one heart, one mind at a time, are how the great Creator works. In this way, the Kingdom is not a wave on the seashore but a holy structure that brick by brick advances in praise of the One who is building it. On the one hand it seems contrary to the nature of a holy God to allow sinful creatures into this divine plan, but on another wholly different plane, it is pure genius to thwart the enemy with such weakness.

As I did battle with wickedness and those

intent on ending Billy's life, I was also able to witness evil on the human plane, in the heart of the man called Clay. Clearly here was one who had lost himself to his lusts, his avarice, and what had become an insatiable need for control. In his darkened and confused mind, he began pursuit of what he believed would satisfy, abandoning himself to the vile and degrading things for which he longed.

Clay had disappeared from the face of the earth after that night. Though a massive hunt was launched, all it turned up was his diesel truck parked by a large bridge that spanned the Ohio River. Conjecture was that he had ended his life and that the waters of the river carried the only clues to his rampage.

Sheriff Preston spoke to Billy later about Clay and told him it was best to play it safe until they found his body. "You don't want that fellow coming back and looking for you."

But Clay didn't return. The discovery of three bodies in various forms of decomposition around the shack was, of course, grisly, and there were many attempts to sensationalize. Fortunately for Callie, her identity was kept covered and she avoided the glaring spotlight.

I did not concern myself with these stories; rather, I remained focused on the task of protecting and observing my charge. And while I was still interested in the things of the past and how they had affected Billy, I came to the decision that I should abandon my intense search for it, as it seemed to be clouding my view of his life. Instead I watched the blossoming of the relationship between Billy and Callie. What had been cradled and stored away in Billy's heart began to emerge. On the day Callie returned from the hospital, Billy met her and her parents at the trailer and showed them a space that had been cleaned immaculately, again, after Billy traded spots to the local Merry Maids. Callie was beside herself at the attention. After their first "date," Callie joined him for dinner on many evenings. Billy would actually order flowers, having traded several sixty-second spots for bouquets of roses and lilies and chamomile from the local florist.

But as time continued and Billy and Callie became used to the new relationship, Callie struggled. Instead of gratefulness at the new life she and Billy had begun, the enfolding of hearts, she exhibited angst toward him. Even when Billy proposed marriage — over the airwaves during a dedication on the morning program — there was a tinge of uncertainty to her acceptance. Of course those who listened and the people at their church were overjoyed at the prospects, but Callie pondered something deeper. A casual observer would say that it was a by-product of the abuse she received or the regret she had for allowing herself to be taken in by such evil. But there seemed to be more. She was concerned more about Billy and his life than about her own.

And to this end, Callie abruptly and with many tears broke off the engagement. Billy, beside himself with worry, pursued her, not as a child weeping for his mother, but as one who does not understand. She would not be dissuaded from her contention that something was holding them back. She suggested Billy meet with a counselor and gave him the name of a man who worked with her own counselor.

Billy approached him, and on the week of their first meeting, Billy's station began running a commercial about the man's marriage and family practice. Indeed, if one were to simply listen to the station's spot load, they would be able to tell much about the life of the proprietor.

I spent much time watching them both, at times following Callie home, other times accompanying her on her route. I had the sense that somehow the enemy had confounded her. But after she returned to work, she was just as productive and her devotion to her church knew no limits. Her sessions with her counselor were filled with tears and frank conversation. But this forward movement seemed to steel her, as if she were digging a sure foundation rather than rushing the construction of their lives. Perhaps it was coincidence, perhaps it was providence, but my seeming rest with the incongruities of Billy's past yielded a stirring in Callie's heart that equally sought answers.

There were tears in the night and anguish. There were sweat-producing nightmares and dark times, which I assumed were from the experiences in Kentucky. And then, on a cloudy morning in late spring, when the earth was full of new life and almost ready to burst, she drove to the counselor's office and sat in the parking lot writing a note. She dropped it in the slot on the man's door and drove away. Billy would arrive an hour later.

I have heard the stories of the Almighty working on people, changing them drastically, moving in hearts and melting the hardness and anger and bitterness and dross away. I was not prepared for what I was about to witness.

# 25

"She won't tell me what's wrong," I said to my counselor. This was another counselor at the same place Callie went every week. "She talks to me, but when I try to get close, there's something between us. I feel we were made for each other in a lot of ways. That we were cut from the same cloth."

"And that took you a while to figure out," he said.

"Yes, sir, it did. I can't believe I was blind to it for so long. I want more than anything for us to be together, but she won't tell me what I need to do to make that happen."

"Maybe it's not about her," the counselor said.

"What do you mean?"

"From what I can tell, she's making progress in her therapy. It's important for her long-term health to heal from the wounds inside, what drove her to look for someone to fill what was missing. But she's dealing with those ghosts and putting them to rest."

"How would you know she's making progress?"

"A conversation or two we had. She's interested in the process we're going through here, Billy. She really loves you. She wants this to work out as much as you do. Maybe more."

"I thought what we talked about was supposed to be between you and me. You said it was confidential."

"It is. I've never discussed anything you've said here. But I find it helpful to get other insights on your life when possible. And it hasn't been anything I scheduled. I just saw her in the waiting room one day and another day she stopped by the office to talk. She says glowing things about you. I wish I lived closer to Dogwood so I could hear your station."

My cheeks were always kind of red anytime I walked into that office. Being with a counselor was the last thing I thought would ever happen to me. But there was a measure of comfort in sharing some of the things I'd locked up inside. Family stuff. The flood. Some of the heartache.

"If she loves me so much, why won't she

marry me? Is it my hygiene?"

He smiled. "I believe she wants to marry you. She's committed to you. But she thinks there are some old wounds of yours that may not have been dealt with. That need to heal before the two of you can become one."

"And you agree with her."

"I think every person on earth has baggage they're carrying around that would be better left at the side of the road. The problem is, we don't leave it behind; we carry it."

"I've told you everything I can think of. The flood, the death of my father, my mother, my brother — I could go into more detail if you want, but —"

He held up a hand. "No, you've been very forthright with me and I appreciate it. Your openness and candor speak well of you. I don't think it's that you're afraid to deal with some things in the past; it's more a question of whether or not you see them as important. As shaping you."

"I'm a simple man," I said. "I live one day to the next and take whatever I'm given and praise the Lord for it. I try not to look back because if you look back, the row you're plowing gets crooked. I don't know what shaping and all this stuff about the past have to do with getting married."

He leaned back, picking up a card from his desk. "I found this on the floor of my office this morning. It's a note from Callie."

"What's it say?"

He handed it to me. It was Callie's writing on a thank-you note that I had gotten her from Walmart right after she came home and people started bringing food and whatnot. Her writing had changed from the diary and was now a kind of elegant scratching.

Dear Dr. Maynard,

I think there is something about a pastor Billy once knew that has affected him. I'm just starting to put it together. Ask him about Vernon Turley. I think something happened with him but I don't know what.

Sincerely,
Callie Reynolds

I handed the card back to him. My cheeks were on fire and it felt like the air had been sucked out of the room, like the canary was teetering in the cage at the bottom of the mine.

"What is it, Billy?" he said. "What are you thinking?"

I shook my head. "I don't know."

"Not a good answer. Tell me what you're feeling."

"Trapped."

"Okay. Why do you feel trapped?"

"I don't know." I wrung my hands. "Why couldn't she just say that to my face?"

"Would you have talked about it with her?"

"I don't know. Maybe. I guess I just don't like other people messing with what we're trying to do. There's something not right about it."

"You're worried about what's right? But the person trying to influence this is Callie. The woman you say you love."

"What do you mean, 'say you love'? I do love her. She's the one who doesn't love me."

"I don't think that's true. Sometimes the people who love us have to say hard things. Get us to talk about what's holding us back. They can see the truth because they're not as close to it as we are."

I took in a short breath and stared at the floor. There was a spot on the carpet where the installers hadn't fixed a seam properly.

"If she were here right now, asking you what happened, what would you tell her about this pastor?" the counselor said. "Was he a mentor to you?"

I nodded. "He took an interest in me. And he let me be part of his music group."

"What did you do with the group?"

"We rode around and played in churches. County fairs and anybody that would invite us."

"You played the mandolin."

"Yes, sir."

"And from what I hear, you were pretty good."

"I tried hard."

"Now, you traveled with this group and played your music, but at some point you put that aside. You even sold the mandolin your father gave you."

"I was running low on money and I needed something for the station."

"But don't you think it was a little drastic to sell the very instrument you had perfected?"

"Nobody perfects the mandolin. There's always mystery to it. Always more to learn and more to get out of it."

"Which makes it hard for me to understand why you would sell it, particularly if it had sentimental value."

I stood up and moved to the window, my hands deep in my pockets. There was something building down inside, bubbling up. I could feel it like pressure against a dam, the black water growing and rising to the top. "I don't see what this has to do with anything. I sold a mandolin. It's not the end of the world."

"Billy, you said that Callie wouldn't tell you what you needed to do in order for you two to get married. Is that right?"

"Yeah."

"Well, if telling me about this event or series of events with this mentor would help you, why wouldn't you want to discuss it? If you knew it could lead to getting together, would you talk about it then?"

I glanced back at him and the look on my face must have given away something. "Is that what love really is? Dragging the past up before you like roadkill? If it is, I don't want anything to do with it."

I turned to the window again. It was one of those West Virginia days with the mist and foggy dew mixing together. Usually it would burn off by now, but the calm wind and the humidity made it hang over the roadway like a ghost. I stood there awhile, swaying a little, getting up the nerve. He sure wasn't in a hurry. He just sat and watched me.

"I don't remember a whole lot of it. It was a long time ago."

"Why don't you tell me what you do

remember?"

A car passed along the road and I watched it round the curve and disappear.

Finally he said, "What are you thinking, Billy?"

I just let that hang there as the clock ticked. "I didn't expect this to be easy, but I didn't expect it to be this hard, either."

"What's hard about it?"

"Remembering. Going back through old stuff. Aren't we supposed to press on toward the mark of the high calling? Aren't we supposed to leave the past behind? You can't drive looking in the rearview mirror."

"True, you shouldn't focus your whole life on history, but if you're dragging a ball and chain, stopping and cutting it off will give you a measure of freedom you've probably never felt. If you don't do it, at some point you'll have to amputate the leg. Or just stop altogether."

I crossed my arms and leaned back against the window frame. He leaned forward with his hands folded in front of him. His voice was soft but firm.

"There's freedom here, Billy. I know it doesn't feel like that right now, but it's available. You don't have to walk around with the weight you have pressing you down. But you have to want freedom. You have to want

394

to be done with the ball and chain."

"It hurts," I said, some emotion there and surprising me. It always caught me off guard. "I thought you were supposed to make me feel better. Talking about it doesn't feel good at all."

He shook his head. "I'm sure it does hurt, and I'm sorry for that pain. But pain is sometimes a gift. And my job is not to make you feel better. In fact, part of why I'm here is not to make you feel good or bad, but to help you *feel*."

"You don't think I feel anything?"

"When you talk about the painful things that happened with your parents — like finding your father in bed that day or what happened with your mother — it almost sounds like it's happening to somebody else. The only time I've seen you weep is when you talked about Rogers."

"You think it's bad to care for an animal?"

"Not at all. But when you have trouble feeling something deep down for the people in your life, it shows me there is something going on inside. Something 'out of whack,' as you say."

I didn't respond, but I could see the sense in what he was telling me. I'd always thought that counselors like this were just in it for the money, but there was something about his demeanor that showed me he really cared.

"Let me put it this way," he continued. "I don't play a musical instrument. I tried when I was young and failed miserably. But my wife plays the piano. And she's pretty good. She says there are two ways to play. One way is that you look at the notes and press your hands down at the right time and you go from beginning to end and try not to make any mistakes. You can get pretty good playing that way. But the other way makes the player part of the music. He's present with all of the others, the strings and the woodwinds and the percussion. Or he might just be playing with a singer. Doesn't matter. She says music really happens when the notes become part of you and you express them not just by following them on a line, but playing them from someplace deep inside. From the heart. Does that make sense?"

I nodded.

"The feeling you have deep inside you is not your enemy. It helps tap into what's real. That's what Callie is calling you to. Not a cheap imitation, but all that Billy Allman can be."

"Are you saying that everything I've done with my life doesn't count for anything because I've been playing from sheet music?"

He laughed. "Not at all. What I'm saying is, until you deal with what's on the back shelf of your heart, you'll be spinning your wheels with Callie and with yourself."

"Why can't we just throw the back shelf out?"

"Doesn't work that way. You can't throw out the truth. Good or bad, it will affect you."

"So I won't be able to get things right with Callie until . . . what? What do I do?"

He lowered his head, like he needed to correct me. "Callie doesn't want to change you so that you become her knight in shining armor. She's got just as much baggage, Billy. This is not about you finding a destination and suddenly 'arriving,' so that now you're acceptable to the rest of society or me or Callie or anybody else. This is about you and freedom. And there's no way to get to that without wading through some difficult stuff. You've heard the saying that sometimes things have to get worse before they get better?"

"Yeah, I've heard it. I've lived it too."

He chuckled. "I know you have. I think it'll be worth it to go through this. So why don't you tell me about him? Tell me what happened with this pastor."

I took a deep breath. Songs and images returned. The other guys in the band. Laughter. Traveling late at night in the van with everybody asleep. Setting up and tearing down in spaces so tight sometimes it felt like there wasn't even room to hold the mandolin in front of me. A feeling of belonging. Coming home late on a Saturday night and getting a little sleep before church. And then the darkness. The impenetrable darkness.

My counselor sat and waited, watching me, as if there was no other thing more important in the world. Haltingly, faltering, I began.

"He gave me a chance to do what I wanted, which was to play my songs. He said I had real talent. And he came alongside me at a time when I'd lost my daddy. Just kind of picked me up out of the gutter and let me stand on that stage."

"And he was also a spiritual influence on you."

"I reckon. He had been music minister at his church for a while. But to be honest, other than the songs we sang, there wasn't much spiritual to it. He knew some verses and could spout them off and make people say, 'Amen,' but there's a difference in somebody preaching what they've read and preaching what they've lived. Just like the music you talked about."

"Exactly. But still, you probably felt a certain affinity for him because he had affirmed you, he was older and was at least moderately successful in music, and you respected him. He was kind to you. He was a father figure."

"Yeah, that's all true. I wanted to make him happy. Which made it all the harder."

"Made what harder?"

"After what happened, I didn't want to believe he was a bad person. I wanted him to think well of me."

"And what happened?"

I sat in the leather chair. I always felt like I was somewhere I didn't belong coming into his office. His chair felt like sitting in heaven itself, and the smell of the place was like sniffing a cow factory, the leather was so strong. The carpet was thick and green, and there was this painting on the back wall of dogs on the hunt and some fellows behind them with guns riding on horseback. I wondered if he had to spray air freshener in there after I left. Still, he didn't treat me as any less than an honored guest, which made it hard not to go back the next week when it was time.

"Maybe you hit on the reason why what happened was so hard," I said. "I put my trust in him. It wasn't just that he pretended to care about me; it was the mix of the Christian stuff that confused me. Abuse is hard coming from a mean man, like what Clay did to Callie, but it's even harder when it comes from somebody who is supposed to have your best interests at heart. He bought me clothes and things I didn't have. He told me I was good at what I did. I'd never had that before. And I felt a certain obligation to him."

The counselor just sat there, looking at me. Finally he said, "What was it like, playing with the group?"

"There was an excitement every time we practiced. I couldn't wait for rehearsals. Sometimes I'd get a ride to his church after school and he'd take me to his house. He'd feed me supper and let me listen to their songs and I'd learn them. He said I was a quick study, a fast learner, and that made me want to learn them faster."

"So you were with older people who respected your talent. For the first time you felt like you fit in with other people and you contributed to the group."

I nodded.

"You said *abuse*," he said. "What did you

mean by that?"

"The things he did. Stuff that didn't make sense. He took this pornographic magazine from a kid in Sunday school and had it in his desk. At least that's what he said. He gave it to me before practice one night. Just handed it over and said, 'Here, take this.' I'd never seen anything like that."

"You know what he was doing, don't you? I mean, you know now, looking back."

"No."

"He was setting you up. That's a classic move by a predator. Let me guess. When he had you alone at his house, he asked if he could take pictures of you."

I stared at the man. "You've heard of this kind of thing before?"

"I hear about it just about every day in one form or another. What did he do?"

"I told you he gave me clothes. They were outfits that we wore onstage. Some of them looked funny, but they were better than what I had to wear. Well, one day he gave me this skimpy-looking underwear and told me to try it on. Said it gave more support or something. I went in the bathroom and tried it on and came out and said it fit fine. He said to let him see. I didn't know what he meant and he said, 'Put it on and come out and let me see.' So I went in and changed again."

"Now let me stop you," the counselor said. "Here's another guess. There was this funny feeling down inside the pit of your stomach that something about this wasn't right. Something didn't make sense."

"Yeah, I thought it was creepy, but then when I was standing there in the bathroom and thinking . . ."

"Thinking *you* were the one who was wrong for thinking bad about him. You pushed the feeling down. Tried to explain it away. This was a man who cared about you. A man you trusted. You're bad if you question his motives."

I nodded. "You're good at this."

"No, I'm not good; I've just heard it before. We push down the God-given feelings that something isn't right and we go along because we're under the 'spell' of the other person. So what happened when you came out of the bathroom?"

My face got red again. "He was standing there in his underwear himself. With a camera. At first I kind of laughed at what was happening because I thought he was just having fun, but he wasn't laughing. He just stared at me."

"Okay, here's another guess," he said. "Nothing more happened that day. You stood there in your underwear for a few minutes; then you got dressed, his wife came home, and you had dinner like nothing had happened."

"That's right. That's exactly what happened. But why? I've thought on it over the years and I don't have the foggiest idea why."

"He was taking you step by step through the process of preparation. *Grooming* is another term. He just took you up one rung of the ladder at a time until when it came time to get off, you were too high up and he led you up one more rung."

"I can see that."

There was an uncomfortable silence between us and I knew he was waiting to hear what happened next. Instead, he spoke again.

"You know, Billy, after all that happened in your life, you could have turned your back on the church, your faith, God. People who have seen what you've seen often decide God isn't there, or that if he is there, he's so mean you don't want anything to do with him. You seemed to run toward God. Why didn't you turn away?"

"I've known since I was young that there are people who just play at religion. They're in it for the power or the money or the good feeling. I think that's what made me want the real thing. I didn't want to settle for what he had."

"So in a sense, this man gave you a gift. Of knowing you didn't want a counterfeit faith."

"In a weird kind of way, I guess you're right. I don't mind telling you I wish I didn't have to go through it, though."

"You don't have to be ashamed of the things in your past that bother you, Billy. Jesus died for the sins you've committed and he can take away the effect of the sins committed against you. The people with a seared conscience don't remember the bad things they've done. That these things keep coming up for you, and I assume they do, is proof not that you're a bad person but that you have a conscience and a desire to live a holy life."

"It doesn't make sense that something can hang on to your soul for so long."

He gave me a sad smile. "What happened, Billy? What did Vernon do to you?"

I took one of the little water bottles he had set out for me and took a swig. "We were on a longer trip. He'd made arrangements not to be at his church on Sunday. We left Friday afternoon and played a church, then had a fair on Saturday, so we drove all night Friday after the show and then checked into a hotel on Saturday afternoon and rested, then went to the fair. That went until late in the evening and it was almost midnight before we got back to the hotel. The other guys stayed in two other rooms and I was alone with him."

"Did that seem weird to you or any of the others?"

I shrugged. "I don't recall that anybody else made a fuss about it. I was just so tired I wanted to go to bed. But he locked the door and turned on the television to one of the movie channels. It was not very family friendly, if you know what I mean.

"He was in the shower, and when he came out, he stood there next to the TV, drying his back and then his hair. I tried not to look, but he kind of strutted around and then sat down on his bed and laid back. I didn't know what to do, to get up and run out of there or pretend I was asleep. To tell you the truth, I kind of wished I was blind.

"Pretty soon he turned down the TV. He said, 'Billy, you're probably wondering what's going on. I've always been a bit of an exhibitionist. Some people think the naked body is a bad thing, but I don't. Male or female, there's a beauty to it because God

405

has made us in his image. Do you believe that?'

"I said that I did. And then he told me to get up from the bed. And I've gone over this a thousand times in my mind and wondered what would have happened if I'd have just run and knocked on the next door. But I didn't."

"Of course you didn't," the counselor said. "He had done his work well. You were tired, confused, and you were more afraid of what he thought than anything. If you had refused his advances, you would have cast judgment on him. You didn't want to do that."

"No, sir, to my shame, I didn't."

"Billy, you were young. He had control over you. You were in a vulnerable position. You wanted to please him. This wasn't your fault."

"I know that in my head. But there's something about it that I still think I could have stopped."

"From what you've just described, this man should have gone to jail. Even if things stopped right there."

"They didn't."

"I'm sure they didn't."

"And I've lived with the regret all these years."

"You've lived with what he did to you. You've lived with the choices he made. Now the choice is yours whether that's going to keep you from freedom."

"You really think there's such a thing as freedom for somebody who's lived with this so long?"

He smiled. "I know it for a fact. You'd be surprised at the number of people who've been freed from things like this. Do you want to tell me the rest?"

"Do I have to?"

"No, but I think you already see how freer you feel in the telling."

He was right. I was surprised at how much better I felt with the little I had already said. Something was happening inside with each new revelation, with every little instance of violation.

Some people think that when you begin telling the stories, it's like a dam breaking and everything behind it just spills out and keeps flowing until the lake of memory is dry. It's not that way at all. It's more like poking and prodding at a backup along a creek. You have to pull at some sticks here and a jumble of leaves and trash over there and get the water flowing, and pretty soon there's something else that sticks and you have to work on that awhile.

He asked questions and just listened as I told him what had happened in the hotel rooms and at the man's house and even at the church where we practiced. When I was done, I felt like I had run a marathon. We'd gone for two hours instead of one and we probably could have gone another hour. He looked at his schedule book and said he had somebody waiting.

"We've made a lot of progress today, but I have to ask you one more thing. What caused you to leave the group?"

I thought back to those awful days. "When I played the mandolin, I could make it sing. I could just make it light on fire. It was how I got away from what was eating at me every time we'd go on the road. A little kid came up after one of our concerts and asked me to give him my autograph. That had happened before, but this time the kid had one of those little pencils they put behind the pews and he opened up his Bible to the front page. I didn't feel worthy to sign one of the offering envelopes, let alone his Bible. I think that was the last straw. That and the bad feeling I had in the pit of my stomach every time the phone would ring and it would be Vernon calling another practice or telling me about another concert he had lined up. I told him I couldn't do it any-more."

"Did he push back? Did he ask you again?"

"Yeah. And my mama pushed me to go with him, too. But after I made up my mind, I was done. After a few weeks he stopped calling and I think he knew."

"That speaks well of you. That you had the strength to break free from that is great. Not everyone could do that." He shook his head. "I'm proud of you, Billy. I think your mother and father would be proud of you too. I'm sorry they weren't able to be there for you through the years."

A mist came to my eyes. I could remember my mother saying that my daddy would be proud of me, but I'd never heard those words from him.

"So what do I do now?" I said. "Do I make contact? Do I try to talk to him?"

"Do you want to?"

"Part of me does. Wants him to know what he did was wrong. And that what happened is not okay. It caused a good deal of hurt."

He nodded. "I think it's a good idea. I think it's part of the freedom you're looking for. You tell him the truth. You say what you know is true and let the chips fall."

"But what's the point? If he owns up to it

and apologizes, I have an apology. And if he says I'm crazy and denies everything, it makes it more painful. Like he's sticking a knife in my back and turning it."

"There's always a risk in telling the truth, Billy. You can't control how anybody responds. But it's always better to get this stuff into the light."

Something moved over me like a cloud and stayed there. Thoughts. Repercussions. "What about Callie?"

"What about her?" he said.

"What's she going to think of me if I tell her this?"

"You think this revelation would cause her to stop loving you? Let me ask you this. Do you love her after what she's been through?"

"Of course. It doesn't make any difference."

"Then why should it make a difference to her what happened years ago? What you went through was every bit as hard as what she went through. Maybe harder."

"That can't be true. I made the choice to go back."

"Callie had an evil man do despicable things to her. You had somebody you trusted use you. He was in a place of authority over you and he violated you. Callie has to work through a lot of things, no question about

410

that. But you have to dig through that coal mine that's been covered over by years of living and hoping it wouldn't come back to haunt you. Your work is just as hard."

"I hadn't thought about it that way."

He leaned closer. "Just know that I'll be behind you. And so will Callie."

# 26

The next week I brought the letter I had written, all four pages front and back on a yellow legal pad. I hadn't talked with Callie about it because I knew this was something I had to do myself. I was doing this for me and not somebody else, but I knew when it was over, things would probably be different for Callie and me. I didn't know that for a fact but I hoped it.

I told my counselor I wasn't much for the written word, that I was mostly a spoken-word man, but when he finished reading it, he had a big grin on his face as he folded it and put it in the envelope.

"I wouldn't change a word, Billy," he said as he handed the envelope back. "But I do disagree with one thing."

"What's that?"

"You said you're not a man of the written word. That's a beautifully written letter. You were specific and descriptive — I don't know how he could argue with anything you've put in there. And it's clear you want the truth out in the open. How do you feel about it?"

"Pretty good, I guess. I wrote it five times. I'd wake up in the middle of the night with something new to put down, some memory that came up. I don't know if I got it right or not."

"Remember, it's not about getting it right. It's about saying what's true."

"Okay."

"Now, make a copy of the whole thing," he said. "He's going to burn it."

"You think so?"

"He's not going to want anybody to see this. He's going to ask you if you intend to press charges."

"Could I?"

"You know all those cases with the Catholic priests. They settled out of court years later, with the grown-up altar boys."

"I don't want a penny of his money."

"What do you want?"

"I want him to say he was wrong. That he's sorry."

"You may not get that."

"But it's worth a shot, right?"

"It's worth following your heart, Billy. And the truth is always worth it."

■ ■ ■ ■

I sent the letter by registered mail that day. Three days later, late in the afternoon, I took a phone call that had nothing but silence on the other end. I said hello two times and then heard the voice that gave me the shivers.

"Billy Allman. It's Vernon Turley."

I paused. "I figured I'd be hearing from you. You got my letter."

"I did. Do you want to get together and talk about this?"

I took a deep breath. "Yeah, I do."

He mentioned a restaurant that was located between him and Dogwood, and I said I'd be there the next evening. That night I didn't sleep, and all the next day I kept accusing myself of doing something stupid. He wasn't that bad. I was blowing things out of proportion. Everybody goes through hard stuff. God can use even the negative.

But the voice of my counselor kept coming back. This was not some little thing. It was life-altering. It had affected every part of me. And I deserved an apology. If nothing else, I was going to get that from him.

■ ■ ■ ■

The Western Steer sits on a little hill just off Interstate 64, a nondescript brick building with a view of passing cars and the changing colors of trees. Wooden tables and chairs rest on faded carpet, and the servers all look like they know they're not going to get much of a tip from folks who wander like cattle through the double doors.

It was cloudy and menacing when I walked in a half hour early. The wind was picking up and turning the leaves skyward.

The lady at the front asked how many were in my party and showed me to a table near the front. I asked if it would be possible to get a booth in the back for a little more privacy and she took me back near the men's restroom. After she left, I caught up with her and told her I'd changed my mind and that the first table she showed me would be a lot better. She rolled her eyes and said, "Suit yourself."

I sat with my back to the front door and sipped a glass of water. My hand shook as I drank it, preparing what I was going to say and wondering what he was going to say. Vernon was the kind of guy who took over a room when he walked in, and I wanted to be in control of the situation.

A few people sat down around me, and when the server asked what I would like, I told her I'd order a salad but I wouldn't take it until the person I was meeting came. The salad was the cheapest thing on the menu. I had made up my mind that there was no way he was going to pay for my meal.

The door opened behind me and I swear I felt his presence. It was as if Count Dracula had swooped down. I stared straight ahead, at the dusty elephant ear in the corner near the bathroom, waiting. He came up behind me and cleared his throat.

"Billy?"

I turned my head slightly, not to look at him but to acknowledge his presence. "Vernon."

He took off his jacket and held it. Then he snapped his fingers to get the attention of the server. "Could we have a booth back there, please?"

The woman came fast.

"No," I said.

He looked down at me, shocked. "Billy, I'd feel more comfortable back there."

"I'm sure you would. I'm good here."

He lowered his voice. "This conversation will be private."

The lady had picked up his menu and was

holding it, waiting for us to follow.

"I'm sitting here. If you want to sit back there and yell across the dining room, that's your choice. I'll be here."

He stood there a minute and I just stared at the water. Finally he took the menu back, placed his jacket on the chair beside me, and sat with elegance. The greatest dignitaries of the world did not have the air that Vernon Turley had. The server walked away and then returned with his glass of water and asked if he would like something else to drink or if he was ready to order.

"Have you ordered?" he asked me.

I nodded.

"I'll have the ten-ounce rib eye with baked potato, no butter or sour cream, medium well. Tossed salad with oil and vinegar on the side." He was finally watching his waistline. While we were on the road, he would snack or have sodas with the rest of us.

He asked about my station and the land and all kinds of things to make small talk, but I tried to show him I wasn't interested in making this more comfortable for him. He pulled the letter from his jacket pocket and placed it on the table.

"So . . . ," he said softly. "What are your intentions?"

My counselor's words came back to me and I stifled a smile. "You read the letter?"

His eyes showed fear like a cornered animal. Part of me felt sorry for him and I pushed that away.

"I did. It was quite a shock. I had no idea you could be this way."

I raised my eyebrows. "*I* could be this way? And what way is that?"

"It would have been more helpful if you would have shown some gratitude for the opportunities I gave you. My wife asked me about the letter. She wonders why you left the group. What happened to you."

"Why don't you let her read it? That would sure clear things up fast, don't you think?"

His eyes narrowed and the muscles in his face tightened. "Because it's not true. Why are you trying to destroy me?"

"I'm not trying to destroy you."

"Do you know what this kind of accusation could do to me? my reputation?"

An older lady wobbled up to the table from behind him and pecked him on the shoulder. "You're Vernon Turley, aren't you?"

He pushed back and smiled, then stood. "Yes, I am."

"I have all your recordings. They mean so

much, especially since I lost my husband. The Lord has worked through you, and I just wanted you to know that."

He took her hand in both of his and looked down at her bent form. It was a surreal moment, considering what was in the letter in front of him. The server came with my salad, and the lady thanked him again, almost in tears, and toddled back to her booth where two other geriatric women sat. They talked loud enough for us to hear what a "blessing" Vernon's ministry had been.

I bowed my head and said a silent prayer of thanks and of petition for the strength to say what I was about to say. After a bite of salad, I said, "Were there others?"

He looked up at me and now his eyes were hollow. "What do you mean?"

"You know what I mean. What you did to me . . . did it happen to anybody else?"

He looked at my chest closely and it was only later that I figured out he was wondering if I was recording the whole thing. That made me wish I was.

"Billy, I don't know what drove you to write such things in this letter. I don't know why you would make such vile accusations —"

"Because it's true. Every word of it and

you know it. And if you're going to sit there and tell me it's not, this dinner is over."

I picked up my napkin, pushed back the chair, and reached for my wallet. He reached out for my arm and I pulled away.

"Now don't do anything rash; just stay here." He ran a hand through his hair and cautiously looked around to see if anyone had noticed the tussle. "This is on me, by the way."

"No, it's not," I said. "You're not going to pay for your sins with an eight-dollar salad."

"I'm not trying to pay for sins. I'm offering this meal as a gift, as a way of saying I'm sorry you feel so bad about what happened. And if there's some other way I can repay you, I will."

I picked up a radish and popped it into my mouth. "You're sorry I feel so bad? That's kind of like the coal company telling our family they were sorry it rained so much. What you did was no act of God, Pastor."

"Please, keep your voice down." He said it with his hands out over the table as if he were conducting a symphony.

"I'm not keeping my voice down. And I'm not raising it either. If we were talking about your music career or the latest ball scores, this is the level we'd be talking at. So if you don't like it, I'll just leave."

"No, please, Billy. Let's be civil. I'm sure we can come to an understanding."

"Well, it's going to be a little difficult to come to an understanding when you don't even admit to doing what I detailed in that letter. And there can't be any middle ground. Either I am lying through my teeth in there, I'm a fruitcake who has no idea what he's talking about, or I'm telling the truth. Tell me straight out right now which of those three things you think is happening."

He took a bite of salad and wiped his mouth with his napkin. "It's not so cut-and-dried as that, Billy. I believe this is the way you remember it and I'm sorry. I truly am. To think that I hurt you in some way is quite painful. I don't know how to say how sorry I am you feel this way. But there are different viewpoints, different perspectives."

I put down my fork. "This is not about perspectives. It's not about anything but telling the truth about what happened. You can tap-dance around this by saying how sorry you are about my feelings, but the fact remains that what I put in here is the truth. And I want you to admit it."

He grabbed the letter as if I was going to snatch it from him. "I don't remember that time the way you do; I'll put it that way."

"Really? And how do you remember it? That we were in that hotel room together watching CNN and drinking root beer?" I leaned forward. "And the morning after the first time, we walked into a church sanctuary and you gave your best performance. You even cried through the reciting of the verses you memorized."

He shut his eyes and shook his head. Then he leaned forward and forced himself to speak in low tones. "Billy, you know I'm not like everybody else. I'm quirky. I might even seem weird to others. But that's what fuels the creativity and the musicality. It's what gets me out there in front of people. You knew that when you signed on for the ride. Am I an exhibitionist? Yes. When I go to bed, I sleep without clothes. Does that make me a pervert? If you were so offended by it or hurt, why did you keep coming out on the road with us? There was nobody holding a gun to your head."

"So it was my fault."

"No, you've got this all wrong. It's nobody's fault."

"You're right that going to bed without any clothes on doesn't make you a pervert. But what I wrote in that letter, if it's true, does. Now I'll ask you again. Was I the only one, or were there others?"

"Of course not. And I don't think that what happened to you — I mean, I can see from your perspective how you might have been offended by some of my tastes in what to watch on TV. I should have been more sensitive to that —"

"More sensitive?" I said, raising my voice. "I don't believe you."

"Please, please," he said, holding out his hands again.

I felt a burst of adrenaline rush through my body and I leaned forward over my forgotten salad. "I could handle it if you just pranced around in your birthday suit. I could handle it if you sang about God's love and forgiveness and watched dirty movies with your wife. And I could handle it if you sat here tonight and said you regret every-thing that happened and that you're sorry and you'd do anything to make up for it. But what I can't stand is having you sit here and say it was a difference in perspective or that you have a special personality and we all need to bow to your genius. What you did was wrong. And what I remember is not just my perspective; it really happened. I've got the scars up here to prove it." I pointed to my head.

His face was red and tight. "What do you

want? I've offered you money to keep your little radio venture going, but you refused."

I shut my own eyes now and shook my head. "That's what you think this is about. And don't call it my little radio station. It may be small potatoes to you, but it's a lot more than that to me."

"I didn't mean to offend you. I think it's wonderful what you've done with your life, especially with all the strikes against you. I just don't understand why you're bringing this up after all this time. I'm not your enemy. I've always had your best interests at heart —"

"Stop," I said. I wasn't shouting anymore, just resolved. And the people around us were getting quiet. Vernon could sense it too. He looked like a cornered rat. "You're going to sit there and listen to me. I'm going to tell you exactly what happened with all of the details. I don't spend one night trying to fall asleep that I don't think about what you did and have to work it through again."

"Why don't we go outside and continue this?"

"No," I said. "We'll stay right here and you'll listen to every word."

"Okay," he said, nodding and pushing his own plate back. Folding his hands, he said,

424

"Maybe I did do some things to you that I shouldn't have. I'm sorry. If I thought for a minute you didn't want me to, I would have stopped."

"Don't put this on me!" I yelled, slamming my fist on the table. The silverware rattled. People stared now, but I had a laser beam focused on him. "If you're sorry about what you did, just leave it at that. Don't blame me. I was a teenager. I was vulnerable. I'd lost my daddy. I looked up to you and you took that trust and you used me."

"You're right; you're right," he said, reaching for his forehead to rub it and run a hand through his hair again. "I'm sorry. Period."

A portly man wearing a sweater vest came up to the table and knelt down. "Gentlemen, is there a problem I can help with?"

"No, we're fine," Vernon said. "If I could have the check and maybe wrap this up in a doggie bag. Billy, do you want your salad saved?"

The man looked at me and something in his eyes led me to believe he was a kind soul trying to understand, but at the same time trying to keep his restaurant quiet.

"I'm finished," I said, pulling out a ten-dollar bill and putting it beside my knife and fork.

"I'm taking care of this," Vernon said.

I handed the bill to the manager. "This is for my salad and the tip. Will you make sure she gets it?"

He nodded.

It was pouring when I walked through the front door, one of those West Virginia gushers that fills the gutters in a minute or two. I stopped for a minute to cover my head with my hood and somebody grabbed me by the arm.

"If it's all right with you, I'm going to shred the letter," Vernon said. "Nobody else needs to know about this, don't you agree?"

I turned and looked at him. He used to seem a lot taller, but with the years he had become bent at the shoulders and seemed to creep closer to the ground. His face was pleading, asking something of me rather than revealing, but even in the asking he was revealing.

"I've lived with the truth of what you did every day of my life, Vernon. What you do with the letter is your business. What I do with the truth is mine."

I walked into the rain and he called after me. "Billy, I need to know. What are your intentions?"

I splashed through the parking lot and the running water across the yellow parking lines. He called again but I didn't turn around. When I got in the truck and started it up, he was at the cashier's station. I pulled through the standing water and down the hill to the stoplight.

Lost in thought, rubbing at the fog on the windshield and trying to peer through the rain streaks, my soul hydroplaning on the back roads of memory, the mesmerizing rhythm of the wiper blades carrying a beat of their own, I drove into the darkness, winding my way toward Dogwood. Like some magnet was pulling me, I wound up in Callie's driveway. I turned off the truck and just sat there with the lights on.

I've spent my whole life looking through the water to hear the music and shut out the pain. Right then, I saw through the torrent. Like when Moses parted the Red Sea, the truth came to me through the downpour. The hurt and pain and everything that trapped me in the little world I'd built surfaced and I decided not to push it away. I'd been running in place trying to get away from myself, not making headway, holding people at a distance, feeling comfortable behind a microphone, talking to people like they were friends when I really didn't know them and they didn't know me. No wonder I felt more comfortable with machines, old radios, and a soldering iron. No wonder I clung to the thought of a girl from years ago and the illusions.

It was like waking up from some long dream with drops of water running down my face, tears and rain mingled down. I was cold and soaked to the bone standing there by the truck, my hair plastered to my head. I didn't remember getting out, but I knew I would never forget what it felt like to finally *feel*. I smelled the wet earth and the worms struggling up through the sod and the muskrats in the holes by the creek. I heard the lonesome dove crying from some dry place for its mate. And my heart beating. And the sting of wet air in my lungs. A deep sadness and joy running through my veins with each pump of the heart. The trickling of water finding its own level.

The door opened and Callie peered into the darkness. She switched on the front porch lights and only one of them worked, but it was enough for her to recognize me. She came out in her bare feet with an umbrella held up high.

"Billy, what are you doing out here?"

Her voice was like an answer to prayer.

She looked close at my face, her feet squishing through the wet grass and mud. There was no way she could have distinguished the rain from the tears, but I guess if you love somebody, you can look into the eyes and see further down into the well-spring of life.

"What is it?" she said. "Are you going low?"

I gave her a sad smile and shook my head.

"Then what's the matter?"

"I think I see now. What you were talking about. The dam over my heart. It's broke. And I can feel everything washing away. Everything in the world."

Her eyes went back and forth over my face. "Oh, Billy," she said, and the kindness in her voice touched deep and the logjam burst. She gathered me in and hugged me tight through all the wet and cold, then took me into her trailer and made me take off my jacket and shirt and handed me a towel that I draped over me. The water just flowed from some cistern of the heart, like it had been trapped my whole life. I put my head down on her kitchen table and let it come, and she stood behind me and rubbed my back, crying herself.

"It's all right. Just let it come on out."

"I don't mean to be this way," I said through the tears.

"This is you, Billy Allman. I don't want anything else."

"Do you mean that?" I said, raising the

429

towel and looking up at her.

It was her turn for the red eyes and puckered chin. She sat down and put her forehead on my back and just let go. "I mean it, Billy. I mean it with all my heart."

If you would have asked me what our problem was before then, I would have said her problem was that she couldn't love me like I was. She wanted somebody else. She couldn't be satisfied with the man I had become. But right then I knew she wanted the real me. She'd seen glimpses from time to time, flashes. I had been in there, covered by the past and all the debris, and the flood that meant to kill me had done its work.

I told her about my meeting with Vernon Turley. I told her everything he did. I told her about the ghosts that haunted me, and as I dug deeper, I remembered things I hadn't even told my counselor. Feelings I had and things I'd been through that had been locked tight. My counselor was right: getting this stuff into the light and telling the truth to myself and somebody else made a difference. Sometimes the biggest enemy you have is down deep in your own soul. It was there in that little kitchen that I began to feel the freedom he was talking about.

Three days later there was a story in the

newspaper about the death of a beloved hometown gospel musician. It had Vernon Turley's picture on an inside section and a story next to the obituaries. The community was mourning a great loss. He was taken too quickly, some said. Others mourned him like he was an angel God had given for a short time and then took from us. The cause of death was unclear. He had been in excellent health but had become moody in recent days and seemed troubled. Still, the family insisted his death was from natural causes.

# 27

The revelations about Billy's past saddened me to the core. I had seen most of his life, except for the period when I was called away to service, and to think a person in some semblance of spiritual authority over him would take advantage of such innocence both sickened and disturbed me.

And I was astounded that a mere mortal like Callie, who did not have my insight and broader perspective, would pick up on his suffering and inner turmoil. Indeed, her love caused her to see more deeply. She did not let her own loneliness confuse her. She truly loved in a selfless way, and I was sure that her actions would pave the way of their future.

However, I could not help but take the logical trip past the choices of others and try to discern how I fit in with these events. You have heard of the angel who wrestled with Jacob. I know him personally. Now I was an angel wrestling with myself.

While this was happening to Billy, I was not only away; I had been *called* away. And I was told by my superior that things would need to occur. Why? For what purpose? If I had been present, I know exactly what I would have done to the man who abused Billy, and it would have taken all of hell's forces to protect him.

But it was not the man and his choices that vexed me the most. Sin corrupts. Sin destroys. It brings death. No, what bothered me most was my own commitment to The Plan. I had spent most of Billy's early life simply observing and, at times, becoming involved surreptitiously in minor incidents of protection I have not herein revealed. His first few attempts to drive were frightening in the extreme. There was an incident with wiring a station's transmitter that might have turned deadly had I not been there, but these I saw as minor instances and the payoff from my constant attention. If The Plan was to have Billy become all he could be, why throw into his life something the Almighty knew would further complicate and stunt him as a person? Why allow this needless occurrence to taint his life and relationships?

As humans would say, it took my breath away. As a warrior, it made me angry. I wanted to inflict harm. It caused me to doubt my role in Billy's life altogether. Why have my protection when it was pulled at the moment of a great trial? Are we, the ministering spirits, simply here to clean up debris?

All of my inquiring of my superiors and doubting of my assignments led me to one conclusion — that questioning the events divulged here questions the ultimate Sovereign upon whom all questioning rests. Each question mark on the back roads of the human condition eventually leads to Him. I am upset at evildoers and how they have confused and contaminated the earth with death. It should never have been this way. And yet, in the counsel of the Holy, there was knowledge that it *would* be this way. He knew the risk of love would demand a price. Life would require death.

I am not getting this down correctly, for I am not a scribe. I do not have eloquence that some do. I am a warrior. But in this warrior's heart beats a desire to know *why.* That is the central question of all heaven and earth.

*Why?*

Knowing this struggle would continue, I was faced with a choice. It is the same, I suppose, as those on earth must make, though their eyes are veiled to a much greater extent than mine. But it is the same choice. Can I live with "why?" Can I exist with the inevitable questions that come when suffering awakens the soul? And if I do choose to live with that choice, how do I accomplish the task?

■ ■ ■ ■

# PART THREE:
# ALMOST HEAVEN

■ ■ ■ ■

# 28

The church was almost full on our wedding day. We decided not to wait and plan a big to-do. We just invited anyone who knew us to come and be part of the celebration. Our counselors were there, and that made both of us feel good. We didn't have much of a honeymoon because of the station, but Callie didn't seem to mind. I promised her that we would go to Pipestem Resort State Park and do an overnight as soon as I could train somebody to babysit the station.

I had my hands full fixing up the master bedroom for Callie. We agreed to sell her place for what we could get for it and merge our disparate lives into my place. It was a tight fit for a while, and our first real fight was about whether or not to add on to the house. We'd been through enough counseling by then to know that we needed to really listen to each other, and by the time I got my head wrapped around what was in her heart — that she wanted to make a nest, a home, and not just a place to lay our heads at night — I came around to the idea. That's why I decided, even before we got married, to build a new studio and shop in the back, separate from the house. That would give Callie the run of the home and me a place to do my work.

I traded out some spots with a local concrete company, and we poured the foundation before the wedding. We used the money from the sale of her home to start construction on the new building. I began with the control room for the board and microphone and then a separate room for the transmitter and other equipment. On Callie's direction, I designed a studio off to the right side where I could interview people if I wanted. I didn't see much reason for it at first, but as things turned out, Callie's dream was bigger and better.

Down the hall was my workroom, and I made it big enough to fit all my old radios and the trinkets I'd accumulated over the years. To save money, we didn't run plumbing out there, and anytime I needed to go to the bathroom, I would just come into the house. We used a loan to finish off the building and to upgrade the music from tapes to digital files that I loaded into a computer.

That was one of the things Callie wanted to see happen — moving away from me getting up twice every night to change the tapes. This way I could program the computer and even download programs to play from the Internet. It made things a lot easier and smoother sounding.

A funny thing happened to my blood sugar around that time, too. My levels evened out and I didn't have so many highs and lows. It probably had something to do with a regular eating pattern, but I contend a loving wife is one of the best cures for what ails you.

It was a big day when I transferred all of the equipment from the house to the new building. A lot of it wasn't finished and there was still that Sheetrock smell to the place, but we made a big deal out of it on the air and invited people to come to our grand opening and take a tour. A handful of people showed up, including Natalie, the little girl who had called and helped me locate Callie. Her grandmother, Mae Edwards, came with her. I learned that the little girl's grandfather had died a few months earlier and the two of them were alone. I showed them through the studio, and Natalie asked a million questions about how everything worked. She was a real fire-cracker.

"I've been wanting to come see your station for a long time," the girl said when she got away from her grandmother. "I ride my bike by a lot, and one time I peeked in your window and saw you talking on the micro-phone."

"You should have just knocked on the door. I would have given you a tour."

"My mamaw said I shouldn't bother grown-ups when they're working, but I sure do wish I could learn how to push all those buttons and make a radio station work."

"It's not that hard," I said.

"Really?"

"No, I started when I was young, putting old radios together and such."

Mae came over to us and asked if Natalie was being a bother, and I told her that she wasn't a bother at all, that I appreciated the questions.

"She's been talking about this all week," Mae said. "She does these little recordings pretending she's on the radio, and it's just the cutest thing you've ever seen."

Natalie told me she had asked for two recorders for Christmas and how she used one player for the music and the other one to record her voice. It was a crude way of doing it, but it showed she understood the concept of radio. As the two of them walked out, I couldn't help suggesting something. I don't know if it was the Lord nudging me, but the way things turned out, I tend to believe it was.

"Natalie, how would you like to come by once a week and do an hour on the radio?" I said. "If it's okay with your grandmother."

She looked at me like I had offered her the keys to the Magic Kingdom. "You mean it? I could have my own show?"

"Sure. I could have you sit in the studio over there and I'd engineer for you. Then, when you get the hang of it, you could run the board yourself. It's not that hard. But I have to warn you about something."

Natalie's eyes got big again, and I leaned down. "Once radio gets in your blood, you'll never get it out. It's just a fact. There's something contagious about it."

She nodded like she understood, but I knew she didn't. Mae thanked me, and I told her to bring Natalie back the next Thursday and I'd promote it on the air. The girl asked what she should do to prepare, and I told her not a thing, that I would help her through it.

"What do you want to call the new program?" I said. "Might be better not to use your real name. Why don't you come up with something catchy and then next week —"

"June Bug!" she said. "That's what my daddy used to call me."

"June Bug it is," I said. "We'll call it the June Bug Hour."

She skipped down the driveway, almost flying like a june bug, her grandmother trying to keep up with her. Her hair was dancing in the wind and the lightning bugs were rising around her. It was like some vision of a perfect early summer evening. She looked back at the older woman and kept talking and gesturing and laughing. I wondered how Mae kept up with her all alone like that.

"That was sweet, what you did for her," Callie said after they left. "You've got a way with children, Mr. Allman."

"Don't go getting any ideas, Mrs. Allman."

The first June Bug Hour did not go the way I expected. Natalie was a natural, but she had written everything out and she stuck to the page like a fly on paper. She wanted "I'll Fly Away" as her theme going in and out of the show, so that's how we started. She told me all the people she'd invited to listen. Kids from her class and teachers and the pastor at her church and everybody on the prayer chain. The kid probably had a bigger audience than my morning show. Mae and Callie listened from the kitchen, and I could tell it meant a lot to the women, but honestly it was the highlight of my week.

Toward the end of the hour, I sat down beside the girl as we played a long tune. "Now this is the last song coming up before the theme."

"Time sure flies when you're on the radio, doesn't it?"

"Sure does. Do you know how you want to end?"

She shuffled the papers that contained every word and thought and breath in pencil. She found the right spot and held it up. "Ready to roll."

"Okay, but I want you to do something for me. And I want you to trust me. I've been doing this a long time."

"All right, what is it? Should I put more oomph in my voice when I say good-bye?"

I took all of her papers from her and put them in a neat stack. "I want you to do this one without your script."

She looked like I had just stomped on her little dog's tail. "But I worked on that a long time. I can't remember it all."

"You don't have to, Natalie. You have a great voice and there's a lot of energy in your delivery. But the best thing about you and the thing people want to hear is right in here." I pointed to my chest. "People don't want to be talked *at;* they want a conversation with a friend, just like you and I are talking now. So don't think of radio as a megaphone where you talk to a thousand people. You're talking to one person. You're making a connection from your heart to theirs. Just be June Bug."

"But what if I mess up? What if I can't do it? Maybe if I try this next week."

Something welled up in her eyes and I knew exactly how she felt. The freedom was too much too soon. I put the pages down and smiled. "All right, we'll try that next week. Now get ready; the song's almost over. I'll start the theme on your cue."

I went back to the control room and through the glass watched as she sat up straight, her hair just touching her shoulders. She had the headphones on the lowest position I could get them and still they were too big. She glanced at me as the song ended and took a deep breath. I could tell she was just feeling the moment. When the on-air light went on, she glanced at the clock and then gently put the pages on the table.

"It's five minutes before seven o'clock and

sixty-six degrees in Dogwood. That's gonna wrap it up for my very first June Bug show. I hope you enjoyed it. And I want to thank Mr. Allman for letting me have the time to come on here and play some songs I like. If you enjoyed it, then tell your friends and family about the station. I've told just about everybody I know. And if we all do that, there's no telling how many people will listen to Good News Bluegrass.

"Mr. Allman said I should just speak from my heart, and so that's what I'm going to do. The last song I want to play is the first song we played — 'I'll Fly Away.' It means a lot to me because my daddy used to put it on every time I got scared. And you might think I like it because of the jumpy way it's played — sometimes that can calm a girl's nerves. But it's not that. It's what the song tells you deep down in your heart: One day, if you know Jesus, you are going to fly away to your real home. This old world is not where our treasure is. It's up there. And I know that better now because my papaw is standing in the presence of his Lord and Savior right now, and I can't wait to see him again and hug his neck and tell him all my mamaw and I have done since he left.

"Now I'm not saying we can't have good things down here and have parties and stuff like that, but this song reminds me that no matter how good or bad things get, we have to keep our eyes on heaven. That will make us better people and more kind while we're still on earth."

She held up a little hand and waved it back and forth, and I started the Alison Krauss version. "Well, I hope you liked the first June Bug Hour, and please come back next week when we'll have more great music for you. I'm June Bug. It's three minutes before seven now and still sixty-six degrees; at least I think it is. Have a good night in Dogwood and thanks for listening. Here's my song."

She hit the post perfectly and the vocals started. I clapped my hands and gave her a standing ovation. Natalie just beamed. Callie came through the door and Mae followed behind her, wiping her eyes and smiling.

"Did you hear it, Mamaw?" Natalie said.

"I sure did, honey. Every second." She laughed. "You just got better and better, didn't you?"

"Did you hear what I said about Papaw?"

She hugged the girl. "Oh, I liked that a lot."

"I was kind of nervous at first, but then Mr. Allman told me to stop reading from the script and just talk, and that helped. It made me feel like I was being myself."

"The most important rule of radio," I said. "She's a real natural."

"You sure are," Callie said. She leaned down to Natalie. "I made some cookies while you were doing the show and they're ready. Just got them out of the oven. You want to come help me put frosting and sprinkles on them?"

Natalie jumped up and ran through the door with Callie following. Mae turned to me and at first couldn't speak. Then she gathered herself.

"Billy, you can't know all that little girl has been through. It's been a tough row to hoe. You've probably heard some things, but you can't know."

"I expect you're right about that."

"This has been the most wonderful gift. I can't tell you what it means to her. I've had to get her to stop talking about it, she goes on so much. But I'll understand if you don't think it'll work out in the long run."

"Work out?" I said, laughing. "Mae, she's the best thing to happen to this station since digital music. I want her to come back every week. And then I'll gradually teach her the board and let her feet get wet. She's like a little sponge, just soaking things up."

"Don't I know it."

I switched to the computer's list, and it took over and began the evening programs and music.

Mae headed out the door, then turned back to me. "Her daddy — well, the man who took care of her for years . . ." She got a far-off look in her eyes. "You don't think you could record Natalie's next show, could you? I'll bet he'd like to hear it."

"You can send him tonight's if you want."

"You recorded it?"

"You think I'd miss this little piece of history? I can make a CD and send it to him tomorrow."

She wrote down his address, and I told her I'd be glad to put it in the mail.

A lot of things in life start out small, and that was one of them. Nobody paid much attention to a little girl playing music on a low-power radio station in the middle of nowhere. It just wasn't on the radar screen of what people would call important. But there was something more going on behind the scenes. Something bigger.

The next week I sent some notes to Natalie explaining how she might improve, and the girl progressed so much it was scary. She used three-by-five cards to jot down phrases and thoughts about the songs and talked like she was sitting across the table from a little friend of hers, having cookies and milk.

"She's going to work me out of a job if she keeps up," I said to Mae afterward.

The woman beamed. "It's like watching a flower bloom, isn't it?"

"I reckon it is."

"I got a call last night from the man you sent the CD to. He has an idea."

"Don't tell me he wants a show too?"

"No, no. I told him about your station and what you're doing here. He was just flying high being able to hear her voice. He said it was like listening to the sun shining. You can imagine how hard it was to give up a little thing like that after caring for her, but I think he knew it would be best for her to be here with us. With me, now. I gotta tell you that story someday."

"Yes, you do."

"Well, a funny thing. He asked if there was any way to hear what you do on the Internet. I told him I didn't think you could do that but I'd ask. Is that possible?"

"Mae, people can hardly hear it here on the radio, let alone the Internet," I said. "It's all I can do to pay the bills. The costs of streaming our signal is just beyond me."

"But it can be done, right?"

"Anything can be done if you have the funds. There's an old boy in town who works on Web site stuff in his spare time. I've talked to him, just dreaming, but it's too expensive."

"Well, this fellow, John, said he wanted to hear June Bug every week and he was willing to pay whatever it cost to get it out where he lives."

"Is that so?"

"And he said people all over the country could hear it if it was on the Internet. I guess if you have a connection, you can do that, right?"

"Yeah. But back up a minute. He wants to pay for the whole thing?"

"Said if you could come up with the charges and what it would take, he'd write you a check. But until then, he was going to send you some money to keep those CDs coming."

The news felt like a gentle rain on dry crops. "I'll see what I can find out."

The next Monday I got a check from Colorado for $1,000. On top of the check it said *John and Sheila Johnson.* John told me how much the CDs meant and asked me to get the costs together about the Internet. He gave me his e-mail address and said he would send the money as soon as I had a plan. It was like getting a lightning bolt from heaven. I didn't do a thing to make it happen; I just did what I had a vision for and the rest fell down. But if it hadn't been for Natalie, it never would have happened.

Which led to another connection. A few weeks into her program, she came to the station to watch me do the morning show and see how I put it together. While songs played, we talked about the man in Colorado, what it was like leaving him, and what she remembered of her life on the road. Then she turned the conversation around. She could ask the most insightful questions.

She asked why it had taken so long for Callie and me to get married. She asked what had made me interested in radio and talking to people since it seemed like I was the kind of person who liked to live on the end of a road and have my privacy.

"What is it about bluegrass that you like so much, because you have to love something an awful lot to play it as much as you do," she said.

"I think it's because it's in my blood. Has been since I was a little kid. One of my best memories is of my daddy having friends over and playing music together at the house next to Buffalo Creek."

"Your daddy was a musician?"

"My daddy was a coal miner, but he loved the mandolin and he loved good music. I credit him with this love I have."

"Did you ever play?"

"Mm-hmm. Daddy gave me his mandolin, and I learned to play it pretty well. Even got to play in a music group once."

"You did? Did you ever make a record?"

"The group had records, but I never got to play on one."

"Where's your mandolin now?"

"Sold it."

"Why?"

"I needed the money for equipment."

"That's sad. I'd like to hear you play."

"Maybe someday you will."

# 29

The summer got hot and the days long. The fourth birthday of the station was coming up, and Callie suggested we launch the Web site and Internet stream to coincide with it. I'd gotten the check from Colorado that covered all the costs and then some.

I could tell Callie had something up her sleeve as we got close to the day. She took off work that day and sat in with me as we had a "flip the switch" ceremony. She wouldn't go on and talk with me hardly at all because she's not that kind of person. But she did lean into the microphone once and encourage everybody to listen to June Bug's show that evening. And that was all she said.

We scheduled dinner at the diner that afternoon, and Natalie and Mae were there, and Callie invited Charles Broughton, the fellow from Charleston who had been such a help. Several people from the community came by and had a slice of cake to celebrate. Our Web guy, Homer Saunders, came by with a printout and a big smile on his face.

"We've already had more than a hundred hits to the site," he said, showing me the states we'd reached.

"I wonder how many there will be to-night?" Natalie said.

"Thousands," I said. "Yours will be the most popular show every week."

She smiled sheepishly like she knew something I didn't. When it was time to head home, I realized something more was up. Callie lingered at the restaurant, and I said we needed to get back.

"Billy, I need to prepare you for something," she said. "The show tonight is going to be a little different."

"How so?"

"It's a surprise. I need you to go along with it."

"How can I go along with something I don't know about?" I put the rest of the cake in the back of the truck and put a brick on the empty spot of the box so it wouldn't slide.

"You have to trust me. Can you do that?"

"You know I trust you. What about Nat-alie?"

"She's the one who had the idea."

"I figured. What idea is that?"

"I said you had to trust me. Now give me the keys; I need to drive you home."

It took me a minute because I always drove. The gears on the old truck were sometimes hard to shift, and Callie didn't like to drive it. I wanted to ask a bunch more questions, but I gave her the keys and sat in the passenger seat. Just before we got to the turnoff to our road, Callie pulled over.

"One more thing. You need to put this on." She took out the little blindfold she used when she went to sleep each night.

"What do I need that for?"

She just gave me the stare of a woman who will not repeat herself. I took it and covered my eyes. "All right, I trust you." I waved a hand in front of me. "Driver, proceed."

We didn't pull into the driveway but parked along the road. That was strange. She got out and helped me through the ditch and the little field beside the house that I told her would be her garden, but I hadn't had the time to plow it.

"What time is it?" I said.

"Almost time," she said. "Watch your step."

She led me into the building, and instead of turning left into the control room, we turned right into the studio. It was warm in there, and somebody snickered and somebody else said, "Shhh." Callie sat me down and handed me headphones, and I could hear the music fade.

"We need somebody to engineer — who's going to do that?" I said.

She pulled the headphones from my ears and said, "You didn't marry a dummy, Billy."

That made the people in the room laugh, and there were a lot more than just Natalie. Men's voices, too. I was trying to piece it together when the music stopped and Natalie spoke without the theme song. I thought it was a mistake at first.

"Ladies and gentlemen, welcome to a very special June Bug Hour. This is our first broadcast streaming on the Internet, and tonight's program is dedicated to our founder and leader, Mr. Billy Allman. And here at the beginning of the program, we decided we would present him with a special gift and then ask him to use it."

My face felt hot. I didn't like all the attention and I hate surprises.

"Hold your hands out, Mr. Allman," Natalie said. "He has a blindfold on, so he has no idea what's about to happen."

"That's normal for Billy," a man said next

to me, and I recognized the voice of Lester Cremeans, one of the pickers for the Gospel Bluegrass Boys.

I held out my hands, and into them came a round piece of wood, smooth and polished, with a long neck. I held it there for a moment, turning it and feeling the craftsmanship. Somebody to my left pecked on my hand and gave me a pick.

"You'll need this, Billy."

The room sounded bigger because there was more than Natalie's microphone on.

"You can take the blindfold off, Mr. Allman," Natalie said.

I pushed up on it and couldn't believe what I saw. It was my daddy's old mandolin — or I thought so at first, but this one wasn't old; it looked new.

Natalie stood there in front of me, smiling, giving the play-by-play of the look on my face, the others in the room laughing. "We tried to find the one you sold, but we couldn't," she said. "But my daddy found this one on eBay. He thought you could use it."

I shook my head and looked around the room at the faces staring at me. I held out a hand to Lester and he shook it.

"It's been a long time, Billy." We called him Lester Round because he was kind of portly and we played off the name Lester Flatt. You would have thought that seeing him would have brought the memories I had of Vernon Turley and set me back, but I was happy to be next to him. He was always kind to me.

"Ladies and gentlemen, we have assembled some of the best bluegrass pickers in the area to join us tonight in a live and unrehearsed performance," Natalie said, reading from her script. She introduced Lester and the others — a couple of them I knew and a couple I didn't. There's something about musicians from the hills. They don't need introductions. They say music is the universal language and just playing together is like having a long conversation.

I could scarcely take it in. And then I wondered who was engineering, and I looked over to see Callie and Mae standing behind Jimmy Stillwater, the man who had taken my job at the radio station so long ago. He nodded and gave me a thumbs-up. That's when I recognized the microphones around the room. He had brought in his own little mixing board and extra microphones to give us a better sound.

"Well, I don't know about you, but I'd like to hear something from the man of the hour," Natalie said.

Everybody clapped and laughed.

"For once in my life I'm speechless," I said. They laughed again. "This is about the nicest thing anybody has ever done for me. And I hate to disappoint you, but I haven't played one of these in a long time."

"It'll come back to you, Billy," Lester said. "It's like riding a bike. I got it all tuned. What do you say we start it off."

"You lead; I'll follow," I said.

Lester counted us off, and that's when I realized I didn't even know what we were playing. But when I heard the first notes, I knew where they were going.

"Here they are, folks, live from Dogwood, West Virginia, for the first time ever, Billy and Good News Bluegrass."

There's something about the feel of the mandolin and picking out the tune at hand that makes a person feel right with the world. As soon as the banjo walked up the steps to "I'll Fly Away," it all came back. I just kind of strummed the chords and let the others run with the first verse; then Lester nodded to me and I took off on a run at the second one. I kept going, really feeling it, the sound going all the way to my soul. A couple of minutes later we were done with the instrumental, and everybody clapped and Natalie about jumped out of

461

her skin watching me.

"I had no idea you could do that, Mr. All-man," she said.

"Well, to tell you the truth, I didn't either," I said. "It's been a long time."

"How do you like the mandolin?" she said.

"It's the second-best present I've ever been given, the first being the Lord's forgiveness to me."

"What about your wife?" one of the boys said.

"Third-best present," I said.

Everybody laughed, and I glanced at Callie in the control room. She had her hands over her face, shaking and crying and just enjoying the moment. The love of a good woman is a wonderful thing, especially one who has held it close for so long and waited. I almost missed it, and right then I kind of choked up.

"What should we do next, Billy?" Lester said. "We have a list of songs here, but this is your day. You call it."

"You fellows know 'Power in the Blood'?" I said.

" 'Would you be free from your burden of sin?' " Lester said. "It's right here on the list. And Terry over there can sing in between the picking."

"Let's do it," I said.

And we did. It was almost heaven. When I closed my eyes and let the mandolin sing, I was back on the creek, back sitting at my daddy's feet, in the front room of the old house that wasn't there anymore. With people who weren't alive, clapping and stomping and playing.

Music has a way of filling in the missing places. It is a gift from God above, who didn't have to provide it, but he did anyway and I half think he decided life just wouldn't be as good without it. Even if you're penniless and on the street and have nothing at all, or if you're shut-in and on a sickbed, or if you're in prison, if you have music, there is something to feed your soul. I guess that's the reason I started the station in the first place. I could stop playing my own music, but there was a need deep down for something real I didn't even understand. So in a way, I started the station to feed myself, for selfish reasons, and it blessed others along the way.

We played for more than an hour before I ever thought about getting tired. I slipped in a legal ID, which you're supposed to do every hour, and we played for another half hour and then did "I'll Fly Away" to end it all. Terry sang and the whole thing lasted more than six minutes. We were all feeling it, and I knew there was magic in the room, the magic of music, and that we'd never have a night like this again because we were making everything up as we went along and it was all coming from the heart. That's the best kind of radio there is, and when the moment is gone, you wish you could get it back, but it's a force of nature you can't manufacture.

After we switched back to the computer, we couldn't help ourselves and we played another half hour, recording an instrumental version of "I'll Fly Away" for Natalie's show. Finally Lester said he had to get home. The other boys all had day jobs too, and none of them played in bands anymore. They just played because it was part of them. So I had them all write down their numbers on a sheet of paper, and before they left, Natalie said, "Why don't we do this again next week?"

"I don't know if we could handle all that excitement every week, darlin'," I said. "What if we shoot for once a month?"

The others nodded, and we agreed on the next date on the calendar. It felt like we'd started something that we'd talk about for years.

As Lester was leaving, he took me aside. "I guess you heard about Vernon."

"I did. That was a sad occasion."

"I never asked you about it, but I always had the suspicion that he was up to something. With you, I mean."

"Your suspicions were true."

He shook his head and winced. "I'm really sorry I didn't say something, Billy. When you left the group, I wanted to ask, but I never did. That's to my shame."

"It's okay, Lester. You were always good to me. And I appreciate you asking."

"Are you doing all right with it?"

"I've learned that stuff like that follows you wherever you go. Follows you the rest of your life. And that's probably why I walked away. But the Lord has a way of showing you that you have to deal with things or they'll eat you alive."

"I'm sure glad you're giving the music another run," Lester said.

"I hadn't planned on it until tonight."

"The Lord bless you, Billy."

"He has," I said. "He surely has."

He patted me on the back, and I watched him load up his guitar and drive away. Jimmy Stillwater said he needed to take his microphones and little Mackie board back to the station, but that he would be glad to come back every month and provide the same setup.

"That's a lot of time commitment without any pay," I said.

"I love the music, Billy," he said. "I'd work just for the pleasure of hearing something so pure and clean. It was like a breath of fresh air. Plus, I feel like I owe you something for the way my brother treated you."

"That's long forgiven and forgotten, Jimmy. I appreciate your heart. Tell Karl I asked about him next time you see him."

Natalie stayed past her bedtime until everybody left. She sat down in the control room while I reset the computer. Mae had gone and Callie said she would drive Natalie home when the festivities were done.

"That was just about the most thrillingest thing I've ever been a part of," she said.

"Me too. And from what Callie says, it wouldn't have happened if it weren't for you and all those ideas you have locked up in that head of yours."

"I do have a lot of ideas, but she was the one who made it happen. Do you think my daddy heard the program tonight?"

"I'll bet he did. And if he didn't, Jimmy made a recording and I'll send it. You miss him, don't you?"

"Yeah. But sometimes I feel bad for missing him because I think it hurts Mamaw's feelings."

"Your grandmother is a tough old bird. I'll bet you she can handle it if you talk with her. She's probably wondering what's going on up there."

"I think I talk too much."

"God has given you a gift, Natalie. And I've learned over the years that your strength can be your weakness. Do you know what that means?"

She thought a minute. "That the thing you're good at can get in the way?"

I nodded. "If you lean on your own strength and understanding, you'll spin your wheels. If you let God use the thing he's given you, and also use the things you feel weak in, your life will be an amazing song sung to him every day."

"How do I do that?"

"There's no formula. Stay close to him. Talk to him. Don't see the trouble as him being mean to you but him trying to get you closer. And whatever you do, give it all your heart because your heart is the best thing. It always will be."

She smiled and gave me a big hug, then went skipping out the door to the house. As I watched her, I thanked God that he would give me something to do that I loved and friends to share it with, a little girl whose life I could speak into, and a wife who loved me.

You can bet that the good feelings that come from such a day will soon pass because of life's troubles, but right then I felt like the most blessed man on the face of the earth. With the mountain behind me and a clear signal on the radio and a wider outreach than I could have ever dreamed and a mandolin to hold again, it was almost too much to take in. I wished my own daddy and mama could be there with me. Somehow it felt like they were.

# 30

I sang the night of Billy's return to music. His was such a small sound, with such a tiny instrument, and yet I felt what I witnessed in that room had been ordered by a divine hand. It took so many pieces falling together to make it happen. I was in awe of all that transpired.

There is rejoicing in heaven when a sinner repents, but we can be captured by other things as well. Answered prayer. Healing. Miracles that spare the lives of the unrepentant who cry out for mercy. And when we rejoice, the music is sweet. It swells over eternity's portals and invades the deepest darkness. I have long wondered why our singing cannot be heard on the earthly plane, except for certain instances like that night in Bethlehem.

But my song drew attention in other areas, and soon a bright light approached. It was such a shimmering, shining presence that I was forced to shield my eyes. He spoke my name. He commended me for my service to the King and asked what I had learned. And I was so honored that I began telling of Billy's life, my observations. I centered on the music and the similarities and differences to our realm.

"There seems to be a sound track to each human's life that runs through every thread and fiber of their being. For some, the music is a dirge, a plainsong that undergirds them through difficult times. For others, the song shifts to major, and life becomes more pleasing. If they harmonize with that sound track, meaning His will and His moving, they are content in every circumstance. But if they fight against it and accuse God of indifference or maliciousness, there is discord.

"To me," I continued, "music is compulsory. It springs from our being. It is the way we were created. And in the same way it springs from them, but it seems to me they have a choice. They can play and sing, allowing the music to flow through them, or they can ignore it, to their own peril. We are given a charge — even the warriors — and we sing well. It is not just a duty; it is a privilege given by the One who made us and makes us sing to His glory."

"But it is mandatory," the shimmering one said.

"Yes."

"And that somehow seems unfair?"

"I know nothing is unfair in the service of the One who calls us, but the humans' way feels, somehow, more organic."

"An interesting hypothesis. Explain further."

"I know of the Almighty's justice. I have seen His blinding holiness. The splendor and majesty. They only see faded glimpses of that on the earthly plane. They can only imagine what it must be like in the heavenlies. But I cannot know or even hope to understand what they do about His love. For all of their deficiencies, they are able to *feel* the love of Him who spared not even His only Son. I have never felt, nor will I ever feel, that inexpressible love. I feel gratitude, of course, for His creating power, His omnipotence and omniscience, but I marvel at the sacrifice. It is the One putting Himself in the place of another that captures me, that makes me sit in awe of their station."

He moved closer, his voice beckoning and alluring. "Now that you have tasted of this human drama, now that you have been enlightened in the ways your King has chosen to work, wouldn't you like to taste true freedom? Rather than following and obeying and the weariness that comes from all of the directives He sends, would it not be better to choose your own way?"

A cold shiver ran down my spine as I looked

471

upon the form of the enemy. I had been deceived into thinking this was an ally. Or perhaps even the King Himself visiting me, and for a moment my pride rose, that I would be important enough to have this dialogue. Instead, I had met the chief enemy of souls and the one whom I had been fighting since he fell.

"Never," I whispered, my jaw set. My hand went quickly to the sword.

His gaze was upon me, and suddenly so were a legion of those from the demonic realm, binding and subduing. I had let my guard down for an instant. I would pay the price. Searing pain shot through my body. But before I could call for help, my mouth was clamped shut, the demons crawling over each other to restrain me. It was then that I looked into the face of the most malevolent evil that has ever existed. In his eyes was desperation that comes from defeat. Insanity that springs from one who can never win but only work against a divine plan.

He laughed in derision. "Your charge is about to meet mine. And there's nothing you or your Master can do."

# 31

After our first live show, a reporter from Huntington came to the house to interview me and took some pictures of the studio, Natalie in front of a microphone, and Callie and me on the front porch holding hands. It was a small piece in the *Herald-Dispatch* on a weekend, and I didn't expect much response, but as often happens, I did not anticipate what God was up to. The Web site count kept rising, and Homer told me we'd probably have to change our server for the Internet stream because of the increased hit count.

On the last Thursday night in September, I was late getting to the studio. It was the day before my thirtieth high school reunion, and people from all over the country were coming back to connect. It was a two-day affair, and part of me was excited about it and another part of me just wanted to skip the whole thing. I knew there would be a lot of people who would crow about all of their accomplishments, and I'd been stuck in Dogwood not doing much of anything. Still, I was looking forward to seeing Heather, who was said to have made something of herself.

Callie and I met at the diner, which was the reason I was late getting back to the station. We'd been talking about our finances and how things had evened out somewhat now that ads were picking up. We even talked about Callie quitting the post office so she could help me at the station. We'd been praying that would happen, but it was still a dream. She had some things to do at work, so I headed home and saw Natalie's bicycle against the house when I pulled into the driveway. She was sitting there waiting like a faithful dog.

"Sorry I'm late," I said.

"No problem," she said. "Gave me time to think. Here's my list of songs."

She handed me a piece of notebook paper with the songs listed from one to fourteen.

"I'll get 'em lined up, and you get settled," I said.

I was focused on the board and getting the computer to cooperate and saw movement out of the corner of my eye. I looked up, and Natalie was busy putting on her headphones. I didn't think anything about it and hit the theme song, the instrumental version of "I'll Fly Away" that the boys and I had recorded. I turned on the microphone, and the on-air light clicked. I usually let Natalie just feel where she wanted to come in, but when she didn't say anything, I pointed at her and leaned back to look through the window. She just stared at the door for some reason.

"What do you want?" she said.

I hit the talkback. "I want you to start the show, June Bug. Let's go."

She glanced at me, and the look in her eyes is something I will never forget as long as I live. A mix of fear and white-hot terror. That type of look should not happen to someone so young.

I pulled the music down and heard somebody else inside the room talking, low and unintelligible.

"Is somebody in there with you?" I said in the talkback.

Natalie nodded, still staring at whoever it was.

"I saw your picture in the paper." It was a man's voice. Higher pitched and whiny.

I froze. I knew I should jump up from the board and charge into the studio, but that voice and the whole situation left me immobile.

"What — what do you want?" Natalie said again.

The man moved past the double-paned glass, and I saw the glint of a hunting knife in his hand. "Just to see you. You're a pretty little thing, aren't you?"

I finally came to my senses and killed the microphone and let the computer take over. The music came up full in Natalie's headphones, and she jerked them off and stood up, moving away from the man. I kept the microphone in cue.

"Billy!" Natalie shouted.

Her frightened voice sent me over the edge, and I jumped up and ran. He'd locked the dead bolt from the inside. The way I'd built it, there was no way I could kick the thing in. He had the upper hand.

The man looked through the double-paned window at me, a scrawny-looking thing with a beard he'd been working on for a long time. A dirty, long-sleeved jacket. Muddy jeans with holes in the knees. And that knife. Long and curved at the end. It could do some damage. Underneath the scruff and dirt I recognized the picture that had been in the paper when Clay had gone missing.

476

I ran back to the control room and picked up the phone, but the line was dead. I really needed a cell phone.

"I don't want to hurt you," the man said. "I just want to get a closer look."

"You leave her alone!" I yelled into the talkback, and the guy jumped when he heard my voice through the speakers. Natalie screamed and looked for a place to hide, but there was nothing in there but the round table I'd made and a few filing cabinets against the wall. She could try to run him around the table, but he had control from the moment he walked into the room. I kicked myself for not locking the outside doors.

I banged on the window to get his attention. The man looked at me with a sick grin, like he knew I was powerless.

"I remember you," he said. He pointed a crooked finger at me that had dirt under the fingernail. "You almost hit me with that truck of yours. I'll get to you directly. First things first."

The Bible teaches you to pray without ceasing, which I take as an attitude of prayer that ought to be part of your whole day no matter what you're doing. And as I prayed, I tried to think of any weapon I had in the station, and the only thing that came to me was a rusty shovel outside the back door. I hurried down the hall and without thinking twice about it brought it back and swung the heavy end into the glass, but the end of it flew off and winged its way down the hall. I shoved the handle into the middle of the first pane of glass until it broke, then did the same with the second that I had mounted at a slightly different angle. It pained me to do that because it cost a bit of money, but there was nothing in the world that was as important as that little girl. I would have blown up the whole building to keep her safe.

I remembered Sheriff Preston's words about Clay, and the memory sent a shiver through me. I should have been more on guard.

Clay had caught Natalie back by the filing cabinets, and when I stepped through the empty window onto the broken glass, he had her out in front of him and the hunting knife at her neck.

"If I was you, I'd put that thing down. Unless you want to be cleaning her blood off this nice carpet."

I held out one hand and propped the shovel handle against the wall. "Put the knife down, Clay. You don't want to do this."

He leveled his gaze and spoke in a guttural whisper. "You don't have any idea what I want to do. I have a lot planned for you and your wife after I get through with this one."

It sounds funny to say it, but I thought about Psalm 121 right then. When trouble comes, where does help come from? It comes from the Lord who made heaven and earth. He is the one who keeps me. He's the one who won't let my foot slip. He doesn't nod off during the troubles of my life. If he really does care, he already knew this was going to happen and had prepared an angel to protect us. He'd protected me all along and I had no doubt he could do it now if he wanted. He was the one who was going to get glory, no matter what happened.

"Everybody thought you were dead," I said.

He cackled and his spotty, black teeth showed. "That's what I wanted them to think. And I bided my time, don't you know. Just waited for a chance to set things straight. After I get done here, I'll disappear again. And nobody's going to find me."

"How *did* you find us?"

He seemed to loosen his grip on Natalie a little, and for that I was grateful.

"That's the funny thing. When I found

Callie's trailer, she wasn't there no more. So I didn't have no way to tell. And then I seen this newspaper article, and lo and behold, there you were. Both of you. Wasn't hard from there. It was just choosin' when. Late at night while you were asleep? Early in the morning? So many choices. You know, you really should lock your house and not be so trusting of people."

"Billy?" Natalie said through clenched teeth. "Help me."

It was the most pitiful cry for help you have ever heard. If I could have taken her place right then, I would have. If I could have lunged at the knife and wrestled it away from him, I would have done it in a second, even if it meant I would lose fingers or a whole hand. But all I could do was talk, and right then it seemed like a poor way of trying to save somebody's life. I tried to put out of my mind some of the things Callie said he had done to her and what the police report detailed. He held Natalie close again, the knife pressed against her skin so hard I thought it would draw blood.

"Clay, she's not part of this. Just let her go. You and I can settle this."

Natalie looked at me, and my heart just about broke for her. I kept trying to think of some way to get her away from him, but one wrong move and it would all be over and I'd have to live with the regret. It seems to me there are times when you have to act and times when you have to wait, but the hardest times are those when you want to do one but you have to do the other and you're not sure which is best.

Clay crooked his arm around her chest and lifted her off the ground, and she struggled and her legs flailed. He was concentrating on her so much that he left the opportunity for me to move in. But as soon as I did, glass crunched underfoot and he stared at me. "Wouldn't do that if I were you."

He was moving to his left, holding Natalie with his left arm, until he positioned himself in front of the window, the shade up. I heard a car pull up outside and tried to cover it with some words.

"Natalie, just stay where you are. Clay and I are going to work this out."

"Where's that wife of yours?" Clay said. "She has a way of disappearing on me. I hoped she would be here."

"She's probably on her way home," I said.

"Can't wait to see her face when she sees me. It would almost be worth it to keep you two around for that, but it probably wouldn't be too smart."

The Lord says vengeance is his, but if I could have gotten my hands around his throat, I would have choked the living daylights out of him. Still, something inside told me there had to be some part of the man reachable with reason or compassion or something akin to it.

"Clay, whatever you've done with your life, you don't have to live in light of that. You can change. God has a way of turning the bad to good if you'll let him."

"God?" Clay said. "You want to talk to me about God, preacher man?"

"I'm not a preacher. Never have been. But I know he's real and he can help you."

"Nobody can help me where I'm going. I just want to take as many with me as I can. Know what I mean?"

He held Natalie up again with his left arm and tightened his grip on the knife. "Say good night, darlin'."

I knew this was the end and if I didn't act, I'd be sorry. I reached for the shovel and while my head was turned heard what sounded like a tuft of air escape. I had the sick feeling that it was Natalie's throat, but when I looked up, Clay had turned and was studying a hole in the window about the size of a peanut M&M. He'd let go of Natalie and she was bent over on the floor.

Another hole appeared at about the same spot on the window, but this time Clay moved back and staggered a little, reaching up to his neck with his knife hand and almost cutting himself.

Natalie ran to me, and I shoved her through the empty window and told her to get outside fast. I picked up the handle, but Clay was leaning back against the table, three more holes in the window and two more showing through his shirt. He dropped the knife and it hit the carpet with a thud. Blood spurted from the wound in his neck, and I moved toward him and kicked the knife away. I waved in front of the window and then looked out to see Callie holding Natalie in her arms, my .22 rifle on the ground. There was a siren in the distance.

"Is that her?" Clay said, choking on something.

"Lie down," I said. "We'll get you some help."

He slipped a bloody hand out to catch his fall, but he dropped to the floor and shook, blood bubbling from his wounds. With Natalie safe and him with no way to hurt anybody, I felt something strange. It was pity mixed with revulsion and compassion.

"Clay, you don't have to go into eternity with all this on your soul. Cry out to God now. He can help you."

He grabbed my shirt and held tight as he cursed. "I don't want his help. Or yours."

His eyes rolled back and the blood that had freely pulsed from the wound in his neck lessened until it trickled down and dripped onto the carpet. I have looked into the face of death before in my life, but never has it seemed so bleak and dark as it did on the face of Clay Gilmore.

The siren came close and a car door slammed. "Billy, you in there?" Sheriff Preston yelled.

"Come on in, Sheriff. He's dead."

Sheriff Preston came in and stepped through the broken window. I was still kneeling beside Clay, closing his eyes.

Sheriff Preston shook his head. "I knew he didn't jump in that river. And I knew he'd come back. I should have given you more protection."

"There wasn't anything you could do," I said. "A more tortured and twisted soul I don't think I've ever seen."

"Is the girl okay? We got a call from Callie as soon as she heard it on the radio. Said she recognized his voice."

"They must be in the house," I said. "He had a knife. I kicked it over there. He was going to kill her, Sheriff. And he would have if Callie hadn't come home."

"Thank God she did." He glanced back at the window and the holes in the glass. Then back down at Clay. "It's a good thing you had that rifle."

I nodded. "I reckon it was."

The two of us stayed there a minute, taking it all in. The wind picked up outside and blew the trees on the hillside in a high-pitched sound.

Mae arrived, crying and shaking. She'd heard the broadcast begin but didn't understand why Natalie didn't talk anymore. Callie had called her and explained, and I drove her and Natalie over there to stay the night. Callie couldn't take the lights and the yellow crime scene tape. It brought up the old wounds, I guess.

Sheriff Preston got her statement at their house, and he assured her it was self-defense and that no charges would be filed. "That's not an easy thing to do, Callie, pulling the trigger when it comes time. There's not anything you have to blame yourself for. You did the right thing, and there's a little girl alive because of it."

She took my hand and held it tight. When she looked up, there was something in her eyes.

"What is it?" I said.

Her mouth opened but no sound came out. It looked like she was trying to pull something from deep inside. "What if I hadn't listened? What if I had just gone on to work like I planned?"

"It's okay, darlin'," I said.

Sheriff Preston leaned forward, elbows resting on his knees. "What are you saying, Callie?"

"I had this terrible feeling. Something just came over me. And then . . ."

"Then what?" the sheriff said.

"You're going to think I'm crazy. I heard a voice. Somebody whispered to me to go home. It said, 'Billy needs you.' "

The skin on my arms got goose bumps.

"It was just as clear as day. And I couldn't think of anything but coming back there. Then, when I heard his voice on the radio, I just knew it. I knew it was him and what I had to do."

I held her close and patted her arm and told her it was okay. It was all over. But of course, it wasn't. Nothing that happens to us is all over when it can stick in your mind and keep spinning.

"I wish there wasn't so much meanness in the world," Callie said.

"You and me both," Sheriff Preston said.

# 32

The next day the first person at our house was Becky Putnam from the local paper. Since I knew her, I talked with her outside but didn't give her any details at that point. She had put the story together and figured out what had happened to Callie. Not long after that, news trucks showed up, and I let them take video of the scene, but I didn't feel like it was my place to do any interviews. Callie didn't want to talk, and I told her she had every right not to. I heard later on that the story Becky wrote got picked up by several newspapers in the state, and maybe that's why not long after that she took a reporting job in Cincinnati.

I drove Callie to her counselor on Friday, and she took some time off work. She slept in our bed and just shook. There was no way I could go to the first night of the reunion. I just held her until she fell asleep, and then she sat straight up and said she heard something outside. It was one of those kind of nights.

Saturday night she said she was sorry but she couldn't go to the reunion. I told her I understood but I wouldn't leave her alone, so I called a friend from church and asked if she would come over and watch a movie or something, and the woman said she would love to.

"You're going to have an extra ticket to that dinner," Callie said.

"It's not a big deal."

"Why don't you take Natalie? She might enjoy it."

"You think people will talk about me dragging a ten-year-old girl along?"

"I wasn't thinking of the other people. I was thinking of Natalie. She has no father or even a grandfather. I think it would be sweet."

I stopped by Mae's house and found Natalie on the front porch playing with her little white dog, Roma.

"Why are you all dressed up?" she said when I got out of the truck. She hadn't seen me in anything but jeans and a T-shirt, so a dress shirt and khakis made me look like I was headed to church.

"I'm going to my high school reunion dinner. Want to come with me?"

Her face lit up, and she opened the front door and yelled for her grandmother. "Mr. Allman wants me to come to dinner with him; can I, Mamaw?"

Mae came outside with her hands on her hips. "What kind of dinner?"

I told her. "Callie doesn't feel much like attending and I don't blame her. I thought maybe Natalie might enjoy the evening."

"Those things have a lot of drinking at them, don't they? You're not supposed to take kids."

"I suppose there will be some who imbibe," I said. "But I got two tickets here for a sit-down supper and only enough insulin for one meal. I think it's a shame to waste good food, don't you?"

She frowned and looked at Natalie. "Well, you'll need to get some nice clothes on. Get your red dress; I just washed it."

Natalie squealed. "That's the one I wanted to wear!"

The girl ran inside. It was amazing how such a little thing could make so much noise bounding down the hall. Mae just shook her head.

"You two doing okay today?" I said.

"Today," Mae said. "Can't say anything about tomorrow."

"One day is all we're given. Does John

know about what happened?"

"He called. He was listening when the show started and knew something was amiss. Said he started praying for her."

"I know it helped. God was watching out for us, that's for sure."

"The evil one is like a roaring lion, seeking whom he may devour," Mae said. "And he seems to delight in devouring the most innocent."

Natalie came out of the house with her hair in a ponytail and a red velvetlike dress that was the prettiest thing. She had on black shoes that tapped the porch and a little white purse with frills. She ran Chap-Stick around her lips, hugged her grandmother, and patted Roma's head. The whole thing took less than five minutes from the time I drove up.

"You be good," she said to the dog.

"I'll have her back at a respectable hour," I said, winking at Mae.

"Thank you, Billy. I know you will."

The dinner was held at a hotel on Route 60 in a sea of green and yellow trees that were just about ready to explode with color. The smell of sumac was sweet and followed us inside. The night before they'd had an informal meeting at a Methodist church. That was just for getting to know each other again, and tonight was for pictures and the program.

Women scurried this way and that, getting things together and directing people where to go and what to do. At the front table was a woman who looked familiar, but all I could remember was her smile and her eyes. She'd been the student body president, valedictorian, and a cheerleader. She hadn't been mean to me back then, just indifferent. As soon as I walked up, she said, "Billy Allman, I would recognize you anywhere." Then she stood and hugged me and gave me my name tag.

"This is not Callie, is it?" the woman said, looking at Natalie and then the list of names.

"No, Callie couldn't make it tonight. This is my friend Natalie. She's going to be world famous someday, and I thought she'd enjoy the meal."

The woman turned Callie's name tag over and wrote *Natalie* on the back and pinned it to her dress. "You have a good time tonight, Natalie. I'm sure glad you didn't have to come alone, Billy."

I walked into the dining room, my heart pounding, not knowing who or what I'd encounter. When you've been working at a job in your own house for so long, it's easy to get in a rut. Some would call it agoraphobic, but I tend not to make it so clinical. And maybe that was why I asked Natalie to come. I needed the comfort of something I knew to lessen the pain of being in a foreign place with people I didn't trust. I was like a fish out of water.

Others were polite and said it was good to see me, but I could tell there were more important people in the room. When anyone came up to me to talk, I would immediately tell Natalie what I remembered about them. Even the people who had been mean, like Paul Davidson, I found nice words for. Of course, that was the Lord helping me and nothing of myself.

The dinner began, and the very first thing to happen was the prayer before the meal, and who was to stand up and say it but Earl Caldwell. As I found out later, he had become a pastor. I just looked at him with my mouth open, and I wondered if he remembered taking my mandolin. He was the most unlikely candidate for Christian service I knew, but there he was, praying for the meal, and I thanked God that he worked on the likely and the unlikely.

The food came and Natalie's eyes widened at the full plate. She had a Dr Pepper to drink and just took in the whole room with wonder. I was doing the same thing, looking at people who'd had success written all over them during high school. Others had seemed destined for welfare. It was interesting that some of the second group were now in business or law enforcement. Some of the first had fallen into the bottle. Of course on the outside everybody looked good, but I could tell from the snippets of conversation that there was a lot of pain in that room. Broken relationships. Kids who'd gone astray. Hopes and dreams faded like wildflowers. People who had come to the end of themselves at the top or the bottom of the ladder like we all do.

I kept looking for Heather because that was who I really wanted to see. Not that I hoped for a spark between us, but after all the praying I had done for her and her husband through the years, I wanted to see if God had held up his end of the bargain.

Just as dessert was being served (Natalie chose the cherry pie), there was a commotion in the back, and several of the women flew like caged canaries. There was squealing and laughter, and most of the rest of us looked around at each other, bewildered.

When she entered the room, every eye was on her. Just as pretty as I remembered and still with blonde hair that cascaded across her shoulders and framed her face. Men and women came up to her and gave her a hug as she made her way to the front. They had kept her meal warm, but as it turned out, she didn't eat any of it.

Before she was seated, she looked around the room and spotted me in the back. It took her a while to get there because of all the people who stopped her to say hello.

"Who is she?" Natalie said.

"Just one of our classmates," I said.

"She's really pretty."

"Yeah."

"Did you know her?"

"We were friends. Good friends."

Heather finally made it to the table and gave me a hug. "Billy, it's so good to see you. I'm glad you were able to make it."

"It's not as far a trip as you had to make," I said. "I want you to meet a friend of mine. Natalie Edwards. She's my date tonight."

Heather hugged Natalie and doted on her dress. Then she said, "Where's your wife? I was so hoping I could meet her."

"She didn't feel well. Maybe next time."

Heather leaned down to Natalie again. "So you're the girl I hear on the radio, right? June Bug?"

Natalie nodded. "You listen?"

"Someone sent an e-mail about your station, Billy, and I've listened ever since. I'm

494

so proud of you."

I felt the red coming into my face and thanked her.

The class president tapped the microphone and called everyone to their seats. "We'll talk later," Heather said.

The rest of the evening was filled with laughter and reminiscing. Someone had put together a slide show with pictures culled from old yearbooks set to the tunes that had played on the radio at that time. There must have been five hundred pictures that flashed on the screen, and I saw myself twice. There weren't many photos taken at the back of the library during lunch hour, I guess.

"Before we get started with the dance," the cheerleader/president/valedictorian said, "we have a special guest with us tonight, all the way from Washington, D.C. You all remember Heather Blanch Hargrove from her years at Dogwood High, but you may not know what has happened in her life since our years growing up. I'd like her to come up now."

Everyone clapped as Heather stepped to the microphone. A hush fell over the room.

"I was asked to speak tonight and put in context what we're attempting at this reunion. A gathering like this can turn into a lot of different things. We could rehearse all of the old stories, the victories in sports, the romances, the defeats at both, and how the clothing and hairstyles have changed."

A photo flashed behind her. It was Paul Davidson and her, who had been voted "best dressed." The crowd hooted and laughed. She made a few more jokes about the lists of "best" or "most-likely" and showed some of the same photos we'd already seen, but it made us laugh again.

"I want to talk about success tonight. Some of you know that I have become successful at speaking and at business and making money, and that I've been able to use that success for what I believe in. Mainly, in fashioning a movement to help young women who are in the early stages of pregnancy decide not to end the lives of their unborn children. And that has led to a work against human trafficking in Africa and the Far East that my husband has spearheaded. And an orphanage in Haiti that we were able to move to this country."

There was applause throughout the room, louder in some spots than others. Natalie was enraptured. There was no question that Heather had control of the room, and I marveled at that because this was not the same girl I had known. Something had happened. She had a confidence and a presence I'd never seen.

"But I want to talk to you about real success, because it's not measured by external things. We normally compare ourselves to others and judge by outward indicators. Do I have more stuff than her? Do I get paid more than him?

"To be honest, this can become quite cloudy, even in a ministry or a humanitarian work. I can do the same, ticking off a list of babies saved or people who've found freedom. I couldn't see this at first. I was too caught up in the trappings, the wrapping paper of charity work.

"Now, if this sounds more like a graduation speech than something at a reunion, you're right, because I think we're at a bigger crossroads now than when we were eighteen or nineteen. I think this is a perfect time for me to reevaluate and put things in perspective."

She took a deep breath and motioned toward my side of the room. "Most of you here remember a friend of mind, Billy Allman."

My face flushed. Natalie looked at me, beaming, as if I were some kind of celebrity just for being mentioned.

"Billy, I want you to come up here."

There was some applause and a few

shouts. "Go get 'em, Billy!"

"Woo, Billy!"

"Yeah!"

Reluctantly I stood and moved toward the front. I could feel the sweat popping. My knees were weak and wobbly, and for once it wasn't because of my diabetes. I stood behind her, but she pulled me close to the microphone and looked up. There were tears in her eyes and I couldn't understand why.

"What are you doing?" I said.

"Just listen," she whispered.

When the applause faded, I looked out and saw a number of women brushing away tears as well. They must have known something I didn't. They must have known Heather's story better.

"This is success," Heather said. "Billy Allman is success personified. And let me tell you why."

She paused. I took the chance. "I want to hear this."

Everybody laughed and she chuckled.

"First, true success is not knowing you're a success. It's humble. It always gives credit to the others who helped achieve that success. And I know, Billy, that you are grateful for those who have helped you through the years."

I nodded. "I am."

"Success is a lot like love, I think," she continued. "Love does not seek its own good; it seeks the good of others. And in that giving, we receive much more.

"Billy was the best friend I've ever had. The only thing I ever did was save him a seat on the bus and he repaid me countless times. He even held my curlers when I'd take them out." Laughter. "After high school, he gave me a ride to the beauty school that I didn't want to attend but my parents had other ideas. He came to the jail and drove me home when I needed help. My father told me that Billy even helped tear down the chairs at my wedding so that my father and brothers could get to the reception."

She looked at me with such love and gratitude and brimming eyes. "But there's something Billy doesn't know. Something he couldn't know."

She paused again, collecting herself. I just stood there, now not as concerned about what people were thinking as they looked at me, but more concerned about what she was going to say.

"It was a night after he'd bailed me out of jail. One of those down times. My parents were gone. I was staying alone at the house.

I'd fallen in with the wrong crowd, and even they had abandoned me because I was out of money. I was at the end of myself. A complete failure at everything. And as young people will sometimes do, I let all of that crash down on me and decided to take my life.

"I had my mother's pills lined out on the bedspread. I had written the note to my parents asking their forgiveness. I picked out the dress I wanted to be buried in. I was ready to end the pain.

"And then the phone rang." She bit her lower lip and smiled. "I just let it ring. I figured it was one of my mother's friends. I didn't want to talk to anybody. I'd made up my mind.

"It rang and rang and finally stopped. So I picked up the first handful of pills and was about to tip them back when the phone rang again. I don't mind telling you, I cursed whoever it was and went to the kitchen and answered it. And you know who it was?"

"Billy!" Natalie said. Everybody laughed at her, and she put a hand over her mouth and sat back.

Heather wiped away a tear. "That's right. It was Billy. He said . . ." She swallowed hard and imitated my voice. " 'It's Billy Allman, and I was just checking up on you to see how you were doing.' "

Most of the people laughed because it did sound like me. She was always good at impressions. But for the life of me, I couldn't remember that call. I believed her, but I couldn't remember it.

"It wasn't so much what he said that night, but the way he talked to me. He didn't treat me like a failure. He treated me like I was some precious creation of God. And all that religious stuff he talked about — God loving me, having a plan, giving his life — all of that didn't compute at the time, but I heard it, Billy. I heard it loud and clear."

She looked back at me and took my hand in hers. "I know I hurt you. I know I caused you a fair amount of pain."

I patted her hand and shook my head. "It was worth it just to hold your curlers."

More laughter. When it subsided, she had regained her composure. "Success is not seen in the circumstances or in the pain or the good feelings. Success, sometimes, is just loving somebody with a love that doesn't come back the way you want it."

My own emotion crept up on me, and I wished I wasn't there in front of everybody. It felt like I was at my own funeral.

"There was another time when I asked Billy what the purpose of life was or some such thing aimed at getting him to say something that would push me over the edge. Something to tick me off about God or the Bible."

Again she imitated me. " 'Darlin', life is a song — a long, winding tune that turns minor at times, major at times, but mostly is just running along in the background. Don't question the purpose of things; just sing along.' "

She looked back at me. "Do you remember that?"

I shook my head. "No, but it sure sounds like me."

"Well, Billy Allman, I've heard about your song that you've been singing. I've watched from a distance and have heard reports of what you've done and how that song continues. And I'm here to say that without the grace of God and your friendship, I would not be here today. And the work that God has called me to wouldn't be going forward. And there are a few people who are thankful you were there at the toughest time of my life."

She buried her head in her hands, and people clapped and then stood up, and it was just too much to take in. Women and even some of the guys wiped away tears. I gave Heather a hug, and she composed herself and pushed me forward in front of the microphone.

"Come on, Billy," somebody said. "Say something."

I smiled. "You all don't know how hard it is for my wife to get me to shut up. Here you are encouraging me."

"Go ahead, Billy."

I held on to the podium and looked at Natalie. She pointed to her heart and I got the message. The same one I'd given her.

"When I was a kid working at the radio station, I used to do the overnights. I would sit at the editing block and edit myself to death because I had a bit of a stutter, and I would try and try to make it sound like I could talk. One night the manager left me a note that said three words: 'Billy. Don't talk.' "

Everybody laughed.

"Well, I didn't follow that advice. I don't think you can call my life a success in the world's terms because all I have is a little station that doesn't go more than ten miles down the road. The Internet has changed that, of course, but we're struggling every month to pay the bills just like some of you.

"But I have to say I agree with how

Heather has put it. The Lord gives us all a song to play, and at first we just play it the best we know how and try to work on it and make it better. Most of the time it sounds awful. But there comes a point where we realize it's not really our song to begin with, and if we'll follow the lead of the one who wrote the tune in the first place, we'll come out all right.

"I don't know what most of you have gone through. My guess is, some of it has been pretty rough. And it's an encouragement to know that somebody at some point listened to something I said."

I looked at Heather and people laughed again.

"May God help you sing whatever song he has put on your heart to sing."

I stepped back and everybody clapped. Then Heather said, "And with that thought, who would like to hear Billy play that mandolin of his?"

The band they had chosen was setting up behind us. They played a little rock and roll, a little country, and even some bluegrass. The fellow who played keyboard also had a mandolin he brought for when they did a Bruce Hornsby tune, and he said I could borrow it.

I knew this tune by Chris Thile, an instrumental on the mandolin that went fast and had lots of runs but needed a little guitar behind it to make sense. The fellow with long hair who played rhythm guitar said he'd heard it but didn't know the chords. Heather said a few more things while I wrote them down and told the fellow to follow me. He was just a young kid with a lot of talent in his fingers and a pretty good ear.

I played it through kind of slow the first time and called out the chords, and by that time the bass player was hooked up and ready, and the second time I just let it fly, my fingers going up and down the neck of that mandolin. There was something about the crowd, old friends and reborn ones, that made the music sweeter. I didn't think of all the pain in that music once. I just let it go.

Afterward, Natalie came up and hugged me. "I never knew any of that stuff that lady said about you."

"I didn't know half of it myself," I said. I looked at my watch. "We'd best be getting you back home, Cinderella."

We headed for the front door, and Heather caught up. "I hope putting you on the spot like that was okay, Billy."

"It was a bit of a surprise, but after I got

used to it, I sort of enjoyed it. Thank you, Heather."

"I've already heard from some others what it meant to them. There's something going on in that room. The hurts and disappointments of people have a way of melting when we share them."

"I keep thinking of the ones who didn't come through the door. They didn't have the chance."

"You reach out to them, Billy. For any of them who feel like they're not worthy to even come through the door."

"Maybe that's the song God has given me."

"I think it is. And you play it well, old friend. You play it well."

I asked about her husband and she said he was fine. He had stayed with the children they were watching from Haiti. Her life had become something sweet and good, and I thanked God that he had heard my prayers.

When Natalie was buckled in, I looked back at the hotel in the moonlight. Heather was still at the front, watching me pull away in the old truck, looking at me with the kind of love and sadness that makes a song richer.

I took Natalie home, and she was yawning when she walked through the door. I could imagine the story she told her grandmother.

It probably took her an hour to get her to sleep.

But that was nothing compared with Callie. She and her friend never did watch the movie. They were sitting in the same spot where I'd left them, a box of tissues between them. After her friend left, I took her place, and she had me tell her about everything that happened. I told her everything I could remember and especially about what Heather had said.

"Is she still pretty?" Callie said. I could tell by her hangdog look that there was something there, and I scooted a little closer and took her in my arms.

"Darlin', she's pretty as a picture. But she doesn't hold a candle to you. I wouldn't trade you for anybody or anything in this world."

I know it sounds unbelievable for a married couple, but we sat up the whole night and talked and hugged and shared the good and bad. When Callie shook and shivered and the fear returned, I read her the Psalms until I could barely hold my eyes open. And when the sun came up over the mountain behind us, we were still on the couch, holding on to each other and to something bigger than ourselves.

# 33

My feeling was that the reunion would be the high point and everything would be downhill from there. Something else would happen financially or the bank would cancel our mortgage and we'd lose the station or some other such thing. It almost felt like anytime there was good news, an attack of some sort was on its way. I don't mean to see a demon behind every rhododendron, but sometimes it can just feel like the world is against you.

But things didn't fall apart. I kept going each day, playing music and talking and working through the flu season. Callie went to counseling, stayed busy at the post office, and continued to improve.

Every Thursday night was like a breath of fresh air with Natalie, and every month we got the boys together. Pretty soon we had interest in people coming to see us live. Some didn't believe we had no practices, but when you've played these songs all your life, they're just part of you. Basically all you need to know is what key you're playing in and you're set.

We held the first public concert in the fellowship hall at Dogwood First Baptist. It's the only Baptist church in town, but I guess they called it that to make sure everybody knew they had the idea. I had to work through the phone company to get us a hookup for the live broadcast and that cost some money, but the pastor of the church and a couple of business owners in town who worshiped there decided to foot the bill.

We didn't charge any admission, but we did leave a bucket in the back for people to drop in a station donation if they wanted. There were probably fifty people at the first performance, and Natalie did even better in front of people than she did in the studio. She was a regular pro on that microphone, and she quickly learned how to talk to the people and get them to respond. It was like watching fireworks go off every time she came onstage. Jimmy brought all the equipment we needed, and I had Callie return to the station and switch to the recorded music when everything was over.

The crowds grew steadily with each concert until we filled the fellowship hall and had to move into the main sanctuary. The Internet hit count went through the roof. I wasn't sure what that meant, but I just kept doing what I felt like God had called me to do. It wasn't the Grand Ole Opry, but it was close enough.

One of the best days of the year was when Sheriff Preston came by the house.

"I've been listening to your station anytime I'm in range, Billy. I love the music. It speaks to my heart like few things do these days with everything going on in the world."

"I hear that from people," I said.

"Well, my wife said I ought to tell you. It was all she could do to keep from running over here last Sunday herself."

"What happened?"

"I'm in."

"Excuse me?"

"I'm in with both feet. Just shows that the prayers of a good woman will go a long way."

I smiled. "I'm really glad to hear it, Sheriff. I don't think you're going to regret it."

"No, don't expect I will. I'll probably regret waiting this long."

"He understands," I said. "And I'll bet

there was some celebration on your behalf when you finally came to your senses."

"You really think there are such things as angels, Billy?"

"I know there are, Sheriff. I have personal experience."

"Well, I thank you for the part you played. I've watched you through the years. I want something genuine like you have. Now I think I've got it."

"One thing about that, Sheriff: once you get it, don't hoard it. It'll spoil if you don't give it away."

Living and dying and everything in between. That's what the music is about. Faith, hope, and love. The glass seems to be growing darker every day. I try to make sense of the world and it just doesn't. All of the pain and the hurt and the leaving and crying and bloodshed.

I still believe in hidden songs that run through us. And I believe the pain has made them more rich and full. I've felt the songs overrun the banks of my life with equal amounts of joy and sorrow. I don't know why all these things happened to me, and I sure don't know what's planned for the future. But I know a few things for sure. One of them is that there is a fountain supplying the waters that both quench our thirst and flood our lives.

I also know that the love of a good woman is a treasure to the heart of a lonely man. And the love of God will change you, if you let it, no matter who you are and what you've done. God cares for us too much to leave us the way we are. He hounds and pokes and prods until we see the truth, and I have loved and hated him for it.

Sometimes in the still of the night, when the train whistle sounds, I sit up in bed and listen for something. A voice. A whisper. Something happened to me back in Buffalo Creek the morning of that flood. My life was preserved for a reason. Was it so I could save Callie? Was it so I could meet Natalie and help her find her way? Was it because of the people who have been touched by the radio station?

I'm not sure if it's one or all of the above. Perhaps God will do something else down the road, though I'm not sure how long of a road I have to travel. But I have come to the point where I don't need to know. That's the best part of my story. I just plain don't need to know.

# 34

I will not divulge secrets of hidden things. I have told you that. And I have endeavored to keep hidden those things that must not be revealed to the earthbound. In a little while you will see fully, but not yet. So I will not divulge the method by which I was extricated from that unholy assembly of malevolent forces who entrapped me, but suffice it to say, the very height of heaven was not ashamed to come to my aid. We rejoiced at the victory, but heaven fell silent with the death of Clay. And not long after, I was given a new assignment and the orders to leave my friend Billy Allman.

I will not say whether angels weep at such partings. However, if we rejoice and sing for gladness, it follows that we can experience the opposite emotion. There was at least a bit of melancholy leaving him, for I knew there would be hardship ahead.

To live earthbound means there are many

questions. For one moment I was able to think as they do, wondering about Billy's future. Would he and Callie have a long life together? Would his diabetes cause irreversible health complications? Would the station continue and grow, or would it — like many things of earth — fade, dim, and wither?

Grappling with life and its many decisions takes the heart of a warrior. After my close encounter with the enemy of men's souls, I see that anew and I am more sure than ever that there is only One who can be trusted with every question mark. As many on earth have found, to cast oneself on the sure mercy and love of the Creator is not an act of blind faith, but a daily act of contrition. For my questions are never answered with an explanation other than the twin beams of wood known as a cross. If I can live with that great question mark of history, I can live each day with the questions that arise from Billy's life and my own.

Still, I lament that I am not allowed to stay longer. I wanted to be present at his last moments, to usher him into the presence of the One he served faithfully. But I know that Billy and Callie and the others will be in the care and protection of the One they serve. As David so aptly wrote, "The Lord directs the steps of the godly. He delights in every detail of their lives. Though they stumble, they will never fall, for the Lord holds them by the hand."

I serve this God of details. This God of commas and exclamation points. A God of questions. It is this God who calls me to another assignment. And though I serve in obedience and seek at each moment to follow the directives of the One who is without compare, it is now not simply a matter of answering a call or following orders. I now live and move and have my being in the fathomless reaches of His mercy and grace, which I do not hope to comprehend, but which I am fully aware exist. I have seen it at work.

What I have witnessed in the life of Billy Allman is a humility unmatched. With all of the pushing and shoving to get to the place of honor at life's table, to see a man so connected to his work and to the Almighty is a wondrous thing. And yet the man has flaws. He is not a saint.

Some believe God chooses the best people to follow Him, ones with fewest flaws, who can do wondrous things for Him. But I have seen the truth of the words written long ago fulfilled. In this case, God did not choose the most wise or powerful or wealthy. Instead, He chose a person the world considered foolish in order to shame those who think they are wise. And He chose the powerless and despised, a person counted as nothing, and used him again and again.

Oh, the beauty of this God who not only fashions the world and makes humans in His own image, but also can take the ashes of their lives and turn them into love. I praise both now and forevermore a God who takes delight in the praise of the least of these and who uses brokenness so that others may see true wholeness. I will forever be mystified by the love of God for sinful creatures that takes them from bondage to freedom and asks nothing more than for them to become sons and daughters of the true King.

I do not know what it is like to have a soul. I will never experience that. I do not understand what it is like to be time-bound and unable to see the truth of eternity with my own eyes. But as I rose above those trees, now bursting with color, away from the world of floods and tears, I understood better what humans feel as they breathe. For every breath they take, and every note of every song they sing from their hearts, originates not deep within, but deep in Him.

# AFTERWORD

Good stories come from real people and real life. There is no fiction well, only people's lives. Since I was young and before I had any good sense to know better, I have dreamed of owning and running my own radio station. I had the spot picked out on the hill where I grew up, in those West Virginia hills. On the other knoll I would build a house.

In January 2009, I received an e-mail from Carmeleta Randolph. She listened to my radio program over station WOTR. The station owner/operator had died the day before, and she wrote to tell me about him. Here is a bit of that e-mail:

Dear Chris,
    I have listened to your program for some time now on WOTR 96.3 out of Lost Creek, West Virginia. Yesterday the owner/operator of WOTR, James William

"Billy" Allman, went home to heaven to be with his Lord. Billy was a unique and extremely kind man and a very close friend to me and my husband. (We considered him family.) He was a good neighbor. He spent his entire life as a servant to Jesus and he did it well. Billy was diabetic and had not been well at all for years, but he pushed on every day to send out the gospel over the airwaves. He was a genius, truly. At the age of five or six years, he built a weed eater out of a kitchen mixer and the beaters! He built an amplifier when he was twelve for his father, who did some auctioneering.

Billy was somebody that I can look at and say that I know without a doubt he worshiped God every day. People look at worship and think worship is singing, but worship is honoring who or what you're living for. He honored God with every decision he made. Jesus Christ was truly his Lord.

He must have had a vision for radio since he was a young boy. I didn't know him then, but my husband did. They lived up a little hollow here. My husband said he would even put speakers outside and he would rig up all these electronics and he would broadcast radio down the hollow so everyone could hear.

There wasn't a lot of support for WOTR, not a lot of people who wanted commercials on a Christian station. It's a very small community. And it's a small station. So he would trade airtime for his services. If he needed work on his car, he would trade airtime, or dinner at a restaurant for commercials. He lived at the station. He put his whole life into it. I keep thinking of the Scripture that God would continue the good work that he started in you. I don't know what will happen, but I keep praying God will do what he wants to do there.

I just would like to say, a lot of people didn't know Billy. But Billy poured his life into serving God. And I know when he walked into heaven yesterday, heaven knew Billy. He was an important person to them.

When I read her e-mail, my first response was "I know this man." I didn't know him personally, but I knew his stock. I knew what drove him to start that station in Lost Creek, West Virginia. I wrote Carmeleta back and asked if she would come on with us for a few minutes and share what Billy meant to her. When she finished, we moved

519

on to another topic, but Billy haunted me. I told my wife later that week, "I think I have my next story."

Everything in this book is from my imagination. As far as I know, there are only shadows from Billy's real life. But I hope in crafting this story that I have captured a little of his heart. I'm grateful to Carmeleta and her husband for sharing their stories of Billy. Of course, I would thank Billy for the way he lived and how he showed God's love. Someday I will meet him face-to-face.

I also want to thank others who have made this story possible. Karen Watson is the top dog in fiction at Tyndale, but you would never know it. She has listened to every idea I've thrown at her and even gave the okay when I asked to put an angel in my story. Sarah Mason performed major surgery on this manuscript, and for that Billy and I both are thankful.

Kathryn Helmers is another constant. Without her encouragement early on, I would still be looking for a publisher.

To my family — my wife, Andrea; my children, Erin, Megan, Shannon, Ryan, Kristen, Kaitlyn, Reagan, Colin, and Brandon — you mean more than life. Thanks to David and John; Susan and Kim; my parents, Robert and Kathryn Fabry; and my father-in-law, George Kessel, for your support through our desert experience. I wish Barbara could have read this story.

Thanks to Robert Sutherland for friendship and more. The dog, Rogers, was an amalgam of our dearly departed Pippen and Frodo.

There is a rich history of bluegrass in the Mountain State, and I listened to a lot of it as I wrote. Thanks to Mickey Halleron for his technical assistance, music, and memories.

And thanks to the one who gives us music, who shows us beauty amid the ashes, and who uses pain to make songs sweeter and more satisfying. To you be honor and glory forever. Amen.

Chris Fabry
Tucson, Arizona

# READING GROUP QUESTIONS AND TOPICS FOR DISCUSSION

1. At the end of the first chapter, Billy finally reveals how he was really saved from the flood. Have you ever experienced a situation like that, where something happened to you that you couldn't explain?

2. What were your first impressions of Malachi? Was he what you would have expected an angel to be like? Why or why not?

3. At the beginning of chapter 3, Billy says, "I have heard that your first childhood memory is telling." What is your first childhood memory, and what do you think it says about you?

4. In chapter 8, Malachi observes that Heather was being pulled away from God by her own passions, and he assumed that

is why the enemy left her alone. Is that reassuring to you or convicting?

5. In chapter 10, Billy faces one of the most difficult decisions he's ever had to make concerning the care of his mother. Did you identify with Billy's actions? Have you ever had to make a similar decision? How did you handle it?

6. Throughout the story, many people extend small acts of kindness toward Billy — Adrian Rogers, Callie, Charles Broughton. Has anyone ever extended similar kindnesses to you? How did it make you feel?

7. At times, it feels like Billy loses just about everything he loves. One of the demons even remarks that everything he touches withers and dies. How do you think Billy feels about his life? Why? If it would have been easier for Billy to stay in his shell, why does he take the risk he does?

8. In chapter 16, Billy says that to many, "God is not someone you know but something you try to get off your back." Have you felt this way at some point in your

own life? How do you see this play out in our society?

9. Throughout the story, how do you see God showing his love for Billy, even at times when Billy doesn't recognize it? Can you think of similar examples of God's love in your own life?

10. An event in Billy's teenage years affects him greatly. How was Billy finally able to overcome the effects of that event? Have you ever faced a traumatic event, and how did you overcome it?

11. In chapter 27, Malachi wrestles with the fact that he was called away by God during a crucial time in Billy's life. Back in chapter 7, Malachi's commander had warned him about this, and told him that the "events to come must occur." How did this make you feel?

12. Though Callie had a strong faith, she reached a time when that faith wavered and she became susceptible to evil. What brought her to that point?

13. What do you think Malachi took from

his observance of Billy's life? Where do you think Malachi was sent next?

14. In *Almost Heaven,* we learn a lot about people like Billy, Callie, Natalie, and Sheriff Preston. How do you picture them five years after the close of this story?

15. After reading the story, what did you admire most about Billy Allman?

# ABOUT THE AUTHOR

**Chris Fabry** is a 1982 graduate of the W. Page Pitt School of Journalism at Marshall University and a native of West Virginia. He is heard on Moody Radio's *Chris Fabry Live!, Love Worth Finding,* and *Building Relationships* with Dr. Gary Chapman. He and his wife, Andrea, are the parents of nine children. Chris has published seventy books for adults and children. His novel *Dogwood* won a Christy Award in 2009. You can visit his Web site at www.chrisfabry.com.